SQUARE
WAVE

A NOVEL BY
MARK DE SILVA

Two Dollar Radio
Books too loud to Ignore

TWO DOLLAR RADIO is a family-run outfit founded in 2005 with the mission to reaffirm the cultural and artistic spirit of the publishing industry.

We aim to do this by presenting bold works of literary merit, each book, individually and collectively, providing a sonic progression that we believe to be too loud to ignore.

Two Dollar Radio
Books too loud to Ignore

COLUMBUS, OHIO
For more information visit us here:
TwoDollarRadio.com

Copyright © 2016 by Mark de Silva
All rights reserved
ISBN: 978-1-937512-39-2
Library of Congress Control Number available upon request.

Design and layout: Two Dollar Radio
Author photo: Whitney Lawson

Printed in Canada

For blood

SQUARE
WAVE

Consciousness is caused by air.
　　　　　　　　—Hippocrates, 5th century B.C.E.

This for certain I can confirm, That oftentimes the Devil doth cry with an audible Voice in the Night.
　　　　　　　　—R. Knox, 1681

Life struggles not with death, spirit not with spiritlessness; spirit struggles with spirit, life with life.
　　　　　　　　—C. Schmitt, 1929

1

THE POWDER WAS DARK AND FINE, REALLY A DUST. It carried into the light in tobacco wisps as he loaded the chamber, packing it flat with the weight of his body, twisting the tamp before easing the pressure. A featureless surface remained. He locked the handle in place and started the pump. Two honeyed streams oozed from the filter head down to the shallow white cup.

The springs squealed. She leapt up from bed, the Ballade in D minor—Brahms, her favorite—following her out of the bedroom as she opened the door and darted to his side. He did not react. Her hands clung to the edge of the sink as she leaned over it, finding a way into the margins of his view as her bare breasts grazed the Bolognese-stained plates poking up out of dishwater, frothless now after three days of attrition.

He stared down into the filling cup. Without raising his head he looked at her. Blue eyes edged with green—they fluttered, fixed his own, released them, and fixed them again. He was unchanged. She swung her head away from him, tucked her chin in the hollow of her shoulder, and swung it back, her face now more flush with light just as cirrus draped the sun. He turned off the pump.

"We should take a trip," she said.

The crema was thinning already. She'd left an entire bag of beans, a Kenyan peaberry finer than her palate, to stale in the unlidded grinder.

He handed her the cup. She tasted it and made a face, crinkled her nose. "You make it bitter." She spooned too much sugar into the drink and sipped at the travesty.

"Why?" he asked as he refilled the basket.

"Why?"

"Then where."

"We could go to Sri Lanka. It's safe enough there now, right?"

"I have what I need."

"Well then not for that." She shut her eyes in concentration or its imitation. "Réunion." The word came abruptly, eyes popping. She touched her thumb to her lip and tilted her head. "Dakar?"

"There might be things I could use back in England. More letters, maybe some journals. We could probably stay at the old house itself this time. If you really have to go somewhere."

"Dakar!" The eyes quivered—that, her manner of punctuation. "Isn't there art in Dakar?"

"In going there?"

"A biennial. I think. Oh, I need to *know* these things."

"Really, though, I shouldn't go anywhere. Not till I've written up these pieces up for the Wintry."

He pulled the second shot and smiled. The pump's din made conversation impossible, forcing her to wait the twenty-five ticks of his Submariner.

"But if you have everything you need, you can do it there."

He paused, though without quite shaking his head. "And do you even have the time for this?"

"Too much. You know that. It is such a strange little place to work, Carl. There's hardly enough to do. Three issues. It's more like half a year's work. And just to go into that office—the six of us. Maybe you'd think, I did, that that would make things intimate, more informal. And it is informal, but not intimate. It's a vacuum. Silence from start to finish most days. And these are supposed to be people you'd actually *wanted* to work with. Really good readers. They write interesting stuff too, smart commentary. But in the flesh, they're false, or tepid, or humorless—or falsely so without alcohol, and even then, the jokes are mostly bad. Paper-interesting, that's what I'm calling them. Halsley's made them that, I think, if they weren't already."

He downed his espresso and set the cup on the surface of the gray water. They watched it capsize and sink to the bottom, trailing dark ribbons that coalesced into a cloud. Her cup sat on the counter, nearly full.

"It's like there's some threshold we haven't reached," she continued. "Maybe it takes, I don't know, ten before you have a staff, any real range. Or else less people than we've got, if you want something concentrated, personal. Ten or more, five or less, and we've fallen in between. But then maybe it's got nothing to do with numbers. There's just so much ego in that room, and less than half of it's paid for." She threw her arms out to her sides as she said this. "And no one stays past five, except for close. That's three weeks a year. And still only till eight."

"I should take your job," he said.

"You should! I can follow the hookers then."

"That's not really my job."

"But that's what you do."

"Incidentally."

"And they pay you for it. That's a job. I don't know what I think of it, but it's sounding better than mine right now."

"But you'd be just as bored. Because most of the time nothing happens. You just walk around, looking for trouble, and you don't end up finding it, the right kind, easily or at all. This stuff with the whores, it could still turn out, probably will turn out, to be the wrong kind. Tangential. Not my job."

She shook her head and ran her finger along the lip of her

cup. "I don't know what to do. Maybe I should start reviewing more. Do you think they'll let me have my old job back?"

"You were replaced."

"I found her for them, though. The magazine could take us both, replacement and replaced." She looked at him hopefully. "No, you're right, they won't. I don't really want to go back anyway. Every time I talk to them, and they still count as friends, individually, every time they mention the magazine, their voices change, they tighten, or if it's in person, their faces do, and I know I was right to leave. I don't like the silence, the sputtering pace now. But the sort of noise I came from… and it only got worse after you left."

"I was pretty bad at the job. The midwifing. The Rolodex. The dinners."

"But you were sort of hoping to be bad. Relieved at least."

"I'm not sure what I was hoping."

"No, I'm not blaming you for quitting. I would have had to leave anyway. But you're too something, for editing. Not just there. Anywhere, probably. Too… yourself. Maybe for the city too."

"I wouldn't—"

"And I love that." Her eyes flashed. "But can't we go somewhere? You'll like it."

"The first essay needs to be done soon. In weeks probably."

"Oh, you'll get them all done. They'll be perfect."

"You haven't seen them."

"But I know."

She must have known most of what she knew of him this way, whatever way it was. She'd never asked to see the drafts, though she was better positioned than most to appreciate them, having once been a graduate student in history, at the same university he'd attended, in fact, in England, and at the same time, though they knew each other only glancingly then. She dropped out before finishing her master's thesis, on literary expatriatism in the Georgian era, with Washington Irving, and his Geoffrey Crayon, the would-be pivot.

It was only after the scholarships, back in the States, in Halsley—in magazines, in fact—that they'd become properly acquainted. But he bore the city's literary world no better than academe. The issue now was frivolity not fustiness. It took him just months as an editor to see this, that wit and bombast would always trump rigor. They liked to condemn it as dreary; apparently this was the worst thing something could be. It didn't have to be, though, applied in the right way, he thought, even if the universities had made it seem so and given them cover for a sloth of mind he was never going to acclimate to, however artful the dress.

She seemed to have run into the same problem. Wasn't that what she was complaining about just now? The fecklessness? Still, he wasn't going to suggest that she quit as he had. Bright as she was, it might be that nothing in the world suited her better. No one, after all, could accuse her of being too herself, only not enough.

"You don't know what the pieces are about," he said.

"They're about your family."

He squinted. "Incidentally," he said, a half-truth, if that. "And that still wouldn't tell you if they were any good."

"Carl, you do everything well," she said, just before threading her lips between his, stifling the demurrals. She gripped him by the nape of the neck and slid her hand upward, lifting the dark curls of hair as she licked the backs of his teeth and sucked his lip.

"Where did you get this impression?" he asked, pulling away and biting the leonine nose.

She squirmed. "You bite too hard." He bit it harder. She whipped her face away, over her shoulder, and leaned against him.

"I can tell by the way you speak," she said, taking the twist out of her neck and tucking her face below his. She gripped his stubbled cheeks with both hands. "Heart-shaped face?" she said. "Let me just look at tickets at least." She shot away from him, to the sofa, and curled up with the laptop.

How did he speak? Since they'd been firmly together, five months now, she'd heard only fragments of anything serious from him. Mostly this was because she attended to his words selectively, just bits and pieces, a phrase, a transition, an odd construction. Yesterday, it had been "a decent shot at regret." Before that, there was "twice-lived" and "something worse than impossible."

While he was thinking aloud, probing, carefully tracing a line of thought, she would pounce on words like these and blurt out, "How well put!" Often he lost the rest of the thought this way, and turns of phrase meant to be means became ends. Even when he didn't, he would break off the inquiry a sentence or two later, seeing that the matter was of no more than private interest. That she didn't mind these abortions only vexed him further. Whatever she got out of what he said, it was hardly ever what he hoped she would get out of it.

This wasn't all bad. The language that drove her to exclaim like this often marked quarries of significance he might otherwise have passed over. As a means of divining these veins beneath his words, she was exceptional. Further meditation was almost always repaid, though she never provided it herself, of course, or encouraged him toward it either. She was thinking of other things by then, the words only an exit onto an avenue leading elsewhere, to a story she preferred. She would be lost traveling this route for some seconds and come to with a silent rattle of the eyes. The praise came then, the tiny kisses laid on his face. It was difficult to stay annoyed.

So it would be left to him, Carl Stagg, to subject these fragments, at a later time, to the maw of his mind, scraping away at their surfaces until a pleasing resistance was met, and what was left in his grasp was hard as stone.

"Tickets aren't so bad, if we buy now—or soon." Her voice, unraised, came from the living room. Immediately she appeared, her face carrying the question.

He stepped on the trash-pedal and knocked out the steaming puck of spent powder. She stopped just short of him and regarded the grocery below in the street as he rinsed the portafilter and wiped down a kitchen counter that didn't need it.

"To England?" He liked misunderstanding her.

"No! Africa. Doesn't that sound better? You've spent enough time—*I've* spent enough time—in England. The house is crumbling anyway."

"It's been renovated."

"And I'm supposed to hang around while you're in the attic digging up old family letters?"

"You could help me if you want." He hung the unsoiled cloth from the oven door and wrapped an arm around her from behind, just beneath her breasts.

"You don't touch them enough," she said.

He turned her around and put his hands on her waist, squeezed her hips, pinched the skin with his thumbs and pointers. Her panties were a shambles. In places the cotton was reduced to just a few crosshatched fibers, and the elastic was dark with sweat and sloughed skin. He pulled it down in front with his thumb and ruffled the dark hair; but he was thinking of Portsmouth, of London, and then of the Fens, where they had both spent most of their time in England, though separately. Finally Kent came to mind. He could see if Oli might save him a trip and visit the country house in Canterbury, send him the last of Rutland's letters.

"I like that you like it." The hair, she meant. Her mouth twisted into a smile that became a pucker. He kissed her eyes shut, right to left, and released the elastic with the lightest of snaps, silent.

"Can we sleep here tonight?"

He nodded.

"So... tickets?"

He laughed. She left the kitchen for the living room, her arms behind her, pulling him along by the fingers in a way that turned his hands into pistols.

Renna's apartment was larger than his, nicer. The living room was a long rectangle lined with narrow boards, maple or ash, varnished and staggered. The wood had gone matte in places: along the path from the kitchen to her bedroom, from the bedroom to the bathroom, and then near the foot of the sofa, the massive gray-green brick covered in a rich fiber.

Besides the sofa there was little else. A parched mahogany table of unknown but apparently ancient provenance served for eating and working. (For him, anyway. She preferred bed for both.) There were cigarette burns all over it. (She didn't smoke, and though he did, the marks predated him.) The table's edge bore semicircular scuff marks from the bottle caps popped on it in its life before Renna. Two folding chairs were wedged under it, and a pair of unstable barstools sat near the kitchen counter. That was it.

The other bedroom, only recently adapted into Stagg's second study, had been vacated just weeks before by the gymnast, a pommel horse specialist. He left in haste to Orlando, to train at a well-regarded program where a spot had opened up owing to another man's career-ending injury. There was some chance of making it to nationals this year, he'd said, but at twenty-three he was already considered old, and his best shot at laud, Olympic qualification, had passed him by three years earlier. He'd finished two places out on the horse.

In the nine months he occupied the second bedroom—he'd replaced a college friend Renna had rented the apartment with originally, a year before, while Stagg was still in England—the two kept things mostly polite and formal between them. Now and again, though, they would eat together.

Stagg once shared a starch-heavy dinner of gnocchi in a veal reduction with the two of them, at the battered table. They'd lifted up the leaves, unnecessarily, as nothing was placed on them. Stagg found the man more of a boy, really. He was not stupid, though his education was soft, his brain, Stagg imagined, resembling unkneaded dough.

That night, he asked him idly about the origins of the pommel horse. Something about Alexander the Great came back, martial preparation. And then, cheaply, he asked him about the *meaning* of the horse, knowing, first, that the gymnast was not practiced in the address of this sort of question, and, second, that whatever meaning might be lodged in the horse, recovering it would be pedantry at its worst, certainly not something worth sullying dinner with, and probably not even a seminar room.

"Knowing" turned out to be too strong, though that is what it felt like. The gymnast's answer, not in so many words, was that the horse was a bounder of mastery. In most things—art, science, politics, friendship, love—success was ill defined, necessarily murky, an always evolving question. Not so, he said, on the horse. A simple mastery was possible. And curiously, he said this was so irrespective of their being anyone in a position to judge the performance, even the athlete himself. Judgment had nothing to do with it.

It was this qualification that complicated the gymnast's answer. The case, and the contrast with the other endeavors, would seem simpler to make with an unjudged sport, track perhaps being the ideal. But the gymnast spoke with such casual conviction, Stagg found it difficult to disbelieve him, even if it threw into doubt exactly what case he meant to be making, and it was not quite possible to understand how what he said could be true, or even how the world would have to be arranged for it to be true.

But wasn't it Catherine, another Great, who'd said that victors aren't judged? The question flitted through Stagg's mind. He let the conversation move on. He would rather explore the thought himself, later, on his own. The gymnast, if he knew anything of this, could only muddle things from here, or coarsely domesticate whatever wayward insight he might have had. Still, Stagg was more impressed by the man then, if only complexly so, than he had ever been, before or since.

The only thing about the gymnast that brought Stagg an unadulterated satisfaction, though not a noble one, was a disastrous day in his life. Renna had gone to see him perform in a state competition, more of a warm up for the season, in his second specialty, the rings. From a handstand, impressively taut and straight, he dipped down into the iron cross, an inverted one, his signature move. But just before he reached the position, a pectoral gave way.

Normally the cross, inverted or not, needs to be held for two seconds for the judges to score it. But his was not a holding of the position so much as a passing through it. He descended from the handstand past the cross, his outstretched arms closing in on his sides. For an instant, with his arms angled back slightly, like wings, he seemed to her a plane flying toward the mat. Stagg found this beautiful. Sometimes he would ask Renna to tell him the story again, go over the feeling she had at just this moment. Once in a while she would indulge his morbidity.

When the gymnast's arms reached his sides, his hands clung tight to the rings and his body whipped around perforce, separating his shoulder and tearing a biceps as he spun to the ground. This was six months ago. But even as he was moving out, Renna remembered him not by the energy drinks crowding the fridge, or the hyperbolically proportioned upper body, or the six a.m. alarms that began even his Sundays, but by that passing, upside-down cross. For her, if not for the judges, it counted. If what the gymnast was saying at dinner were to be believed, it simply counted, for no one in particular.

They were in her bed now, she under the covers, he over them. "*You* can be my roommate," she said, caprice speaking.

"I like my apartment."

"Compared to this one?" she asked, as if that were insane.

"It's chastening is what I mean. I have a lot to do right now, to write. It will go faster there. And anyway you don't want my notes all over the place. They've got a way of taking up as much space as there is."

She frowned but it was mostly show.

"The sooner I finish, the sooner we could go somewhere," he said, taking her expression in earnest. "Maybe we'll get a place together when our leases are up."

"I can edit them. They're like short stories," she said, passing over, or through, his words to his work.

"More like fragments, of fact. Patchworks of fact."

"Bricolage." She drew the word out in a faraway whisper, as if speaking to her own past in graduate school.

The mattress shifted. She was on her side now, away from him, texting, and then up and out of bed.

"Oh I thought he'd cancel. I have so little to do and I'm still doing it terribly." She dressed twitchily, pulling on lint-ridden leggings, Chelsea boots, and a cream blouse. "*And* I have a dinner tonight." She ducked into the bathroom to fix her hair, so short now it didn't need to be fixed.

"Weren't we going to see Larent play tonight?"

"I know. You go, though. He wants you to hear his new stuff, he said so."

Stagg's interest was wholly dependent on hers.

"Tell him I'm sorry," she said. "He knows how I am. Will you go, for both of us?"

With a sucking sound a kiss came at him from the doorway.

He stared at his feet. Then she was on top of him, sprawled. "Let's *move* to Africa."

"Who's the writer this time?" he asked.

"The dinner? Tim Heath. He hasn't written much yet. But what he's written! Have you read anything?"

"What's he write?"

"Short stories mainly."

"Stories, no, I don't—"

"You just *write* them."

"That's what you keep saying."

"Okay, so they aren't stories! They don't sound at all like essays, though. Something beyond that. Beyond even history maybe. Right?" She rubbed her face against his and her hair poked at his eyes. "I know they'll be you—all you."

She pecked his lips twice and sat up on the edge of the bed, facing away from him. "Anyway, I want to get something new from Tim, before his story collection comes out. A reported piece even. He has some pitches. Could make him a regular contributor, if things go well. It would definitely help the magazine."

"That *is* your job."

"It's the only interesting part of it right now. He's very good. He's like you."

She stood and turned just her face to him, over her shoulder. "Oh, do I love you," she said, in a tone that placed this just between a statement and a question.

He pulled her hands to him and kissed the tips of her fingers. "Okay, so, home late, I'll miss you."

The door rattled shut and a pattering of feet faded in the hallway. He lifted the window. The draft stung his face, whipped the door closed, and vanished. There was only a plastic lighter in the blue and white cigarette pack on the sill, next to the dark bottle and the trails of ashes like crumbs. He tossed the empty box, cellophane still girdling its lower half, into the morning outside. It caught in a gust and hovered a moment before the wind pinned it to the other side of the alley, leaving it soon to tumble into the weeds of pale green and the beer bottle shards of a darker hue below.

Without fantasies he licked his hand and lay back on the bed. Just before he came, soundlessly, he turned on his side, toward the floorboards. He turned back and waited for the medicinal effects to take hold. Immediately things seemed simpler, mercifully abstract. Philosophical. A natural refuge.

He rarely leaned on fantasies now. When he faltered, and a blank slate wouldn't do, the only ones that helped were of her. But he didn't want them. They were the wrong kind. There were times, though, when nothing else sufficed, and, helpless, he would let his mind, till then a vacuum, fill with the men who had, in her own strange and potent description, metabolized her.

Thinking of her this way, as an instrument, satisfied something in him. He was slow to accept this, but the link between imagining her so and the stiffening of his cock had grown too strong to ignore.

She herself spoke with something close to pride about being a notch in the right bedposts, the ones of the Casanovas and cads, the elegant rakes. Mostly she would describe these men of art through the beauty of their apartments, the ubiquity of their friends, the perfection of their seductions. There was admiration, envy, and only a little disgust in her voice when she did, and on the occasions when scorn did come to the fore, the more she poured on them, the more pleased she seemed to be to have lain in their beds.

It gave her something, to play a part in their stories, any part, the more public the better. Though she liked gossip, she liked being its object even more. And as she seemed to measure her worth not by anything inhering in her, but by the company she kept, the surroundings she could work her way into, it was lucky she had a knack for ingratiation.

Generally all of this nauseated him, and though he didn't like to think about it, it must have been one of the less lofty reasons he'd dropped out of publishing so quickly: that he might not have to know these gallants of empty graces and Cheshire smiles.

In fact, she too wanted to feel she was something apart from these men, that world, especially its charlatanry, which in quieter moments she allowed, in the soft, slow monotone she did her thinking in, was part of its essence, maybe even part of its allure. You were never really expected to show your hand.

His affection for her, though, was the proof that she had a hand to show. After all, she thought, he'd done the work—not just intellectually, in books, but introspectively, in himself—that they mostly pretended to. If she could hold his attention when they could not, that must mean something: that though she spent much of her time swanning around, disappearing in the froth, there would always be a remainder. And this, the solidest bit of her, was something that he had to take seriously.

But did she really want that, to be truly seen? Wasn't that seriousness, the very one he was applying now while she ran off into that world, already beginning to undo them? The closer he looked, the more she squirmed, the more the remainder receded like a mirage. Even if it existed, she did nothing to honor it. And was that what drew him to her anyway? He stepped around the idea that her appeal might be grounded in bone structure. Perhaps they both needed the conceit then.

None of these thoughts, of course, helped in bed with her. But alone, with his hand on his cock, they brought him not just nausea but pleasure. Solitude activated their sexual potential. He came hardest this way now, without her around, only a notion of her and him, and not a flattering one.

It occurred to him then, in that swell of endorphins, that really her history with men was derivative, an effect emanating from a cause broader if not deeper than sex. She was shot through with a flutter.

The skittering and lunging, more than her beauty, had a near unassailable force on him—near only because, like bad hearts, her attention too had a flutter in it. The order of explanation, though. Was it just that she was a perfect conduit? The impressions the world made on her, lighting the eyes, tickling the skin, was their transmission simply uncorrupted, and all her buzz and bloom merely the reflection of a chaos woven into the world itself, an irreducible manifold? Was it, then, only his own sensorium's deficiencies that rendered the world smooth enough to still his mind? Could this distortion, the soft focus, be what provided for the possibility of sustained attention, and so of art, love, friendship, and the rest of the things the gymnast had spoken of?

But then it might have been the other way around. Maybe the flutter dwelled in her, sent a tremor through the world. *It* might have been what governed the flitting that so transfixed him, if "governed" was the right word.

What whiskey remained he tipped into last night's snifter till the better part of the balloon was amber. He took four overlarge gulps, brimming mouthfuls that sent trickles of liquor down his chin. Sparking the flint of the lighter continuously, he sat back on the bed and returned his eyes to his feet, waiting for the soft and familiar burn of the stomach and a still airier texture to the world in his mind.

Sometimes he wished simple condemnation were an option. But there were spasms of awareness in her as rich as any he'd known: the times, say, she could tell he'd had four drinks not three, or more preternaturally, ten drinks not eight, by the slightest variations in the clatter of his words as they left his mouth; or sense the strength of his misgivings by how their hands fit together when they walked; or weigh the gravity of his thoughts by how his head lay on her shoulder, in bed.

There were the times too when she seemed to recall every detail of his boyhood, however quotidian, or of his sexual history, however odd, that he'd ever conveyed to her, even if only implicitly. She would seem more at home with his life than he was, more able to flip through the facts, his facts, and arrange them into significant wholes. She couldn't do the same for herself, of course. She could be you but not her. That was her perversion.

Then there were the times, when she was excited for a stretch, for whatever reason, that she would effortlessly absorb the tiniest things he did, chart the place and nature of every object around him. Long after he'd let go of the occasion's minutia, she could recall just what he'd eaten, what he'd passed on, and in what order; or where the power outlets were or weren't in a country house she'd been in just once, many months ago, in another country; or the exact page on which he'd given up on a book forever, setting it face up and open on the kitchen table, its spine broken.

In all of these moments he felt transparent, and something like parity would reign between them. For the grain of his own attention, she admiringly granted, was unobservable, only a postulate; and it seemed always pitched that way, toward her, toward anything—except, as she'd ruefully pointed out more than once, when he made himself hopelessly drunk, and understanding was no longer an option.

But her awareness undulated. Like a square wave of terrific amplitude, the crests would drop precipitously into troughs no less remarkable, but for the purity of their oblivion. She was made of nothing then, as was everything around her. Nothing counted, not even things that meant the world: her work, his writing.

His own being would begin to flicker. Sometimes she would smile. It terrified him, the voided eyes. He would look into his hands and croak, "Anyway…" She would say things then they would never remember, not because the words didn't reach their ears, but because their sense, so slight, seemed to die with their sound.

He couldn't help but anticipate these slackenings. They contaminated the tauter stretches, throwing them in relief, making them more acutely felt and then immediately missed, even before they had actually gone. Sex was no different—towering spikes of communion plunging down toward onanism until it was only that. She'd get herself off lying next to him, eyes closed, having only just got off on him. "I like it when you're selfish," she'd say. He liked it when she wasn't.

So things went, in an endless oscillation. She was as close to him, then as far from him, as one might be, and it was rending him. It made him wonder what exactly he was to her. Once, she'd cheerfully volunteered that he was like a stone at the bottom of a pond. He was still thinking about that. She, on the other hand, she was the lizard that walks on water, she said. Or not walks. It couldn't do that, not without crashing through. Certainly not stands. Only runs. The surface was just firm enough for that, shattering only after she had moved on.

You slow me down, she said. That must be how she'd arrived, falling to him, beyond the dappling light above. It was new. She liked it, seeing in the dark, without the glare. And what was she to him then? An emissary? Of that same light?

The whiskey continued to disperse him. He considered now how the crests of the wave might be dilated, if that was the key between them. Perhaps it could be accelerated, he thought, its frequency increased, its period compressed, so that the gaping voids at the base might be elided from experience, as the black between film frames is, and her attention might appear a continuous succession of peaks.

Perhaps, though, he would get used to the pairing of states, learn to take what he could from both. To take the flutter out of her mind, even if he could, might take it out of her body too, and he couldn't be sure he'd want what remained. She might be an alloy, not an element. There might be no space, when it came to her, between purity and dispersion.

■ ■ ■

The thin blond light turned to gleaming gold, the chill stiffened in a rising wind, but still the whiskey pulled him under. Lately his dreams were duller than his life. They embarrassed him, their triteness, their risible symbolisms. They were also countable, and this redeemed them for him, at least a little.

There were five. Or else five acts of a single dream. In the first, standing, he eats a cold Reuben just peeled from the plastic wrap, the meat stiff, the striations of fat congealed, the rye disintegrating in a bath of Russian dressing. He throws a quarter of it out, but on its way past the swinging door of the deli trashcan, a twisted rope of plastic gets stuck in it. The man behind the counter, the one without a paper hat, stares at him as he decides whether he's expected to push the sandwich through. Often he would wake after this, and once he even fixed himself a sandwich.

When he returns to sleep, invariably he's high above half-court watching basketball. He can taste salted beef cutting through the barley of arena beer. A lanky guard on the wing sheds his defender off a high screen but runs into a forward, arms wide, legs low, waiting at the elbow. He's forced toward the baseline, where he starts backing down the bigger man. The help comes, a passing lane opens, but the clock is at four. He picks up his dribble, holds the ball against his chest, and puts up a turnaround fade-away over the fingertips of the forward and the center. The horn sounds and the backboard is framed in pipes of red light. The ball skips across the rim. The half is done. The score stays tied. The stadium monitors replay the shot three times, each one in slower motion than the last.

Before the close, two intervening acts: the first, at a latrine, listening to the drumming of piss on steel, and the second, in an enormous crowd molded in the shape of an avenue, on New Year's, creeping down the Las Vegas Strip. Sometimes he can only manage to keep his feet beneath the spot where the crowd steers the rest of his body, but sometimes he feels as if, for a moment, it is his feet, his body now driven by them, that moves the crowd.

And then the finale, which is without all sound. In the midafternoon sun he walks four blocks, through empty streets, in the city's red light district. When he arrives at the river, he sits on the front slats of a bench, right on the edge of it, with a Parliament behind his ear. He pulls the box of cigar matches from his shirt pocket and lights one, large like the tiniest torch, with a gentle stroke. The tall teardrop of a flame fails to bear a twitch of the air. Four matches go the same way. The box has many more. But he sets it down on a slat, bites down on the filter, and hunches forward, resting his chin on his hands as his thoughts turn to nothing especially. There the curtain drops.

In these dreams he is only half there, sometimes less, though he does not for that recognize them as dreams. If the cycle fails to complete in a night, usually it begins the next day afresh, with the sandwich. However many times his rest is broken, the sequence nearly always resumes with the next dream, as if waking were merely a scheduled intermission. It has been like this for weeks now. He anticipates them before he dozes, the acts he knows await him.

But this morning, this afternoon, just traceless dreams, or none at all, it is impossible to say. He awakes beneath a mass of blankets, piled high and twisted, overlying each other at odd angles but failing even in their totality to cover him. The sheets are damp. The cold has taken the feeling from his feet, as the bedroom, window agape, is now only an annex of a half-formed night. He shuts the window with a struggle, needing to lean on the frame with both hands, which are numb like his feet. It opens more easily than it closes.

He sits on the bed and studies the painting in translucent white on the floorboards—apparently his own work from this morning, just after Renna left. Three Newman zips. But it's the only abstraction left. Sleep has cleared away the rest.

The bottle is darkening with the afternoon. He pictures the stripped mattress on the other side of the wall, a queen covered, head to foot, only in his papers—the scattered Dutch records, dug up in a minor Viennese library indifferently pointed out to him by his father. Haas's journals.

He rises. If nothing else, there is work. Bricolage.

2

WITH BOTH HANDS ON THE STOCK, AND THE BAR-
rel nearly vertical, Haas lifted the arquebus (*haakbus*) above his
head. The grain of the heavily wooded arm, descendant of the
handgonne, flashed copper in the light infiltrating the canopy.
The sterling serpentine, engraved with boar and crossbow, held
the slow match, and from its ends, narrow streams of smoke
rose without curling, revealing the light's architecture, the crisscrossing, odd-angled channels by which it arrived at the canopy
floor.

Haas rested the tip of the barrel in a tree fork, smooth
and black and eight feet high. Along the blade sight, with his
left eye shut, he regarded the thorn-gate along the mountain
path, and beyond that, the fortified walls of a highland village,
Detumbeneram, not far from Kandy, center of the island kingdom of Lanka (*Zeilan*).

The village had been sealed off in anticipation of his
approach from the south, the Dutch strongholds of Colombo
and Galle. The Portuguese had claimed these cities in 1500,
more than a century and a half ago. It took the Dutch, newly
arrived in the next century and working with the Sinhalese from
1640, a decade or so to dislodge them. By now, though, in 1663,

the allies were enemies. The Dutch were at least as interested in controlling the island as the Portuguese they'd helped drive off.

The North Country remained in Portuguese hands. Strangely, they'd made no progress in the Highlands separating them from the south. Had they found it impossible to take Kandy? Or had a tacit understanding formed since the Dutch-Sinhalese alliance collapsed, that the island belonged to them both now but no other, that the common enemy was the Dutch?

That was beyond Haas's ken. What he knew was that ten years ago the Portuguese ably defended the north coast against his Dutch ships descending from India. He'd had to circle back from the south of the island to gain a foothold—at the time with Sinhalese aid—against more porous Portuguese defenses, unfortified by the European forces stationed to the north, in India.

He also knew that some of the soldiers he'd been fighting lately, in the Dutch effort to take Kandy, had a complexion neither native nor European. They fought a bit like Europeans, more than the Indians did, though with a greater ease with ambush. There were also some that fought alongside the Sinhalese who seemed to Haas purely Portuguese by blood, though they spoke, and cursed, only in Sinhala, the native language, even in the moments before death, with a bayonet twirling their guts, when one's mother tongue ought to be irrepressible.

Haas cocked his head toward the other Dutchmen—some soldiers, but many merchants, stand-ins for the severe casualties suffered only months ago. They all stood in a line beneath the giant palm leaves that overlay the tall wood frame bound by twine. The shelter was less for their protection than for the powder's. A pile of round ball, another of buck, lay just behind the men, and a large sack of powder lay beneath still more leaves. These also served as wadding for the guns.

The men held a collection of cheap flintlock and wheel-lock muskets, with the odd matchlock among them. Haas's arquebus was of another era: unwieldy and requiring a rest to fire, though forked branches could play the role, as now. For all its faults, it was of altogether better class than the muskets.

The large-bore barrel had been re-rifled just a few years before at a distinguished Rotterdam smithy, at the request of Haas's uncle, the weapon's last custodian. The original owner had been Haas's great-grandfather, Hendrik Velte, whose family, tracing to Alsace, formed a minor aristocratic line of Etichonid blood. Though settled in the Netherlands for generations, Haas's surname, his father's—High German rather than Low Frankish—left them feeling mildly, proudly, transplanted.

Hendrik's service as an army officer had been mostly symbolic. In any case he had little need for a weapon of a foot soldier. The training he had was proper to his class: in longbows and rapiers, and in horsemanship, not guns. But he was far from alone among officers in having fine versions of infantry armaments made up, not for use, nor even for show, but simply for possession. The felt need for them seemed to grow just as that weaponry eclipsed the rarefied martial skills of the nobility on seventeenth-century battlefields.

The Velte collection was extensive. It held, among much else, ancient hand-cannon, elegantly wrought pikes, and an array of arquebuses of various bores. Some had been lost, dispersed, or sold over the years, but the arquebus in Haas's hands was the best of Hendrik's: uncommonly accurate owing to the rifling, and potent, with a bore twice the size of the newer infantry muskets.

The gun had never been fired on a man before it came to Haas, who was the first in several generations to serve actually rather than symbolically. His mother had been reluctant to see him do so on the other side of the Earth, if he had to do it at all, and then only in defense of crass commercial interests. But that was the modern world. The son had wanted a part in winning it; that is, in winning whatever there was left to be won, even if his kind were no longer in the ascendancy. So he'd left Europe to extend the reach of something between a business and a colony, the Dutch East India Company.

Almost from the start there was local resistance. It turned armed and absolute as soon as it became clear they were occupiers not liberators. (The Portuguese had already given the game away; simple trade could never be the end of it.) Haas found himself helping raze Colombo, when the Portuguese still had a hold on it, then rebuilding the same city after the Dutch won it.

Since then he'd been making ever-deeper incursions into the bush, toward Kandy, winning and losing the same ground several times. At one point he took a nine-month trip back to Europe, as a sort of extended constitutional. It included a marriage, to a second cousin of equal birth, or slightly better, as the last century or so had been kinder to her family's fortunes than his own. But the woman, the girl, was far from his mind, now that he'd returned to Lanka. Love would matter one day, he thought. It would be everything. But first there was blood, and there was plenty of it to be spilled.

After several recent losses of position and personnel, they'd managed, almost magically, to hold the ground they took. He thought he must have solved something, even if he couldn't say what. It must be showing up in his tactics, moment to moment, a finer calibration to the environment, one he couldn't describe or know of except through the raw fact of their success. Lately he'd heard rumors that the Portuguese were making trouble to the north, perhaps drawing the Sinhalese away from the southern front of the kingdom. *They* might be his magic. He put it out of his mind. It didn't help. And they were only rumors.

Haas and his squad found themselves on Kandy's doorstep now. Fifty miles, maybe less. But their victories, coming consecutively, were beginning to cripple them. The men, and he especially, as commander, had been left starved of sleep and, far from Colombo, short of munitions.

By rights Haas could have led from a distance. He was fourth in command of Dutch forces on the island. His rise hadn't been hurt by his family name, the distant echo of clout it carried. But mostly it was down to his relentlessness in the bush these past years.

Probably he should have been relieved at this point. Leading a charge took the kind of clarity it was very hard to conjure in a state of exhaustion. But when the kingdom finally fell in Kandy, he thought, when the natives would submit or be annihilated, he wanted to be there, not Colombo. After the years he'd given, he couldn't imagine it otherwise, not taking his men to the center.

Haas tested the trigger's pull. An even pressure sent the serpentine dipping back toward the pan, the smoldering match in its jaws. He took a small blackened cloth from his coat and wiped down the flash pan and the touchhole. From the horn he drizzled powder until there was a cone of it in the pan. He flattened the charge with his thumb and the powder stretched to the edges.

He raised his eye to the sight but there again was only the broad barricade of the village. For hours now he and his men had watched little but the sun rise. It might have been a religious observance that kept the Sinhalese so still and silent. Or else they were just waiting for him.

His arms were burning from this same stillness, holding up the arquebus in the fork of the tree. Finally, there was movement: fifty yards above, high on the rock face, an eagle with chestnut feathers and a face mostly of black rose from its nest. Without a thought he swiveled the gun's barrel in the fork and set the sight just below the neck of the bird. His arms and his senses revived. The bird stared down from the mountain with unfazed eyes. The men turned to Haas and his peculiar engagement. Their bleary leader only returned the look. They busied themselves with their muskets.

The eagle shot from the cliff, its wings tucked tight to its body, down to an ancient tree whose branches hung above the path. Near the base of a giant limb, the wings flared, the claws extended, and a twisting wire, iridescent green, took flight.

The weight of the snake slowed the bird. Haas nearly took a midair strike at it, but just then it swept up the mountain face to its nest. A scrum broke out. He pivoted the barrel in the fork toward the animals, the bloody snake lashing out at the bird lunging at it with a cleaver of a beak.

Now he bore down on the trigger with stiff fingers. The serpentine struck at the pan in one blinding motion. An ochre flare, the crack of a fifty-yard whip, and a thrashing snake and bird. There were two or three flaps just above the nest before the bird dove into the gray-green underbrush. Caught in its claws in the escape, the snake was thrown from the nest, weltering along the smooth gray face in increasingly vigorous twirls and spins. Finally it arrived at the base of the great tree, directly below the nest from which it had been snatched. It was dewy and raw and still.

The men stared at it. The chance at ambush was dead, for no reason they could discern. Haas slipped the gun out from the fork in the tree and stood it on the ground. The barrel warmed his hands. It was no clearer to him, really, exactly why he'd fired, except perhaps that the threat of silence, the fatigue it brought, now exceeded that of open combat.

As he reached for the ramrod to reload, two Sinhalese in long cloaks appeared on the path above, beyond the snake and tree—with muskets raised. Dutch muskets. Spoils.

Haas's men scrambled to take aim. He himself knelt behind the rocks that made up the front wall of their outpost, bemused by the contempt and cruelty that suddenly filled him. He heard the thick, resonant pop of four rounds discharged at once, not far off from the sound of cannon-shot, but more complex, chordal. His men played no role in it.

Petr, the gangly metalworker-cum-soldier Haas had sailed

here with years ago, seemed to hurl his gun against the rock front. It clattered about and fell at the base of the short cannon. He went to his knees and into the pile of round ball, scattering it across the wood beams undergirding the fort. With his good hand he clutched the wet red one with too few fingers pointing in too many directions. The other four Dutchmen returned fire, but blindly, discharging their muskets with stocks held at their waists. The volley came to nothing.

A fine buckshot, almost a mist, came in then, from the barrels of a different sort of musket—Portuguese ones, judging by their angular stocks. They'd been fired by two Sinhalese who'd crawled partway out of hatches in the barricades.

The buckshot washed over one of the Dutchmen. It was too fine, and fired from too great a distance, to kill outright. Instead it scoured his face down to an oily translucence. Swatches of bone shone brightly where the skin had been ground away, around the chin and cheeks. His nose had become a small fibrous nub overhanging raw lips and cracked teeth. From his eyes came a feeble glare that fixed on Haas. The man seemed to choke. Petr caught him with his good hand as the man's knees buckled, but he could bring him no comfort, and the two lay among the pile of round ball.

In the dark before dawn, Haas's men had already primed the cannon. The vent brimmed with the coarse powder, and a thin flax fuse dangled from it, just a few yards from where Haas still knelt. He laid the arquebus down beside him in the soil heavy with water and began to unthread the slow match, still burning from both ends, from the serpentine. The other two men in fighting shape had laid their shortswords down next to them as they reloaded their muskets. Haas held one end of the match to the soil and it sizzled to a silence. He twisted it around his thumb and held the lit end between his fingers.

The Sinhalese were quiet now. More were surely positioning themselves, and his own squad was in shambles. Once again they would have to give ground to the heathens. If not, there would soon be none left alive to hold it.

Haas made a hammer stroke in the air to Petr, who pulled a sliver of steel from his boot in response. He tossed it across the other soldiers to Haas, who raised his hand and held it a moment. The two soldiers reloading their guns laid down their ramrods and weapons. One moved to help the two fallen men to their feet.

Arquebus in hand and the other soldier in tow, Haas crawled toward the cannon. The barrel began to fill with the thick black mud all around as the butt carved a trailing wedge in it. The match's tip poked up from his hand, safe from the water in the soil. The men got to their knees and with two sharp, coordinated tugs, Haas from the middle and the soldier from the tip, raised the cannon twenty degrees so that it faced directly onto the barricades. Haas took one more look at the target, which could barely be seen through the shrubs surrounding the cannon. Two musket barrels peeked out of the hatches, and behind them he thought he could make out their shadowed faces, the black, animal eyes he was going to blind.

He turned to his men behind him, at the fort. The others propped up the half-faced one. Haas was disgusted not by his injuries, which were catastrophic, but by his uselessness. He couldn't imagine him surviving the week. Minutes ago he looked a spectral white and pink; now there was only a crimson visage. At the equator, the fetid was the state toward which everything raced. It was the center. The infection that would finish him had probably already taken root in that mass of pulped flesh. The sooner the better.

In one motion Haas turned and touched the match to the fuse. There was a hissing, then a rumble. The cannon convulsed, seemed to deform under pressure. The ball came out low. It ricocheted off the dirt and punctured the wooden barricades, leaving them convex and gaping just above the hatches. One of the Sinhalese was in slivers. The other seemed to have been halved by the collapsing wall. The fluttering of his arms slowed, the rhythmic heaving of his chest petered out, leaving only the top of a man, still as stone, clutching a gun.

Haas dropped the spike in the vent. He lifted the butt of the gun high in the air and smashed it with it. The spike twisted and dug into the barrel base. He struck it again, pushing it further into the hole. He struck it once more and a long split ran up the stock. The spike was nearly flush with the vent now, its mass having been molded by the strikes to the dimensions of the hole. The cannon was crippled. If they had to accept defeat, they might at least leave no spoils behind.

For an instant, looking at the ruined stock of the ancestral weapon, he thought to bring it down on his own man, drive his nose like a spike. In the next, he thought to dump the gun. But in the one after, he came away with it—perhaps it could be fixed—down the mountain with his men, the broken ones too, to ground that was still solidly theirs.

3

THE LOW-E RUMBLE OF BOWED DOUBLE BASSES
filled the space. Sustained Es in higher registers, from a pair
of cellos and a viola, joined those nearly subsonic tones, a timbral complication to the accord of pitch. Of the basses, Edward
Larent's was distinct. It was miked. The signal ran through an
overdriven amplifier coupled to a nondescript speaker cabinet
belonging to the little Halsley café. As the sextet held the E,
Larent leaned into one of several pedals at his feet, loosing a
pitched growl, still an E. It enveloped the few dozen guests. He
drew the volume down with another pedal, level with the other
instrumentalists, though the tone was still thick with distortion.

A seven-note figure in a minor key cascaded from his bass.
The rest—first the viola, then the cellos, and finally the other
double basses—adopted ascending figures of the same length,
interlocking with Larent's, and a guttural counterpoint replaced
the droning Es.

Stagg sat at one of the tiny metal tables at the edge of the
darkened café, consumed. The sextet navigated a series of variations, Larent's bass growing rawer, more ragged, from one to the
next. The phrases crowded Stagg's thoughts, reoriented them,

brought them the veneer of structure before collapsing them down to a measureless point.

The music quieted for a moment, but given the circumstances, her voice could only be remote.

"I never said I wanted to meet them," she said. "As if I'd have anything to say."

He looked hard into the dark and made out Renna's face in the fringes of lamplight at a table three from his. Her chair was pulled back from it, and her words were for a figure, a woman, he thought, by the silhouette of hair, standing even further from the penumbra.

The music stopped. A wave of applause rose and fell as the players cleared the stage, all but Larent. The cellists came down the three or four steps on the left of the stage and sat at a table near Renna, nodding at her as they sat. The contrabassists joined them while the violist, a squat man in a woolly blue sweater, headed toward the door, lighter and cigarette in hand.

"You've been here," Stagg said, standing above her now.

"Yes and where were you!" She got up and kissed him, grabbed his hands, wrapped up his fingers and squeezed. He brought his hands together, hers in them, and extended his forearms to keep her where she was. The nausea, the buzzing head, the discarded afternoon, all for naught. At least he'd salvaged what he could, writing through the hangover, after he'd woken as night was falling.

"You said you weren't coming."

"Why didn't you answer? It was just drinks in the end, no dinner. But you weren't even here!"

"I was." He pointed over his shoulder vaguely.

Her eyes rolled but she was smiling. "You didn't check your phone."

"I left my phone at my apartment last night. You remember this?"

"Oh!" she said, angry with herself, or him, he couldn't tell.

She hugged him. "Can't you just be glad I'm here?" She put her cheek flat against his chest. "And how much have you had, my love? I can smell it through your shirt."

"Some." He grinned to no one, without choice or pleasure.

"Did you write today?"

"Yeah. Just before I came."

"The Dutch stuff?"

He nodded. By her face, he couldn't tell if she believed he'd done anything but drink. Anyway, if she didn't, she would never say so, even if nothing could help him more than to be called out. That would mean tension. Nothing was worth that.

Larent set his bow down against the amplifier and started in on a delicate pizzicato line, his right hand snaking over the fingerboard as his left pinched the strings. For a moment it took Stagg away from her, put him in mind of Bartók's strings. It was a mutual respite.

He and Renna sat at the table. "Another sherry?" he asked without raising his eyes from the empty copita in front of her.

"Sure, yes," she said.

He lifted his hand in the light of the hanging brass lamp, signaling for the waitress. "And the writer, how was he?" he asked.

"He was good."

Stagg waited for more but she was absorbed with Larent's hands now. "Very nice." He felt his mouth tightening into a smile but conquered the urge.

The waitress, dressed crisply in black, crossed into the yellow cone of light.

"Another sherry for her," he said, leaning close to her ear. "And I'll have, what, an Ardbeg? If that's something you've got." She gave a sharp nod, all surface, and withdrew.

The room clouded over in the harmonics Larent drew from his bass. The music's complexion had changed. It seemed beyond comparison now. Perhaps that only underlined Stagg's ignorance.

As the piece wound down in intricate double-stopped glissandi, he took in Larent's face: the long jaw, the very short, very brown hair, the eyes of the same color, and the delicately freighted expression—with what exactly Stagg couldn't tell—on which applause, twice now, had no effect.

Renna and Larent had been great friends in prep school, then something more afterward, though at a distance. He was in a conservatory in New Hampshire, and she was in grad school abroad.

Now they were something less, though exactly what Stagg felt it hard to know, given how little she volunteered. The two kept up, that much was clear. There were his performances and her readings and panels. Renna's silence about Larent annoyed Stagg, but prying was just the sort of indignity he wouldn't bear. Perhaps she thought she was saving him from more mulling. Of course it could only have the opposite effect.

Larent's manner was a challenge. The literary set might be nauseating, yes, but it was possible to feel that way only because reading them—"marking the axes of their being," another phrase he'd run into that Renna had seized on—was not very difficult. It was a nausea born mostly of boredom.

Larent was different, opaque, and even that without making a show of it. Translucent. It wasn't just that he was a musician, although that wasn't irrelevant. Notes could give away less than words. It was that he didn't flaunt who or what he knew, or what he was or thought he was, or what he thought you ought to think he was. Maybe he didn't have strong ideas about any of this, though there was plenty to have ideas about. He *was* interesting. That was just a fact about him, like height or weight. Partly this was because he seemed less interested in himself than in whatever he found himself doing. If only Stagg's own engagement with his work might be so natural.

There was none of the theater, then, the performance of character, that could give away the shape of your soul—a shape, incidentally, almost always distinct from the one you were trying to project.

In one sense you could say he was without charm, but in a way that had an abiding pull on Renna, it seemed, and, grudgingly, on Stagg too. It's what set him apart from the people in her world. Charm, after all, was always a bit of a racket. And he wasn't a racket, though he wasn't exactly earnest in the ordinary sense of the word. He didn't appear earnest, not consistently. But that might be what it was to *be* earnest, in the same way that the truest gentlemen have no truck with etiquette. Only imposters do. Gentility was in the bones—there was nothing to be done about it—and not being regulated by a concern for appearances, it could surface in ways that looked distinctly ungentlemanly to those who didn't know better. It wasn't merely sprezzatura either. There was nothing studied about it. It was the thing itself. Larent's artlessness might be of the same order.

There was silence. Larent leaned the bass against the speaker cabinet and joined the table of musicians. Five minutes later he saw them off.

"So?" he said, looking at Stagg and tapping Renna's shoulder. He was brighter now.

"That was weird!" she said.

"This is your group?" Stagg asked.

"No, no, just people I know from school," Larent said. "Sick of their orchestra gigs, for the night, anyway. It's the only time I can get them to play my stuff."

"They don't like what you write?"

"Well, they like *me*. The music, well, they'd play it either way. Do you like it?"

"I think I do."

"Interesting," he said. "It's not Bach, though—any of the Bachs—is it?" he said to Renna, the tiniest smile cresting on his lips. "Or Brahms."

"No, I liked it!"

"The distorted parts too?"

"Yes… but the last thing was more me."

"I know," Larent said. He turned to Stagg. "I think the straighter pieces reassure them I haven't lost my mind. But actually I want to send that one through the effects board—infinite delays, chorusing, pink noise—just to see. Make it unbelievably loud too."

"You'd see them in pain," Stagg said, gesturing at the tables around them.

"Well, as long as they clap."

"Why shouldn't they."

Larent shifted in his chair. He set his hands on the edge of the table, his long fingers arched as if at a keyboard. "So what, drinks?" He caught the waitress's eye and ordered the house red.

Stagg woke Renna's phone, which lay on the table, and checked the time. In truth it was a pantomime. He already knew he had to go. He lifted the tumbler to his lips and claimed the last briny drops. "I should go," he said as he put the glass down.

"Work," Renna said without looking at him.

"Sure," he said.

Larent seemed puzzled but before he could say anything Stagg got to his feet and bent over the table toward him. "I've thought about it. I did like it. Good luck."

"Thanks," Larent said, almost to himself.

Stagg took Renna's arm brusquely in his hand. "So I'll see you around, I'm sure." She gave him a look of exasperation, real or faux, and was about to speak, but before she got anything out, he was away from the table and through the smudged glass doors into the bracing night.

■　■　■

Larent's bass lingered in his ears as he cut across two narrow lanes, down the sloping avenue leading to Halsley's longest canal. The moon had turned the water a viscous black. A stiff breeze rippled its surface, drawing shallow crests toward the banks. The flow was always slight, and in the summertime the canal spawned great swarms of vermin. Now, though, entering fall, the waters were colder, the winds were brisker, and the canal was clear of rot.

Tall streetlamps fluorescing blue unevenly lighted the asphalt path along the water. Stagg paused in a long unlighted stretch and watched. On the other side of the canal, their bikes laid in a pile, several boys passed a pipe. One moved off to the side and seemed to do an impression. He paced with an exaggerated pigeon toe and swung his arms in eccentric ways that had no meaning to Stagg. But as the smoke swirled, and heaving coughs drifted across the water, long laughs did too, showing it meant something to them. He could see the impressionist's lips moving, hear a softly articulated garble coming from them. But his words never made it across, not as words, and the scene remained unreadable. At least in its details. The larger picture was clear enough. There was no larger picture. Knowledge lost any further purpose here.

He turned away and carried on to Fenton, a broad street running perpendicular to the canal that was lined with squat one- and two-story buildings, mainly bars and strip clubs, as well as a couple of taller buildings—well-trafficked hotels. The street's name was built on the backs of its escorts and its traders in pharmaceuticals.

Tonight it seemed empty. But even the impression of emptiness was more vivid, and equally, more confused, than it might have been. It was fresh. Without much explanation, Penerin, his supervisor, had altered his route again. Its newness was undermining the light trance Stagg usually did his rounds in, where perceptual reflex would suffice and his mind would be left free to work over other matters, like the knots in his drafts, or his relationships. That was watch-work's appeal. After a time of tracing a fixed route, you hardly watched, not in any active sense. Though you were paid all the same, you might as well not be working at all, just daydreaming, and with the peculiar agility of mind only an ongoing closeness to violence can grant.

Everyone, in fact, was on better terms with violence now. But watches more than most. He couldn't remember a stretch of more than a few days in which he hadn't come upon a car smoldering or a building collapsed. Less than two months before general elections, the country was wobbling in a way it would have been hard to imagine just a decade ago. Stagg had to admit, though, the infirmity was nourishing him, intellectually and financially. His job wouldn't exist if there weren't a desperation for eyes now.

He had no feelings about this. After all, he'd never had any special faith in democratic processes, not of the usual liberal sort anyway. He wasn't even totally sure he was an egalitarian. If anything, he was surprised the pieties of his age hadn't frayed sooner. Wasn't that the norm, certainties succumbing to doubts succumbing to new certainties, ad infinitum? Whatever it was, life now felt as though it was being lived on the cusp of fresh certainties, just when the doubts were deepest. Their nature, though, had not yet emerged.

One thing that could be safely assumed: if it was going to steady belief in its authority, the current government needed a landslide. First past the post wouldn't do. Turnout too would have to be far stronger than usual for the results to carry conviction, if not in the eyes of all—that was an unrealistic target at this point—then at least in those of most. The ruling party, and the president, would settle for that—so long as they won, of course. Whether their democratic commitment might fray if they managed to lose, no one knew. That just wasn't the sort of thing that could be known anymore.

The spate of attacks against the city's infrastructure and its public spaces was putting in doubt the government's claims to control, and especially its capacity to stage elections. Among the targets—schools, government offices, convention halls—were many prospective polling stations. This threatened turnout, of course, which must have been the point.

Stagg was the tiniest element of the effort to counteract this, though it was often far from his mind as he did his rounds. He took a more immediate interest in the novelties each new route introduced him to. Today it was The Lioness, the largest club in the area, and the best of its kind: two stories, four stages, and a tangle of VIP rooms. Nationally regarded dancers, their reputations spread by skin flicks, frequently headlined. The club was anomalous, though. If not for zoning laws consigning it to Fenton, The Lioness would have been built closer to its mostly upscale patrons. As things were, these men were forced to experience first-hand the grit that lay behind their entertainment.

Its sign was formed by narrow tubing shaped in diminutive lower case: "the lioness." The phrase shone a dark gold. Stagg pulled a soft pack of Parliaments and a convenience store lighter from his shirt pocket and drew a weak flame through a cigarette, watched the tobacco wilt in the heat. He shot the first pull of smoke from his nostrils and regarded the sign. There were four more drags, hard and quick. He dropped the half-cigarette into the rain gutter and went through the club's wide black doors.

"Thirty tonight," said a scrawny man in a cheap printed tee behind the glass panel. "Violet Skye is featuring." Stagg swept his phone across the face of the scanner mounted on the glass. "And it's a drink every hour," the man said.

"I get one?"

"You get to buy one."

Stagg turned into the darkened corridor past the window. Two giants, one white and broad, one black and tall, stood in front of the entrance to the club's main lounge. He waved his receipt at the blue-black African, who must have cleared seven feet, and paused before them both. Neither deigned to look. Stagg squeezed between the two into the room.

The stage seemed to recede indefinitely. It was as wide as the room itself, with an irregular, wavy lip like a designer pool. Three poles were aligned diagonally across it, front to back, and large screens ran across the back wall. All showed an ample-breasted Japanese dancer collecting the last of her tips from the men lining the stage.

Several hallways led out of the room, presumably to the smaller stages and private rooms Penerin had told him about. Stagg walked along the perimeter and sat far from the stage, at a table of lacquered wood. Most were empty. By strip-club standards, it was early.

Still in a glittering purple thong, the woman left the stage as glam metal resounded through the space. A waitress, beautiful only in her past, offered Stagg a wanton smile dull from use.

"And how are you?" The steel locket between her collarbones dangled as she bent down toward him.

"Yeah, fine."

"We have a drinks special on—"

"How about tomato juice."

"Sure? Everything's fifteen, even Coke, so—"

"That's fine."

She looked at him with an expectation that briefly eluded him.

"Pay first? Right." He pulled a loose twenty from his pocket.

"Or you can get it yourself from the bar."

"No."

She left with a more natural smile. Stagg slid his elbows onto the table. He cupped his mouth in his hand, pinched his nose lightly, and closed his eyes as the music played. "18 and Life." Skid Row. This was hair metal's afterworld, places like this. He'd never heard it anywhere else, except on Internet radio, when he used to listen to it sometimes for ironized laughs. (He was mostly done with that kind of laughter.) The frontman, Sebastian Bach.

He probably shits in a pan in some Burbank nursing home by now, he thought. Still—not a bad song, at bottom.

The room began to fill. Suited men in their thirties and forties, twenty-somethings in exquisite sneakers and cashmere hoodies, they flowed into the room through the various arteries linking the club's lounges. The undulating edge of the stage disappeared from view as the men gathered next to it, some sitting, most standing. Without waiting for his drink, Stagg got up and took his place among them.

As he approached he surveyed them, as he was meant to, but without knowing what to note exactly, except to note everything, which was impossible. He was there to detect change but lacked the baseline to do it. Tonight, and probably the next weeks, would be about establishing one, bit by bit.

Some of the men held wads of twenties; others, of fifties, though slightly thinner. Star money. A voice came from the speakers, interrupting Bach and introducing the dancer. The MC closed with a flourish, drawing out her name as a ring announcer would a fighter's.

The room went dark, then silent. In seconds the faders came up: "The Ballad of Jayne," another ghost of a song that had died decades ago. But again, not a bad one, if one had the stomach for the gratuitous. Still, it was an unlikely pick. It was wistful, or an attempt at it at least. Was it possible to strip wistfully? And even if, under the right circumstances, it was, can one really *begin* to strip that way, cold? Perhaps it was an eccentric challenge Skye, quickly becoming as porn-star famous as anyone, had set herself, to stave off the boredom of routine.

It was still dark, and it stayed that way for an uncomfortably long time, so long one couldn't tell if it was the indulgent whim of the dancer or a technical failing. Finally heavy white light fell on a girl, just post-teen, inverted a yard off the stage. Her tanned, stockinged legs clasped the center pole; her dark curls dangled nearly to the floor. She loosened the lock and airily descended, her azure skirt falling upward. With splaying legs she carved half a circle in the air, gripped the pole tightly and brought her patent leather heels, an explosive black under now-strobing light, to the glossed floor. She sprung up and pranced to the front of the stage, her flowing proportions now appreciable. She was just feet from Stagg, burnishing appetites with an opaque hazel gaze.

With that the men were in her thrall, proving it possible to begin wistfully. He wondered about the makeup of that rapture, though, its less gleeful elements.

Skye's repertoire seemed vast though her moves were mostly classic. The impression must have been achieved by small details—how else to explain it?—but he couldn't pinpoint them. He wondered whether they would show themselves over the next weeks, or whether he would come to find it was only an impression.

Piece by piece, she shed the black blouse, the skirt, the lace bra and panties in white. The club's DJ threw her a promotional tee shirt with her picture and their name emblazoned on it. She drew it slowly up her legs and held it between them. A spotlight appeared just in front of her and then the shirt was in it, a dark, wet patch on it against the bright white of the rest. She tossed it into the crowd as the men tossed cash onto the stage—small bills, large bills, everything. Stagg felt then there was nothing to fear from them or their rituals. And nothing to learn either.

It was too early, really, to say. One grasps so little the first time through, which was the way most of life was lived. But here was his peculiar advantage. He could bank on recurrence. It was his job. He would see and re-see all of this many times, a rerun with variations.

Skye made her way along the edge of the stage, taking a last round of tips and kissing each man on the lips as she leaned down and pulled the bills from his hand. She came to Stagg and looked at him with practiced sweetness.

"Was that fun?" she asked.

Stagg dug in his coat pocket for cash but came up with two quarters and a nickel. He looked away, felt himself shrug. "I think, I don't..."

Her lips curled. She dropped to her knees and picked up a crisp twenty-dollar bill from the stage, folded it in two, and pushed it into his pocket. "Here," she said. The staginess was gone from her voice. It was flatter now, but neither cold nor upset. "The next girl that comes on, you'll be ready." She leaned over the edge of the stage and kissed Stagg like the rest, her breasts pressing against his neck with the telltale firmness of silicone. Perhaps the kiss was different, though, he thought. She would have been racing through the space between personas when she gave it.

A young man appeared next to Stagg in a lush herringbone sport coat and a pinpoint oxford, his breath reeking of mixed drinks. "I loved you," he slurred to her. "I did."

Stagg retreated through milling patrons as Skye exited that space and claimed the young man's money. At his table he found a short glass of tomato juice sitting on a five-dollar bill.

He thumbed the rim of the glass and sipped at what seemed almost a sauce. "You ready for another? Something else?" His waitress's voice came from behind him.

"No... I don't think so." He lifted the glass into eyeshot.

"Oh. You haven't done much with that one," she said. "But take your time, you still have a while till the next one."

"Thanks," he said. He reached into his pocket and dropped the twenty onto the five and left.

■ ■ ■

The wind had grown stout on Fenton. Stagg fixed the throatlatch of his coat and squinted as the gusts drew tears from his eyes. He walked toward Harth, where the familiar portion of his route began (eventually this too would be shifted). A dust of plaster and wood filled the air as he approached a stretch of buildings under renovation. The sidewalk scaffolding shielded him from the worst of the thickening winds, though it also narrowed his vision.

The ovoid headlamps of a Lotus blinded him, just before bringing light to the grainy currents whipping about the metal framework. The car, of a dark, indeterminate shade, drifted down the street, and as it passed, he made out a long-faced man in a blazer behind the wheel and a woman with small bones and bronze skin beside him. Only the future could tell him if this was worth knowing, if it suggested anything, or if it was just one more of the thousands of observations that pointed only to themselves.

Stagg left behind the thin stream of people walking Fenton for its more sparsely populated cross-street, home to walk-ups punctuated by the occasional convenience store or gas station shining gauchely in the night. He came upon very little tonight on Harth: a few streetwalkers, a car parked with a small-time dealer he recognized behind the wheel, waiting, and two red-faced drunks, possibly a couple, in skullcaps and oversized coats, sitting on the curb collecting cigarette butts that had been stubbed out early. Nothing worth reporting.

A hundred yards on and the street darkened. The blue lamps gave way to dim yellow ones that appeared at ever-larger intervals. Finally the overpass came into view. The headlights of cars streaming along the bend in it combined to throw a pulsing beam over the edge, perpetually twisting leftward, as if on a pivot, with no clear terminus in the night sky.

The beam disappeared as he entered the passage beneath the overpass and walked alongside the short gray brick wall that ran the length of the massive structure. Long tubes of light encased in PVC lined the walls. Many had burned out; some only flickered. There were also those that had been diligently smashed by vandals, their casings caved in at the joints between lights, their weakest point.

The cement sidewalls bore a deep aerosol patina. Whirling outsize letters and images in washed-out colors that carried the trace of a former garishness, layer upon layer of them, applied over many years—they sealed the pocked surface like a primer. Scattered atop this base were more recent images, vivid, sharp-edged, soberly stenciled rather than freehanded: parasols, perched birds, nimbus clouds, and mathematical operators, the integer, derivative, and inequality signs among them. Other stencils were built from phrases in non-European languages: Japanese, Hindi, Arabic, and several African scripts. These palimpsests brought Stagg's other work to mind, particularly his would-be draft about the Buddhist monk, Darasa. Even after months of mulling, that scene was no more than notes and thoughts. Maybe, he thought, he could just start at the fortress wall, the monk's own palimpsest, and let the material find its own shape from there.

So far all his conscious efforts at tracing a vector between the monk and Haas had failed. Including Darasa in the series of writings always felt essential, though, and perhaps this was precisely because Haas's cultural "mission" in Sri Lanka was so radically different from his—a mirror image almost, destroyer and preserver. There must have been a personal aspect to the inclusion as well: the monk, after all, was metaphysician, exegete, and historian in one. Just what Stagg was becoming, it seemed.

Every time he came through this passageway, he wondered why he didn't carry the weapon he was entitled—encouraged, even—to carry. It routinely brought him across the fear-worthy. But tonight there was no one, just a chain of decrepit parked cars dotted with pickups and vans and the occasional over-worked subcompact racer. He slowed near the other side of the overpass. A maroon sedan, the right side of its bumper collapsed, sat behind a pickup whose body appeared tiny and frail above its own gargantuan wheels.

The tailgate was down, which was odd. Odder, though, was the woman beneath it, lying against the hulking tire in a bra and a silk skirt the color of straw. She forced the draft, the monk, from his thoughts.

Were it not for the peculiar way she was dressed, Stagg would have taken her for another unsheltered alcoholic and let her be. Instead he swung the tailgate shut and watched harsh purple light flood her face. Her eyes were open but so vacant he wouldn't have thought it a mark of consciousness had she not eventually blinked. She stared out at the length of walkway he had just passed, her head down on her shoulder. She must have seen him coming.

Her face, her forehead especially, was swollen and bruised, her nose scuffed and crusted over with blood turned black. She drew shallow breaths and her chest jerked with each arrhythmic pull of air. Stagg knelt beside her, brought himself into her line of sight, trying to extract the true form of her face. Beneath the swelling and cuts and shifted bones, beneath the heavy eyeliner and thick rouge, there was symmetry.

Their eyes were very close now, but she said nothing (maybe she could not), and he obliged with silence (anyway he could think of nothing to say). Her chest was swollen and red in patches. He put the palm of his hand beneath her breasts, near the sternum, and felt the skin inflated with fluid. He was searching for the articulated firmness of ribs but finding only a vague mass of tissue wrapped in torn skin. His investigations made her squint, but still no words came, just a slightly heavier breath.

He lifted her head and set it against the treaded tire beneath the bed of the truck. With his thumb he cleared away the hair that had slid across her face, and her eyes shone green again under that strange light.

Soon he found himself pulling her from the shoulders,

disregarding everything he had just confirmed about her condition. Her collarbones seemed to flex as he tried to raise her to her feet. She squirmed violently. It seemed to encourage him, this first vigorous sign of life, and he could think of nothing else, if he was thinking at all, than to pull her out from below, onto the sidewalk and up against the brick wall.

He wrapped his arm around her waist, leaned her upper body against his thighs, and dragged her toward the wall. She clasped her arms around her chest, closed her eyes, and mumbled or moaned as Stagg pulled her up the curb, her legs vainly kicking.

As soon as he released her she curled up on the sidewalk on her side, stretching her legs along the length of the wall. He didn't try to right her. Instinctively he searched his pocket for his phone. It was at home, he remembered now, the source of his trouble earlier with Renna, or the excuse onto which it fell.

There was a phone booth at the end of the passage, though he'd never noticed it till now, and was unsure whether it actually worked, or if it were merely the remains of a dead technology too costly to bury.

He had none of the numbers he would have liked to use, so the call was to 911.

"Yeah, I'm under the freeway at Harth. There's a woman, a hooker, I think. She doesn't look great. Second Watch. We'll need a car too. Carl Stagg."

From the booth he could see warehouses, some converted to apartments, some still serving commercial functions: textiles, lumber, paint. His eyes settled on the four-story directly across. The building's framework stood exposed at the near corner. The bricks had broken away unevenly. The matrix of beams, once precisely arranged along several planes, had wilted into a jumble of iron, soot-covered and twisting into the evening sky. An intense blaze must have shriveled the metal, but the beams, tangled almost sculpturally now, meant there had been combustion as well. A flammable inventory, probably. Whatever it was, the building was unsound, unusable, abandoned. Its lower windows were boarded, as were the doors, as of course were many others now throughout the city, not only warehouses but restaurants and shops and public facilities.

Through the building's charred scaffolding the moon was visible, a brilliant white haphazardly fragmented by metal. He walked back down the passage and sat on the wall, waiting, with the woman at his feet.

4

LIGHT ARRIVED AS A PLANE, PROJECTING THROUGH the slit between drawn curtains, cutting the bedroom in two. Stagg sat at the foot of the twin bed, on a short pine bureau intersecting the light. He passed his hand through the beam and watched sun-kissed dust swirl within its borders. He pulled the thick curtains apart and two dimensions became three, the light broadening until it was nearly the width of his little studio apartment.

In the street below, a small child and an older one, not quite a teen, hurried along with brows pulled low and heads whirling. The woman from last night, her broken body, the picture came to him. What will Penerin want to hear?

His shirt was heavy with sweat. He pulled off the black tee and balled it up in his hand, felt the damp in it before wiping it across his neck. It took some of the stickiness away. He reached down to the tiny metal handles and opened the second drawer of the bureau beneath him, sliding his legs out as far as the drawer itself. The clothes, overstuffed in the drawer, plumped as he did. He'd not looked at this surplus in over a year, ever since he'd moved in, after returning to the city from England. Everything in his closet was on the floor at this point, and as filthy as the tee shirt. At least these were clean, he thought, even if they looked like someone else's clothes to him now.

Along the top layer he found a crushed blue button-down with a mangled spread collar and flannel trousers. He opened the drawer below with his toes threaded through the handles and kicked a three-pack of generic boxers to the floor. They looked as if they'd been bought at a drugstore. Why he'd bought them, he didn't know, but he wasn't troubled by it. When you drank like him, little oddities like this lost their oddness.

It was only after piling the retired outfit on the bed that he noticed the small loaf of olive bread on the nightstand. It must have been there, sitting on the red plastic plate, since he'd last slept here. Two nights—three nights—now. One of the two chunks was nearly eaten. Only a hard beige crust covered in semi-elliptical ridges remained. The other chunk formed a complete half, its exposed interior a gauzy white punctuated by oblong streaks of purple. The sight of it seemed to hollow out his stomach. He felt a weakness in himself he hadn't known only a second before.

He pressed his arched fingers against the white of the bread, but like a cast that had set, it was no less firm than the crust itself. He gripped the half-loaf with two hands, his fingertips lining up in parallel along the white. One twist and the shell gave way. He pulled the quarters apart, put one in the palm of his hand, and dug his fingers into the crumb as close to the crust as he could. This was not so close, as some of the crumb had also staled. Leaving the husk on the plate, he pulled out the small core of cottony crumb. He did the same with the other quarter and pushed the husks off to one side, exposing the ridge at the edge of the plate in which olive oil had collected. He swabbed the chunks of bread until they turned a greenish-yellow.

Breakfast in the Spanish style, he thought. And who was it, the curly-haired golfer, who'd been known, decades ago, to eat bread and a shallow bowl of oil before each round? His father had told him about him, presumably as an example of Spartan values. But the name didn't come back.

He turned to the second chunk, warily eyeing the desk across from him, overwhelmed, for months now, by legal pads with most of the sheets torn out; xeroxed journal articles, some pristine for not having been read, others bearing the underlines of successive readings, such that virtually the entire paper was lined, restoring its balance; loose papers and index cards carrying unassimilated notes; books, open (Collingwood, Bentley) and closed (Barnes, Burnyeat), stacked and scattered, concerning several projects; the disintegrating letters and journals on paper of varying constitution and age; and the little hand-drawn maps, water-stained and mottled in every shade of orange and yellow and brown.

These materials spilled onto the floor, reducing by half the walkable area of an apartment already compromised by scattered clothing. At the very center of this mass was a laptop, with a cursor blinking on the last line of a document, the one that would make sense, or a kind of it, anyway, of all the ones surrounding it.

Obscuring the keyboard were his notes from last night, the flashes he'd had of the monk, just before he'd found the wordless woman. There were still a few hours till he had to brief Penerin. His real work, the next part of it, was glaring at him: charting the axes of Darasa's being, if not Larent's, or Renna's, or his own. Although if he could find his way to accounting for the men peopling his histories—and they were all men—they might well end up accounting for him, given his ancestry. He was, after all, only the latest branch of the tree. He swallowed the last of the bread and pushed on toward the center.

．．．

Squinting into that bright stretch of rock, his own reflection obscuring the fine scrawl covering the wall's mirror-black surface, the mendicant Darasa, poet, chronicler, exegete, and priest, would have wished for powers of vision greater than men are granted as he searched it for sense.

Whatever he could make out he transcribed into a book of palm leaves. The uncommonly curly script, a thousand years old and part of a language caught between Pali and Sinhala, had been molded by these leaves. Where straighter lines would have separated the plant fibers, rounded ones, running across rather than between them, did not. The writing of Darasa's day, less rounded but distinctly curvy, answered in its own way to the same constraints.

The graffiti covering that wall at Sigiriya was only partly intelligible to him, first, because his grasp of the continuum running from ancient Pali to seventeenth-century Sinhala, his own tongue, was strongest at its termini and progressively less certain toward its midpoint; and second, because the inscriptions were multiply superimposed, sometimes in seven or eight layers.

They'd accreted over the twelve centuries since the island had been ruled from here and not Anuradhapura, the ancient capital farther north, or, as now—1664—Kandy, to the south. At the time each inscription was made, it would have appeared more distinctly than the ones overwritten, the marks sharper, more pronounced. But little had been inscribed here since the monks re-founded the monastery two hundred years ago, though at the base of the rock this time, and not on the palace grounds themselves, which had served that purpose as recently as 1100. The monks' maintenance, high atop the rock, was thought too costly by recent kings, so the grounds were left to decay.

The years had flattened the writing. A kind of visual parity had overtaken the marks, making it difficult to say which inscriptions came last or first, or even to say which stretch of words or symbols went together with which others. Depending on how one grouped them, there were dozens of ways of reading the inscriptions. All of this only compounded his difficulties.

The monk had, some months back, cut a few words into the wall himself, in a blank area near its foot, discreet and permanently shaded from the sun. Mostly this was to test the tactile properties of the rock, the ease or difficulty with which the original inscriptions would have been made; and to see how the wall held a perfectly new inscription, in the hope that this might help him date the layers.

But perhaps he also did it simply to leave a few words behind, like the rest. His translated as "A lesser chronicler." He wondered how the phrase might someday be overlain, misunderstood possibly, and taken up, perhaps, into something greater by that misunderstanding.

He folded the palm book and placed it, along with the thin, plain stylus, into the sheath he kept at his waist. The day's transcribing was done. He would add these notes to the rest back at the temple.

For all the complications, he'd managed to give sense to some of the scrawlings. Most seemed addressed to the paintings that covered the rock fortress during Kassapa's reign, particularly those of women, "long-eyed," "golden-skinned," whose essential features, judging by the inscriptions, were stillness and silence:

> *Those ladies of the mountain*
> *They did not give us*
> *The twitch of an eyelid*

The paintings had been done after the fall of Kassapa, around 500, when his deposer, Moggallana, moved the capital back to Anuradhapura. Those living in the villages surrounding

Sigiriya would have made the massive rock (and the wall at its base) theirs again, while the palace proper was converted into a monastery.

A few of the paintings, smaller ones, remained along the path spiraling hundreds of feet into the air, ascending the fortress's edge. They would have survived for their location in the recesses and caves, which shielded them, along with the sentries of that era, from the elements.

There were also other inscriptions Darasa had at least partly interpreted, ones of a more mundane sort: declarations made between lovers, light rhymes, nicknames, and simple identifications (so-and-so from such-and-such). Amid these were the more significant ones, the ones he was after, carrying intimations of life in Sigiriya across the centuries. They dated as far back as 500, around the time of the death of Mahanama, the leading scholar of his era, and the primary compiler of the Great Chronicle (the Mahavamsa), a clerical history of the island covering the thousand years preceding his death.

Some of the graffiti spoke of noble families and their scandals, others of the lack of rice or meat, still others of populist discontent and the deposing of kings—and indeed of the fall of the fortress kingdom itself, to Moggallana, the rightful heir, apparently.

Darasa hoped these records might enrich the commentary he was preparing on the Great Chronicle. More to the point, though, what made the task pressing, was how they might inflect his contribution to the Lesser one (the Culavamsa), the still-living record of the kingdom. It had been accumulating in fits and starts from the time of Mahanama's death up through to the arrival of the Dutch envoys thirty years ago. That arrival had disrupted the keeping of the record, and a handful of the most senior priests—Darasa, not yet 50, being the youngest of them—was charged with updating it, through a portrait of the most recent decades of the kingdom. When it finally arrived, he would say to himself sometimes, the light of the past, even the very distant past, must change the complexion of the present.

Interpreting the inscriptions was arduous and uncertain work. As was simply collecting them. He'd only begun to account for the many inscriptions carried by the architecture of the court and palace above. So he ascended again. This was his third trip. The monk left the mirror-wall behind and edged his way along the path. In the guard stations he passed several renderings of the Buddha, in bleeding shades of red, orange, and yellow. The path narrowed as it wrapped around the interior face of the fortress, which was hidden from both the entrance to the court and the nearby townships, partly by the thick forest at its base.

Further toward the top, the cliff turned sheer and the path narrow, in some places reducing to mere foot-holes. The shallow steps ascended at a radical angle, as a great height had to be scaled in the smallest distance. He leaned against the rock. At this height, already two hundred feet from the forest floor, the winds were muscular, death-dealing. He'd knotted the loose fabric of his robe to give the currents less to work with.

In previous eras, rope bridges had crisscrossed this part of the mountain, connecting various levels of the fortress on the exposed top, where the palace lay, to the plateaus, embankments, and interior caves below. As Darasa stepped from foot-hole to foot-hole, pressing his weight against the cliff, he wondered, as every person who had ever got to the palace above must have, how many would have lost their footing, been snatched by the winds, toppled from the bridges, only to expire in the coconut palms and shrubs below.

The sun descended from its apex just as he reached the top. The palace grounds had stood unoccupied for over four hundred years. It was a site for research only now, and so far, beyond the reach of the Europeans. Just as Kandy marked the southern stronghold of the kingdom, Anuradhapura, though more vulnerable, did in the north. Sigiriya lay safely between the two. It left Darasa free, in a less fraught space, to make sense of things, which was what monks of his rank chiefly did.

Scattered throughout the grounds were staircases of varying widths leading only into the sky, the surrounding structures long ago having been dispersed by the elements. Several well-preserved buildings with broad balconies lined the plateau's far edge, each with eccentrically shallow stairs: sixty of them rising just ten feet.

The largest building, the palace proper, stood to the right, along the southern edge of the plateau, five stories high, each floor narrower than the one below. The inner wall had long ago collapsed, leaving behind a cross-sectional view.

The interior was mostly debris. The outer wall, facing over the cliff's edge, was in better condition, but large patches of it had fallen away, leaving gaps of a leafy green—forest surrounded the great rock out to the horizon—against the pale gold of the remaining stone.

The vast quantities of rock had been quarried miles away and brought up the sheer walls by an elaborate system of pulleys. All supplies would have been carried on the backs of servants, dragging many to their deaths. The king himself would only occasionally be shepherded from the palace to the long rectangular pools at the foot of the rock, where members of the extended court, and further out, the priesthood, resided.

The walls were engraved with lions and other animals, alongside geometric patterns and what seemed an uninterpreted language. Darasa entered the ruins to finish recording these markings. They might shift the meaning, he thought, of King Kassapa's description in the Chronicle, and perhaps send a sort of interpretive ripple through the ages down to the current regime and Darasa's own king, Rajasingha II.

He climbed to the third floor of an adjoining structure to take down the exterior markings on the palace walls. The angular inscriptions seemed to him clearly more than decorative, patterned as they were with something like a syntax, though not of a language like Sanskrit or any of its descendants.

The more he studied it, the more the writing came to resemble not a language but a shorthand, one that would have been filled in contextually during Kassapa's reign. On either side of the writing were elongated etchings, some of a creature that was a man below and a lion above, depicted beneath a broad parasol, and adjoining other images of palm trees and scabbards.

He copied down the three-inch-high script bounded by these drawings. On the fifth and narrowest floor, a pair of interior columns within the king's chambers was similarly marked. He kneeled near one of the columns and transcribed the text that wound its way up to the low ceiling in a spiral. After finishing the other column, he sat against the wall and put away the stylus and the palm book. The day was not unusually hot, but an ordinary day was fiery in the midlands, far from the cooling seas.

The king would inquire about the commentary on the Great Chronicle the monk would prepare back in the Highlands, the core of the modern kingdom. He was sure of this. Rajasingha presented himself to the Sinhalese, and to the Europeans equally, as a champion of historical inquiry—perhaps he was—and, more certainly, of the notion of lineal rule of the kingdom tracing back to Kassapa.

The king would be even keener, naturally, to know what the committee of monks was preparing to add to the Lesser Chronicle about his own reign over the last decades. But here Rajasingha's inquiry could not be direct. By tradition the clerical records were not to be interfered with. If influence were to be exerted, it would have to travel by subterranean channels.

For the moment, Darasa thought, the king might be occupied by more pressing matters—the intensifying Dutch raids from the south, and the more ambiguous, mature standoff with the Portuguese to the north—to bother much with this. Any sort of respite from his "vigilance" would be a relief.

The monk took a sesame ball from his satchel and ate in the heat, thinking of the trip back down the mountain, to the village temple where he'd spent these last nights.

■ ■ ■

Stagg rose from the desk and pushed open the bathroom door. He tugged on the beaded metal chain that hung at eye-level. The bulb hummed then flickered. It stabilized a faint white and revealed a mirror stained by a mist of toothpaste and a tiny oval sink ringed with millimeter-length hair. He put his hand on the hot water knob of the shower. But he was late. In the many months now since he'd started writing the pieces in earnest, stopping only when the scenes trailed off in his mind, he always was.

From the medicine cabinet he pulled an uncapped bottle of mouthwash, bright green, and gargled with his head held back while pissing into the stained bowl. The sound of disturbed water confirmed his position as the burn of alcohol grew in his mouth till he had to spit it out over the last trickles of piss. He dressed quickly in the clothes on the bed, sank his feet into loafers, and squeezed his laptop into a briefcase, a gift from Renna, that was stiff from underuse.

The air in the hallway was an improvement, cooler, smelling faintly of sawdust. The trip down three flights seemed longer than usual, and he caught himself limping slightly. His Achilles was sore, though he couldn't think of when or where he might have strained it. Perhaps dragging the girl.

The foyer was flush with sunlight. It streamed through the glass doors and reflected off the concrete stairs outside and the glossy speckled tiling underfoot that smelled of disinfectant. For a moment everything disappeared in the glare.

5

"THIS IS WHAT," THOMAS PENERIN SAID, STUDYING the manila-foldered report on the last assault. "Jen Best. Found... Harth, right, well, that says almost nothing. This is what, then? For us."

"I've seen a lot of girls now on that route," Stagg said. "And no one's turned up like this." He picked bits of lint from his sock, which rested on the opposite thigh, his legs being crossed. "Maybe that doesn't say much. Either way, though."

"Not really, no. One way counts, Carl. The other is simple assault. Run-of-the-mill police work. We'd turn that over. Even a string of beatings—if that's *all* it is, we're wasting our time. So, does this woman, what happened to her, have anything to do with anything? Jenko, say. Or the elections—"

"Does it matter who wins anymore?" Stagg said. "Sometimes, for a few seconds, I can forget who's president now. Which is crazy."

"It matters," Penerin said.

"A third of them voted last time."

"And that's what we're trying to fix. We have to make it matter to them. Obviously it already does to the ones destroying every-thing. So as long as you work for me, as long as the government keeps picking up both our tabs, it'll have to matter to you. So, from all the months you've been with us, Carl, can you tell me something?"

A sneer overtook Stagg's face. "Look, this girl, she got seriously fucked up. But it looked like, to me, she was meant to live, the exact way she'd been fucked up. That's it. She didn't say a word, not when the police and the ambulance came either. They must have gotten her name after I left, or from something she had on her. I only know what you're holding in your hands. And there's not all that much in the report, beyond the few details I supplied. What's there to interpret yet? Her empty stare? If it's speculation—sure, a less-than-murderous ex, maybe. Or a warning for the check that bounced. Or just a dissatisfied customer looking for a refund. There was nothing obviously about... politics—the 'State'—if that's what you mean. That I can say."

Penerin got up from his swivel chair. "Your impressions, even the faint ones, are why you're here. If that's all you have, then fine, that's all. But did you check this against the earlier incidents? That at least could mean something eventually—that they're definitely all related, if they are."

"I wasn't working here when they happened, though."

"But the reports. Did you look them up?"

"This happened yesterday. No."

"Then we need to check now."

"I'm going to get something just from comparing names, images? I need to talk to her."

"We'll do both," Penerin said as he got up from his desk. "Anyway, here's the thing. I have another watch here, from Henning, who's seen prostitutes harassed or worse recently. I sent him a copy of the report this morning. He thought we should compare notes." He walked past Stagg to the door that looked only a little like wood and gestured for him to follow.

At the end of an underlit corridor they came to a room of glass. The ceiling was painted a cool green. In the corner was a small desk with a fax machine and a printer. Three folding chairs were laid out around a coffee table in the center of the room. A South Asian sat in the middle chair, slender-framed, long-fingered. His eyes livened when he caught Stagg's.

"This is Ravan, this is Carl," Penerin said without gestures. Stagg extended his hand and Ravan received it happily, though without standing.

"So you've seen what I've seen, something a bit like it anyway," Ravan said, still shaking his hand. His accent confounded. England was in it, but in a complicated way.

"Really there hasn't been a case like this in months, in Easton," Penerin said.

"But yeah," Stagg interrupted, "I found a woman, beaten but not mugged. She lost nothing," he said, scanning Penerin's copy of the report. "Her bag, money, ID, everything was found on her. Just yesterday."

Ravan pulled on the collar of his polo with two fingers. His sneakers were battered, offsetting the curiously sharp creases in his gray wool trousers. He turned his eyes to the floor and then quickly back to Stagg. "Lately there's been quite a lot of this, in the more unpleasant parts of Henning, where I keep an eye out, the way you do here, I understand. Some even in the better places. Mostly it's among the girls, the escorts, this."

"And what's 'this'?" Stagg asked, staring at the heavy glass windows that were the room's walls. There was a small speaker next to one of them, but the glass was untinted and non-reflective, ruling out interrogative uses for the room.

"This violence, that's never quite fatal," Ravan replied. "I've had at least four of these. You've had at least four, even if they were a while ago now. And the report you've sent—the physical description of the man is basically consistent with one running across most of the cases for which we have one. There is also the car, its make and color. An uncommon kind of green, actually. You'll have to check further with her, but it sounds as if your victim is describing a vehicle from another case of mine. I'd have to know more, of course, but I can't help thinking she's just the latest. The meaning of it, though, I've no idea.

"Some of the beaten girls have disappeared since. That's worth keeping in mind. We can't say, of course, if they've just left town, gone back to some relative or boyfriend or whatnot. That's the thing with tarts, isn't it." He looked up at Penerin. "A couple of dealers, cocaine mostly, have been roughed up. Put in hospital actually. There have been a few firefights too, which have put them on notice. In a way, well, I tend to think it's all had its use."

Penerin shook his head with a resigned smile.

"Well, the police can't be bothered with this at the moment, right?" Ravan said. "Bigger things afoot. That's true. And there are certainly, visibly, less girls working now. That must be good. And it can't not have something to do with this force that looms."

"Force," Penerin repeated the euphemism.

"Violence—its possibility," Ravan said. "Mostly that's been enough. Except when memories need refreshing, like this, maybe. And isn't that what the police ordinarily provide? That possibility? Doesn't someone always?"

No one said anything.

Penerin closed his eyes briefly, as if clearing Ravan's words from his mind. "Carl is going to talk to Best as soon as he can," Penerin said. "We'll be in touch after, Ravan."

"I think she'll be out of commission for a while," Stagg said as he stood. He shook hands again with Ravan, who seemed settled just where he was.

"Whenever you can get access," Penerin said. "Maybe before she's discharged if we're lucky. She can't disappear on us."

Stagg and Penerin stood near the door. Finally Ravan got to his feet, almost reluctantly, and the three of them filed out of the glass room with the green ceiling.

6

A HUNDREDTH OF THE CITY'S SUBSTANCE VOIDED, sixteen months in, and hardly any deaths.

Idle police cars, a fleet of them, rendered down to a veil of sheltering smoke, itself lost in the broader black of night. It took the large-bore beam of a scrambling chopper, gyrating above, the beam and the chopper both, to expose the shroud. A few minutes pass and a gas tank yields to the simmering orange and blue of the lot. White flames dilate twenty feet, spraying metal and glass, plastic and leather, puncturing another tank and setting off another round.

That was the first crack. June of 2027. Stagg had seen it presented with rare pomp, if it could be called that, at a friend's parent's place, a duplex downtown. This was in the weeks after Easter term. He was just off a flight from Heathrow, back in Halsley, to work on the closing chapter of his doctoral dissertation, which was not in imperial history but analytic philosophy. There'd been a tie he had yet to find, and he thought it might lie at some distance from the library's stacks.

That night, though, there would be no writing or reading, no rewriting or rereading, no reflexive mulling, no deleting and restoring verbatim from memory alone. Instead there was

Hour of the Wolf. He was told, for this director, that scale was the essence of the thing, his somnolent figures defined in light-eating blacks and silvered whites.

But before they could get the film onto the pearlescent vinyl sheet the very same shade of white as the living-room wall from which it hung, cable news and its smoking lot of police cars came blaring through the digital projector. In the small hours, the two of them would make their way back to the film, to Johan's chafing spirit, to his arched fingers pinned against the temples. But by then one magnitude had displaced another. Plates were shifting. Bergman could make no impression.

In the months to come a pair of abortion clinics, one attached to the city's most distinguished university, the other to a Jewish hospital, were abolished by floods, ceiling-high and sewage-laced—the reported cause, exploded mains. A tax court, and across town, an employment office and several check cashers, were razed in sequence. Then it was the churches and mosques, collapsed in alternation, transubstantiated, burned down into shells soon boarded up, some of them metamorphosing along the way into shooting galleries and heroin dens. Simple backpack devices sufficed to cripple the subways and buses. But through all of this, no deaths, just paralysis, erasure, a neutron bomb in a mirror.

Arrests were made, but mostly at the lower levels: the ones who dispatched the devices, lit the fires, sprung the waters. This slowed nothing. Frequently it was impossible to tell whom any of them served.

These negations and nullities wound their way through the city, across its bridges, penetrating its outer districts, laying ellipses everywhere, relieving Halsley of an analog fullness, or anyway disenchanting people of the notion, and of the very idea that the state was any longer in a position to make guarantees.

Strangely, there were no claimings, only denials. They grew fiercer as accusations sharpened and rote as they diffused.

Motives, originally few and imputed confidently (not to say correctly), metastasized, every effect guaranteed by several causes. A building saved from one attack—many were foiled along the way—would soon fall to another, often bearing the trace of difference, the activity of a rival body.

The government only added their own scars to the city, exploding hives of alleged factionalist activity, sometimes preemptively and on little grounds.

A half-dozen interests stood to gain from the laming of every building, the stilling of activity within, whether libertarians, religious fundamentalists, direct democrats, socialists, antiegalitarians—even some anarchists who felt they'd found their moment, with a faltering central authority. (There was also the mention, among some, of democratic dictatorship and what it might mean.)

But the manner of gain, the precise aim, the strategic or cathartic value, grew less obvious by the month, its significance emerging only against a backdrop, itself perpetually expanding, of hundreds of crisscrossing antecedents and an ever-growing list of factions.

With each disembowelment, government security thickened, necessarily so, and without much complaint from the citizenry: the arbitrary checks and searches, the shows of force, the rapid and continuous diffusion of officers and agents, plainclothes and otherwise, the reserves on permanent domestic deployment. A crosstown bus trip, the purchase of a phone, the filling of a theater, all of these proceeded at half or quarter speed. The city clotted, and as it did, the day, unit of life, contracted.

Now, with elections approaching, the disruptions were peaking.

The expansion of security, and the gradual mutation of the National Security Administration and the Federal Bureau of Investigation into a clutch of allied and semi-autonomous intelligence agencies, was the bit of luck Stagg needed, the stopgap income between academe and the think tanks that editorial work couldn't provide, not without exacting a toll anyway, socially, intellectually. For the Second Watch, his own division with this reorganization, there were the eight weeks of training to deal with: target-work with the G17, techniques of spontaneous interrogation and dissemblance, a few self-defense maneuvers (chokes, grips) he was sure he would never actually find the idealized conditions, or the calm, to use. And with that, he was paid to do little besides wander and watch. His mind was mostly his, to dispose with as he liked, which generally meant mind-writing, as he liked to think of it.

Generations ago, wasn't it Matthiessen, Stagg thought, who'd written his first book, and even helped found a once-significant literary journal, a bit like this? That was on the foreign side of the intelligence community, though, the CIA, which itself had splintered. Now it was Stagg who was searching for a book, and something like a new historiography, even a new identity, but right here at home.

The Second Watch assigned and continually modified three or four basic routes for each agent, to prevent detection, but also, by disturbing the monotony, to re-sharpen the senses. No more than four, though. Too much familiarity was blinding, but so was too little, especially in picking up minute deviations from one night to the next. Most days his walks were the mildest permutations of each other, a story written over and over, intercalated with a few novel clauses here and there.

Still, he was more valuable to them than a camera eye, which anyway they had stationed at most segments along his routes.

He could catch the atmosphere of an exchange, the charge carried by a tone of voice, the way the same stretch of words might be variously inflected on seven occasions, five innocuous, one obscure, one toxic.

The watches' logs were processed a level up, by veteran staff who sifted them for useful patterns. But the ground-level reports were the critical inputs to this process, which was in effect a kind of echolocation.

Penerin valued the capacity to discriminate in these, his lowliest of charges, quasi-agents at best. It was not strictly a job requirement; the country's needs now were too great to make it one. A degree from the elite colleges, though, had become a common point of entry, in a way it hadn't been in the days when domestic intelligence was considered child's play next to the foreign side. Now that it was, by anyone's reckoning, at least as complex, pedigree helped, even if, as for many, there were only gentleman's Cs to speak of.

Still, some watches managed to distinguish themselves. Their reports came to be relied on, sometimes as much as the experienced investigators on staff, though they saw no more pay. They would be shunted toward paths thought information-rich, and also—the qualities frequently coincided—to places where the signal-to-noise ratio was low, and an uncommonly fine capacity for discrimination, whether learned or innate, was a boon. It helped no one to raise red flags everywhere. It was about noting the shifts of consequence. In this respect Penerin had begun to trust Stagg, his sense of significance.

Stagg would later learn that his and Ravan's reports, in particular, had been critical in mapping the whore beater's activities. (Despite his insouciance, Ravan had the kind of consciousness that registered much.) Stagg's discovery of Jen Best under the overpass had not been simple chance then. Penerin had had his suspicions, though he kept them to himself, about the possibilities of political meanings attaching to the assaults, and had been funneling Stagg toward a hypothesized perpetrator. The route that took Stagg under the bridge had been suggested by information coming in from him and the other watches. Penerin was continually recalibrating Stagg's route, of course. He just hadn't told Stagg that this man was already one of its targets.

That he'd come across Jen, and Ravan had come across two other girls in even unlikelier places—just off from a heavily trafficked pan-Asian restaurant, up against transparent garbage bags of rancid bok choy; and on a dank emergency staircase in a subway station, next to faltering industrial-scale elevators—also meant that between them they had likely come face to face with the man, or men, though they believed he was one and not many.

Probably Stagg had seen him several times, among the regulars along his route, people who recognized him as much as the reverse, though he hoped, of course, they didn't recognize him qua watch. A subset of these he'd even befriended in limited ways, leaching data of unknown quality. Some of these were surely other watches, the sensoria of other agencies whose domains overlapped, or even tiers of the same groups, where jurisdictions were often structured concentrically. Responsibilities intersected.

Somewhere within the twin penumbras, the shifting loci formed by Stagg's and Ravan's movements, was the man (or woman, though the history of violent crime all but ruled this out). Or if it was not the man himself, then something that shadowed him.

But it was always possible, and Stagg would frequently think about this, that all their calculations were for naught, and it was only something like dark, useless chance that brought them upon those beaten women, giving them the sense, and only the sense, that they were closing a distance.

7

A CHURNING VIOLET CYLINDER OF SMOKE, A thousand feet tall and growing with no compromise to its proportions, rose off forty smoldering broadleaf acres on a windless morning on the Indian plateaus. The second millennium had seventy days left to it.

The younger son, twelve, the father, fifty, and a lineup of atmospheric researchers, military officers, and statesmen all waited near a temporary station cluttered with meteorological devices. A heavy crackling, the cavernous thud of collapsing trees, and most of all the rumble of rushing smoke—it filled their ears.

The sky was dawning an uninterrupted cobalt, cloudless. The dew point was thought adequate, the upper atmosphere appropriately turbid, to stoke this enormous immaterial engine, one whose operation, it was hoped, would induce a torrent.

Deep in the Orissan jungle, every ten miles, for forty miles, another cylinder fired and another group clustered a mile from its base. It was the father, though, Menar Peshwa, deputy head of the country's military weather bureau, and Indian representative to the World Weather Watch, who led.

The hard edges of the towers gave way. The smoke dispersed

laterally at the tops, where the atmosphere turned violent, merging into what looked like gray nimbostratus underlain by scuds. This, as the sky was losing its green and going a truer blue in the half-light of a sun cresting the horizon. The jungle, a thicket of shrubs, airy bushes, lanky trees, all brown where they were not a searing orange, had been scanted by the monsoons, as had, more important, the rice paddies woven through the base of the mountain range, the Eastern Ghats.

Within the station, Menar studied the atmospheric data coming in from the probe, the small blimp they had sent up five thousand feet. The advanced metrics rolled across the screen, forming patterns whose significance he could read off the matrix like a map. The assistants, the sergeants, and the other officers all watched the data percolate through the display, but they could apprehend only elements of it. For a synthetic interpretation, a final diagnosis, they turned to Menar.

Intimates could sometimes see the answer in his face before Menar could turn it into words. This time he was blank. He rose from the long metal desk and strode between the men out of the station. "The readings are fine," Menar said, the men gathering behind him. But on the fringe of the horizon they saw something unwelcome: a thick sheet of nimbus headed in. Menar disappeared into the station. On the radio he pressed the Bhubaneswar weather monitors for news. A voice explained that the fast-moving storm had unexpectedly kept much of its force as it made landfall. It had brought significant rains to the paddies among the Ghats—that was the good it had done—but it was now on its way, at great speed, to the plateau. In ones and twos the men trickled back into the station. Now Menar wore the news on his face. Only his boy, Ravan, remained outside, watching the convergence of clouds, natural and artificial.

The smoke had risen to seven thousand feet and now descended, as hoped, to three thousand, as nimbostratus clouds about to storm normally would. But the men stood at the monitors, indoors, and watched the incoming monsoon explode the experiment. A fine drizzle came down at first, then, in minutes, heavy rains. But the two clouds had by now become one, and the precise origin of the water became unknowable. Menar came outside again and called the boy's name. Ravan looked back, drenched. Nothing more was said as he followed his father inside. At the cost of one hundred and sixty acres of scorched forest, the storm engine would have to remain hypothetical.

There were, and would be, many occasions of this sort. Like the time, in 2010, in Andhra, south of Orissa, that they covered a hundred acres of fallow fields in carbon black, and an adjoining area of the same size in chalk, hoping to promote thermal updrafts. For Ravan, who was now finished with university, art was overtaking science. So he couldn't help but see the project under two aspects, as the atmospheric experiment his father intended, and as the Earthwork triptych, or else the field painting, unwittingly created. From the mountains running down to Andhra, Ravan and his older brother, who was also their father's chief assistant and namesake, looked down onto the fields: an immense black against an immense white against an immense blue (the Bay of Bengal).

Menar had decided the project was worth a try. It was much less expensive than the others, and it destroyed nothing. The fields were already empty, and the carbon black might even rejuvenate the soil. The Babylonians, he told his boys, would burn their old fields to stimulate new growth, and rain too, for the next year's crop. These ancients were, to the father, progenitors of a thermal view of storms.

He hoped the pattern of heat absorption and reflectivity produced by the dusted fields might stimulate ocean winds and condense water into low-lying marine clouds. Rain did come, and the blackened fields received a substantial share. But so did the white fields. Moreover the effects showed themselves only over weeks, making it hard to trace the causality. It may have been that the black was responsible for bringing rain to both, given that a storm's trajectory couldn't be precisely controlled. Or it could have been, as the skeptics at the weather bureaus at home and abroad thought, that the matter was, once again, simple coincidence.

There was the time, too, they set the sea on fire. This was even before they torched the forests of Orissa. They cleared a mile of beach, floated fire-retardant buoys, and applied refined oil to the ocean's surface with six boats that covered the field in the manner of lawn mowers tending a soccer pitch, strip by strip.

At his request, Ravan ignited the slick. Aiming slightly upward, the boy, just ten, pulled the flare gun's heavy trigger with three fingers. The stick shot out of the broad barrel of the pistol and ignited within yards, trailing red sparks before exploding in a ball the same color, shimmering from then on as it cut a path through the air toward the center of the slick.

As the flare struck the ocean, the smaller flare acted as the spark to a vastly larger one. Because of the slick's expanse, the flaring proceeded as if in slow motion, the flames traveling methodically in all directions from the center. The breeze riffled the waters in the bay. It gave the flames a topography. Burning waves rolled in toward the shore, while the wind sent smaller, more fragmented waves laterally, intercepting the others. The path of the fire itself was unaffected. The flames rose over all of it, and for a moment, under the midday sun, a translucent, rolling red overlay the aquamarine of shallow bay water, just before smoke, charcoal black, came up off the tops of the flames, cloaking the red and blue beneath.

They kept the burn alive by piping fuel in just beneath the surface of the water, from tanker trucks stationed on the compacted sands of the beach. Within hours, stratocumulus formed and returned a steady drizzle to the sea. The clouds drifted inland on air currents aided by the flames, bringing rain to the rice fields, as hoped. A layer of larger cumulonimbus began to deliver a true storm.

They regarded the trial as promising, an advance over the last time they tried out the idea, in a slightly different form, inland, just a few months prior. A pool of oil, Olympic-size in width and length, but just a foot deep, had been set alight, sending a thick sheet of black smoke drifting into the lower atmosphere. No correlation with rain emerged. The humidity might have been inadequate. The sight of the flaming pools would stay with Ravan, though. They reminded him of the burning oil wells of Iraq, from the second American war there, though the flames had less clear purpose then. Still, as he drifted away from science, into art, music, the two, war and weather modification, would merge for him like clouds.

In the sea trial, the timing between the burn and the storm seemed better than luck could provide for. But consistent replication eluded them. Though the burning slicks appeared to increase the odds of rain, they couldn't be depended on to produce them. Unaccounted variables remained.

There was the environmental cost to consider too, the sheer amount of fuel necessary, at best, merely to increase the odds of rain; the oil invariably seeping beyond the buoys out to sea; and the smoke itself, which was possibly an aid to rain but certainly a pollutant.

Storm generation ex nihilo proved hit or miss. But Menar's results were good enough for his governmental sponsors. They pledged continued support of his experiments with weather, including newly begun interventions in existing clouds. There were other incentives in play, after all, beyond bringing water to rice fields during drought: military ones that remained hazy, still notional. There was also the perennial problem of flooding in the north of India, which meant there was as much to be gained from destroying storms as there was from creating them. It was thought the processes involved must be related. So Menar's program grew.

8

EDWARD LARENT AND HIS COULD-BE DRUMMER were thirsty, and the bar was not far now. Their first rehearsal over, the two had walked from the drummer's loft, lodged in the dying industrial heart of the city, to the large cobblestone square that was Carrell Plaza. In a recent renovation, the facades forming the square had been lined with massive high-definition screens, each assembled from smaller screens of the same proportions. Usually their faces gave you incandescent Dodges, Sprite cans, MacBooks. Today, though, a live newsfeed offered up a different kind of vision. Thick gray-brown billows, twirled by a corkscrew wind, rushed out of a battered fountain. From beneath chunks of pale yellow marble, clouded water spewed along the stones and across the benches edging the fountain. A pair of marble legs, one severed at the patella, the other at mid-thigh, remained upright, stoutly projecting through the shards from the whirling fountain floor, where the feet remained bolted.

The two of them didn't know what face to make. Something less than shocked. That would have been unreasonable at this point, after everything that was happening. More like unhappily curious, the sort of look that didn't last.

"Must be Brandt?" Larent said.

"I think," Li Moto, the drummer, said.

Hundreds were collecting in the plaza, all caught in the imaged wreckage of another, Brandt Square. The density of pixels marginally exceeded what the eye could resolve, so it was only the lack of a third dimension that disqualified these immense pictures from the status of self-standing reality.

In front of them, at the base of one of the screens, a pair of sneakers shone absolute white. Fraying jeans draped over the tongues and laces and led on to a Redskins sweatshirt; atop that, a pair of dry yellow eyes and a roiled mouth were affixed to a small black face.

"This," the rasp came, the man looking into the screen behind them, "I'm telling you, this is real. This shit." His left heel shook in a quick rhythm, pivoting on a sneaker toe. His thigh bounced and rippled his loose, stained jeans. His eyes surveyed the crowd and found only Larent's and Moto's. The rest were on the screens, the skies, or the cobblestones. The man's face went blank and stiff before an easy grin came across it. "What do you think of this?" he squeaked.

Moto reflected back something of this oddly timed grin, though his was milder, and its cause was the man not the circumstance. Larent, for his part, only stared into the brightness of the man's shoes, observing the double-stitched, unscuffed uppers, the "14" inscribed on the tongue in a tall skinny font. High-tops, just out of the box. How many jump shots will they see? And how many Crip walks?

Larent had clicked on "Crip walking" a few weeks ago, a link in a history of blacks in American music that was itself only something he had fallen into in a search for free jazz. It took him to a clip, a tutorial in fact, according to the tag: black teens in perforated football jerseys, bandanas just above the eyes, in a circle in the middle of a residential street, taking turns bisecting the ring in a sort of languid shuffle. Their upper bodies were slack and slightly hunched, but their legs were in constant motion and seemingly autonomous, carrying the rest of them in tow. Loose legs and bent knees turned stiff and straight in alternation, right then left. Their shoes, like this man's, whiter than white, or else a perfect black, went toe to heel, then effortlessly across the asphalt as the other leg tautened. They crossed at all angles, sliding past each other but never colliding. Having made their crossings, they would take up positions on the perimeter, reinstating the form of the circle as others broke off from it and floated through the space within.

The clip seemed to end just before perfection had set in and their movements had the chance to jell into some broader choreography, an organic orchestration. That was just beyond the tape, probably. Or perhaps gunshots were, and everything had turned to chaos. Whatever it was, Larent had felt compelled to watch the clip at least a dozen times.

"Why you looking at the ground, man?" the black man said to him. "There's nothing there." There was no menace in his voice.

Larent wished he would do the walk there, a perfect dance in those perfect shoes.

"Can't you see?" Moto said, playing along with the man. He grasped Larent by the shoulder and gestured at the screens.

"That's right, man. Now he's got it right." The man's face got smaller as he squinted at Moto. He drew the back of his hand across his stubbled chin. "You Chinese? Japanese?" he said, pushing one of his sleeves up to the elbow and dropping his head slightly as he studied the stones underfoot, yellow and gray.

"Yeah," Moto said.

"Which?" the man said, lifting his eyes but not his head.

"Yes, which?" Larent said. With a jaded look he grasped Moto's forearm and guided him off his shoulder.

The extent of Moto's glibness troubled Larent, more than the destruction itself almost. Perhaps he could be so playful, so detached, because it wasn't his country being sundered. He could always jet back to Japan, or Monaco, for that matter.

At Deerfield he'd been a parachute kid. But a gifted one, Renna had said. She'd re-introduced Moto to him just days ago as a possible bandmate. He'd been in her class, one behind Larent, and though, according to her, the two musicians had met before, neither could remember anything of it.

Moto's money, the leisure it brought, had freed up his gift for unprofitable things like experimental music. (From the little Larent had heard from him, earlier in the afternoon, he had to agree, Moto had talent, though he was unsure how or if it connected up with his own.) A few years after finishing at Deerfield, Moto went back to Japan with the noise-rock band he'd formed across the country, in San Francisco. They'd broken up for no good reason, as far as he was concerned, and he'd only just returned to the States, to that artfully spare loft—paid for, Larent assumed, in yen. He had no reason to begrudge him, though. Larent's family's money had done much to free his own creative impulses. There just wasn't quite as much of it, none to carry him now.

Larent regarded the black man, who along with Moto was grinning more freely. Really it wasn't his country either. He could never be free here. History, the sugar trade, wouldn't let go of him. And unlike the drummer, there wasn't much chance of his escaping. This, Larent thought, might have darkened the man's amusement with this chaos that was rolling in waves around them—*all* of them now, not just his kind, and for months.

The black man pulled his sleeve back down and gripped his face. He started tapping his pockets with his other hand, searching. The screens emptied. After a long moment they were reanimated not by a ruined courtyard but a razor blade, as tall as a man, briskly circling the plaza's digital perimeter. The blade shimmered as it flew through the deep black nonspace of the screens and glided into place alongside several other blades in a cartridge. A razor flying in the opposing direction met the cartridge, fastened to it, and fell into the palm of a waiting hand the width of three men.

Just in front of this race-indeterminate palm, the black man was lost in concentration, on a point inches from his nose. He flicked his thumb along the strike strip of a white book, dragging the crumbling pink match head across it. Still attached to the book, but with its cardboard stem bent around to reach the strip, the head combusted as his thumb withdrew into the space . beyond the book. The stem held the flame as he maneuvered it to his unwavering point of focus, the tip of a short filterless cigarette.

The digital hand behind him and the razor in its palm faded. The first traces of the razor maker's name gathered in their place. But a thousand footfalls were already echoing through the plaza. The crowd had lost interest, had perhaps never had any, having probably seen the ad many times, on many screens—just like what had come before it, the billowing smoke, the dust of another detonation.

Larent and Moto pushed through the crowd toward the edge of the courtyard. The man, smoke swaddling his head, lurched toward them before they could make much headway. A pocket of space enveloped him, but it moved with him owing to the fire jutting from his mouth.

"I bet I can help you," he said.

"I'm fine, I think," Moto said.

"Why?" Larent asked the man. "Why would you think that?" Larent didn't know quite why he'd asked the question, though the man offered a creditable answer.

"Because." He held out a crumpled soft-pack of Camels toward him. "Because can't anyone?" The pocket around the man hardened in place, penning him in, just as the two of them drifted away on a current of foot traffic toward the shops beyond the screens.

They stepped through the beaten doors of Moto's haunt, The Round, a pedigreed rock club on the courtyard's eastern edge. The bar itself was no more than a low-ceilinged corridor line with a dozen cherry stools. Behind it were three local drafts that Moto attested never changed, and a modest shelf of spirits, mostly common stock, though spiked with a few rarities the owner apparently enjoyed, things like Green Spot, or Yoichi.

No one was tending bar. Moto scraped past the two vintage Rickenbacker F-holes hanging on the wall and clutched the shoulder of a bearded man on the farthest stool. Larent, who had slowed at the head of the bar, near the door, searched the eyes of the four men for the bartender, the one indulging his regulars in the slow hours of early evening, he assumed.

Before he could single him out, Moto caught his eye and waved him on past the bar. By the time Larent entered that cube of a room at the back, Moto was comfortably seated at a long unvarnished table near the entryway. Larent looked over the stray music gear that demarcated the small stage beyond: the Korg keyboard, the well-used twelve-string, two pre-war steel strings in slightly worse shape, and the powder blue Fender bass with oversize tuning pegs like cloverleaves.

Clustered near the gear, around what looked like a plastic patio table, were several twenty-something girls, all of them in threadbare sweaters, one in white jeans, and two more like twins, though not, in leggings and gauzy skirts. A bottle of Campari sat on the table, and their mouths moved violently, probably with gossip. What else inspired that kind of passion? But all he could hear was the Fahey record jangling through the sound system. The music soon vanished the girls from his mind, and as it did he began to study what was left in that peculiar blue-walled space, what Moto would later point out was actually a white-walled space bathed in pale blue light (hence the peculiarity).

You couldn't say what Fahey was, really, Larent thought. Or how exactly he'd arrived at the music he did. Probably Fahey couldn't have told you either, even afterward. Or he'd give you the wrong explanation. No one seemed to think that was a problem. Larent liked the thought. Maybe he needed it too.

He hadn't sat yet. He looked back at the bar from the doorway. "Drinks, yeah, he knows, he's coming," Moto said over the music as he ran his hands through his hair.

Finally Larent sat, still bemused. Moto began to tell him of the bands of distinction who'd played there—The Fall, Embrace, Can, and twenty years on, Gastr del Sol, June of 44, Polvo—often to audiences that were, though modest in an absolute sense, large enough to make the room, not the audience, seem to be what was too small.

All of this was mostly lost on Larent, preoccupied as he was with the musical failures of that first rehearsal. It was fine to talk of seminal bands, but what could the two of them hope to achieve, if *that*, the flatness of the afternoon, was ground zero? Beginnings mattered. Nothing was just practice. Or you could say practice told you more about everything to come than you would ever have wanted to believe. And he hadn't liked what he'd heard. He could remember this same feeling, with other musicians, on the cusp of stillborn projects.

The worthiest material Larent played that day was never heard. It came in between, after they'd let a feeble improvisation shrivel and die. He was hunched over his double bass, with his right hand blindly fingering chords, or if not quite blindly, then in the dimmest light. Nothing could be heard because nothing was sounded; his left hand lay flat along the strings. He had that talent for hearing unsounded notes, and what he was hearing seemed to him to make more sense than it strictly should have. It was something to unravel, these new instincts his hands were turning up more and more now.

It helped him ignore what he was actually hearing, with his

ears. Then, as now, it was Moto. He was retuning his drums, directly behind Larent, with what must have been, judging by the sound, little quarter twists of the drum key, moving from one lug to the next along the smaller tom's perimeter, tapping his stick against the center of the head. The pitch dropped as the drum deflated. He kept loosening the head until it fell a whole tone above the larger tom he'd already tuned. There was a pause before Moto smashed the open hi-hat. The rattling alloy cut its way through Larent's silent song.

He bent his head around to Moto. The drummer's hair seemed to glow under the white lights crossing the loft's ceiling along a concrete beam. He was expressionless, or perhaps he wore the thinnest-lipped smile, and it seemed as if he had finished adjusting his setup, though the differences looked meaningless to Larent. Now, the splash cymbal was just to the right of the hi-hat, and the crash hovered over the left tom, overlapping it slightly. The ride was still on the right, and for whatever reason the china had been pushed away from the set.

Moto dropped Larent's gaze and stared through the transparent heads of the toms. A deep, compact note answered his taps of the bass pedal as an eighth-note pulse took shape. The snare flams came next, interlaced with a roll so slow you could pick out every strike.

Larent returned to his silent fingerings, though, to the inner music that seemed to be leading somewhere. But Moto persisted, and eventually he relented. He set aside the baffling chords he'd been toying with and returned to the scales of earlier, bowing every third note, sounding ascending fourths and sevenths, flattening and sharpening notes as he crossed through several modes. Having won Larent's interest, or at least his commitment, Moto distilled the thick rhythms down to a quiet line on the toms, a tapping of the ride, and a sharp snare.

Larent switched on the amplifier and the delay pedal. The notes collected in layers, mode on mode, his route through one superimposed on the others. A kind of aural fog emerged, with only Moto's snare-work, increasingly central to the sound, making it through.

It was painfully indistinct. He threw the bass onto the bed in the corner and dropped to the floor, his back against the night-stand, facing Moto, and his arms wrapped around his knees. The bass notes continued to flow from the speaker, though slowly the haze thinned as the layers fell away, one at a time, the delay being less than infinite. Moto carried on unperturbed, his stare deep into the drums unbroken. It wasn't clear if he'd noticed Larent had stopped playing or whether he assumed this was the bassist's intention, a piece that, once set in motion, faded away in its own time, a release of potential energy.

The bass notes finally disappeared. Moto carried on a few more bars and let the loft go silent.

"Well?"

"Nothing, really," Larent said. "That's the problem, I guess."

Moto paused a beat, raked his hand through his long black hair. Four cracks of the snare and then his sticks were on the floor. They rattled and spun, settling into circular sweeps that barely began their motion before being interrupted, one by the wall in a too-bright yellow, the other by the olive couch pushed up against it, across the room from the bed. Moto smiled and sat down on the couch.

"What were you expecting?" Moto said. "We barely know each other." He laughed into the empty space between them.

"It's been half a day and we've found nothing at all, not even the beginnings of something."

"We could go back to something unamplified, really clean, simple, start from there."

"A single instrument—a melodic instrument—and it's a bass. It's too little." Larent put his hands on the bed behind him, pushed up, and sat on its edge.

"And these?" Moto asked as he tapped the tuned toms with his fingertips.

"We need more, however you want to put it," Larent said, the curtness growing in his voice.

"Well, if you want a fuller sound—"

"Every group you've played with had horns, guitars, keys. Usually all of those, and other things too. There's not enough friction here, even for harmony."

Moto stood up, pulled his black long-sleeve taut along the bottom. "I don't mind the change really. My drone groups, these ensembles with lots of friction, however you want to put it, started to outnumber the audiences. They just kept shrinking. Scaling back, even way back, to something just a little bigger than nothing, that doesn't seem so weird to me now. But it takes a while till you're okay performing to yourself."

"The composers, the poets. I'm aware."

"But even a form of rock. All of it's arcana now."

"Drone was always, though."

"Oh that's not true. Maybe here. But in Tokyo you could actually have a show with a sea for an audience. You didn't have to play to a hundred ABDs in a gallery or a factory loft. But that was a while ago, in another country. Now we're just like you, the conservatory crowd. I don't have a problem with small, even very small now. But then I'm not against some expansion either. We've got to play around more, I think. The ideas will come."

They'd left for the bar after that, the amplifier still on, humming in the empty room, its power light shining red in the dark as Moto shut the door.

And maybe the ideas *would* come, Larent thought. But there were still no drinks.

"You know," Moto said now, expertly accommodating the silence Larent clung to, "the best show I've seen here, or no, the one I remember most clearly, here or anywhere, maybe, I actually saw with Renna. It was Dianogah. Almost a reunion show. Definitely a band on its last legs. Maybe that made it even better.

"We had these fake IDs. This was a decade ago. Even more than that. I didn't know the band that well—I still don't, it was really a band other musicians turned me on to—but the first thing I heard as I came in were these two basses, one clean, with very light gauge strings, I'm assuming, because it seemed to be tuned in a higher register than a regular bass. The other was fuzzed, rumbling beneath, maybe in a dropped tuning. Behind both was this frenetic beat that was still precise somehow. Made me think of the Minutemen, D. Boon. Slint just as much, though. Classic, before-our-time stuff. And for those first songs there wasn't a guitar on stage.

"The place was slammed, nauseatingly full. We watched most of the show wedged in the corridor. No one much moved, no one could, I guess. So we all just took it in. There was a constant stream of speech from both bassists. I couldn't make any of it out, not sure that it mattered, but after a few minutes they turned to singing this simple melody—which they could barely hold, of course. Part of the charm.

"The clean bass started sounding overtones. This entrancing line. He held it for a long time while the rest of the music dropped away. Just this little five-note figure. And as the rest of the band sat around, paced, smoked, whatever, out of the audience steps this man: short black hair, long-sleeved polo, red canvas shoes.

"He lifted the strap of a black bass over his head, holding the cable in his free hand. The other Dianogah bassist set his beer down and started picking a steady stream of As. All the while, the overtones kept sounding.

"Now this third bassist—Bundy K. Brown—plugs in and strums across the strings. Nobody'd seen him in years, post-Tortoise, but there he was, the anti-legend, and the crowd playing it off like it was nothing. So he keeps strumming, head down, twisting the tuning pegs in big turns, all in the same direction, bouncing between them, loosening the strings haphazardly, sending the notes, already low, plunging. The amp can't even resolve these notes, they're so low, and what comes out is this sort of unpitched roar. Bundy catches the strings in his hand—they were wobbling, visibly—and pulls his head back up, as if satisfied with the tuning he'd arrived at, if you could call it that.

"The drummer had returned to his stool by this point. He taps out this delicate beat on the tom and snare, no bass, pumping the hi-hat. A final overtone rings out, and Bundy starts picking this really intricate riff that's right on the lower border of what you can hear.

"He *had* been tuning, or detuning, and even though those notes were mostly gravel, texture, they were still pitched—barely, but still. And what I assumed we were in for, a blaring noise piece, this cacophony, never came. It turned out to be this carefully shaded tune, with Bundy supplying the deepest layer of the harmony, through a sort of percussive melodic line. And the drums matched this with the opposite, a melodic percussive line.

"So these three post-rock bassists gave us ten minutes plus of something not far from counterpoint, in the lowest registers, at immense volumes, and in rumbling, near-inharmonic tones you took in through your chest, your skull, more than your ears. This place just shook, everything and everyone. It made me a little sick. But I guess there are good sorts of sickness. Renna didn't feel quite the same about it, I think. But there was nowhere to go, we were packed in too tight for that. So she waited through it."

Moto brought his eyes in line with Larent's. "Or I guess I don't really know how Renna felt. Just that she hardly talked, when we were getting drinks afterward with some of her friends, or with me, on the train back to Massachusetts, to school. It's hard to believe it didn't make an impression. She was probably preoccupied. With you, I'm thinking now. *Like* you, right now—this entire time, really."

Larent smiled. "Just listening." Moto was right, of course. But he was dwelling on more than musical failures. Renna had been on the fence about him then, in school, and he was already in love with her. After that, they'd had their few years. Then not. Now, she might be back on that fence. Or else, he thought, what they had was all they ever would. It looked like a lot. It was a lot. But if nothing changed, it would shrink to a blip in the years to come.

"No, it's fine," Moto said. "Maybe she was listening too. Not to me, but just playing it all back in her head. I don't think we actually talked about the show later. Anyway, Bundy did play another couple of songs, the opener off the first Tortoise record, and then 'Dreams of Being King,' which was, I'm remembering, the perfect summation of Dianogah. But none of that sticks in the mind like that first piece with Bundy."

In the far corner, behind the gear, a young man with hair poking out beneath a logo-less baseball cap got up from a table and in one motion hopped over a couple of drums inverted on the floor. Their silver snares rattled from the Fahey. He flipped the power switch on the Korg; the speakers popped and the Fahey cut out. With the palm of his left hand he rocked the modulating wheel back and fingered a minor seventh with his right. The wheel drew the chord smoothly down a step to D minor. "Like that?" he yelled over the Korg's pipe-organ tones. He let go of the wheel and the chord snapped back to E. The three at his table nodded vaguely as they swigged from dark bottles of beer.

While holding the chord he put his cap on the keyboard and leaned over the keys, brought his face close to them. His hair, three shades of brown distinguishable under the stage lights, fell over his face. He brought his head back up and rested the cap lightly on it, with the bill angled down over his forehead, obscuring his eyes.

Several long rows of buttons ran above the Korg's keys. Above them was a narrow screen, as wide as the keyboard, flashing parametric data: pitch, amplitude, attack, decay, and such. He riffled through the presets and the chord showed itself protean, incarnated by turns in violins, in guitars, in trumpets, in piccolos, in vibes, in oboes, and finally, in tinny synth tones. The screen showed a timbral profile for each in green, broken down into a few dozen categories. The last preset displayed most simply. The graphs were smooth, the mathematics of the sound free of natural complications like the overtone series.

He blinked heavily and brought his left hand back to the keys, away from the buttons. In those planar tones, with his cap covering his eyes and his shoulders raised, he sounded the opening bars of Satie's third Gymnopédie. The rendition was airless, free of heat or cold. But the score wouldn't submit, not wholly, to the slightness of its dress. Gravity remained.

Larent studied the player's hands, perhaps for a meaning of some sort. He ran his thumb across a broad knot in the wood of the table, pressing his finger into a divot.

"Ridiculous," he said.

Moto laughed. "I don't know," he said. "Yes."

"And still no drinks?" Larent asked.

They turned toward the doorway. There was no one.

The music ran its course.

9

ALBERT COTEN, ANDERS JAIKIES, FRANK RELLEAU, and Harold Kames—the four sat in a row. On one end was Coten, his cuffed flannels, tailored in gray-purple Super 150s, falling finely over his crossed legs. He sat up in his chair and pulled it imperceptibly forward before settling back. An old Montegrappa cut across the blank legal pad in his lap. The ruby celluloid of the pen held the light, glowing as if lit from within.

Kames, at the other end, reset the sleeve of his blazer to a half-inch of his shirtsleeve. He fingered a cufflink as his watery gaze met the broad doors at the back of the auditorium. Relleau and Jaikies, sitting between the other two, only looked into the stage lights.

Men and women, middle aged and primly dressed, had filled most of the seats, except for the rows in front, which were occupied by younger men, mostly students wearing the off-duty uniform of the well bred: loafers, shaggy-dog sweaters, and button-downs with rumpled collars. Two generations of Halsley wealth.

The hundred odd seats, arranged in several tiers, were three-quarters full now, and the flow through the doors had slowed to a trickle. Kames stood and took the podium.

"Let's begin, I think," he said. "To start, then, a brief statement of tonight's theme. My colleagues and I—some of you will know this—have been thinking through, over the last months, a few of the contrasts that give shape to political orders, social orders. Tonight we want to see if we can throw a bit of light on that between the mercantile and the martial. By mercantile we mean not the economic theory of that name so much as the broader orientation of the merchant toward life, and of societies that take the merchant's outlook, if only implicitly, as the primary mode by which to apprehend the world. Societies that treat the merchant as offering a template for citizenship, you could say. In the same way, by martial we mean the outlook of the warrior—not only the brutish or rapacious conqueror, but equally, the defender, the guardian.

"Except for our revolutionary period, and not even then, really, this country has never known anything resembling a martial order, or its common descendant, the royal order, the earliest monarchs often being triumphant warlords themselves, if they are not backed by them. The martial and the noble, the royal, these are really one category.

"Now, to put it in the crudest, quickest way, one which I can only hope we will improve on tonight, the merchant's life is built around a particular ethos, we can say, one that invests certain notions with special importance. Among these: exchangeability, trade, consumption, profit, calculation, consensus, negotiation, persuasion, dissimulation, connivance.

"The values of the noble are, as we said, molded by the demands of war. So we have the knights of Europe, the samurais of Japan, the kshatriyas of India. The appealing qualities first: courage, honor, loyalty in action. And then the less approachable ones, which are nonetheless bound up with the others: an acceptance of the necessity, and the permanent possibility, of violence; of the unequal distribution of virtue and wisdom among men; and of the reality of unexchangeability—of seeing some matters as musts, whatever the cost, personal or social, which you can call, in a language that will be familiar to our philosophers, the deontological limits on action and citizenship, ones that cannot be gainsaid or inputted into any broader moral calculus.

"This is much too simple, of course, but it gives the flavor, I hope, of what's to come." Kames looked back on the other three and lifted his brow. "Anything to add, then, just at the start? Surely I've muddled things. Albert, will you help?" There was mild laughter.

Coten put his hands on his thighs and cleared his throat. "Sure. My own training," he said, still seated, "is in the philosophy of politics, as Harold's is in law and history. I would just add the following. If—if—you think virtue and wisdom should have pride of place in our social decision-making, there is, and it's distressing, there is no guarantee that decisions made that way will yield popular consent. The 'wisdom of crowds' is reassuring, and if you look hard enough you can find cases that seem to substantiate it. But there are too many negative results to sustain the idea. It just doesn't look like the popular bears an inherent correspondence to the good. We take this as a truism in domains outside politics. In art, of course, but also in science. We don't take polls to decide on the load-bearing capacities of bridge designs. We leave it to the people who know better. Should we assume politics must be different?

"So this is another way of seeing the dispute between the noble and the merchant, for whom popularity, in the end, not goodness, accuracy, quality, strength, beauty, and so forth, must be the guiding principle. And that's just because the most valuable product, from the merchant's point of view, must be the one that sells. Otherwise, well, he goes out of business."

Relleau, a political correspondent for Halsley's newspaper of record, with a master's-level training in both history and anthropology, brushed blond curls from his eyes before taking his turn. "If one looks at our situation, where conceptions of the good are now beyond number, and where the communities answering to many of these conceptions are perpetually stymied in the elections, simply for lacking scale, numbers, it's difficult to tell them that our political arrangements are as they should be. Anyway they aren't listening, are they? Coalitions in the legislature, and between interest groups, are the obvious route in situations like this, and we have gotten that for some time. But what is more interesting, and newer, is how the last decade has seen a kind of turn toward other approaches, in particular, to certain forms of aggression, not always of a bloody sort, or mounted directly against the people, but against state institutions. Infrastructure—assembly halls, schools, and so forth. But that is still violence, dead bodies or not. And it might be a more potent one in the end, we don't know. The elections, in November, might tell us. We'll see how many are brave enough to show up at the polling stations.

"In some ways, however, it isn't an altogether different approach, because this extra-democratic aggression has itself turned coalitional. We hear of libertarians, and also the advocates of direct democracy, collaborating in some of the destruction—in its funding and sometimes its execution—of voting booths, subways, public monuments. We hear even of Muslim and Christian groups acting jointly. And they are targeting not just abortion clinics, but scientific institutions more generally: the flooding of UCLA's genomics center, most recently. This sort of collaboration was unthinkable just ten years ago. But today they are agreed on something, the substance of which isn't totally clear, even to them, one feels.

"But this is getting pretty speculative, so I think I'll leave it there. What do you make of this, Anders? Your research intersects with this in interesting ways."

The young sociologist with the burgeoning reputation, formerly of Bonn but now full-time at the Wintry Institute, leaned over the arm of his chair toward Relleau. "For just the reason you mention, I'm going to save my remarks for the discussion. If that's all right," he said, smiling broadly.

"That's just fine, Anders," Kames said. "I think they've had all they can take of general remarks, anyway. So, we'll all do just twenty minutes or so, and at the end we will open up the discussion to our very patient audience, for an hour or beyond, whatever we are feeling like.

"And I did mean to say at the start—I'll say it now—thank you, to our guests, fellows, and regular attendees, for coming to these sessions of the Wintry Institute. And of course to our founding donors, who have put us in a financial position to forget about finances. It's left us free to follow the argument wherever it leads, to examine our homilies open-endedly, without thumbs on the scale. We are very lucky to be what we are. Let's see where we go tonight."

10

THE FIRST INTERVENTION WAS NOTHING OF THE sort. Thirty floors up, at the Four Seasons, Lewis sat on the edge of a California king, slugging Caol Ila from a crystal lowball short on lead. The door was ajar. The desk sent her up, a Junoesque brunette with a bronze clutch, wearing silk the green of those portraits of Laurette (Matisse was still the master, Lewis thought). He felt he ought to be in tails, not this linen blazer that could use a pressing. The cut of the dress—high-back, ankle-length, flowing around the legs with a matchless drape, subtly pleated above the waist—played nothing up or down, neither flaunting nor withholding. Distortion was needless. The dress was her equal, and together they formed a pair of autonomous beauties, as handsome couples do.

She sat on the bed at his beckoning, not too close to him, and laid her hands in her lap decorously. The watch flashed in the low light of the nightstand lamp. Breguet. He studied its face, the immaculate guilloché work. The hands, at eleven and twelve, blued, not painted. The case too, it glowed whiter than stainless, in a way peculiar to gold. And the strap's irregular crosshatchings, the crispness of the black, bespoke alligator.

Lewis rarely confronted finery anymore, only when he saw

friends from the old life, or his mother. The august materials, the fabrics, hides, metals, and minerals, the aura of ultra-skilled labor emanating from their rendered forms—these were woven through the mise-en-scène of his youth. Their reappearance, though, in these circumstances, attached to this woman, left him of several minds.

Through a college friend, son of a pop icon and now a practiced layabout, he'd made these arrangements with Life, Halsley's top escort service. Three grand for ninety minutes. Utterly wasteful. But Lewis felt life telescoping. They'd asked him if, for another fifteen hundred, he wanted to include dinner; for five figures she could even be rented out for the weekend. He'd declined. The girlfriend experience didn't appeal. He liked Janus.

She ventured a few pleasantries, sustaining that dazing restraint. The faux-gentility—there was no question of authenticity, given her vocation—it only estranged him. Her tony clientele must have expected this, at least initially, especially at dinner, if they took that option.

He remembered speeding the encounter past these awkwardnesses: first a rote offering of a drink (she declined) and then, while holding her by the Bregueted wrist that still lay in her lap, a wordless unzipping of the dress. She leaned her face against his, only grazing it, letting her breath fall on his neck, which he could just barely feel. She went no further, and she said nothing. She was merely keeping his pace, letting him lead.

He pulled her to her feet and disrobed her with a care that seemed directed more at the dress than at her. The stitching was close to invisible, patently hand-done. The silk was even finer than he thought, with a pleasing weight. Givenchy. He folded it over the desk chair and turned back to her. She was standing in matte-black bra and panties, smoothing the copper-brown curls that fell just beyond her lightly freckled shoulders. To the smallest degree possible her eyes had brightened, and they fixed on him without the hint of the coquette, calibrated to project only gentle desire.

The seamlessness of her performance, the longer it went on, only deepened his bewilderment. He stripped with haste and pounced, hoping to slow the process, even reverse it. It worked at first. Sex grounds. But quickly her perfection in bed was manifest and impossible to ignore. He started to drift again, and as he did, the urge drifted too.

It wasn't long before he found himself slapping her breasts, hard, then very hard. From behind, he did the same to her ass, her ribs, her thighs. Her twitches and cries took on a new ring of truth, breaking the illusion so troublingly convincing up to now. With that revelation, his desire, the species of it he needed, returned.

He got her on top and, using her neck as a grip, threw her down onto his cock. She accepted this, mouth open, eyes closed. He tried to take her bobbing breast in his mouth but found it just out of reach. His hands tightened around her throat as he stilled her body. He pulled her up, toward him, and found the nipple as a rasping escaped her. Her hands clutched the backs of his, prying at them, scratching at his fingers, as his teeth came together around her nipple. Her chest jerked away from him, her fingernails dug into his face. She coughed as his hands convulsed from the pain, and as they did her own sprung from his face back to her neck.

He threw her off him. Her nipple swelled, and blood didn't look far off. She kept both her hands around her neck, as if she were wringing it herself. In language he would never deign to use, she cursed him. He knew it was there, beneath the veneer. Reality seeped back into their exchange. Lewis had made it happen.

In stiff cadences he apologized, thought an outsize tip would prove he meant it. Sullen and silent but not teary, she dressed and left, leaving the door ajar and him to wonder whether there would be trouble from Life.

Everything was over in half an hour. He sat in the chair, feet up on the bed, taming the fifth of scotch two fingers at a time, swigging from the tumbler and a miniature can of macadamia nuts in alternation. By the time he left the hotel, at two in the morning, he wasn't sure what he'd meant. He felt less sorry. He hadn't come. In the back of the cab, Lewis weighed the glint of the watch, the drape of the dress, against the dinginess of his life, and with purpose, lost himself in the brake lights of passing cars.

■ ■ ■

This was a year ago. His profile had grown since. Or that of his deeds had, which was better, and what mattered. Lewis's person remained opaque, or multiple, which came to the same. The sketches were various: a raven-haired man abundantly goateed, a mustachioed blonde in aviators, a brunet longhair with beard untended, witnessed only under low light. Twice he'd come ski-masked. Twice he'd managed entirely in the dark.

Locations too were diverse: hotel rooms, cars, deserted parking lots, the bathrooms of failing restaurants, the smaller subway stations, far into the night, and once, just as the sun peaked, at the site of a partly razed building. He would arrive by bus or train or otherwise car—a Corolla with a missing bumper, an Audi gleaming white, a windowless cargo van—all rented or with out-of-state plates. For its purity, though, he preferred, when possible, to come on foot.

Eleven girls in Easton and Henning, not counting the two he let go, judging them self-correctors. There were limits to masquerade and he was exceeding them. But between the spells of panic and the unleavened reaches of despair he would sometimes find an affectless calm. He struggled to worry about his fate then, felt it frivolous to do so, even pretentious. A kind of absolute selflessness, as he saw it, would follow. It was then that he made his "interventions."

From each woman he would extract a biography. The inquiries all began from certain generic angles of attack, there being only so many to a conversation, but from there, each rapidly became its own, and the path forward had to be improvised.

Occasionally matters were simple and quick. In minutes they would begin releasing their histories. These, he supposed, were the women who weighed their stories, or whose stories weighed on them, perpetually or nearly so. There was no introspection called for, the tale was always at the ready, for better or worse.

Sometimes he suspected deceit. They were too quick to share, the narratives were too neat, either brimming with pathos or a frosty insouciance about their past and present both. But even their fictions, if they were fictions, could suffice. He would take these stories both ways, once as truth and once as lie. In all but one case, his conclusion was the same. If you told certain sorts of fictions about yourself, you might warrant the same treatment as those for whom those fictions were facts.

More often, though, unlocking their tongues took a fine probing; it could take hours, a half-dozen tacks, to find it, the key. But he had yet to fail. The accumulated detail could be extravagant, but he had little choice. He had to see the shape of each case, the precise trajectory of descent.

The eleven cases remained with him vividly—his memory was prodigious—so that when it came to them he had no use for pen and paper. He held them all in his mind, calling them up as he pleased. But on late drives home, like tonight, to Janice, or Janus, his preferred endearment (not hers), the stories would start to mingle.

He imagined that there might be, even must be, women in the world whose stories matched these permutations. As they all shared an endpoint, it was not always clear to him what difference it made how exactly they fell—whether from drama society walk-ons or orphans, state-school freshman or dressage champions—or what to make of the minutia of their lives, the many blind alleys.

But though the inputs were clear enough, the calculus itself was only partly conscious. At the moment of decision, when he would gather all he had been told before him, perhaps these trifling details were not so trifling. There may have been borderline cases, he thought, where everything turned on the girl's mother being Jewish and the father not, or on her preference for ketchup not Tabasco with her eggs. He couldn't say. All the same he felt his judgment unerring.

Beyond the histories, his mind held snapshots of the girls, before and after, along with ones of lower resolution, during. Like the histories, they would start to mix, and he often wondered then what one would have to do to turn one woman's before into another woman's after, what the intermediate stages would look like, how far he would have to denature them before finding the highest common factor. The lowest was easy; matches and gasoline sufficed. But that sort of reduction didn't exercise the mind.

The most luminous images were the after-after ones, the women returned to a finer state. (Except for one case, which, if her unthinkable account was true, marked not so much a return as a first ascent.) Though these images weren't stamped on him by the world, as memories were, they were clearest, most vivid, perhaps as only unmoored idealities can be.

The girls were never subjects for him—artistic subjects. He found the notion morbid. There was simply no art about what he was doing, nor should there have been. He hadn't painted anything in months. Some charcoal line drawings were all he'd managed, of Janice on the fire escape or in the kitchen, and even those were more for her benefit than for his. He'd left art behind for life.

He had in fact descended too, like the girls. His father, Leo Eldern, had invested much of his personal assets in far more aggressive ways than the money he managed for a midsize hedge fund. Most of his fortune was lost this way, shorting the currency markets. The fund itself performed well, though, frequently surpassing the market by meaningful margins, sometimes very large ones. There were very few truly poor years.

Had he approached his own investments as he did his fund's, he would still be beyond wealthy, given the size of the inheritance that had come to him from his mother, the lone child of a Midwestern auto-parts magnate.

Instead he was reduced to his salary at the fund, for a year or so, anyway, until several investors who ran in his circles couldn't help but note the sharp contraction of his prodigality.

As he was being dismissed, he protested that he'd never subjected them to his personal risks. They granted that that might be true; the fund's long-run success was sterling evidence. Still, they were unwilling to stay with him, not believing a bifurcation of character could be absolute. Leo's life, with his son's, was recast. All the money in his name was a play portfolio Leo had given him, perhaps to entice him into the trade, worth several hundred thousand dollars.

Early on Lewis had plumped for the impractical life, one in the arts. He'd wanted to fill it with the kinds of meaning his father's, by his own admission, lacked: moral, aesthetic, intellectual. Moral most of all. Politics seized him even before college. He'd sensed the early signs of rot everywhere in Halsley, the kinds his urbane friends mostly ignored or felt at some remove from, though it was happening right in front of them, *to* them, to everyone.

But Lewis's unease was shapeless. He could convince no one of the problem, nor offer any real explanation as to what had gone wrong. At least he noticed. Brilliant wealth seemed not to blind him. That was a talent. Since some things can only be achieved through brilliant wealth, all the better if you could see too.

It was Kames who first gave form to Lewis's intuitions. Lewis attended a Wintry lecture on literature and politics simply to accompany a friend whose father was close to Kames. After the meeting, Lewis felt more himself, and it was through someone else's words. Here was a man, self-effacing, unpretentious yet bold of idea, who might help him arrange his thoughts. In this sense Kames was an architect.

He spoke that day of the mythologies of a pat secularism; the seductions of the managerial state, of taking ways of life for lifestyles and ethics for a mostly private affair, which was in truth impossible. Ethics implicated the collective, it couldn't be cordoned off, and political morality was quietly, sometimes silently, at work in the functioning of every public institution. The only question was of its truth, not its existence. Could we do better, once we gave up the fool's errand of collapsing the domain of "ought" in the world to a private sphere? Was that narrowing of the concept the very reason for the slow loss of credibility that every modern republic had experienced?

Remarkably, all of this was extracted from a critical reading of *A Farewell to Arms* and *The Crying of Lot 49*. His friend didn't seem to take much from the night, but Lewis was invigorated, by Kames and his manner especially, though he grasped only some of what he'd heard. A slew of Wintry lectures over the next years fixed this. His sense of the political grew as rich as his feeling for art, painting, in particular. He got his father, Leo, to come along to some of these talks, which pleased them both, for different reasons. After a time they got to know Kames, to the extent he was willing to be known. He'd been bred the same way they had, but in an intellectual register, not a commercial one. Leo, who was roughly his age and in fact had friends in common, admired, even envied Kames. There couldn't have been a shortage of meaning in *his* life, he thought.

There were other shortages, though. Like the liquidity to extend the recently founded Wintry Institute beyond Halsley (the endowment was still tied up by its executors). It was the sort of thing Kames wouldn't canvass people about, for fear of tainting the institution's intellectual credibility. But friends were another matter. Here Leo could do something for Kames, and more important, something for his son. Lewis headed off to Brown and RISD and Leo financed a Providence chapter of the Wintry. Kames even came up to lecture there occasionally, and Lewis helped organize speakers from the nearby universities: sculptors, biologists, philosophers, anyone with a heterodox point of view.

Lewis would take degrees in political science and visual art, but halfway through college it became obvious that art was his real strength. It was where his natural capacity for invention lay. He was best off filtering his political imagination through his paintings, he thought, as many an artist had. So, with some reluctance, he abandoned plans of a senior thesis in government.

He also stopped attending lectures at the Wintry. He'd learned a lot through Kames and the Institute, but after a point, there was no use in talking, thinking, politics anymore. You had to do something, whatever it was. He felt that was the implicit point of the Wintry as well.

What Lewis knew how to do was paint, so that's what he did. His senior show consisted of a dozen diptychs of B- and C-list actors on unprimed canvas, in which the expressions on each of a pair of faces was balanced against the other in peculiar ways. Uneasy resonances resulted. Partly this was because the expressions were ones never seen on those particular actors' faces before: a pneumatic bimbo looking scholarly, a sitcom comedian looking noble and detached. But a kind of interaction was also present, though the actors occupied separate spaces and looked out from the canvas only toward the viewer, not each other. Somehow, you could read Hollywood's schizophrenia off these pairs, Janice said. Lewis's mentors in the art department agreed. His show received a distinction.

And then his father fell into ruin. Since Lewis was no longer financially assured, Leo urged him to reconsider his chosen vocation, transform it into an avocation, and use his A.B. in politics, coupled with the value of his portfolio, as a stepping stone to a career in business or law.

Lewis balked. Unlike his set, which treated work in the arts or at the nonprofits as luxury pursuits to be quietly set aside when capital, the life-giver, the buffer and balm too, waned, he had always thought (and declaimed) that art couldn't properly be a hobby or diversion, whatever the change in circumstances. If it was art, it was life.

His father's financial collapse would be the test of his conviction. Lewis was determined to pass. After graduation, he nursed his portfolio, living only as the interest allowed, so he might devote his energies to painting as completely as possible. He moved in to a tumbledown apartment in Halsley with Janice, who'd transferred out of RISD and graduated from the culinary-arts school at Johnson & Wales after finding that her real talent was with food not paint. At the time, she might have been even more impractical than he was, though nothing in her background entitled her to it. They made sense to each other, together.

Leo eventually found a place at another fund, but he refused on principle to grant Lewis any support after he'd set a course so reckless. In fact it took only a few years for his father to grow quite wealthy again. But there was no thaw. Lewis spoke to him only cursorily now, though without hostility or open resentment. He refused to ask for anything more from him.

Lewis's mother was gentler toward him, and it was her affection that underwrote a future reconciliation between father and son. But Lewis felt the affection was sustainable only for being generic, blood-fueled. She had little understanding of his projects, being mostly consumed by her role on the board of a charter-school fund and not something in the arts. He didn't hold this against her, though. He barely understood them himself anymore, and he doubted whether working with the museums, say, would have helped her with this.

He'd been living this way now for a decade, in an aging, underfurnished apartment, in a manner entirely at odds with how he might have lived had he been willing to seek rapprochement with Leo. The only virtue of the place was its fourteen-foot ceilings. He and Janice had converted the second bedroom into a studio for him, and the correspondingly tall windows ensured that his canvases would be awash each day in the creamy light of late afternoon he liked to work in.

Besides Matisse, his early hero had been Paul Klee, that painter with few ancestors and fewer descendants. In college, he flirted with Bacon, whose canvases, though formally rich and possessed of a cultural resonance that was unlikely soon to fade, struck him as indefensibly sunless. There were fewer ideas in them, and less feeling, than they at first seemed to hold.

Lately, though, it was the work of Denis Peterson that occupied him. He was taken first by the hyperrealist paintings, where signage dwarfed subject. But it was the homelessness series that reshaped him, through its moral demands, the urgency Peterson brought to his subjects, though in a peculiarly clear-eyed way. The series lived at the nexus of pathos and precision: compassionate, yet insulated against all sentimentality by its exactitude.

Up until now Lewis had been trying to find room for abstraction within a hyperrealist frame. He liked unprimed canvas, a holdover from his Baconian phase originally, but now a useful means of sending the faintest ripples through realism. It just slightly materialized the image, degrading its resolution much more finely than Warhol's Marilyns. Keeping one foot in each realm, the technique yielded artifacts—canvases—that appeared literally stained by reality. And one way or another, in everything he did, reality was what Lewis was after.

The painting that sat on his easel now, long unworked, was of this sort. It depicted a heavily tattooed bike messenger standing on the pedals, sideswiping a hansom cab pulling onto an avenue next to a grand city park. The bike's rear wheel is elevating and the messenger is taking flight over the handlebars, just as a postal tube is falling down between the spokes of the cab's wheel and the bike. The cab driver, a bushy-haired Arab, has his head swiveled into a bunch of crassly arranged flowers. He looks irked rather than surprised. The horse, still unaware, remains placid.

The last painting Lewis actually finished was a truck-stop bathroom that imperceptibly merged with a slightly abstracted woman in yellow rubber gloves, kneeling and cleaning the toilet. Only inspection revealed figure to be less tangible than ground.

He had found his way into some noteworthy group shows, both in America and in Europe, and had two shows of his own, with small but generous write-ups in the art journals. But the biennials eluded him, and it pained him to acknowledge that this was not unjust.

By now he'd imagined he would have made some sort of aesthetic breakthrough, if not in the art world, then at least in his own mind. The world could catch up later. But no, the world was spot on. His canvases hinted at something they didn't quite deliver, even he saw that.

Formally they weren't uninteresting. But transfiguring a quality of paint into a quality of spirit, as Peterson, as all the meaningful artists had, he hadn't managed. It was alchemy. Maybe it was voodoo. Whatever it was, he wasn't even close.

The lack seemed not to be one of talent, or of imagination or craft, but of a certain power of synthesis. Vision in art was, at once, idea and experience, a joining of thought or affect with perception. He could conjure beautifully fresh sensations from paint. No one doubted that. And his ideas ran deep, as did his feeling for the world and its order. No one doubted that either. But he couldn't seem to integrate them, not without seams. And eventually the stitching would give out, no matter how tight. Was it, in some sense, a lack of nerve? He didn't know. If it was, though, he was in trouble, because day by day, summoning it got harder.

His work stalled. His financial state was weak but stable. Painting earned him little more than the occasional four-figure sale. Sometimes he was tempted to take a more aggressive market position, swap the index funds he'd converted his portfolio into for more volatile securities. But he held off, knowing that Janice would eventually earn a reasonable income; that his portfolio, even as it stood, would last some time still before inflation eroded the capital; and that his desire for more was a desire for the superfluous, one which could only be pursued by putting the necessary at risk.

So they remained, living in a false poverty, with no sign of improvement on the horizon. They had both thought this acceptable to start, and Lewis's opinion hadn't changed. He could have tolerated real squalor even, at least he imagined so, and they were probably heading for it. At times he took a stolid pride in this. But he sensed Janice's growing unease with their present course, and this divergence was starting to color their relationship in ways that defeated expression.

She'd noticed, of course, that he had mostly stopped painting. It had never happened before, and this must have added something to her worries about him. As did the weeks he would spend in bed. There were also the many nights now he was out until morning, and the increasing rate at which his appearance changed. New haircuts, new clothes. When she would ask about this, he would chalk it up, plausibly enough, to type-two bipolar, the condition that had hounded him since college, even high school, though it went untreated then.

Still, she'd seen other episodes of his over the years. None was this peculiar. As for the stalling of his work, he passed it off as a deepening lack of inspiration, and the late nights as a search for some. The first part of this was true, the second not—or not in the way he meant it.

In fact, he'd taken to whoring. The practice came with an illustrious artistic pedigree, which made it easier to dip his toes. It took away some of the sense of betrayal he felt. Self-betrayal. He couldn't see it as a betrayal of Janice. She would think it trivial.

It began, then, as a simple diversion from his unpromising present. But his spirit interfered from the start, from the time of that cab ride home from the Four Seasons. Here were women, many of them intelligent and for the most part not without options, humble though they may be, living in far greater comfort than him, purposeless comfort, on the basis of their orifices alone, not their talent or sacrifice or effort. *These* were self-betrayers on a Platonic scale, who refused all paths but the one of least resistance.

More than anything, there was an absolute vacuum of belief in these women. They might be the most secular people on Earth. It was this recognition, of their etiolated spirits, that prevented him from actually having sex with most of the women after the Breguet girl. His own spirit wouldn't submit.

There were artists, like Peterson, supremely suited to giving substance to the deformed; their art in turn became the body of fellow-feeling. Perhaps nothing was more transcendent. Ruskin would have approved. But it wasn't in Lewis. That's what a decade of work had showed. His gift was limited, in the end, and cruelly bestowed, in that it was large enough to tempt him to try to scale the heights, but small enough for him not to be able to make the climb. And he would only understand this after falling from the mountain's face.

What was left for him? He had Janice, but she must be disappointed, though she would never say so. How to incarnate spirit, if not in art? Hadn't that been his fount of meaning? Life seemed only to flicker with significance, and the gaps between flickers were growing.

The Breguet girl was the start of the turnaround, though he'd felt only despair and confusion at the time. Through the next two girls, he unearthed a new fount. This one might even exceed art. Rather than give flesh to spirit, he would give spirit to flesh, re-enchant it. After the first four girls, there was no more sex even. But none would get the easy money they'd expected. Not that they didn't get their money; he was too conscientious for that. But it was hard money—too hard, he hoped. If there was no true change without crisis, well, he would bring them crisis.

He beat them to life, that's how he liked to think of it. He also liked "beaten to a pulp," since pulp was the kind of thing you reshaped into something of value. You pulped airport paperbacks and printed Shakespeare. Or if not Shakespeare, then Updike at least. That, more or less, was the idea.

His powers of synthesis no longer seemed inadequate, as they had with painting. Each intervention seemed to him to embody his feeling for the world, the purity of purpose, the honoring of self, more seamlessly than the last. By the eighth girl, he'd felt he'd reached a kind of perfection. Maybe his talent for politics was not of the Wintry's sort. It was for lived politics. Personal politics. Micropolitics. And maybe that really was greater than his talent with a brush.

But there was second synthesis, of course, a more important one: an alignment of flesh and spirit in the women. How to know if he was succeeding? Or even improving? Tonight's drive was evidence, wasn't it? It was becoming harder to find streetwalkers in Halsley since he'd started. It was the same way with finding escorts, for him or anyone else, he understood. He'd brought things to a boil. He'd taken away their shortcuts, through fear. They would have to find another way. They'd have to kick, if they were strung out. They'd have to go humbly back to their families, if they'd run away. They'd have to learn how to make actual lives for themselves, however modest actuality proved, whether it meant Starbucks or Target or community college. This is what the new emptiness of the streets meant to him.

What was certain, though, was that the most recent intervention, carried out days ago beneath an overpass, was a regression. It was as impenetrable, as confused, as the first one. It lacked all form. And it was worse than any botched painting.

The girl—she went by Lisa—she'd been clear-eyed. There was no defensiveness or callow defiance, as with the intervening girls. She pursed her lips thoughtfully when he spoke and seemed to accept the fallibility of her stance. It was discomfiting, the possibility of wisdom in her.

He might have let Lisa go had it not been for that, the easy cogency of her replies. They were familiar enough at their core, and he'd rejected versions of them in other girls. But their dress, her even-handed delivery, was unusual. It seemed to reform their content. Pinpointing her bad faith became impossible, which undid his sense of purpose and returned him to that first night at the Four Seasons, where there had been almost no talking at all.

Lisa couldn't be accused of elementary misapprehensions or a jumbled mind. But her notions were cool and neutral, and they threatened to ablate his own, in the way the sublime can menace beauty. Maybe too, in the shadow of the sublime, he sensed the monstrous. The feeling had hastened his decision. He aborted the inquiry, and for the first time since the Breguet girl, was tempted to have her. But he stopped short, striking Lisa instead with a rashness that embarrassed him now. He rolled her out of the car and pulled away after he'd finished.

He tried to flush the memory of this episode from his mind as the back of a convertible, its top down, expanded before him. Lewis tapped the brake. A police SUV was parked roadside, its tailgate pockmarked here and there. The upper edge of a sheet of fine gray grit traced a line halfway up the back window and the mounted spare tire. On the other side of the road a squad car's light-bar strobed.

Lewis had yet to be stopped at a checkpoint. They were springing up with a confounding arbitrariness, never staying put for long, shifting throughout the city and the wider region. Halsley's district borders were only sometimes used. Just as often, police cars would flank small roadways like this one that didn't make it out of town without merging with the larger arteries. Whatever pattern there was, it was illegible, and anyway underwent continuous mutation, presumably in an attempt to trap trouble, or more frequently, its mere potentiality, which of late had become necessary, supply having grown so great. How many of these movements were addressed to the future? How many the past? He liked to think prevention and retribution were on a par.

In the early days Lewis could safely assume his exploits could effect no change in the movement of the checks. He wasn't serious quarry, given all else. But the assumption grew less secure every day. He wondered now if the net was sometimes recast to bag him, and at times, studying the newspapers, he couldn't avoid the feeling that his deeds were making deeper impressions than even he intended.

The quality of his masquerade was being tested. It made grasping the pattern urgent. There were websites devoted to mapping the checkpoints, but when he superimposed the locations of his encounters on these maps, he couldn't settle the question. Sometimes he thought he saw influence, but quickly he would see nothing at all.

The convertible, unstopped, drifted past the officer standing astride the road. The resolution of his face rose as Lewis approached, the details filled in: squat neck, wide ears, sharp nose, bad skin. His eyes remained unchanged, though, black voids from a distance and the same up close. The laws of optics appeared to have no bearing on them. Lewis fixed on the officer's slack arm, looking for a twitch of the sinews running along the back of his hand, or perhaps some tightening of the forearm. Nothing.

On the other side of the checkpoint, heading home to Janice, untested again, he assumed a swell of satisfaction, however small, a lightening, however transient, would arrive. But there was nothing. The eyes of the officer stayed with Lewis on the rest of the drive while he wondered what laws of affect his mind had just flouted.

11

STEPHEN RUTLAND STOOD AT THE TOP OF THE
path, well water in hand, peering down into the narrow Kandyan
valley below, which was in truth not much more than a ravine.
A stream, small but running with some force, passed through
the rocks and tall grass of the valley floor. A wood frame twice
his height and nearly half that wide lent shape to his view. A
door was propped up on the cross-post of the frame, with ropes
holding it in place, so that it formed a sort of inverted draw-
bridge. Rather than being fashioned from a solid piece of wood,
it was woven from thick branches and vines radiating four inch
thorns.

The gate was open, and the thorn door projected over the
shoulders of the Rajasingha's sentries stationed on either side
of it. All comings and goings were kept track of at these checkpoints. Unless those passing were from neighboring villages and
recognizable to the gatekeepers, they would produce identifi-
cation issued by their village councilmen, or, in extraordinary
cases, by their county governors. The ID would be impressed
upon a small clay table. There were twenty-four recognized
stamps, indicating caste, village seniority, marital status, as well

as the sort of business they had that required passing the gate, whether personal, trade, or official.

The Ceylonese councilmen or governors would modify these twenty-four if they needed to express something the stamps couldn't accommodate. The meaning of these alterations—a set of x's along the bottom of the tablet, say, or a red swatch cutting across a stamp—was often not known to the travelers, so that frequently they carried information about themselves and their journey they were not in a position to decipher.

In times of little threat the gates were kept open. The sentries merely ensured that only locals freely passed. They could often be found chatting with them, joking, chewing betel-leaf. But whenever security was a concern, which was often, and even more often in the king's mind, Rajasingha would send messengers, or else military scouts in the threatened areas, to have the gates lowered. Since the paths through the Highlands were typically narrow, falling away steeply into deep rocky crevasses, the kingdom was nearly impassable with the thorn-gates shut, and any part of it could be isolated from the rest.

The gates, in fact, and the mountains they were built into, were a good part of the reason there was an independent kingdom left at all; whereas the coasts, north and south, where geography gave no advantage to the Sinhalese, had fallen easily to the Europeans.

Dutch or Portuguese incursion was nearly always the given reason for closing the gates, and probably that was always a genuine concern. Still, had that reason not existed, it seemed to Rutland that the king might have been driven to do much the same for others. The people's rebellion against him, for one, must have changed things. Rutland was still piecing the story together.

He approached the sentries and half-waved. They smiled and followed him with their eyes as he walked through the gate with his pail of water, down toward the village of Belemby, his home for the past nine months. He'd seen this particular gate closed only a few times. The sentries' mien had been altogether different then.

■　■　■

Four years had passed since the Ceylonese had seized the *Ann*, their East India Company frigate. That was 1659, at the eastern port of Trincomalee. He, his old friend Robert Knox, and the rest of the crew were kept near the sea for weeks afterward, in a windowless military shed carved into the side of a mountain. It's where Knox's father, the ship's captain, went delirious and died.

Later Rutland learned that the seizure had been unusual. It was, in fact, only their slowness in presenting the king with gifts that brought it on. Knox Sr. had been preoccupied with getting back to England, and thought they might simply trade for the supplies they needed for the return voyage and get going toward home. But this wasn't India. The rules were different.

As mere merchants, they were thought to pose little threat, so the conditions of their captivity were mild. On Rajasingha's orders, they were separated (to prevent collusion) and dispersed around the kingdom, to be housed and fed by locals on a rotating basis. Recompense for these families, when it came at all, came mostly as food, a few measures of rice or lentils. When it was time for a rotation, each family hoped it would not be chosen to maintain the men.

Belemby, Rutland's fourth village, sat in the western county of Hotteracourly, about twenty miles east of Rajasingha's emergency residence, which he'd taken up only recently, after barely surviving a populist rebellion. Though it was now almost nine months ago, Rutland still knew few of the details, as they were kept from him. What he did know was that the king believed foreigners like him may have helped spur it.

So this was his punishment. Belemby was easily the most

unpleasant place he'd been kept. The terrain was arid, craggy, given to drought, and frequently short of grain. The cattle, emaciated in the best of times, would die off, or else the families would have to lead them to relatives living in the more temperate lowlands, if they had any.

Though food and lodging were provided for, no allowance had been made for clothing. Except for his boots, which coconut oil had saved, and his heavy leather gloves, which served him now not on a ship's deck but in the paddies, bringing in the neighbors' harvest for a share, Rutland's garments, mildly supplemented by old garb villagers had given him, were in tatters.

He carried the pot of water along the main avenue bisecting the village, past the row of houses of the wealthiest townsmen. These were seven- or eight-room affairs—two rooms being reserved for the servants—built around handsome courtyards, whose short walls of clay limed white were covered with engravings of birds and lions.

Further along, the houses scaled down to three rooms, then mostly two, and then, for the lion's share of the avenue, just a single large room. Rutland's did not even reach this standard. It was just large enough for sleeping and sitting; cooking had to be done in the yard. But it was his, which was new. Through his efforts it might grow.

He hung the water from a vine strung across a pair of coconut palms, above the twigs and woodchips and charred branches of last night's fire. He picked up one of the sticks and turned for his neighbor's house, one he had slept in many nights, before he'd been able to shelter himself.

A fire burned in a ring of stones in the grass outside Rajarathnan's house. He too would be cooking soon. Rutland planted the charred stick in the fire and caught the eye of the man and his wife, Priya, sitting in silence in the house. All nodded.

Rajarathnan had been a natural host. He bore the burden

of the Englishmen lightly, especially Rutland, whom he'd once assured was great company next to Francis Crutch, a stormy shipmate of Rutland's he'd had to house for two months. He said this neutrally, though, as if really he didn't much mind him either. Rutland himself had always liked Crutch, his irascibility, which even good breeding could not mold or mask. He had known him in boyhood. He was no different now.

The stick smoldered an earthy red. Rutland took it back to his own yard and plunged it into the pile of firewood. It began to smoke. There was enough wood to start a fire, but he'd have to collect more after he ate to take him through to dawn.

Near the outer wall of his little hut he found two small sacks of rice and a large basket full of limes, raw pumpkin slices, coconut meat, and wild leaves he didn't know the names of, nor seen elsewhere, not even in India. Next to it was a smaller basket of sweet fruit, which the villagers were not obligated to provide. Four purple mangosteens. The supplies would have been left by other villagers—Elara and his wife. It was their turn.

He took one of the sacks and tossed it onto a pile of three others. This was his currency. The idea had not been his but John Loveland's, another shipmate. Though he lived just fifteen miles away, Rutland hadn't seen him in almost a year, from the time their various keepers, being known to each other and seeing no harm, allowed several of the *Ann*'s crew to lunch together. The men converged on Loveland's village, where they'd learned, though they couldn't quite believe it, he lived independently.

Each arriving man got a jolt seeing Loveland in a pristine white tunic. It gave him a clerical appearance, though no one could say the church or the god. More than that, it was the starkness of the contrast with their own rags that surprised them. That and the scale of his home: three rooms, like a middle-class townsman. Rutland remembered the faraway look on Knox's face; the way he wandered through the rooms and the yard, as if private property were a miracle; and the way he stared into the white of the foreign tunic.

Before any sort of gulf could open up between the men, or misunderstandings could multiply, Loveland gave his method, which had nothing to do with religion: "Do not take your food dressed."

It was simple commerce. The king had ordered the towns-people to provide food for them; he hadn't said they must prepare it too. After some argument with the councilors, Loveland's abjection, which they were beginning to find obscene anyway (this perhaps *was* a religious matter), persuaded them to go along with his plan, so he might earn enough from selling the rice to clothe himself decently. From then on his daily grain came raw. A year of that, Loveland said, had led to this, gesturing to the wealth around him.

From that day, the other Englishmen of Hotteracourly followed suit. It meant they had to go hungry sometimes. But it also meant they had an income now, one that could be transformed in principle into anything at all. A burning stomach, Rutland thought, was a fair price for that sort of alchemy. Bartering had its limits.

Rutland poured the other sack of rice into water on the cusp of a boil. He added a few thick flakes of sea salt. The starch of the rice thickened the water. There was no meat tonight, though the flesh of the coconut was as good as meat to him now. He poured off some of the froth and put the coconut and pumpkin slices in with the rice to simmer.

He turned to the half-knit cap he'd started on the day before. Caps were the real wealth-makers now, for him and the crew. This idea traced to, of all people, the unruly Crutch. When he'd bought some clean clothes at the village trading post with money from raw rice he'd sold, Crutch saw knitted caps for sale. Badly chafed by the equatorial sun, he wondered how he might acquire one, not having quite enough money for it.

So he bought some cheap cotton yarn, in red and yellow, and some needles, on the condition the shopkeeper would show him how to make a cap of his own. He sat down with Crutch and did. After several aborted efforts, Crutch produced a comfortable, imperfect cap with a wavy brim that managed to keep the light away.

But the caps could offer more relief than this, he saw. Sinhalese traders frequently wandered through the villages selling them. Crutch would do the same. He, and later his shipmates, began knitting and selling these caps on long walks through the villages, offering them for a bit less than the shops and the other roving traders.

Through the sale of rice and caps, Rutland himself had found his way to some small amount of independence. Whereas the Englishmen had previously been passed around the village as unwanted lodgers, they were now in a position to buy building materials, and even the labor of the villagers, to house themselves.

Trade had been only a pretext for Rutland when he'd first joined the crew of the *Ann*, a merchant vessel, in London, in 1658. Now, though, this well-bred man of privilege was finding that commerce could ennoble your life when pedigree failed, and you found yourself scrabbling with common stock for survival.

Rutland's place was mostly built now. The walls were made of rattan-fastened boughs, which he let stand without the usual clay plastering, as he'd not yet adjusted to the exceptional heat (nor would he ever). The roof was thatched with banana leaves and tall grass in an oddly patterned weave that the villagers were expert in. The oddness, apparently, made it watertight.

Rajarathnan had been most helpful of all in building the shelter, and he asked for nothing in return. It was his floor Rutland had first slept on in Belemby. Rutland would stay in a room separated from the main house by a thatched wall and take his food on a small table and stool—an honor the family paid him, as they themselves, like most others, ate on the floor. He slept on a mat, as they did, and after a time he found it no less comfortable than any bed in England.

Knox hadn't adapted so readily. He was the worst, in some ways, seeming stubbornly lost, as if he didn't understand this world and didn't think he should. But then, he'd had to watch his father die. Anyway, Rutland thought, Knox's eye was sharp and might evolve. Maybe he'd even start trading like the rest of them and get himself a house.

Rutland returned to the pot dangling above what was now a crackling yellow fire. He stirred the mixture and tipped the pot into his usual basin. The night was only beginning to perfect itself. He sat in the light of the fire and took his meal. Before the sun was lost entirely, he got to his feet with two mangosteens in his waist pocket and one in his hand. He squeezed the fruit and the thick purple rind split along a seam. A clear juice ran down to the dirt below and swelled into muddy lumps. From the shell he pulled the fruit whole, a tiny white orange. He took the segments into his mouth and headed out to the forest in search of an armful of wood as the fire wound down.

12

ONE WHORE PUSHED THE OTHER ALONG THE sidewalk leading out of the city hospital. The wheelchair wobbled and bounced along the cracks, and with each impact Jen's body came throbbing back to life. She was swathed in gauze, soft and hard, for the three cracked ribs, the two snapped clavicles, the broken orbital, the dislocated shoulder, and the subluxated elbow of the opposite arm. (These were just the injuries above the waist.) Her limbs felt as if they were not quite hers, as if a slightly firmer shock might separate them from her altogether. Perhaps that's what was needed, the thought came to her and went.

Mariela, the other whore, born Ecuadorean into respectable circumstances but long since transplanted to the social fringes of North America, led the chair down an incline to the pavement. The jolts came in a triplet, the first and third accented. The chair crossed that neat, narrow avenue, freshly corrugated after a recent collision, under heavy rains, between a Camaro, a Kawasaki, and an ambulance carrying victims of another car accident. The motorcyclist left with a bruised femur and a wrecked bike. The Camaro's passengers, four teenage boys, were effectively cremated on site, their bodies being inextricable from the flaming car. Those in the ambulance escaped unscathed, though the two in the back died shortly after of their original injuries.

"I need a couple of things," Mariela said. "We do. But I can do this after, if you want." Jen's head shook and then bobbed fractionally. Her eyes held a long blink as her head came to a rest, slumped.

Mariela steered the chair through the propped double doors of the grocery. The clerk gave her a glance before fixing on the blue rubber wheels of the chair. He made his way up from the loose sweats Jen wore (Mariela's), the billowy sleeveless shirt, the soft cast at the elbow, the sling, and the figure-eight splint peeking out at both shoulders, to her right eye, watering lightly, the lens saturated with blood on the outer half. His gaze flicked back and forth between the splint and the inflamed eye.

"I'll just get this stuff real quick," Mariela said, mostly for the clerk. She picked up a green basket from the stack beside the door, leaving Jen near the deli counter. Wax paper separated the slices stacked into squat towers, of beef, of chicken, of sausage dotted with bright white fat, and of hams and turkeys, honeyed, baked, boiled, smoked, and cured.

Around the towers plastic wrap had been hung, so that the top slice, not being papered over, could be plainly seen. Despite the wrap, the meat on top had suffered; the edges of the slices had dried and darkened. Near the center the textures were more natural. Each was a signature, each played on Jen's eyes: the slick marbled surface of rare roast beef, heavy with blood; the fine uniform density of ham; the coarse grain of roasted pork; and the lighter, airier textures of chicken.

Behind the stacks, more tightly wrapped in plastic than the slices, was a small slab of the corresponding creature, prepared just so. In the case of the chicken slices, it was a half of a chicken behind them, the only animal whose form remained.

At the other end were the sausages, where the shapes of the creatures going toward them had been entirely erased.

"Turkey, right?" Mariela returned with a full basket.

"Thank you," Jen said, with a gravity that seemed to transcend turkey. The clerk came around and took off the plastic wrap on the slices. Jen motioned to the slab instead. "Thin."

He hoisted the animal and pushed the saw pedal. The blade whirred, the teeth flashed. The man drove the bird through the ring, shaving nine or ten limpid slices from the slab that collected on the far side of the blade in a translucent pile.

"That it?" the clerk asked the women as he wrapped the meat in paper and dropped it in a plastic bag.

"Is that it?" Mariela asked.

Jen turned to the basket. Tuna, skim milk, English muffins, a six-pack of Michelob, a small bottle of Advil, then cold udon in a ginger sauce and a bag of green apples under that. Her eyes lingered on the fruit, though she had something else in mind.

"Cigarettes?" she said.

"Yeah," Mariela said.

"Dunhills," Jen said.

Mariela gave her a funny look. Jen had started smoking them as a joke, back at UVA, when as a sophomore her interests seemed to have turned a bit tony in her friends' eyes. She'd declared in classics that year. She'd always loved to read, to disappear—in fiction, in plays—so why not find out where it came from, how it first happened? And if you didn't actually use a pipe, like a don in an old leather chair, weren't Dunhills what you smoked reading Aeschylus?

Now she enjoyed them. Somehow they smoked as if they weren't even burning. But the tragedies ended up unfinished— she dropped out in her junior year. Or took a break, really. Even three years later, that's still the way she saw it, still the story she told her family, even if they didn't put much stock in it anymore. But that last year in school, she hadn't even been able to make it to classes, let alone pass them. So why hang around campus pretending you were in a condition to do what you couldn't?

The origin of that condition was still obscure to her. One thing she knew was this. Over those months, nights reading the ancients sipping wine had turned into mornings swigging vodka curing hangovers. At the same time she remembered an encroaching feeling of uselessness, uselessness to herself. Her family had picked up that something was wrong, her brother especially, but they avoided the questions—about the missed Christmases, the sporadic silences, the slurred speech—for fear of the answers.

Was drinking a cause or an effect, though? AA people liked to say booze always masked other problems. But often it seemed to Jen the only problem she had with alcohol was the *grace* she found in it. She was perfectly fine without it, no tears, only a little lifeless perhaps, a little bored. But with it, and especially in the hour-long window before she'd had too much, she felt as if her inner life perfectly aligned with the one outside. Nothing was left out of place. She became *herself*, the best version of her. And if you discovered you could turn into yourself like that, wouldn't you do it as often as you could, come what may? The only time she saw surprise on the face of her college psychiatrist was when she told her this. It frightened her friends too. She had trouble explaining the thought any further, but the words never felt wrong.

Maybe now, though, crippled as she was, she'd have to find grace in the books again, to go back, to disappear properly. The clerk found the cigarettes on the shelves. Mariela paid for everything and hung the two plastic bags on the handles of the chair. She pushed Jen out the door, the bags swinging forward a few degrees, then back, as they crept back out onto the uneven sidewalk.

The sun was low and large outside. It gave light without heat. They trundled five blocks, across bone-white sidewalks and charcoal pavements, past public basketball courts, a narrow slate chapel, and a towering parking lot, almost a fortress, to 384 West—Mariela's building—a walk-up in white with green accents, simple lines, eight floors. Mariela rolled Jen into the shallow retrofitted elevator and the doors grazed the blades of her shoulders as they closed. Jen's slippered feet, wrapped in heavy black socks, pressed against the back wall and took on its angle from the ball up. They got out at the sixth, onto a hall lined with pastel green paper crisscrossed with long curlicues in a lighter green.

The apartment was shallow but very wide, with wood stained peach. Jen had been here before, though not in a while. Mariela was not a close friend, really. She'd arrived at *this* by a route so different, so much commoner, true intimacy seemed out of the question. By American standards, Mariela came from bona fide poverty, and her family was far away, in Ecuador, with so little connection to her now Jen couldn't remember Mariela mentioning them more than once in the time she'd known her. Meanwhile Jen had a radiologist for a father, and her family was just in D.C., a few hundred miles away, waiting, probably, for that first honest phone call from her that could turn all of this around, almost overnight. They'd bring her home, or start sending real money again, make all this unnecessary. In just months she could even be back in school, as if she *had* just taken a little break.

This made her the exception in Mariela's world. Sometimes Jen would marvel at how it had all happened, how, with so much opportunity, she had ended up just as alone. Wasn't that common ground between them at least? That life had managed, for the moment at least, to reduce both of them to wraiths? Life was doing that to all sorts of people lately, though. Which meant you couldn't take it personally, even if you wanted to.

Still, Mariela was here now, and Jen had very distinctly felt some of the tightness come out of her face when she appeared beside her bed in the hospital. Mariela didn't pretend to really understand her, that's probably what Jen liked about her most. Maybe refusing a false communion had established a different kind of closeness between them. In truth, Mariela probably understood enough of Jen, everything that counted now.

Mariela's place had been in worse shape the last time, with clothes and an unusual number of shoes strewn about the living room, beer bottles in the sink, half the lights burned out, and everything reeking of several types of smoke, each of them illicit. Now it looked vigorous and right, prim even. Maybe Mariela was different. Or maybe it was just a matter of courtesy, and had just been made up. She hoped it wasn't courtesy.

"I think someone will be here today, to talk," Mariela said while splitting the noodles between ceramic plates. She flipped the plastic box and poured the ginger dressing, loose as water, onto them. It splashed against the ceramic and dribbled onto the countertop. Bits of chive floated in these black pools. "Erin had to talk to them—"

"They came by the hospital to tell me." Jen's lips twisted. "It's fine." Mariela had left her by the long line of latticed windows. The view was not especially interesting—a jagged row of prewars—but she had a lot of it. Mariela was good at what she did, and she worked six days a week.

The steam radiator, painted a burnt orange, provided what the light could not. But the pale wash fell on Jen all the same, in a grid that located her in its lower quadrants. She turned her head toward the facing buildings. Her eye shifted off a bar of shadow and filled with too much light as her damaged iris failed to adapt to the change. She shifted back by reflex and the buildings were replaced in her view by the lamp and table at the far end of the apartment.

"She's fine now, pretty much," Mariela said. "She got out right after you went in." She held the plate out to Jen but she didn't reach for it. So she lowered it onto the sill, a third of it hanging over the edge, and tucked the tines beneath the noodles.

Mariela ate. She stood at first; then she sat on the sill. The noodles, bloated with dressing from their time on the store shelves, dangled from the fork as she conveyed them from plate to mouth. They sparkled in the soft sunlight, and they dripped, having absorbed what they could. She finished most of the plate and set the remainder next to Jen's.

"You're okay staying here?" Mariela asked.

Jen took in a short, sharp breath through the mouth. Her thoughts scattered at the question, forcing her eyes from the lamp to the blue-green fingers on the hand of her slinged arm. With her good hand she gingerly picked up the plate and, shoulder stinging, balanced it on the armrest of the wheelchair. The bruised fingers steadied the plate but just as they did the fork fell from its edge, lifting droplets of oil and soy onto the window and taking the noodles that were to have held it in place to the ground. They stared at the udon caught in the tines. Small rivulets of dressing formed.

Mariela held out her fork to Jen. She took it and began to eat.

13

STAGG NAVIGATED THE AVENUES AND BYWAYS downtown, scrolling through the map, looking for the place, 384 West. The pulsing arrow leaped miles at a time, first here, then there, then somewhere else again, triangulating his location. But wherever it landed, the compass direction stayed true, even when, going by the phone, it was leading him into the river, or on toward Boston, or out to the prisons at the edge of town, or sometimes even through the Atlantic, on course to Europe.

As at sea, direction alone counted. So he held the phone out in front of him like a dowsing rod and followed. It took him across Knoll, the wide avenue near the cul-de-sacs abutting the city's essential services.

The fire station rose up on his left, in gray brick, stolid. There had been three firebombings in as many months, all stillborn. Molotov cocktails punctured the upper panes of the windows only to be retarded by metal grills. The fires burned themselves out in the windows, on the steep iron escapes, carbonizing black paint but nothing more.

The department would soon succumb, though. The garage, two fire trucks in it at the time, fell to the flames just weeks later. Several firefighters came rushing up to the second floor after midnight, talking about an inferno below. As the smoke wound its way upstairs, they took to the escapes and made their way down to the asphalt outside. A neighboring fire department was called in to put out the blaze. The cause was never determined. The tanks of the trucks were double-lined steel and the garage itself was heavily insulated. Of the men, the night watchman, a junior firefighter, was dismissed pro forma.

The arrow leaped again, haloed in translucent powder blue and locating Stagg in the middle of the river. It swiveled around, holding course. He was close now, he felt.

He rounded the corner of a twisting lane and a sourness tore at his face. A spasm ran through him from the chest down. The phone slipped from his hand and somersaulted across the metal rain grating. He stumbled on a deep fissure in the sidewalk, a hand across his mouth, and nearly followed the phone to the ground. The loss of balance, the fallen phone, they displaced the odor of waste at the core of his awareness. Instantly it reestablished itself, filling not only his nose, but his mouth and chest. It seemed to penetrate his eyes too, like light, but passing through them altogether, filling the space beyond.

Stagg climbed up a short stoop with a hand on his forehead, instinctively separating himself from the street. An agitated water flowed across it, some vanishing down the sluice, but most flowing around it, toward the corner he'd just turned. Granules, whorls of fine sediment, and bubbles, some barely visible, some large, ballooning and popping, traveled in the flow. He took a snort of air through the nose and choked.

Having landed in the middle of the grating, the phone was mostly safe from these waters. He snatched it up and felt the grit on it. The screen bore a spiderweb crack but the arrow still pulsed, or really, it shimmered, through a halo extended by refraction. It guided him onward. He gauged the shallow flow and checked the time. The woman, Jen, would be waiting. He walked as briskly as he could, his course unchanged.

The source of the foul water seemed to be only a few buildings down, at the turn in the alley. The trouble would be over once he'd cleared it. The smell, of stool fringed with urine, bloomed as the building came into fuller view. But as he approached, it became clear the water came from further on, from the apartments near the next turn in the switchback.

Things went the same way with this building, though, and the one at the turn after too. For a time the source seemed always deferred. Stagg's incredulity grew with each turn in the lane, each false origin, as the air grew fouler and the water flowed stronger and thicker with sediment. It splashed about at his feet as he chased the arrow, and by the time he finally came to the end of the passageway, his shoes were sopping.

The alley opened onto a wedge of industrial outfits: a body and tire shop, a small hardware store, seemingly family-run, a seller of insulation materials, and several others. An aquamarine billboard adorned with shortboards and blond cigarettes, its skin wrinkled, being imperfectly laid, loomed over the shops and angled out toward the freeway. The whir of traffic mingled with the manhole's gurgle as it shot sludge and stained water up into the middle of the street like a fountain. The epicenter.

On the other side of the wedge was a tall chain-link fence topped with razor wire, and behind it one of Halsley's smaller waste stations. The fence gaped—the hole made with bolt-cutters, it appeared. A dozen officials, some uniformed, some signifying their connection to the police force only with caps, but all masked for the pungent air, milled about, assessing the damage. Two others stood near the center taking sharp pulls from cigarettes held like joints. Another pair stood toward the edge, near the fence, silent and blank, with their phones pressed against their ears.

Several police cars and a fire truck were parked on the station lot as golden smoke streaked with rust billowed from the hydraulic pumps. The smoke enveloped a ten-yard stretch of the freeway; the cars shot through it unperturbed.

Beneath the billboard, some of the workers had their shirts pulled up to their eyes. Another held a grease-streaked rag over his mouth and nose. The flow had so far left their shops untouched, the slight incline drawing the filth down the lane Stagg had come by. His loafers were a mess, and his eyes began to water lightly, whether from the excrement rushing out of the manhole, the gauzy twists of smoke, or the ruined shoes. Cordovans.

Further up the road, past the filth, he could see a gas station. He would hear all about the incident soon enough: the demographics of the neighborhood, a public utility compromised in a poorer district. There was no rush—only to the interview with Jen. He'd left in plenty of time and now he was going to be late anyway. It was a pattern that wouldn't break.

He walked around to the back of the station in shoes squeaking wet. He snatched the air hose by its neck and twisted the copper nozzle. A hiss turned to a whine. He knelt and untied his shoes with one hand while holding the hose pointing skyward near his ear, shooting air into air. Once out of the shoes, he took the hose to them, blasting away the crusting debris and dirty water. The shoes deformed. They shrunk flat when he shot them from above, looking almost like covered slippers, and the uppers ballooned when he pushed the hose up into the toe box.

Having left the socks in a stinking pile near the pumps, he did to his feet what he'd done to his shoes. The skin shuddered as their structure surfaced under pressure.

The hose took his shoes and feet from wet to damp and that was the best he was going to do. He twisted the nozzle shut and flipped the air hose to the ground, not bothering to hang it up. With the water hose he rinsed his hands and walked off from the station, sockless.

He dug the phone out of the pocket of his blazer and wiped

the cracked screen, still beaded with water, across his sleeve. Apparently its brains were intact. The face glowed in the weakening light, and the arrow trembled back to life, pointing him further up the lane—away from the piss and shit—to 384 West.

■ ■ ■

The woman swung the door open at Stagg's weak knock. Her flaking, lightly pockmarked face, the crevices filled with matte makeup not unlike cream spackle; the contrasting sheen of her forehead; the wide eyes offset by a narrow rhinoplastied nose; and the feathery shoulder-length hair, a brown leaning orange— for a moment his lungs locked up. He could think only of the cocks that would have bruised her throat over the years, the heavy mucus they would have drawn from her, fortified by precome, the demands, as those heads crashed against her tonsils, that she swallow. And then the trains she must have ridden to get here, the paperlessness of her life, the money better than she'd ever seen.

"She's over there," she said, pointing to the tan leather sofa near the windows. Stagg could see only a woman's bare feet dangling over the edge of it in the last bit of light. They slipped off the sofa's arm and fell out of sight.

"I'm Mariela," she said. "Jen'll be with me for a little."

"Good."

She opened her eyes wider.

"I'm from the agency. Carl Stagg. We just need—"

She backed up into the apartment and he passed through the doorway.

Jen was sitting up now, with her sling resting on an oversize sofa arm, and her figure-eight brace coaxing uncommonly good posture from her. The sight of her face, now largely healed except for the bloody eye, seemed to transform into the disfigured one he'd seen under the truck. This was an inversion of that night, when her true face, one he could now see he had correctly imagined, even in the finer details, had seemed to surface from behind the blows and cuts, the froth of blood along the mouth and chin. He wished he could leave the other face behind. But it remained as a kind of spectral superimposition. He couldn't hold her eyes.

Mariela leaned on the sofa arm farthest from Jen. Stagg raised his eyes to hers, but the throat reaming came back to him. He turned away from her too.

"Okay, I'll be back in an hour, maybe two?" Mariela said. "Enough time I hope."

Looking only at the peach floor, he nodded with a delicacy of significance lost on the Latina. The door was noisy, the hinges on the jamb squeaking, the metal of the loose knob rattling and clicking as Mariela twisted it and pulled the door closed twice to get it to shut.

From an inner pocket Stagg pulled a spiral pad of unlined paper, pale green. He scrawled the date on the first blank page. "You wouldn't mind," he said, moving toward a tall halogen tower near where Mariela had stood.

"It's dark," Jen said, nodding at the tower. These were the first words she'd spoken to him, now or at the crime scene. He twisted on the light and followed her gaze out the slatted blinds, still open, a second geometry overlying the gridded glass. Dusk was passing. The apartments were mostly lit.

Stagg sat down in a cavernous chair the color of cognac and faced Jen across the coffee table.

"You know the man that did this?" Stagg asked.

"No. Or only by reputation." A pained half-smile flitted across her face.

"And this issue, the violence, it's well known."

"To the girls?"

"Right."

"You couldn't not know, really. I don't see how you could. Well, *you*, I can't say. But us."

"I'd still have to start somewhere, whatever I know."

"There's been no chance to forget either," she continued. "Two months go by, then this," she said, with a look at her braced collarbones. "And the start?"

"Yes?"

"That must go back a long time."

"The first woman you heard about like this."

"Oh, that's simpler. Nine months, I think. Mariela will know better. She's been around longer."

"And you?"

"Yes?"

"You started when? The workers involved, who might have information, the department's not going to bother them."

"The workers."

"The sex workers."

She brushed away a long dark curl of hair that fell from behind her ear across her mouth. "Not long ago, at least around here. Three months maybe. Three and a half months."

"You started working the neighborhood where you were found."

"I'm not a walker."

"Okay."

There was a tightening in the exchange. Stagg could smell his shoes lost to the deluge, the rot. He wondered if she could too.

"He took me there," she said. "I was working out of a club. No dancing, just escorting. Most of the dancers do it. The club's mainly a brothel. The dancing is for show."

"It has rooms."

"The usual private dance ones. But not that many, and not the kind a lot of johns want, real bedrooms. The girls will go with them then. The hotel we use is down a few blocks. Someone had called and scheduled with me, asked for me, from the club.

The hotel knows what we use it for, so it's safe for us, in a way, because of that. So they sent me off to meet him, in the lobby. But he was waiting for me at the intersection, outside the hotel."

"In a car."

"He was standing outside it with the door open. And he called me by my name, my work name. Lisa."

The ordinariness of the name struck him hard.

"You knew it was him?"

"I thought I recognized his face. But not really. I hesitated near the car. He said we could just do things there, down the road, no need for a room. Normally you don't do that, it exposes you, like the girls in the street. But this was arranged through the club. Anyway I couldn't really deal with a cancellation that night. I couldn't. And he was clean cut, a pressed suit, seemed like a businessman or a lawyer taking care of himself for the night. Handsome too. The tip was going to be good. So I got in, this sedan, a Lexus, I think."

"And the color?"

"Green, but like it was black. It took lights to see what it was, and—I'm not sure how to put it—it had this depth to it. Then inside it was all white leather. He started the engine, I asked him what he needed. He said he was thinking about it, had to see the girl before he knew, and maybe we should drive, find the right place first. That didn't sound so strange, from a man looking like he did. So he took me out past the tenements, the cash-check shops, all the dust and dirt, toward the freeway. The luxe hotels were just across the way, two or three exits. Maybe he only wanted something nice.

"But just as it looked like we were going to get on the free-way, he pulled up under the overpass. I looked at him, a little surprised. But not really, he hadn't said we were going anywhere in particular.

"He said he'd figured it out, what he needed. 'From what,' I asked with a light little laugh. 'You haven't looked at me since we got in.' He said just from breathing me in. The air, that was all it took, most of the time. 'What, then?' I said. He said he needed to talk to me. 'That's all?' He said he wasn't sure, that 'the air doesn't settle everything.' Which was a pretty thing to say, I thought.

"Finally he turned to me. He hadn't looked at me once yet in the car. His eyes were calm. There was even a warmth in them, on and off. He started asking me how long I'd been working, doing this, the reasons, how long I intended to carry on. You know, up until the questions, I hadn't really been concerned, but I started to think—"

"He spoke with the other women at length too," Stagg said, thinking aloud more than talking to her. "That's what they've said."

"But that wasn't it, some pattern. Even if nothing at all had happened, the questions, the extent, it would have still stuck out as... unnecessary. From a john. They do want to talk sometimes, even *just* talk, that's not that strange. But there was no charge, no tinge of sex in his voice. There wasn't any pain in it either. He wasn't looking for a listener, confiding in strangers—that happens too. He just seemed interested, intellectually, I guess, in my... history. And that doesn't really happen. So I started to feel a problem coming, whether it was actually him, or just someone like him.

"You're already all nerves if you're sleeping with people for money. That's what the drugs are for, the ones to sleep, the ones to get out of bed. And now, what's happened to ten girls, your nerves, they're just searching for a trigger."

She coughed and put her hand to her eye. "But I was right. And it was too late."

Stagg stirred. He looked at his pad and a bear stared back. He'd been doodling, apparently, though only now, scanning the immediate past, at the margins of memory, could he recover any experience, and even then it was faint, of laying down the lines of the animal's face, its wide tongue, its teeth drawn tiny.

It was difficult for him to see the drawing as his. He'd been listening carefully, raptly, to her story. He was paid to listen, after all, and he wasn't going to lose this gig. But it was more than that. Her story, her way of telling it... he liked the way she spoke. That's how Renna would have put it. Everything was balanced just so. Whatever exactly he asked, she would look inward the way you could only look outward, at someone else's situation. It's how he was too. You saw more that way, even if after a while, you looked around for something to blind you. A pill, a drink. Still, before that happened, you could see the art in things that were ugly and vile. Like tragic verse. That's what she'd been making him see now.

But as hard as he'd been listening, by the looks of it he'd also been drawing, and quite carefully too. It seemed incredible to him, but there it was: the contours of the bear's head natural and subtle, the expression of the beast equanimous, if beasts were capable of such. The eyes, though, had not been finished. But then, being unsure of his intentions, he couldn't say if this wasn't the full picture. Whatever it was, the eyes were mere circles in the pale green of the paper, not the black of the pen. Perhaps that's where the equanimity resided.

Stagg turned back to Jen. She had paused, noticing his involvement with the pad. Probably she thought something important was written there, about her case. Perhaps a relation to the other cases, or some interpretation of her words. A key. Even he expected better of himself: something about his essays, if he had to drift. Not a bear.

He flipped the sheet. "And then, the attack itself?"

"I answered his questions, told him I'd been doing this for a while, on and off, that I didn't know how long I would keep doing it. It depended on what alternatives came up. He said he knew young women who worked as clerks, waitresses, baristas, that sort of thing, and aren't those alternatives. I told him I had done some of those jobs, that they humiliated me in certain ways that felt worse than giving head.

"He gripped the steering wheel tightly and stared out the windshield. He said, 'Then why don't you do that, right now?' I was a little surprised, given his tone up to now. But that's why I went on the ride, right? So I leaned over his lap and undid his belt. He gently put his hand on my shoulder. I pulled his cock out and started stroking it. I was about to put it in my mouth when I felt a terrible pain in my back. He'd hit me with a blackjack.

"I knew it was him then, and my fears—some of them—grew. I knew there was going to be pain. I knew there'd be the hospital. But some of my fears shrank. I knew I'd be left alive like the others.

"Anyway, that's how he pulped me that night, with the black-jack. I thought it was like an especially bad beating by a loan shark, except you'd never borrowed money from him in your life. I think he kicked me a few times too. I can't remember everything after it started. I gave way at that first shot, collapsed in his lap, with my face resting on his cock. He pulled me from the car, from the driver's side, and lashed me with the sap, all over. I remember seeing the tool, the woven leather, the springy handle.

"And the sting of each hit. It would ripple out until it met the stings of all the other hits, until eventually, these circles of pain, they overlapped, turned into one thing. And then it stopped. He left. I started to feel less. It was very cold, and I remember feeling grateful for that. Then, later, I was dragged along the ground again, but more gently, by a different man." She looked at Stagg as she said this. "And I remember being unloaded from the ambulance at the hospital."

"He said nothing to you, during or after."

"I don't think he had anything left to say."

Stagg started to summarize these details in his notes, the bullet points Penerin would want, how all this might compare to Ravan's cases. But the image of Jen collapsing on the man's cock, at the strike to her back, divided his mind, and half of it turned toward the double-axe handle.

His freshman-year roommate once told him about someone he grew up with, Chris, who was, at the time, a Sigma Chi brother at Cornell. He'd met a thick black girl one January night—Lena, a student at Ithaca College, he thought—in a pickup bar in town. She wore a bob cut, with shiny, waterproof hair, the sort that had been relaxed in an attempt to mimic the hair of other races. But in this respect it failed. It looked only like distressed African hair. She wore black skintight leggings, and a black blouse meant to be flowing that was instead packed tight with flesh. Her belly appeared to begin at her sternum and it rolled in waves down her front as she moved.

Chris showed up at the bar already loose from the four pints he'd had at the frat house, around the pool table. It was Sunday night and the bar was less than half full. He sat down, asking for a double Maker's, one cube. Lena was three stools down talking with another black woman, this one of more common proportions. There was a moderately attractive white girl next to Lena, then an empty stool, then Chris. The girl reminded him just slightly of an ex, her small breasts pressed against a fitting wool sweater. He caught the ex's eyes—they might as well have been—and nerves seemed to stir in her. A sense of possibility came over her face; he let it be for a minute, in small talk. He made it grow when he asked if she'd like to move down a stool. She did.

The bartender came to see if she could use a drink Chris would pay for. But as she ordered, he slipped around her, bourbon in hand, to the stool she'd vacated. He thanked her for moving and watched vague hopes seep from her face. Seamlessly he chatted up Lena. A few vodka spritzers, some talk about the formative influence of *Good Kid, M.A.A.D. City* on his life, and then outside, pushing past six-foot snowbanks on the narrow road. To an Ithaca dorm? No, turns out she's not a student anywhere, just a townie. The fraternity was no place for her. So they made their way to her apartment at the base of the hill.

He watched Lena jiggle up the stairs from behind. The place was clean, it surprised him to see. But the materials were poor: linoleum, plywood, dollar-store spackling, wood-patterned plastic for the table, chairs in aluminum with vinyl cushions, and a couch upholstered in cloth only slightly smoother than burlap.

He thought of his ex as he pulled the clothes from her. The mess of rolling flesh made him smile. He pulled out his cock and pushed it between those heavy lips. Too much tooth. Can't even suck a dick right. He reverse-fishhooked her with his thumbs, felt the grooves of her molars worn away by ten thousand Slim Jims. With his hands gripping her face, he wrenched open the jaws and pushed himself into the space he'd made. She gagged and tried to close it, but his thumbs were there. He carried on in her mouth this way until she began to froth. He rolled the woman over, told her to fold out the burlap couch. She said some words that didn't interest him. He was more concerned with the two condom coins he'd pulled from his pocket, for double bagging. The diseases he imagined she had then were many, and the thought of each brought more blood to his groin. He finished his preparations and worked her over from behind. She rocked and rolled and the couch threatened to collapse, but he was determined to finish before the fall.

He did. But as he came, he gave her two sharp shots to the kidney, gripped his hands high above his head around the handle of an imaginary axe, and launched himself into the air with a roar. He brought his fists down on the stem of her neck, his full weight behind them. The metal struts of the couch seemed to crumple as her arms splayed out and she came down in stages under him.

He rolled off her with an athlete's grace and pulled the sheaths from his cock. He flushed them, taking care not to leave any semen on the bathroom floor or the rim of the toilet. It was five a.m. and the radiator had just come crackling to life. He dressed before her overturned body and the bent couch.

She moaned softly, whether from orgasm, alcohol, or simple blunt force, he couldn't tell. That was the point, to leave without knowing the meaning of her quivers and coos. The beast had been felled by cock, or fist, or bottle. How she would rise again, in what state, how much she would remember, how she would explain this night—these were questions for other men: brother, father, officer.

Jen had been felled by a man of privilege too, it seemed, someone idle enough for such lovingly scripted cruelties—even if he hadn't actually fucked her. Though that did make the story odder. They always fucked them. But not this man, a good-looking man at that.

"Okay." Stagg finished his summary and flipped the page in the pad. "How many girls have left over the last months, would you say, because of these assaults?"

"Left Halsley?"

Stagg nodded. "Or the business."

"A lot. Half maybe. More all the time."

"And are they still sex workers, as far as you know?"

"I can't really say. I don't know these people, this community, if you want to call it that, very well. But I don't see why not."

"Right—but you would think there'd be a lingering fear. Do you know of any who've definitely gone in another direction? Away from prostitution."

She swept the hair from her face as that word came from his mouth. It kept cascading down when she shook her head, yes or no. "Sure. A few. When you go as far as moving, you consider a lot of things."

"And of the victims themselves?"

"I think at least half are doing other things. Back with family or friends, some in NA or halfway houses, some working regular jobs, retail, that sort of thing."

"And that's pretty well known to the other women, what they've chosen, you would guess?"

Jen paused and squinted, searching the apartments across the street. "Yes. That I know, actually."

He stood. "A lot of people are working on this, Ms. Best," he said. "I'm hoping there's something to tell you soon."

She yawned as he spoke. "Can you get me my pills? They're on the counter."

He picked up the translucent orange bottle from the kitchen counter. Percocet. He thought to bring it to her but paused between kitchen and couch. He twisted off the white cap and tapped a single oblong pill into his hand and set the bottle on the counter.

"They gave me so few," she said.

The glass of water Mariela had set out for him remained on the coffee table, untouched. He picked up the chilly glass and condensed water dripped across the table. The last of the ice, just milky slivers now, was dissolving. He held out the pill and the glass to her, one in each hand, as if she might receive them the same way, though she had only one good hand at this point. She took the pill from his palm and pushed it into her closed mouth, between her lower lip and teeth, like chewing tobacco. She returned with the same hand, the good one, for the glass. Before he could lower his own, she put the glass back in it. Only after all this did she look him in the eye, and then only briefly, in a sweep of much else.

Her phone chirped twice.

"Your friend?"

"Mariela. She's here almost."

"Good."

She dropped the phone on the couch and put her feet up over the arm. "Bye," she said in something just above a whisper.

"Should I wait for Mariela? I can."

Jen lay there with her eyes half open, willfully oblivious to him, with the very mien the opioid would anyway force on her shortly. Perhaps she learned this at the hospital, he thought, that it was better to adopt the look of lassitude than to wait for it to seize you. Just as well.

He drank the rest of the water and left.

14

LARENT SAWED AT THE STRING, THE OPEN E.
A continuous tone rose from the double bass, and from it sprang
further tones, harmonics, an infinite ascending series, growing
ever fainter. He'd trained himself to hear it, though, a portion
of it at least, as Stockhausen could in even the roar of taxiing
airplanes.

The series came as a mix of ratios to the fundamental, E,
all whole numbers, and small. Loudest, most resonant, early in
the series, were the superparticulars: $(n+1)/n$. Two to one, the
octave; three to two, the fifth; four to three, the fourth. Larent
followed these tones up through the registers, fixing the intervals with his ear, tracing an elemental order. The first thirty-one
harmonics, more than he could resolve, produced a *pure*, a *just*—
a Ptolemaic—version of the common twelve-note chromatic
scale.

He stopped the string a pure fifth above the open E. He held
the B against the E still ringing through the amplifier on a delay
pedal. The dyad was glassy, luminous, and fragile. Shaving just a
fiftieth of a semitone off of it, as the usual tempering did, managed to shatter its coherence, sending waves of sound beating

in and out of phase, canceling and strengthening each other by turns.

He carried on forming dyads this way, twelve of them, taking each rising fifth as the new root, locking it in place with the pedal, and bowing a fifth above. He made his way through the circle of fifths, climbing seven octaves this way, seven and a remainder. The E at the top was not an E, could not be. It overshot E by a Pythagorean *comma*—less than a quarter of a semitone, and nowhere close to superparticular: 531,441 to 524,288.

This wasn't his mistake. The glitch was in the mathematics itself. You couldn't return to the root pitch through pure fifths. The circle wouldn't close. Instead it spiraled upward, a comma for every twelve fifths. To close the loop, to make E meet E, you had to narrow that last fifth by a comma. This was how a wolf was born, a howling, beating fifth.

The spiral wreaked other havoc. The major third you got from building the chromatic scale by stacking pure fifths, the way Pythagoras did, was much wider than the pure one (5:4) drawn directly from the harmonic series. So, to capture those pure major thirds, they tried *tempering* Pythagoras's scale. This was two millennia later, during the Renaissance.

That just relocated the problem. Tempering the scale to achieve pure thirds meant that some of those previously pure fifths had to be narrowed, which is to say coarsened, not so much as to breed vicious wolves, but enough to steal the brilliance from the scale you were left with. And even then, a true wolf sat there at the tail, making most of the keys unusable for their dissonance.

If instead you tempered the twelve fifths by different amounts, so that the interval between notes varied throughout the scale, you could make even more keys playable, as Bach did in his *Well-Tempered Clavier*. All twelve keys become usable to one degree or another, and each takes on a distinctive character, depending on the precise spacing of intervals to be found in it.

You have fewer true wolves this way, but then, you also have fewer pure intervals.

What took hold in the nineteenth century, what still reigned today, equal temperament, went the whole distance with tempering. All the keys became equally playable, because all of them became identical. Each of the twelve fifths was tempered by the same small amount. Flattening the spiral in this way made harmonic motion, modulation, effortless. But nothing from the harmonic series—the very origin of the scale—remained, less the octave. So you'd chased away all the wolves, yes, but then you'd done the same to everything pure.

■　■　■

Larent saw the gap between pure scales, drawn from the overtone series, and the tempered scales that prevailed not as a musical problem but an engineering one. It only afflicted instruments like the piano, whose centrality to the conservatory repertoire neatly explained equal temperament's reign. While each piano key must be tuned to a single frequency, stringed instruments, and many brasses, can in principle produce notes of any frequency. Just like the voice, the first instrument. Note-space is made continuous, spectral rather than discrete.

Observations of this sort led Larent, halfway through his studies at the small but distinguished New Hampshire conservatory that had produced a string of notable neoclassical composers, to move from piano toward his second instrument, the double bass, his fondness for which, up until then, had been based on its access to the lower frequencies. Just as singers had natural registers, whether baritone or alto or the like, it seemed to him that each instrumentalist had a natural inner range, one where his musical sensibilities were most fully at home. For him, this was in the bass. There was also the physical aspect of it, the kinetic pleasures of standing and bowing with his whole body as compared with that of sitting on a stool and striking bits of ivory.

The conservatory's curriculum emphasized classical forms to the near-complete exclusion of more recent developments: musique concrète, jazz, nonwestern musics like Gamelan and the Indian classical tradition. The American minimalists, who'd long interested him—Young and Reich especially, and more lately Basinski—were hardly treated at all. The teaching tapered off with Stravinsky, Bartók, and the serialists, whose work, though radical, was defined almost wholly by its negative relation to the classical tradition rather than by any affinity with exogenous forms. Certainly just intonation—a tuning based on the natural physics of sound, the harmonic series—got scanted, and it wasn't even a foreign tradition so much as a historical one that had been prematurely buried.

After three years, Larent left without his degree. He didn't want an orchestra spot, or worse, a post in a conservatory where he might pass on the very same theory lessons he'd chafed at. In the seven years since then, he'd felt even less regret than he imagined he might when he left. That didn't mean he was pleased with himself. There'd been four groups in those seven years, and he was the prime disbander of each. Mostly the other members seemed to agree with him a little too easily. At that point he would walk away, unhappy with his own ideas, which they didn't seem able to test in the right way.

What encouraged him now, apart from his own ripening views on music, was a certain *dis*comfort with Moto he'd noticed in their most recent practices. Their bland start had been misleading. Moto *had* ideas, and they were in productive tension with his own. That's how really interesting things happened, Larent thought, even if no one exactly enjoyed the process.

When his father tired now and again of sending him checks, Larent gave private lessons in bass and piano. These were more about technique than theory or composition. They might be applied to any sort of music. What that meant was that although most of his students would go on to staid classical careers—if they went on to a life in music at all—that fact couldn't be laid at his feet. There wasn't a single student of his who didn't have some settled musical question unsettled for him, who wasn't given some inkling by Larent of the sheer variety of scalar strategies, even if only through hearing him play Bach on his bass, using the alternative temperaments the German had used in a faraway era before industry or ease.

■ ■ ■

Larent set the bass in its stand and let his mind whir ever more furiously, almost without him. Geometry was a dead end, he thought. Pythagoras didn't offer the right constructive principle. Better to start with the physics of sound and let the mathematics fall out from that. But when you looked at it, the physics seemed to favor something like an arithmetic principle.

Naturally produced tones were always complexes, subsuming a series of simple harmonics, or partials—sinusoidal waves. The harmonic series gave you a set of naturally occurring intervals from which to build scales. And as Larent was realizing, if you were serious about cleaving to the harmonic series, what mattered was saving the smaller integral ratios, especially the superparticulars, as Ptolemaic scales did. They did far better in tracking the harmonic series than Pythagorean ones, yielding pure versions of the chromatic and diatonic semitones (25:24, 16:15), the minor and major whole tones (10:9, 9:8), the minor and major thirds (6:5, 5:4), the fourth (4:3), the fifth (3:2), and the octave (2:1).

That the notes of a Ptolemaic scale can't be pinned to specific frequencies—well, why should they need to be? Certainly it's a problem to realize them on fix-pitched instruments. The variable semitones and tones make any standard piano keyboard inadequate (and split keyboards are too cumbersome to consider).

But with variable-pitch instruments—the voice, strings—you could maintain the pure intervals even through harmonic progressions. Modulation too. You just adjust the pitches of chords built on a given scale degree so that the notes sit in the right ratios to the root. Ratios—relations—not absolute frequencies, are what count.

Riley, Young, Harrison, Blackwood, Johnston: they'd all tried to accommodate just intonation or its approximations within the fixed-pitch orbit of the piano. Even if they did manage to arrive at music that was interesting, sometimes beautiful, and once in a while sublime, the instrument forced them to contort.

Only instruments with an *analog* structuring of note-space could realize just intonation fully. The piano, the harpsichord before it, these were really digital instruments. Either you sounded A or A♯, nothing in between was reachable. It might as well have been zeros and ones.

String quartets and vocalists sometimes try to approach just intonation, but they mostly shy away from the harmonic complications. Certain chord structures, five-note tone clusters, say, can't be realized in pure intervals. But tetrachords can. Take the justly tuned dominant seventh, the so-called harmonic seventh. It's common in a cappella music, since the voice, being variable pitch, can adjust to the 7:4 minor seventh involved—the seventh partial in the harmonic series.

Maybe then we need a more flexible approach to harmony. Couldn't we take our cues from the overtone series itself? Building chords by stacking thirds is a geometric method. But if we've already parted ways with a geometric approach to scale building, we could do the same with our chords, our harmony.

It's true that many of the more complex chords formed from pure scales turn out to be more dissonant than their equal temperament cousins. That can't be ignored. But why think of just intonation, of "pure" tones, as entailing the avoidance of dissonance or the creation of beatlessness, rather than simply a fidelity to scales composed from intervals found in the overtone series—in nature, that is—whatever consonances, whatever dissonances, they might lead to?

Larent's head was light now. He sat on a speaker cabinet and calmed himself a bit. How, too, to fuse all this with features of music that had no echo in the concert hall? Things like heavy amplification, inharmonic distortion, the full repertoire of electronic manipulation, the primitive rhythms of rock even. Glenn Branca had come closest, he thought, in the middle symphonies, three, four and five, deploying an army of guitars, twenty or thirty, most playing single sustained notes without distortion, right alongside violins. And all of it set to primal beats. Mostly it involved stepwise motion through the intervals of just-intoned scales, this miasma held together by percussion not far from punk rock.

Couldn't heavier use of melody, more formal orchestration and harmonic structure, produce something less numbing, more agile? And could it even be set to words, not as Partch did, but in more vernacular forms—Dianogah, Slint, Boris, all the bands Moto was so deeply schooled in. Something that could escape the ghettos of art music, the concert hall. Something continuous with the decentered brutishness of the city and ripe for unintended consequences. Everything depended, though, on finding the right musical cohort.

■ ■ ■

Eight vintage analog synthesizers, bought on the cheap from Columbia's Computer Music Center, which was set to scrap them, sat on a long table across from Larent. Here was his lab. As he surveyed the equipment Larent thought of Alvin Lucier's famous experiments at Brandeis, back in the 1960s: the construction of feedback loops, recorded voices that descended into unintelligibility, overtaken by their own constituent frequencies, reinforced unevenly till they fell into a chasm of static.

And what about Steve Reich's lab from that era? Larent seemed to remember hearing that it was really the mechanical defects of those tape loops, their incapacity to sustain any sort of constancy, that was at the core of the phase effects Reich was renowned for. More remarkable to him, though, was the idea of Reich spending much of the noisy sixties—maybe the last time society had seemed so malleable—painstakingly splicing tape loops in a soundproof lab. Yet he was never not political. *It's Gonna Rain* and *Come Out* proved that. As a performer, Larent had spent most of his time out in the world. Somehow that hadn't done much to clarify the nature of his engagement with it.

He switched the synths into oscillator mode, where they produced *un*natural tones, simples, the equivalent of partials—single frequencies uncluttered with natural overtones.

He flipped the first of them on. It hummed and buzzed and then produced a disembodied C, akin to a flute in the higher registers. Above this, at a lower volume, he added the second harmonic, the octave. To these he added six more partials: the just fifth, another octave, the just third, and so on through the overtone series. This naturalized the C, incarnated it, forced it into the unsynthesized world.

He altered the amplitudes of the partials, pushing some of the faders up, others down, all in slow, continuous movements, waves, mutating the texture of the C. None corresponded exactly to real instruments, but all corresponded to possible ones. First the tone fluttered and roughened in the direction of a trombone. Another distribution of amplitudes turned it breathy and woody. Then the breathiness fell away and the tone sharpened into something like a violin. Finally he pulled the faders down, all but the first, and the glassy sheen of a fundamental defeating its overtones returned.

With enough oscillators to recreate ever-higher partials, and with enough time, the entire timbral range could be mapped. Every route through this terrain corresponded to a continuous manipulation of overtone amplitudes.

The materials for a performance, perhaps. Moto on drums. Electric strings, a guitar tracing a justly intoned horizontal line, low leading tones with enharmonics restored, all set against a simple vertical construction. Promising, yes, but it would take a very particular sort of guitarist to make it work.

He turned the oscillators back into synths. A middle C sounded from the first of them, an E a pure third up from the second, a pure fifth G from the next, and a B♭ on the one after—the greater minor seventh (9:5). Between the third scale degree and the flattened seventh was an interval now slightly wide of a diminished fifth (64:45). So Larent dropped the seventh down by ear, through heavy beating, and arrived at the consonant dissonance of the *lesser* minor seventh (16:9). The diminished fifth took shape.

More corrections. The minor third from the G to the B♭ was still wide, so he took the seventh down still further, the pitch slider drifting down the oscillator's base, the tone wobbling quickly and then less quickly, settling into an even flatter version of the minor seventh (7:4). The lesser septimal tritone (7:5), the purest, most consonant type of diminished fifth, locked into place and the chord rang out, the overtones reinforcing each other, creating the effect of a distinct binding tone.

Larent sat back down, away from the oscillators, and let the chord draw him in, the harmonic seventh: the barbershop chord, so called for its a cappella uses. He imagined the Crip walkers then, asphalt dancers with picks buried in lightless hair, isolating this constellation, the background hum of another world, together, a dozen of them in that circle. All the while, their immaculate sneakers kept gliding across the pavement, and the men kept whirring about the circle, their motion counterpointed only by that peculiar chord they would hold until their lungs were raw.

15

THE SPOTTED SLATE TIE IN WOVEN SILK, CROSS-knotted between the spread collar of a bespoke oxford; the single-button, summer-weight Huntsman, cut long, in gunmetal blue; the flannel trousers, chocolate, unpleated and uncuffed; and the whiskey brogues, one dangling—Kames's legs were crossed—its sole scraped down to an ashen canvas speckled black and tan.

He clutched the papers with both hands: a few draft essays, a letter of introduction from Hade, a vita. Thirty or forty sheets in all. The high-armed chair, lacquered maple wrapped in blue leather, softly whined as Kames shifted forward and, studying the CV, returned a curl of hair to the place behind his ear.

"Intellectual history," he said.

"Well, more history of ideas, I think," Stagg began. "Told, it's true, through the history of Anglo-American philosophy. Basically, the evolution of modern moral thought, political thought, alongside ideas about the mind—action, personal identity, consciousness—within the analytic tradition, from the mid-nineteenth century on. Which means Mill through Sidgwick and Moore, down to Williams and Parfit. And then for the mind,

Brentano, Frege, Russell and Ryle, through to Quine, Austin, Davidson, Dummett, and McDowell."

Stagg waited for Kames to speak, but the director kept his head turned away from him, apparently in concentration.

"And then there's some discussion," Stagg continued, "though it's not really enough, of how this all relates to wider ideas of morals and minds in Britain and America, the ethical sensibilities of the culture, its sense of itself as a political body and as a collection of individuals. But that was more of an afterthought. Future work, I think."

Kames turned back to Stagg slowly. "But is there any gesture toward more classically continental thinkers?" he asked. "I'm thinking first of Freud, but also, politically, of Habermas, Strauss… Schmitt even."

"To a degree. Only if they mark the philosophical tradition I'm working on. Usually the influence, for the continental thinkers, runs through the general culture, whatever it soaks up, and then back to analytic philosophy. So, Freud. Unignorable stuff, not necessarily because it has intellectual credibility—I'm not sure it does at this point—but because it became common sense, a feature of the culture, to be explained like any other. Even its mistakes need an explanation. Nietzsche, the same thing.

"But Schmitt, say, or Althusser, not really," Stagg said. "They haven't been absorbed by common sense, not so deeply, not yet, anyway, so they've never had to be dealt with by the other tradition. Even if they might have a lot more going for them, intellectually speaking, than Freud. I don't know. I do have some material on Schopenhauer and Hegel, and also Foucault, since they helped form the ideas I'm looking at, negatively at least."

"It's been submitted, I take it," Kames said. "The dissertation."

"I've had my viva, actually, though I haven't gotten the official results yet. There'll be the usual corrections, I'm sure, the examiners always ask for some, but I assume I'm basically done. It went well."

"Good. You know, your supervisor, James Hade, is an old friend of mine," he said. "I hadn't talked to him in years, until your application came in. He thinks well of you, all in all." Kames smiled. "Anyway, we don't always see eye to eye. He's a very good teacher, though." The next words came haltingly from his mouth: "So, this proposal. Imperial history. The first thought—actually, the first thought I had, I have to say, is what's this got to do with philosophy?"

"Not very much, really. But then, philosophy is never very far away from anything, so—"

"But how would you bring your learning to bear?"

"There's a history of ideas in play. Just in a different way."

Kames ran his thumb up the edge of the papers. "Not much discussion of intellectuals, or ideas as such, though. It's not very clear, anyway, from what you've given me. These drafts." Kames set the papers on the table at his side, beneath a darkened lamp.

"There is some of that, actually. I can show that to you soon. But it's about the intellectuals of another culture, the monks, their methods, their ideas of history and interpretation. As far as the West, though, that's true.

"But that's what I think is interesting," Stagg continued. "The intellectual history here works in another way. It's a break with the classical sort, which is closer to history of philosophy, but with a wider range of thinkers. The ideas I'm interested in tracing here, and they're mostly political and moral, they were first formed not just, or even mostly, by intellectuals, but by explorers, traders, soldiers. Marco Polo is the obvious example. Their impressions are like ideas in embryo.

"The European sources I'm drawing on most heavily are from a Dutch soldier and two English traders, their journals and letters and, in the case of one, his published chronicle. Mostly I'm trying to see how ideas can develop in a totally concrete way, not as some broad current in a culture, but down through the generations of a single family."

"Yes, and of some political and intellectual influence. Your family."

"Well, the pieces would also form part of my genealogy. Literally. But given the specifics of this family, I think the genealogy doubles as a history of ideas. And that would be the interest."

Kames riffled through the pages and found the brass marker he'd laid. "Carl Rutland Stagg."

"My mother's side."

"And Haas, the warrior."

"On the other side. A slightly less direct relation, but yes. The Dutch-German part. My father's family."

"And how far back are you planning to go with all this?"

"To the time of Rutland's stranding in Sri Lanka, 1660. But with some mentions of Rutland's grandfather. And Haas's. So maybe 1600."

"The civil war in England too, then, or do you consider that distinct? Perhaps the Rutland role in it."

"Cavaliers, defeated in the end. That's about it for their role, I think."

"That was the pejorative, for a Royalist. Cavalier."

"Right. But it doesn't strike me that way now, not so simply."

Kames looked past Stagg to the windows behind him with eyes that seemed to have gone bluer. "Nor I. But most people still balk. The dictionary does." He put one hand on the sides of the knot around his neck. "So, these lectures are personal."

"That and something more."

"Your motivations, I mean."

"I do think you can recover something of yourself like this, through genealogy. Sure. But once you get started, blood's never the end of it. The Buddhist monk, Darasa, there are things he's doing with history that speak to me. He's the main non-European source I'm using."

Kames raised his other hand, put it at the back of the

hourglass-shaped knot, and stretched it slightly. The weave of the silk caught the light. "Well I'm certainly intrigued by what you've said, and by what you've given me. Still, I can't really say I grasp the meaning of these drafts. They read like scenes from a novel. Not essays, really. The richness of the details—"

"That's the other break. But the details are actually all in the letters and journals. There are drawings as well, full of information."

"You've supplemented them in some way, though."

"By other texts of the time, yes. The clerical record, Knox's chronicle, Dutch and Portuguese documents."

"More than that. The perspective is so deeply integrated, and the language, it's not the historian's. Not the modern historian's anyway. Maybe Herodotus, who was almost a novelist."

"Well, there is something ancient going on, you're right. Herodotus matters. He wrote first of all to be heard, to be experienced by a gathered audience. And these pieces are meant to be heard too. Thucydides, say, he wrote more to be read, studied. It's very smart but also clinical, as he would have it. He wanted a certain sort of 'scientific' history."

"So then how much of this is, well, reconstruction, imagination?"

"Well, the prose, the diction, the point of view are mine, however close I come to occupying their standpoints at times. It's the binder, the frame. I haven't tried to recreate the past, only represent it, in my terms. That's all Herodotus. He is a master of form, I think. And it also means I haven't attempted the kind of philosophical history Hegel wanted. I don't know if that's possible, to go native in the distant past.

"But I've followed Herodotus only so far. There's something right in wanting a properly scientific history. Certainly we can't go back now to the older, more poetic form. So, the details, I haven't taken the liberties he did. They're all strictly culled from the sources. So it's not an imaginative act at all, if that's what you mean by 'reconstruction.' I haven't filled anything in. Whatever gaps there are in the sources are still there in the presentation. That's why they're fragments."

"I noticed that."

"That's because I've stuck with the known facts, as far as they can be known, anyway. I've looked for convergences, checked one voice, one account, against another. Any details that ended up in dispute I've left out or signaled. But for a lot of the material—most of the psychological details—there just aren't multiple sources. The records are spotty.

"But unless I had a reason to suspect error or deceit, I've let them stand. If I'd stripped out every detail that couldn't be corroborated, there'd be no texture left. And the texture isn't really incidental, for me. It *is* the history. To thin it out in the name of some sort of definitive history would be a mistake, I think, when there are so few conclusive facts. It would reduce it all to this trivial nub of truth. I'd rather let some of the impurities remain."

Kames stared into him. "I'm not asking you to change them. I'm trying to get a handle on what you're doing. It doesn't sound like you're imagining things in the ordinary sense. But there's a kind of precariousness to it, don't you think?"

"'Precarious' is just right. It's history out on a limb, at least some of the time. But there is always a limb, at least. Nothing's being included just because. For all the elements, and their selection and arrangement, narratively, there's something in the documents that lends them support. That sounds impossible, given the level of detail, but that's what's so odd about the evidence, especially what I have from Rutland, and also from the monk. They're so rich in sense details, internal and external, it's made a scenic style possible—without having to imagine anything.

"The only imaginations at work here, if there are any, are the ones of the authors of the source documents. What it is, really, is a completely granular history. Around that, I've supplied some of the more general details about what we know of the time and place, and bits of analysis or explanation where it's well supported.

"You see writers, sometimes historians, sometimes journalists, attempt this sort of thing with contemporaneous histories. This is history in the manner of Thucydides. But they can gather any amount of details on the subject they like. Everything still exists. But for a history of four hundred years ago, from a remote part of the world, where what we've got is mostly all we'll ever get? Either you go the way Herodotus did, or you write a threadbare, schematic history. Or you get very lucky with your sources. And I've been lucky. Mostly by birth."

For a moment Kames looked appeased. Then he leaned forward slightly, put his hands on his knees. "So what are you finding exactly? I see that you aren't, in these pieces, much interested in explanation. But if you were to compose an accompanying commentary—you could do that later—what would you say, to begin, about the knots in the moral and political orders of the period?"

"That's still hard to say. I don't know how all the pieces fit together, or that they will. There's a king besieged not just by the Europeans—the Portuguese, since he came to power, and then the Dutch, the more recent arrivals—but by his own people, in a rebellion. There's a scholarly class of priests, linked to the nobles, who are themselves linked to the upper echelons of the military. There's this mix of commercial and martial conquest in Sri Lanka, and behavior in the kingdom that in less strange times would have to be called paranoia. At the same time, in England, there's a royal, Charles II, being restored after a fallow period, and then London being eviscerated by the bubonic plague soon after.

"Then the political dynamics: Rutland and Knox and their crew having left from Cromwell's England, watching another ruler try to keep his kingdom in one piece, sometimes, but only sometimes, against the will of his people. And the king's seeming admiration of the Europeans, their manner. There are all these less sinister relations between the natives and Europeans—admiration, respect, in both directions—some through force of circumstance and others based only on misunderstandings."

Kames seemed to frown. Perhaps he was simply thinking hard.

"If you mean more analytically, almost everyone involved, in incompatible ways, is trying to start certain things over, on better footing. Clearings, you could call them. Conceptual or political ones, not ethnic ones per se. So they aren't obviously irrational, any more than the Glorious Revolution was in sweeping away absolutism."

Kames dropped his head, twisting it to the side. "There is that view."

Stagg narrowed his eyes as he stared at Kames's fallen locks. A grin formed on his face, though Kames, face still down, couldn't see it. Kames lifted his head suddenly and pursed his lips. "And these martial and scholarly orders, you have a chapter, or a scene or whatnot, on this? The ties there interest me, and many at the Wintry, actually."

"Well, I have some description of the martial strategies used by the Sinhalese against the European outfits—'Christian armies,' Knox calls them—who of course had the better arms. But better techniques, that's not so clear. The Sinhalese used the terrain to their advantage, relied on deception and surprise and speed. Like any overmatched opponent, really. And they played the Europeans to a draw for a long while. 310 years. The end game was very drawn out. Which is victory of a kind."

Kames nodded and blinked heavily. "And what's the end date, for you? How far do you plan on taking this?"

"For the talks, we could stop at 1680, with Charles dissolving Parliament, and Rutland and Knox returning to England. Eventually I'll take it further, as close to the present as I can, I think, with the other sources I have from later centuries. Those are still mostly back in England, in my grandmother's country house, actually. I'd also like to include the British return to Sri Lanka a century later."

"For now, though, five talks are what we are thinking?"

"If that works for you. I think I'll include some sort of commentary, as you mentioned. A supplement I can save for the last lecture, a gloss on what came before. Or is it better to present them with no explanation? Maybe that's too much," Stagg said, fingering his trousers.

"Why don't we see how things shape up first. Say we tentatively schedule the talks for the last week of October. Six weeks' time. You can show me the drafts before then, and I will pass them on to the board. On that basis we can consider you for a fellowship. We can also think about publishing the pieces, as revised lectures or something else, in the Institute's monthly journal. For the talks themselves we can pay you a small commission, and your status for now will be affiliated researcher. It's not enough to live on, of course," Kames said with a tap of his pen on the papers. "But it's something anyway. Perhaps you have money left from your graduate stipend?" Kames got up from his chair. "In any case."

"I have some saved from teaching. But most of it's coming from freelancing," Stagg said, rising.

"Ah. Commissions like this one? Maybe adjunct labor?"

"No adjuncting. Really it's whatever assignments I can pick up right now. The commission definitely helps—thank you—and if I can turn this project into a full-time matter with the fellowship, even better. The part of school I miss. Now I'm juggling research with mundane things. Earning a wage."

"Right. Yes," Kames said without listening. "Actually, you know, there is one other thing we should discuss." He sat down again.

"Yes?" Stagg said, doing the same.

"About the Institute. I have this chat with everyone who wants to research here, whether on a provisional basis, like you, or as permanent staff. Most of it you'll know, but I feel it's a responsibility I have.

"The Wintry isn't celebrated in all quarters," he began. "The casual indifference that greets standard think tanks and research centers, we don't seem to get that. That's a mark of distinction, in a way.

"The universities are bothered by the public debates we've set off about education, the blinkers we've raised on the entrenched way. It must be a little unnerving, to see us producing work that isn't socially and politically inert, invisible except when reinforcing the established ways, fit only for the conference circuit, the academic presses, and, finally, the mausoleums, the university libraries.

"And we've done it without sacrificing any seriousness. The proof of that has been their concern for our poaching. Many of our senior fellows are drawn from their highest ranks. Our credibility is mostly unassailable at this point. We are neither a practical policy think-tank with the usual ersatz scholarship, nor simply a first-class research institute that's insulated from the broader culture, like the Institute for Advanced Study, say. We're a kind of hybrid, unaffiliated with any external body, with no reigning political doctrine, where thinkers can come to conduct unusual or contrarian—potentially paradigm-shifting—research. The number of MacArthurs our people have won, for instance, it's exceptional. So what's unique about us is temperamental almost. The focus is on giving uncommon ideas a hearing without repercussion.

"More than that, though. It's also the way we open out onto the world. The atmosphere here, the chance to intercede in the culture, which our fellows take seriously, and the very generous endowment our donors put in place early on, means we are the ideal place for a certain sort of intellectual.

"You've known of our satellite discussion groups and lecture series, springing up around the country, I take it?" Kames asked.

"I attended a talk—in London. On Fourier's flaws."

"We are there too. The endowment funds all of this. We're injecting ideas, complex, careful ideas, but bold ideas, into the world with a speed no university can match.

"But our mission's considered problematic. And not just by the universities. Why, I don't know. That we don't take politics, democracy, to come before philosophy? That's a very anti-Socratic view. That we don't mind testing truisms? Probably it's that we don't do it in a way safely disengaged from actual life. Corrupting the youth, they'll say."

Stagg felt a buzz in his chest.

"But what has really changed, I think, is the surrounding circumstances: 'at a time like this.' The attacks at the turn of the century, 9/11, then the ones in Spain and England, for all the tragedy they wrought, seem to have freed something up in people—peoples—who substantively couldn't be more different. The discord, this interminable collision of interests that will not yield, the impossibility of any course sticking for more than a moment, until the next election, and, more than anything, these voting blocs that are persistently defeated, cycle after cycle. All this has left people… primed.

"The planes, the falling towers of World Trade, were the sparks to this charge. Then there was an exploded space, a place from which another look at our political mechanisms, the entrenched methods of coordination and decision making, became not only possible but unavoidable. They stood exposed.

"It's taken a few years—almost three decades now—but not that many. The Wintry was quick to recognize that space, I would say, and we've been effective in suffusing the atmosphere with, well, reconceptions of the social world, ones that aren't definitively aligned with any active political tradition, and certainly not with any of the parties and their ragbags of ideas and policies. It is confusing the order, what we do. Clouding any Archimedean vision of political process. We are not so easily forgotten about."

The buzzing recurred—Stagg's phone, in the inner pocket of his blazer.

"I tell you all this, as a prospective fellow," Kames said, "because these are complicated times for the Wintry, or really anyone looking to scrutinize form, the shape of things. You are doing that, it seems, but obliquely: the collision of several historical orders, the trajectory of a family, and then, in an enacted sense, of the form historical inquiry might profitably take. All this interests me, us. I'll be curious to see what your genealogy unearths, tells us, now, about today."

"I should be able to get something polished to you in a few weeks, the first talk, or piece."

"Fine. Very good."

Kames walked Stagg to the oak doors flanked by enormous bay windows, concave like eyes.

Outside, on the honey cobblestones, Stagg checked his messages. A text only: "Jenko billiards. Downtown ASAP."

16

THE CUES WERE IN THREE AND FOUR PIECES, ragged spikes of maple shorn by an undetermined force. Several of the tables closest to Stagg were on their knees, half their legs having been blown off at the joints, leaving them buckled, with cloths sloping. The balls were cloaked in soot, mildly discolored or worse. Most were numbered, stripes and solids, meant for games of eight- and nine-ball. There was also a small share of unnumbered balls, continuous pinks, reds, blacks, greens, browns, blues, and whites.

In the back of the hall, beyond a sodden curtain fallen to the ground and a line of sharded glass, lay the remains of a table of great dimensions—for snooker, and billiards as well, judging by the white ball resting against its edge. The table had lost all its legs and lay flat on the ground. The cloth had burnt off, but evenly, completely, and the dense wood had turned a rich charcoal tone. The plane of the table was still flat and smooth, and though the airier wood of the cushions was only ashes now, the metal frame, marked by pockets at its joints, skeletally cordoned off the space. Stagg thought it looked as though it were meant for a different game entirely, perhaps one played with clubs instead of cues; or if not that, then a kind of billiards where players lie prone like snipers to shoot. The posture might not suit the billiards clientele. But then, he thought, they did enjoy the hunt traditionally.

Further back, there were a couple of pocketless carambole tables for defunct games like straight rail and balkline. The entire area had been shielded from the common eight-ball tables by a frosted glass partition, though Stagg could only see the indeterminate remains of it, and would have to confirm the fact later, with Emile, the Jenko who owned the hall.

The Jenkos were Slovenian transplants, but several generations past now, first to London in the 1920s, then to Boston and Halsley in the 1960s. They were an educated clan, mostly in law and medicine, though they were businessmen at heart. Emile himself had taken an LLB at Imperial, in London, where the broadest branch of his family remained. He never practiced, though. After returning to the States, he passed up the LLM or JD and went into business, with money his grandfather had made with a series of snooker halls in North London: Jenko halls, as they came to be called.

He opened one downtown, in this space, which originally housed a small factory. As a child he'd enjoyed the antiquated table games, dead like Latin, especially carambole, where the balls were few and even then unsinkable. He'd first learned them in the small London halls that carried those embalmed traditions forward. Cue-sport connoisseurs were their custodians.

Thanks to Jenko's efforts, Halsley was home to a cadre of well-heeled enthusiasts, one already familiar with billiards. The glass partition, though, hadn't been their idea.

Emile's father, a doctor but also a businessman in medical supplies, had gotten some of his friends to frequent his son's club. But the humble clientele jarred them visibly, so much so that they would rent out the entire hall for the night.

Emile put the partition in thinking they might come more often that way, since the whole hall would not have to be rented.

They could treat it as a private club of sorts downtown, which was close to the banks but somewhat far from the best recreation. But even the mute, blurred presence of the eight-ball players turned out to be unbearable to them; they kept renting the whole hall for a single table.

The glass was functionless, then, except as decoration. Jenko had commissioned the frosting at some expense, for the way light refracted through the etched pattern: a coat of arms slashed with Habsburg quills, the only nod to Slovenia in the building. Lit from behind, it produced a vague illumination sharply articulated only along the clear shafts of the arrows, which gave them the look of being on fire.

The curtain that ran along the partition was almost always left open, mostly because both sides of the hall were rarely occupied on the same night, but also because when they were, the carambole enthusiasts would be of less benighted origins, and they felt no need for distance from the common eight-ball players. On nights when the common hall became particularly rowdy, though, the curtain was closed to discourage curiosity, which drink had a way of darkening.

Stagg was the first of the extended intelligence forces to arrive. The police had taped off the basement staircase and given the hall a first look, making note of potential evidence, dusting for prints. At the top of the stairs they stationed two men to watch over the place. They IDed Stagg and left him to examine the hall. Through the blown-out windows behind the stairs, he couldn't make out the specifics of the damage. But its complexion was heavy.

The door was cold and damaged at the hinge. He wrenched it open. The room tasted of smoke, its wood base made acrid by phenolic resin. He stepped past the centerline of the hall, scanning the floor. Ambient sunlight fell from the street above, through the long narrow window frames set high against the wall. It was the only light there was.

He counted at least a half-dozen balls in various states of abjection. One was melted away into a hemisphere that had recessed itself into one of the long floorboards lying atop the concrete factory floor. Some of the boards were burned away, but many remained, at least in fragments, especially on the far side away from the bar. The "2" on the ball was partly effaced, the resin presumably subjected to extended and extreme heat.

Three other balls were similarly deformed, having been liquefied to varying degrees, one nearly completely, so that it was only a smudge on the floor, and another, a green one, only fractionally, so that it was like a standard ball with a flat spot, a bruised apple. There was also one that seemed abraded, as if something had scraped at it viciously, or immense jaws had seized it. Though the innards of the ball were rough, looking of raw marble, portions of the surface remained lustrous and perfectly enameled.

There were also those that were more than deformed, that neither a forensic worker nor the imagination could reassemble. Shards of resin, and flakes too, like arrowheads, were clustered where the pool cues and racks once hung but now lay crushed. This, near a pool table that was itself in shards and flakes. Green tangles of cloth were strewn across the mess of wood and metal like bandages, and it was only by the quality of the cloth, the fineness of the nap, that one could say it had once been a pool table at all.

The fire apparently hadn't reached it, as there was no hint of soot or char. Stagg imagined the force that would have had to visit it, exert itself upon it, the outsize impact it would have had on this part of the room. Looking over the surrounding tables, the force's vector—its destructive signature—was obvious.

The arrangement of the damage suggested a single detonation. He'd visited over a dozen venues like this now, which equipped him to make such diagnoses reliably. It would have altered atmospheric conditions for only an instant. The air would have been still immediately after. But the fleeting change had transformed every object within the walls. Fire finished the job, consuming the shattered tables, bottles, benches, and balls at a rate that was always accelerating, each object that succumbed to the flames increasing the odds and speed with which the rest would.

The firefighters managed to defeat the blaze quickly, which explained why much of the room's contents were, if hardly intact, not ashes either. No one had died here. The officers confirmed this later, but Stagg knew by his nose. The air had much wood, resin, plastic, even glass in it, but not a trace of denatured flesh, or the iron of blood. Nor was there any of the usual visual evidence, no chunks of femur, pelvis, and skull; no encrusted circles of burnt fluid; no crimson spatter or mist on the walls.

The hall was struck at night, the fire put out in the morning, the investigation conducted at noon. The evening prior had been a busy one, Jenko would say. The tables had all been pushed up against the walls, so the room looked like a rectangular slab bounded on all sides by tables: in other words, a larger table, dwarfing the snooker table behind the glass.

Two hundred builders filled the space. The sliding glass doors of the partition were open, and on a small podium, Javier Celano, recently elected leader of the largest labor union in the state, spoke in resolute tones. Emile provided kegs of cheap lager gratis at these biweekly meetings, but on this night, they would not be tapped till after.

It was the substance of the talk, and equally Celano's measured cadences, that kept them from the treacly beer. He was not himself a laborer, unskilled or otherwise; nor had he ever been. He was also not an American, but a Spaniard, and an Old Rosean, if dropouts could be counted. His father was a construction magnate based in Seville, with concerns extending as far north as Denmark and as far east as Russia. Jenko and Celano had become close in London, both scions, both sympathetic, genuinely so, to the swaths of people they felt their money had compromised.

Celano spoke in an English not of the workers, and his accent had an inscrutable transnational quality to it. He tried to limit the more ornate syntactic constructions, the rarified diction he was given to, but in moments of greatest concentration—as his mind was consumed limning a Gordian thought, and lacked the resources to dress it simply too—he would drift toward the baroque language natural to his station. When he was not probing in this way, though, and merely telling what he knew, what he'd settled on, his language was limpid and plain. By register alone, then, one could hear where his mind was.

Even when they turned tortuous, though, the urgency of his words was usually enough to win the workers over, however alien they found Celano in these moments, however little success they had in so much as parsing the grammar of his ideas. More than that, it was his grasp of construction in its global dimensions, the niceties of the trade, and indeed the joints where it might come undone, that overcame their bemusement and earned their interest.

On that evening, Jenko later revealed, Celano had urged them to make their ancient grievances visible by new, still-forming means, that this was the lesson in the air, the meaning of Halsley's rot. The security they lacked, the static wages, the uncompensated injuries, the part-timing, the lack of training programs—by being pressed in familiar ways, these concerns barely registered as having anything like the gravity they did. There was protest, of course, and for a time that could hold the attention of the media, which could in turn hold a nation's. But no one can stay attuned indefinitely. Protest becomes noise. In any case, given the rigors of redress—no less than the remaking of a country's self-conception—it couldn't happen at any speed. It let their case be tabled.

Strike could have had more bite than protest. But hadn't it

lost its teeth to the old cowboy, Reagan, in a battle over air traffic decades ago? Their own situation was even worse, since Celano's workers were mostly unskilled. It was nothing to replace them. So the pain they could induce, the attention they could command, was also nothing.

Both tactics, strike and protest, had their place, Celano granted. They'd done much good for labor. But their own historical moment, he said, seemed to ask them to reach further, to discover what lay beyond. Or before, primordially.

Their problems might not be exclusively, or ultimately, with the *substance* of the law. They might be with the very manner of its making, the mechanisms of the state they'd been taught to call democratic. It was no longer clear, if it ever was, Celano intoned, that voting your interests and living with the results, come what may, was a conscionable course. Democracy—rule of the people—might not be so simple as majority votes.

That meant shifting the point of attack, or expanding it at least. More than that, it meant a fresh translation of *demos*. Everything would flow from that. Now, the alliances brought with it, the unities created, they would be unfamiliar, unstable. After all, a lot of people were busy reinterpreting *demos* for a new era, each to their own purposes—the rich, the poor, the devout. The liberal, the statist, the autocratic too. Why, after all, should democracy exclude certain forms of dictatorship? But who exactly would count as the *demos*? There were Athenian notions to revisit. It wasn't so obvious who was what.

These alliances might also be as unavoidable as they were unfamiliar. There was overlap in these redefinitions, yes, but even more discord than agreement, so that wasn't why. Really it was the act of redefinition itself that arrayed them all against the state, which was itself happy enough with the old understanding and doing its best to stamp out the shifts of meaning the factions were floating. As far as the government was concerned, they were the same. Revisionists.

The particulars were still shrouded, Celano said, but the mist was burning off every day. He said no more. Which was wise, Jenko thought.

Celano's abstractions quieted the room. There was a coded charge to the words, though the code was neither one he had encrypted nor one he was necessarily equipped to decipher. A murmur came from the workers as Celano stepped down from the podium and re-entered the partitioned space. They clapped with calloused hands. The taps shot beer into chilled mugs. They returned the tables to their places and began to play games of nine-ball, in teams.

The footfalls came on slowly, the soft slapping of leather on stone. Stagg twisted toward the staircase: a descending pair of unshined wingtips, then seersucker trousers, then a heavy wool cardigan a deep green.

"You got that text too, yeah," Ravan said.

"I did."

"And what've you found?" he asked, surveying the damage casually.

"Looks like a police raid. Same contractors, at least. Same matériel." Stagg pointed to a charred strip of tempered vinyl that appeared military grade.

These raids were sometimes as destructive as any wrought by the factions they were meant to subdue. The government had already exploded several hives of the agents of opposition and their alleged abettors, on grounds of national security. Of course, political license for this kind of violence wasn't easy to acquire. It depended on the sustained appearance of sedition.

There were certainly clear-cut cases of it. Lately, though, the basis for these interventions appeared to have grown thinner, more preemptive, even reckless. It was consuming credibility, and questions of this sort were losing their paranoiac ring: How many involved embellished charges, only to justify the tightening of control? Worse, how many of these police raids were passed off as the work of factionalists, for the same purpose?

Jenko's hall looked to be one of these confidence-eroding cases. As far as anyone knew, alongside more mundane discussions of procedural matters, only Celano's almost philosophical talks went on at Jenko's. There was no history of violence to point to, and no manifest incitement to it either.

In the wake of the attack, the government had the usual choices: claim that the evidence of violence, or the intention to it, had to remain classified—this did not ease anyone's worries, not at this stage—drum up some evidence, or disclaim the attack and count it as internecine warfare between factions.

The angle to be taken on Jenko's hall was not yet established, or anyway known to the two agents.

"The meetings might have been a bother to the government—to us, I mean," Ravan said. "They'll have to make the case for going this far, though," he said, gesturing at the wreckage. "Or implicate some enemy of labor in this. A pretty sophisticated one, by the looks of it. Anyway, I've just come from talking to Emile, the owner, at the station." He relayed the substance of the workers' meeting to Stagg, as told by Jenko.

"And where is Celano?" Stagg asked.

"He wasn't there, but Penerin's looking for him." They walked through the space, the debris. "You know, I don't think I'm seeing anything you're not. It does look like our work—the same sort, actually, I've seen in other districts lately. That's really why I'm here, to compare. But I don't see a difference. Not one that makes any."

Ravan paused over a shattered cue ball. A blue dust coated it. "The explosive traces, the shrapnel, the placement and timing—maybe the motives too—generations of R&D behind them all. That's the way it looks, anyway. They're convinced these are framings, Penerin and all. Not actually government work. The *appearance* of state oppression. That's what they're designed to give."

"*We* are convinced," Stagg said, touching Ravan's shoulder with the tips of his fingers. His voice was flat.

"We are?"

"It's not so easy to make the case, I guess, when things look like this," Stagg said. "So... to form."

"Well, yes, how does it play?" Ravan said. "And what do I know, we know, about what Penerin and my supervisor are convinced of? We know what they tell us. And they might not even know as much as they think, never mind what we do. I don't see how any of us can be convinced of anything much, really."

They ascended the staircase, leaving a precisely established chaos behind them.

17

"I HEAR YOU'RE DOING BETTER," STAGG SAID OVER a crackling phone line. "A little bit better."

"The wheelchair's gone," Jen said. "They took it back."

"That's good. You can walk."

"Is that what you mean?"

"Well—"

"No more rolling around."

"And your eye... I remember. It was painful."

"I have whites instead of reds again."

"Good."

"I still see double at night, brights against darks. Everything haloes, and text, especially text, like on a computer screen, it doubles."

"You're not done getting better. That's what the doctors tell me."

"My ribs get sore, they're sore now, when I've coughed too much, or laughed too much the night before."

"Laughing is—"

"It's happened once."

"They take time. I've broken mine."

"Have you. And your collarbones too?"

The line flickered with static.

"I'm sorry. What I—"

"My fingers work. They didn't for weeks. They were all these colors. Green, orange, blue, red…"

"The bruises must have been deep."

"Must have been."

"But they're gone."

"My grip's still weak. All my fingers tremble when they come together. I drop a lot of things."

"That'll change."

"The stitches have all come out. I had twelve above my right eye."

"I remember."

"Left a scar along my eyebrow. My head just split there. And I've got stitches along the edge of my wrist. Odd place to get them. I don't know how a lot of it happened."

"That's okay."

"It wasn't, though."

"To who?"

"At the interview. You didn't say it. But it wasn't okay."

"That's not true. You were very helpful."

"I was on drugs, for the pain."

"You were helpful. And you have a copy of your statement. So if you did want to add—"

"See, I knew you would ask me that. That's what I mean. It's not okay. But nothing's clearer now. I read it over four times. I could have been clearer, more direct, answering your questions, but the facts are the same. The tiny ones are sharp. But the big ones are dull, soft. The facts are the problem."

"We aren't expecting anything more from you. But yes—this is why I'm calling, mostly—as helpful as you were, we still don't have anything concrete. I'm sorry to have to tell you that."

"Nothing."

"Though there are a dozen or so people under special watch."

"There's a profile, you mean."

"And what you've told me has contributed to it."

"But it fits twelve people."

"Well, yes. Even they aren't hard suspects. I don't want to mislead you."

"So it fits even more? I helped you put together a picture of a person—"

"Not a picture—not a physical description. Parts of it are that."

"No, but a picture of a person, an idea of a person."

"You did. It was vital, what you added to it."

"But this idea fits twelve, and not even them so well you'll call them suspects. Maybe it fits a hundred, really."

"That's true."

"A thousand."

"I don't know."

"And this was vital."

"It could be. You were vital in creating it."

"How is that even an idea of a person? What sort of picture matches everyone? What sort of picture is that?"

"Look, Ms. Best—"

"I think 'Jen' is better."

"We haven't had any incidents recently. Nothing in weeks, in any of the districts."

"And that's not good?"

"Well, of course it's good. It's—"

"But for the case. You need more. More beatings."

"No. We don't want to see any more—"

"You don't *want* more. Obviously. Of course. You're not evil. You only need more. It would help. And you wish I had more. But that's what I mean. I can't tell you very much about how it happened, not the way you want to know."

"That's not your fault."

"Well that's just idle. 'Fault.'"

"I don't know."

"Maybe you are evil, Carl." She laughed and it mixed with the static and made the phone clip. "And my experience, my pain, it hasn't moved anything, changed anything."

"I just said it has. The profile."

"It really is a stupid word you brought up."

"Jen, we are going through what we have. What we know, in all sorts of ways, from every direction. Something can emerge."

For a long time, they listened to each other breathe.

"You seem different today," Stagg said finally.

"Different how?"

"Terse."

"Just like you. Maybe it's being off the pills. Or just the phone."

"Maybe."

"And does that mean you found me awfully chatty at the interview? You *can* be strange. Just like she said."

"She?"

"My friend. The one who let you in."

"Mariela."

"Dress shoes and no socks. Wet pants."

"The legs. She mentioned that?"

"You looked at my fingers the whole time I talked."

"I don't remember that."

"The colors maybe."

"I was listening."

"You ran into Mariela on your way out."

"That's right."

"She thought you were so strange."

"Well, I'm not a cop. Maybe that's who she's used to dealing with."

She laughed. "I'm sure she is. But there are lots of you now. Watches, I mean. That's not strange, Carl."

"Maybe I was bothered by your story. I'd only just heard it. It might have showed."

"*Maybe* you were bothered?"

"Jen—"

"Do you have a girlfriend, Carl?"

"Your story—"

"Do you?"

"Yes, but this story—"

"She must be very understanding."

"I'm sorry, if I didn't—"

"Or she just tunes you out. I bet that's it."

"I was taking it all down."

"I guess you've already got plenty to worry about, don't you?"

"It's a terrible story."

Again there was a pause.

"You know," Jen began, "what someone should seem like, why they should seem like anything in particular... Mariela's ideas are definite. Not like the profile. The opposite problem. But maybe I've missed something. She's managed to stay on her feet the whole time. And I'm still not better. Still, I was glad to go in the end."

"Go?"

"Mariela's too worried, too aware, whatever it is, to live with for very long. Does it even help? I wonder whether she took me in partly for that, to size up this threat. From a toll. I'm a toll. I don't think that's true. She did ask me a lot, though, long strings of questions, stretched out over days. She would pick up out of nowhere. About friends of hers I may have worked beside, people I saw that day, any signs there may have been, what did I miss, what did I not see. Or the lack of signs. Maybe I missed nothing, he was that good, or lucky. And how quickly I knew, and now that it's happened, what will I do. She's been trying to get me to call you, actually."

"Strange as I am."

"But I didn't call you. You had to call. And that's because I don't think there's much I know. She just assumes I must, that it's only got to be fished out. I don't mind talking about it. But the angle, the way it's always a piece of a bigger puzzle. I can't think like that."

"You don't."

"Not as that. A reign of terror or whatever. And over a bunch of sluts."

"But you're worried about the profile."

"I want to be useful, Carl. You aren't calling me for personal reflections, ones that end there, tell you nothing about the future."

"What about just *your* future?"

"I don't think about that either."

"It would be pretty hard not to."

"It is hard."

"Impossible almost."

"No. But it doesn't help, so I don't."

"And Mariela?"

"She thinks only of the future, as far as I can tell. That must be hard too. She has a kind of concern for the group at the front of her thoughts—her among the many. She's helped me because of it probably. She might have helped anyway. But she thinks about things in this way I can't. Like you."

"About the city, the community."

"The future of it."

"Well, professionally, yes, I think about it."

"This can't seriously be your profession. This is about convenience. I'm sure of that."

"It's one of them."

"Right, so there are others."

"They pay me to consider the whole—"

"They pay you for the particulars, like these."

"Yes, but for the benefit of the whole. I keep it in mind."

"Professionally."

"Right."

"Maybe that's what Mariela meant. That it ended there for you. Just a job to do. Or is that impossible too?"

"It could be. I'm not sure."

"Anyway, she needed the space back. It was always temporary. Her boyfriend made it from Quito. Mariela's the breadwinner now. Proud."

"And—"

"I'm in my place, for weeks now. With my brother, for the meantime. He's in the other bedroom. He's helping me cover rent."

"So things are okay."

"He can work from here. Coding identity software. It's kept our parents out of it. I think they think I'll eventually go back to college. That's what he—Reed—tells me. But they are less sure now, it's been three years, not the year off they signed on for."

"You were studying what, before you left."

"Really?"

"Yeah. Anything can help."

"Classics, while it lasted. Is that funny? Is it strange?"

"They get you to pick something. Why not."

"It's more than that. But the incompletes were piling up."

"And they think what?"

"My parents? Traveling, partly. And I am. I spent about half the time, less than that, in California, between San Diego and L.A. And then a bunch of places around here. I assume they think I'm figuring things out. That's never totally false, I guess, whoever says it."

"And nothing unusual, no trouble."

"Things aren't good between us, just in the last year really. My father won't take the phone anymore. I'm not mad though. I see it. They're wondering about college. Officially it's odd jobs— waitressing, tutoring even. I've done a little of those things too. They don't know why I want to keep doing this, though, and I've said some things along the way about writing. I guess that's another thing you can say and never really be insincere. Everyone has that wish in them, somewhere. But I've written nothing. No journals. I don't really think I will, when it comes down to it. I think I prefer reading."

"I think I do too."

"When I've been able to. And they say, can't I write after the degree? How could studying classics hurt a writer? I don't know if that's right though. But it doesn't matter really, does it, since I don't actually write. But I do still read them. Or I've started again. Ovid, last."

"Oh."

"You've read him? Your other profession maybe."

"No."

"Then?"

"Of ancient things, Gorgias last."

"I knew I knew you. The *Gorgias*. Plato."

"Actually, his *Encomium of Helen*."

"He's there in Sextus Empiricus too, right? *Against the Professors*."

"Right, but second-hand again."

"I don't know Gorgias, really. Except from the *Gorgias*."

"He doesn't really show up there, though. No one shows up in Plato but Plato. But Ovid, yes, I have read bits of the *Metamorphoses*. Not so different… your family, though, do they help you, financially?"

"I don't expect help from them anymore. They used to send money, sometimes through Reed. They still do, but less regularly, less enthusiastically. It's not enough anymore to help. He says they're pretty desperate, wanting me back in Bethesda. I called them from my hospital bed, actually, in the middle of my stay, as if everything was fine. My body was just pieces after the beating. My mother asked me to speak up. That was the jaw. The drip kept me together. And the Librium."

"Detox."

"Yeah."

"You've stayed that way."

"Mariela kept carting me to meetings in the wheelchair. NA, CA, AA. All I really needed was the last of those. The other things aren't, well, entirely 'unmanageable.'"

"You still go to AA."

"I'm not drinking."

"But the—"

"The point is I'm doing better. That was your point too, wasn't it?"

"You won't go home."

"Not a solution."

"For a stay. It could be easier to be sober."

"Well, I spent two summers there during college, and every night I'd end up drinking this plastic pint of vodka out on the driveway. It's no different now. And there'll still be the decisions I can't make."

"Outside of that, since the hospital, nothing unusual. We haven't heard from you, so that's what we've assumed."

"No."

"Things are getting back to normal? I'm not interested in interfering, it's not what I'm supposed to do. Same as the last time."

"You only watch, I get it. Not normal exactly. Hooking was never normal. Anyway, what I'm thinking now is different. It's safer."

"It is."

"It's legal. I haven't started. Reed won't stay forever. He won't stay more than a couple of weeks now really. I need to do something. I might move. Perk of the job."

"New profession?"

"It's definitely an improvement. I haven't even told Reed what it is. If he knew, he'd be happy, or maybe he'd be sad, and then he'd be happier. You know, it's been strange not needing to find money these last weeks, to have so much time. I sleep and read. And talk to Reed. I like him more than I remember. A lot more. Maybe I'm just not remembering. Or I just like him more now, and I remember fine."

"But you won't level with him."

"Not now."

"You can't trust him."

"I trust him completely."

"It's probably easier to tell—"

"I'm going now, Carl."

"Okay."

18

THE LIGHT WAS DIMINISHING IN THE FORESTS
surrounding Belemby, but more slowly now, almost asymptoti-
cally, as if the night were unbreachable. Rutland searched for
the thin branches he might light with the bark he'd scraped as
kindling. Most lay in damp undergrowth, moss-covered, rotting.
But in a small clearing he found the stones and barely singed
wood of a fire that looked as if it had been made and unmade
immediately after. He fingered the branches, wispy and abun-
dant. He pulled twine from his pocket and tied some of them
up in a bundle.

The monk appeared at the edge of the clearing, his rust robe
catching in a gust of wind. Rutland rose, leaving the wood on
the ground. His fire, perhaps. Beyond the monk, in the distance,
Rutland made out a narrow, tall building in gray stone with a
steep roof tiled in the Portuguese style. The village *vehar*, its
Buddhist temple.

Belemby was small so the temple housed only a few priests,
and most rotated from this site to others in the region. To mark
its autonomy from the kingdom proper it was placed on the
outskirts of the city, though by a centuries-old arrangement

between the priesthood and the royal court, the king paid for its construction and upkeep, beyond what the locals provided through a temple tax.

Rutland raised his hand and the monk came forth. In a mix of English and Sinhalese he explained his bundling of the wood, the assumptions made. He started to untie the sticks but the monk, Darasa, held his hand out flat and received a nod in thanks.

Over the years, Rutland had picked up enough Sinhalese to survive on. For his part, Darasa knew substantial tracts of the invaders' languages: Portuguese, Dutch, and already some English. He asked the Englishman if his needs went beyond wood, light, heat. Rutland scanned the undergrowth before seeing the stylus and the folded parchment next to it in the monk's hand. Darasa unfolded the parchment, revealing the script, alien to Rutland. He gestured for him to follow him back to the temple, explaining he may have something he might like to read.

I cannot trouble you, Rutland said. He thought to return, with or without the branches. The villagers would soon wonder where he'd gone. The bending of patterns brought unease. Darasa smiled and explained that he would escort him back to the village himself afterward.

They walked toward the spot the priest had emerged from, making parallel prints—Darasa's feet, Rutland's boots—in the dirt. The monk had acquired more than a few books over the years from the foreigners: navigational works, texts describing proper seamanship, collections of maps, and a very recent account of a plague crippling Europe. There were also religious works, like the Gemara, portions of the Mishnah, the Koran, and two copies of the New Testament. At the mention of the Bible, Rutland's eyes got large.

They came across a shack. Rutland recognized it at once—a *covel*, a temple of the *jacco*, the devil's house. They dotted the country. The resident priest (*jaddese*), pious in his way though of low birth and little learning, was absent. A boy with neatly combed hair sat on the stone steps, looking faint and ashen. Darasa touched his head with an impersonal warmth.

The two men entered the front room of the covel. Plates of rice, loose betel leaves, and overripe mangos stretched across the floor. Along the walls men were drawn in reds and blacks. Lying behind the offerings were arrowheads of flint and bone, one affixed to a long branch. They found two poorly wrought shortswords next to a door leading on to a space with room only for a bed. The blades were so blunt and tarnished Rutland couldn't tell if they were weapons or relics.

They crossed out of the opposite door and came to the yard. Four birds, all short-feathered and blood-red, moved about the pen, pecking at the grass. Each represented a healing, or anyway a patient's recovery by one means or another, ague being the common malady. The birds would have been gathered for a mass sacrifice to the governing devils; or else for a sale, depending on the scruples of the jaddese.

In trips through the country selling caps, Rutland had seen red cocks of this sort sold in bulk by these lesser priests. A dozen years later, during one of several escape attempts, Knox and Loveland would bring six of these birds, gathered on a reconnaissance trip, back to camp. They'd got them from a jaddese for an iron pan and a few coins. Having lost their common blade fording a river, Knox twisted the necks of some of the birds, rotating them two revolutions until he heard the pop. Loveland, disturbed by the noise and feel of cleanly snapping bone, preferred to smash their heads with a rock. Rutland recalled the plucking vividly, the luster of the feathers, the patience involved. Once the birds were all gooseflesh, they tore out their bowels with their fingers and spiked the gutless creatures on long young branches, roasting them with only the salt they had for sale.

They gorged on the pink meat, the skin sweating fat and blood. They dug out the marrow from steaming bones. There was too much. Two of the birds were tossed into the marsh. Their crisp bodies, their taut, charred skin shrunk tight over bony scaffolds, their gaping bellies, they watched it all sink in brackish waters. Manaar, the northernmost province where entry and exit were possible, was close now, and they had the full stomachs that might carry them through this time.

But the king's men had not been far behind. They were soon overtaken in the swamps. Their lead had been lost roasting birds. The Englishmen saved their lives by playing off the dash as an especially wide merchant wander.

Darasa took Rutland through the covel only for contrast with the proper Buddhist temple they were headed to. He related how the jaddeses sometimes appeared mad, and it was then that they were taken for gods, not devils. Advice was sought. The people would pose questions of many sorts, practical, metaphysical, political, personal. The priest would answer all in the same tone, riddling and frenzied by turns, and his words would achieve a gravitas they could not approach in saner moments.

Unlike the jaddeses, Darasa said, the people could be inhabited only by devils, not gods. But they talked much the same as the priests then. Rutland had seen a man in the forest writhing and shaking. First he thought it a case of the sacred disease— epilepsy—or snakebite, perhaps; but as he approached to give succor, the man started mixing local sayings and proverbs, and indeed some European ones too, into novel, unimagined maxims, deforming and inventing meanings, so much so that though the grammar of sense remained, Rutland could not follow him.

He was convinced that something intelligible was said, if only his capacity to comprehend could keep pace with the man's capacity to pronounce. He couldn't call them ravings. Rutland had heard those many times, in Yorkshire and St. Andrews, by his ostensibly possessed countrymen. Maybe it was they who merely had the sacred disease. For the Sinhalese man's speech did not bear much resemblance. In the British cases, there was just the simpleminded repetition of a few phrases, invocations of the Devil and of God: nothing nearly so complex and creative as what he was hearing from this man.

He wondered whether the Sinhalese possession, then, was the genuine sort, and what had come before, in his homeland, were merely the babblings of the mentally deficient. Or could it be that the devils possessing the Sinhalese were simply cleverer than Satan? Perhaps this was owed to their multiplicity, their regional grounding, each devil having his province and jurisdiction. Might there be spiritual specialties, smaller expertises exceeding any single intelligence, ones that issued not in universal claims, but in both ones tailored to the region of origin and ones that were crossbred, the most fertile of all, which correlated to the various routes one might traverse the country by?

Rutland conveyed to Darasa what he could of these thoughts, which put the monk in mind immediately of the prophet of the god without name. The god, or anyway the prophet, first made himself known by a trail of fallen *dewals*, temples of the gods, which were bound to the covels by a common commitment to idolatry (both sorts were held in less regard than the vehars, the proper Buddhist temples). The prophet claimed, through his messengers—he, like his god, was never seen—that the nameless one had commanded that the other gods' temples be razed.

Over several months, collapsed temples appeared across the north, from Trincomalee through Anuradhapura. Chunks of clay with branches running through them lay scattered about, no less than the people's offerings. The relics included arms (some of them European), clay figures (some of them Virgin Marys), and collections of household objects that were also the symbols of embedded gods. These were all carefully defaced, the clay figures dismembered, the swords bent in two and displayed in their abasement.

The people shrugged off the nameless one at first, but as his destructive powers grew, and the wreckage accumulated, their allegiances shifted. Next to the rubble of the dewals the villagers would leave fresh victuals and new items to be enchanted by the god.

The prophet, finding so much success, thought he might be not only a god but a king. Through his messengers, prophets of the prophet, he declared his intentions to establish a northern kingdom that would overlap Rajasingha's.

The king had been happy enough for the prophet to rule over the next world. But not this one too. He dispatched soldiers to the north to monitor the remaining dewals. Eventually, in the night, the prophet and several of his disciples were discovered undermining a temple. The squat Dravidian and his assistants were brought before the king, who asked his name. Munjan. This incarnated god was bisected. The resulting aspects of the man-god were incinerated in the center of town, just outside the royal court. In the morning, in front of the smoldering pit of Munjan's bones, there were flowers, victuals, and relics.

Rutland and Darasa came to another clearing, this one with rice paddies, clusters of coconut trees, and livestock, all managed by local farmers. They paid their taxes in harvests, Darasa said, and not to the king but to the vehar, where they maintained its monks. The king provided men to help collect the produce, look after the livestock, cook the meals, and serve the food as needed, when the farmers themselves could not.

At the center of Ratukela, holy satellite partner of Belemby, was the vehar, just as the administration was at the center of the king's townships. None but the townsmen were admitted to pray. Women, even the best of them, were thought in some way unfit to affirm the destruction of want, the prime doctrine of the Buddha.

At noon the townsmen would serve the monks food and give offerings to paintings or drawings of past ones. The monks arranged themselves in a row, with space for the likenesses that were interspersed among them. The men would move down the row, ladle in hand, each offering a different dish to the monks. With a nod a monk accepted, with an extended hand he declined. The plates of the likenesses were always piled highest, as only they never refused.

Rutland and Darasa regarded the stone vehar, sober yet grand. The roof's lime-whitened edge was inlaid with onyx in a pleasing but inscrutable pattern. The temple dated back centuries at least, and the current Sinhalese builders could not match the skill of the originals, which meant that every renovation was also a defacement, an aesthetic and perhaps spiritual diminishment. So the Buddhist priests, the senior ones especially, liked the vehars restored as little as possible. As long as the walls didn't collapse, and the roof mostly held the rains at bay, they preferred the unreconstructed shelter, vulnerable though it was. Rajasingha was pleased to go along with this, as it came at a savings to him.

They entered the temple from a side entrance and went up a set of stairs to a long, narrow room full of loose papers and bound books stacked on the tables, the benches, and the floor. Darasa headed toward the back, but just inside the door, Rutland saw what looked like an Arabic scroll with a set of calculations in familiar numerals at its center. A trader's tally sheet. Next to that was a small book of recipes in a Germanic language, probably Dutch, he couldn't tell.

Beyond the stacks were several sea charts laid out on benches, the oddest of them being a map buried in the face of a jester. A hood—the left half yellow, the right orange, with belled tassels—was pulled tight around the world-face. It merged with the jester's suit, which was in the same colors, trimmed with gold piping, and decorated with medallions at the shoulder, as a ranking army officer's might be. There was an inscription to the jester's right:

Democritus laughed at the world,
Heraclitus wept over it,
Epichthonius Cosmopolites portrayed it.

Epichthonius Cosmopolites—"Everyman"—a name that did not name. The picture didn't give away its tragic element easily, though Rutland's heart sank infinitesimally the longer he stood over it, studying the geography of a clown's face.

Mercator's map, from decades before, was there too, up on a table opposite the main stacks of books. Next to it was a kind of update of the *mappa mundi*, Desceliers' plane-chart of 1550, but with significant interior detail, beyond the coastal outlines and seaports. In this way it was more than a mere sea chart.

On the table near Darasa Rutland found the double-hemisphere of Jean Rotz. On one corner of it lay a small atlas with further maps: the charts, Rutland knew, of Battiste Agnese.

There were more, and it astonished him to see them all here. Beneath the Mercator was Martin Waldseemuller's *Carta Marina: A Portuguese Navigational Sea Chart of the Known Earth and Oceans.* A true mariner's map. Unlike the Ptolemaic map he'd made earlier, the *Universalis Cosmographia*—Rutland wondered if there was also a copy of this in the room—with its scholarly deductions, this was a deeply empirical depiction, which meant there was an unruliness to its lines. There were the tensions thrown up by conflicting records coming in from so many sailors. A priori maps elided that sort of complexity, or more likely never knew it.

Rutland recognized all but the jester map (the *Fool's Cap*). His grandfather, a high-ranking officer in the English army, was something of an amateur mapmaker, not only collecting copies of all the watershed maps from Ptolemy onward but drafting his own. In doing so he would conjoin rational and empirical principles, thinking this was the key to definitive cartography. Most of his creations, in fact, were composites of ones in his collection. The results were as visually interesting as they were unusable, by sailor and scholar alike. The principles, it turned out, were incongruent. Still, he'd managed to pass his grasp of the history of the discipline to his grandson. It was some part of the reason Rutland had taken a sailor's path.

Above the books, hanging from the wall, was the 1502 Cantino World Chart, an accretion of hard-won Portuguese seafaring knowledge from which the *Carta Marina* was derived. For its martial and commercial value, the Portuguese royals had carefully guarded it. The Italian spy Alberto Cantino, Rutland recalled, was sent by the Duke of Ferrara to find a copy of the map. Ultimately he did, by an unknown hand, and smuggled it out of Lisbon. The Italians' worldview immediately grew: the Cantino map of 1502 depicted outlying areas unknown to most other Europeans, regions that might serve as trading posts to bring mineral wealth and exotic foodstuffs into Lisbon—or else be annexed outright in the name of the empire.

As the priest continued to search the stacks, Rutland examined the depiction of Ceylon on the map, the tiny teardrop, here more of a circle. The Cantino was published just three years before the Portuguese arrived on the island. It was this map that many of their sailors would have helped create, contributing fresh details, improving its fidelity bit by bit.

Later generations would have steered here with its help; hence its presence in the temple. It was fitted to a wooden board, to preserve it, Darasa would tell him. The deep yellow of the map contrasted with the stark line drawings of the shores in brown ink. Mostly seaports were noted. The interiors were largely voids. They had not been much explored at the time, as it mattered little to merchant sailors how exactly the interior was arranged. They needed only to understand the edges of continents, where exchange was conducted. They would oversee the loading and unloading of cargo, and occasionally help military personnel secure the port. But they spent their time thinking of the ocean, or of home, not of the lands they found themselves in, or the precise origins of the goods they carried. Martial sailors and the explorers too held different maps, different thoughts, ones that traced their inward steps.

Darasa set a copy of the King James Bible on top of the *Carta Marina*'s Africa. Rutland half-bowed to the monk as gratitude washed over him. The book's burgundy covers were worn so smooth the leather appeared grainless, though the vellum stock had stood up quite well to the marine air it would have seen in transit.

He fingered the slices of calfskin inscribed with the word of God, but strangely, without quite the conviction he expected to feel, given the many months since he had last seen a Bible. Carrying the residue of vast terrestrial movements, their geometries and schemata sketching historical trajectories without meaning to, the maps gave little ground, in his mind, to the Word. Most stubborn was the *Fool's Cap*, at once a simple guide to the world and a shaping of it, an inscrutable transfiguration of history and futurity, both, into geography.

The Bible was something different. Cartography enforced a leanness of meaning; a coastline, a bay, or a mountain range could carry only so much sense. The Book, holy poem, was a thicket of sense, making it impossible to read its implications off cleanly.

The air had gone blue black outside. Rutland insisted he would make his way back alone, and asked only if he might have use of a lantern, which he would return the next day. Darasa pulled a sheet of paper from the shelf. It was decorated with the emblem common to the temples, which resembled those of the kingdom: the seal of the lion, descending from the ancient north-Indian kingdom of Kalinga, where the Sinhalese, it was held, originated.

He inscribed a few lines, signed and folded it, and held it out to Rutland. He was to present it to anyone in the village, especially the village councilors, who might be suspicious of the evening excursion. He walked Rutland back down to the vehar's side entrance and took up an unlit lantern, its twine wick poking out of yellow goat fat.

Rutland took the ball of twine from his pocket and dipped the end of it in the flame coming off the hanging temple lantern. He lit the one Darasa held with it and left through the tall grass, the letter tucked in the book.

When he reached the clearing with the abandoned fire—he'd never asked the monk why he'd made it, or why he put it out, or even if it was in fact his—he set the lamp down and opened the Bible to the page of the letter. It had settled in Leviticus. He opened the letter, and though he could read bits of Sinhalese now, he found the characters strange.

Later he would learn the letters were Pali. Understood only by the Buddhist monks, the characters would be recognized by the town's officers as Pali, but they, like Rutland, would have no sense of its meaning except for the numerals indicating time and date. Its meaning, then, was effectively just its form. If he presented a letter in Pali with the right date and time, and with his name on it—he could see that much, as it was written in English—on temple paper with a senior priest's signature, the officer would not bother to have another priest decipher it, and Rutland would be left alone.

But what did it mean, in Pali? Was it nonsense? Perhaps the priest had a sense of humor. Or maybe it was meant to be deciphered someday, when his descendants found it among his papers, in England, God willing.

Rutland tucked the letter back into the book and held it with the lantern in one hand. He picked up the bundle of sticks and headed home.

Stagg closed the laptop and drank deeply from a coffee mug full of flat champagne so cheap that it was hardly worse for having lost its life. He shut his eyes and blotted out the light of afternoon.

Rutland would truly head home, Stagg thought, only many years later, in 1680. But the London he fled to would be two-thirds the size by then, hollowed out by the bubonic plague, and with a king, not Rajasingha II but Charles II, the Stuart, restored. The Lord Protector and master Roundhead Oliver Cromwell had lost the confidence of his people and left them longing for the comforts of monarchy.

Rutland's father, Harold, a prominent Royalist, had relished the restoration of the Stuarts in 1660, though Stephen himself was always more cavalier than Cavalier. Certainly he was at the time he'd left London, in 1658, after a military training, for a life at sea, ostensibly in the name of the commercial interests of the East India Company but really more for the adventuring. The conflicts he'd been enmeshed in on the island had altered his politics, his sense of justice, though he couldn't say just how, except to say he could be neither Royalist nor Roundhead now.

Stagg's own predicament, the inchoate strife that surrounded him, how different was it, finally, from what Rutland had experienced abroad? It must be making his politics mutate too in unknown ways. Officially he stood with Penerin and the ruling order. But if the elections, or else a less peaceful force, were to undo it, there was no saying in advance which of the competing actors might earn his sympathy, or what new attachments he might form. This mercenary instinct seemed to be growing in Stagg, and he had to consider whether, beyond the turmoil all around him, his research too might be a catalyst, just as its object, a long-lost Sri Lanka, had been for Rutland.

A century and a half later, as if to revenge his captivity, the

Rutland line would return to the island. Lt. General Andrew Philip Bartley Rutland led the final thrust into Kandy and was a leading signatory, in 1815, to the Kandyan Convention, that British treaty of annexation.

In the Uva rebellion that followed, he brought an end to several leading Sinhalese bloodlines, ones very much like his own back in England. He was always of the view that Bulwer-Lytton would articulate years later, and Disraeli would endorse: an "aristocracy of shopkeepers" was not to be preferred to an oligarchy of nobles. Abroad, of course, these English shopkeepers were out of sight, so A. P. B. Rutland was less dispirited by them than by the killing of nobles here in Ceylon, swiftly, brutally, knowing it could only speed the conquest of the commercial classes, however exactly they chose to dispose of the island.

Later, around 1900, Andrew's grandnephew Gareth Robbins Rutland would serve as deputy governor of Ceylon. He had been an Apostle at Cambridge, at Peterhouse, in fact, where Stagg had been a doctoral student. Gareth's ascendancy was swift. His family name virtually assured this.

Stagg himself was nearly tapped to be an Apostle, before he told the would-be tapper, in the sincerest tones, how important it was to follow your dreams. His friend readily agreed to the platitude. Then Stagg told him he'd dreamed the night before he'd pushed a child down a flight of stairs. What to do then? Baffled laughter came back. It was a fine joke, but Stagg had to pursue it. Would he help him memorialize the realization of his dreams, by filming it? he asked. And where would they find the right child? After a surreal debate over the meaning of the platitude, whether dreams in the clinical sense could possibly count, Stagg held firm to his position, his tone never straying from earnest. It froze his friend's face in the end, stunned him into silence. At that point Stagg patted him on the shoulder and laughed, left him to watch Arsenal F.C. finish off Chelsea in the middle common room of Jesus College. There would be no tap. The friendship was finished too.

Where to trace this taste for terror? Probably the question itself was a dodge. Yet he liked to think he was finding the form of an answer in Haas, a commander who seemed as much at war with his own squad as with the enemy, who seemed to need to visit arbitrary cruelties on those around him to keep his mind level. In a diluted way Stagg's father seemed to share in this unknowable need, at least when Stagg had been younger and more fully part of his squad. The family had disbanded now, or retired maybe, on neutral terms. The old wars had been too much. The mother remained in California, the father in Vienna. The child was still finding a territory of his own.

Gareth Robbins Rutland came to Ceylon with a fellow Apostle, Leonard Woolf, Virginia's future husband. Soon after, though, Woolf returned to London, and Bloomsbury, troubled by the mechanics of colonial administration. He wrote a novel about it: *The Village in the Jungle.*

It was a bad novel, narratively clumsy and evincing nearly as much contempt for the Ceylonese as for the British administration. Still, like the best undistinguished novels, it remained useful to the historian mapping the shape of an era.

Robert Knox, who escaped to England with Rutland on a Dutch military vessel, composed a chronicle of his experience in the mode of the traveler's tale: *An Historical Relation of the Island Ceylon in the East Indies.* It was published in 1681, sold very well, and unlike Woolf's book centuries later, managed to have some literary merit as well. Though roughly formed in places, there were affinities with *Gargantua and Pantagruel* and *Moby Dick.* It's said to have exerted a direct influence on the writing of *Robinson Crusoe* and *Gulliver's Travels.*

But for Stagg there was much more to admire in it. It *can* be called a traveler's tale, but the records from other merchants and soldiers, and from the monks and statesmen of the island, corroborate large portions of it: the native habits and customs, the horticultural explanations, the translations of pregnant Sinhalese phrases. It was closer to a travel memoir, really, than a tale.

Detailed records of daily life in the 1600s are few on the subcontinent generally. It forced you to rely on imperfect foreign reports like Knox's. Of course, there were the clerical records, the Great and Lesser Chronicles. They did offer a continuous history of Sri Lanka *of a sort*, from the time of its settlement in 543 B.C.E., when Prince Vijaya, it attests, sailed to the island from Kalinga, in the north of India, with seven hundred men and women, through to 1815, when Kandy finally fell. But, being composed and maintained solely by the priesthood, the account was profoundly incomplete.

For one, the customs and practices of ordinary people go almost entirely unrecorded, as do any matters of neither practical nor metaphysical interest to the monks. Instead, the Chronicles give you the evolution of successive royal orders, the unfurling of aristocratic lines, in tandem with a history of the priesthood, its influential scholar-monks—the *tirinanxes*, as Knox and Rutland called them—and how they related to the successive regimes. Their record of the royal court, though, was of less value, as it was known, from other surviving documents, especially those of dissident priests, to be written in a manner unduly favorable to kings who were concessive to the priesthood.

The Chronicles, then, are a history, and in the main a panegyrical one, of two institutions, church and state. What doesn't bear directly on either or casts them in too harsh a light would have been left out, or even redacted by later generations.

Centralization was partly the source of its unreliability. Each change of regime seems to have forced rhetorical and substantive shifts on the two books. So it fell to documents like Knox's, composed by the marauders, the imperial and commercial outfits, and to the few surviving private journals of monks and distinguished members of the court, to give ballast to the official domestic record, a fraught task, the difficulties of which, it was growing ever clearer, Stagg had probably undersold to Kames.

For one, the copious notes Stagg had collected of Darasa's spoke to a narrow range of issues, or at least spoke about matters from a narrow angle: metaphysical, or philological. Not that they weren't fascinating to Stagg. Probably he studied them most closely of all, but as much for historiographical as for historical reasons. At those times he felt more kinship with the monk than with his less cerebral blood relations, Rutland and Haas.

As for the history itself, sometimes he suspected he was only checking falsehoods against further falsehoods. Even less than Darasa's writings could he take the European records from Rutland and Haas and Knox at face value. Beyond the usual problems of transcultural interpretation confronting any historical anthropology, there were several more: the literary license taken in some of them, like Knox's book; the commercial and imperial ambitions, latent and nascent, that lay behind these documents; and the religious coloration, the apparent sight of moral inferiors, heathens, everywhere.

A greater range of representations might have eased the problem. Stagg could then have started to solve more precisely for the nature of the history itself, the properties inhering in the world that might explain how these various impressions came about: a meta-representation that could account, possibly uniquely, for the more partial ones, just as the Cantino map systematized the observations of generations of sailors.

But the data sometimes seemed to Stagg too impoverished for that. Too many frames could comfortably accommodate it. Reconciling the inconsistencies was no less difficult. Often there was simply the word of one against another, or the preponderance of evidence would come down to a single datum leaning ever so slightly one way. The outcome could be that precarious.

Part of the poverty of information was induced by the

island's climate. The swelter quickly rotted any document that wasn't expressly preserved. In the great vehars and the royal court, manuscripts would be stored in rooms lined with the spongy roots of a rare native shrub growing along the Highland mountain peaks. After a few months the roots would become fat with water, at which point they would be replaced. But the root's scarcity meant that little was preserved that did not pertain to the priesthood or the court.

Most commoners didn't believe the everyday was worthy of collective remembrance anyway. Crises, denouements, counted for more. So the quotidian, Stagg felt, went unrecorded and something like Freytag's pyramid, its legs and vertices—the five acts of a classical drama, like his own recurrent dreams—were taken up into the space of myth through the gateway of meter and verse. That was the structure of the Chronicles.

Rutland's letters and journals, which he'd kept religiously during his captivity, were Stagg's primary British counterpoint to Knox's book (Haas's more fragmented diaries formed a Dutch one). For years the letters to Rutland's wife had lain in the old country house in Canterbury, the one Stagg had spent half of June researching at with Renna; and the rest, the ones to Rutland's father and to his invalid sister, along with most of the journals, in Rutland's childhood home in Portsmouth, still owned by the family.

Some of these records, the ones relevant to legal matters surrounding missing cargo of the East India Company, say, or compensation for men lost on the *Ann*, were made available to the British courts. When their historical value came to trump their legal significance, some of the letters went to the British Library, others to the Fitzwilliam Museum, in Cambridge. But there were many more that were neither needed by nor disclosed to the courts, and these came down through the generations almost as family heirlooms. Gareth Rutland had organized and archived them a century ago, and in fact considered undertaking the very study his descendant, Stagg, was now conducting.

Together, the letters and journals chronicled the unfolding of Stephen Rutland's hopes. From them, Stagg thought, the scope of his talent for suffering might be recovered. There were over four hundred letters, not really so many given the many years of captivity. (Very few of his crew, just he and Knox, as far as Stagg knew, made it back to England in the end.)

The letters were carried back home mostly on English and Dutch trader ships, sometimes light military vessels. They were taken first to the Ceylonese ports on foot—Colombo, Manaar, Trincomalee, and Jaffna—by Dutch messengers, Arab traders, and French explorers. Rutland had sneaked many of them to Sinhalese villagers he'd befriended over the years of captivity, years correlating precisely with the Bubonic plague's sweep through Europe. Captivity by God's grace, he would write later. Taking pity on him, the Sinhalese would find ways to get his letters into the right hands when he himself could not.

The letters were generally five or six pages, written on a local paper, not palm, that was pressed by the Dutch. It was made from coarse plant fibers that flecked the cream of the paper with gray, black, and green. The imperfections distorted Rutland's wide script, which he'd applied in a heavy ink with the feathers of those red cocks native to the island. His line jittered, being pushed to one side or the other by the topography of the pulp. His mind might have jittered too.

Each sheet was housed in polythene now, and stacks of them sat all around Stagg's apartment. Most were in good shape, not only because of the efforts of various Rutlands over the centuries, but because the coarse pulp was naturally low in acid. A more refined stock might have been dust by now.

They circled around just a few issues: the resolution of business matters back in England, with his father; how the affairs of his house should be handled in his absence; and, most important for Stagg, what his life was like in Ceylon, offered through small sharp glimpses of the island, as if they, more than anything more systematic Rutland might say, could most effectively close the distance between them.

Rarely were they explicit about the depth of his anxiety. Yet the only feelings he omitted were the ones he had about himself. His affection for his wife, father, and close friends was everywhere in evidence, always in the tone, and sometimes in closing paragraphs and postscripts, where he would describe an experience common to their lives he was particularly fond of, the contemplation of which now brought him pleasure.

Anxiety and despair, these were reserved for the journals, though even his lamentations were crosscut with precise physical description. Stagg had so far located only six of these books, in palm paper. Their pages tell that more were composed, probably too many to carry through the mangroves of Manaar in the escape.

That he carried any at all is a surprise. They were thick volumes, together weighing some twenty pounds. They would have compromised his chances of escape by some margin. But, Rutland writes, leaving without the journals would be like leaving twenty years behind, mercurial ones, and in all likelihood, he recognized even then, the most interesting ones, if also the most difficult, he would ever live. He'd kept them at the bottom of his rucksack on the escape through the midland swamps, not allowing Knox to know he hadn't left them behind, as Knox had left his own.

Knox's *Historical Relation* was composed mostly from memory back in London. So, for all its texture, it had to be more abstract than Rutland's contemporaneous chronicle. (It was unclear when Haas's records were composed, or even how exactly they'd made their way to the Austrian library Stagg had found them in.) The density of detail in Rutland's unpublished writings easily outstripped Knox's work, whether about village architecture, the structure of the court, flora and fauna, hunting techniques, or trade with the Europeans.

Where events appeared in both accounts, how could Rutland's not be given more weight? His words, after all, were temporally closer to the objects and events described, and conceptually closer as well, perhaps, in that Rutland gives us scenes, sequences of his experience, inner and outer, unfolding in ordinary time. Knox condenses and generalizes from his. Supposing their powers of observation were commensurate, and that neither had more reason than the other to distort matters, it seemed natural to give priority to Rutland's words.

But the first assumption: How to measure their perceptual acuity without being, yourself, in a position to check it against your own, observing the same things, beyond the correspondences with other documentary evidence? And did aesthetics insinuate itself here, as it did in mathematics? Perhaps it had a place, and the great maligned classicist Richard Bentley and his heterodox approach to interpretation—really his gifts as an exegete were beyond question—was right, to a point at least. A great aesthetic intuition could recover the true and fullest form of a gap-ridden text, even when it was *Paradise Lost*, and the world snorted with laughter at the emendations.

There would also be immanent clues to consider. Too many inconsistencies in an account might suggest a weak eye. But too few might suggest the same, the missing of distinctions, of tensions, of the minute irreconcilability of events along their edge that every glassy text and tale polished away.

Even if the matter of priority couldn't be settled, an equilibrium might be sought. Rutland's words could light Knox's, and Knox's Rutland's. Similarly for the rest—the Chronicles, the trader balance sheets, Haas's and Darasa's words—until everything was bright, light dawning "gradually over the whole," as he'd read once in the carrels of the Wren library, in Cambridge (Bentley's library, too). The pages of that original manuscript,

Wittgenstein's, were tinged blue, he recalled, by the light falling through the library's tall lead panes.

In Berkeley, the preferred term was semantic holism: the fixing of the position of one term by the fixing of the position of others. Perhaps, then, Stagg's work was just historiography as an extension of radical interpretation, recovering the past as one recovers the meaning of sounds leaving mouths, a world, an idiolect, on every tongue.

Then the second assumption: Beyond reconstructing the life of a nation, to what extent could Knox's private view of the Sinhalese be discovered? There were far fewer letters to go on. Apparently he didn't think there was much hope of their reaching home.

Rutland's records, the journals and the letters, were private documents, which meant he would have had little reason to mold them for public effect. *Historical Relation*, on the other hand, was written to be widely read, and was.

As one of the first Britons to be so deeply acquainted with South Asia, Knox offered one of the first detailed reports on the land; there is an early mention of cinnamon, for instance, and other endemic spices. So he might well have been tempted to sculpt his account, in an effort to shape the dawning imperial consciousness of a nation. The irony being, though, that through the influence of his family through the generations, Rutland's account almost certainly had a deeper effect on that consciousness than Knox's in the long run.

Knox more than Rutland took an impersonal, quasi-anthropological approach, and this suppression of subjectivity created a further hurdle for Stagg. Knox was steeped for twenty years in the country's atmosphere before writing the book, though. Whatever his aspirations toward being a dispassionate witness, time would have molded his sensibilities, structured his account.

But teasing out the normativity, uncovering the moral architecture of the book, and of the British Empire—all the things that interested Kames—how was that to be done with *Historical Relation*? The book rarely engaged with matters in a straightforwardly moral way, so Stagg would have to detect their subtextual operation. And then, as before, how far could the moral framework be prized apart from the reality it framed? A kind of notional separation of scheme and content, to whatever degree it could be effected, was required, a double interpretation, of Knox's consciousness and of the world it embraced.

All this made him grateful for the private jottings of his ancestors.

19

STAGG MOUNTED THE SUBWAY STEPS NEAR CAR-
rell Square, his ears still throbbing from the train. Only some
lines had it, the crushing squeal that came on far from any platform, deep in the tunnels. Every conversation halted, and the
sound, like a jet engine overlain with trebly polyphonic squawks,
made itself the lone object of the car's attention. It might have
sprung from the tracks, he thought, something warped or worn
in the black spaces between stops.

A wall of wind met him at the top of the steps. His stomach,
rekindled half an hour ago by a swig of vodka as he walked out
of his apartment, burned pleasantly. Still, he was feeling prickles
and running with sweat, so he welcomed the frigid wind, which
numbed and dried him. It was hard to outrun a chronic hangover. Whatever you did, however much you drank, it was right
behind you, waiting for you to fall off the pace.

The grinding noise grew rather than faded as he walked away
from the station. A tower of scaffolding stood in the distance,
in the square. Though it was partly lighted along its edges, it was
still too dark, and there were too many crossbeams blocking his
view, to see exactly what it scaffolded. He wondered whether

work somehow might be going on, even so late. The sound only got louder as he walked, before suddenly falling away.

The fountain in the square was dry, and under the dim construction lights circling it, the concrete was pitted and scaly. Plaster stained the bottom in swirls, especially near the base of the statue. It had been annihilated in a blast that came right on the heels of the one in Brandt Square, just weeks before. He'd assumed the statue at its center would be replaced, as the Brandt fountain was going to be, not restored. Circumstances must be different.

He jumped the massive lip of the fountain and approached the statue. Plaster, or some sort of binder, was spattered along the fissure beneath the ribcage, where a curving chunk of the torso had been reset. The same had been done to one of the arms, though the hand, which was meant to rest on its waist, was still an absence. The wrist simply hung in the air, falling short of the body. He studied the legs, veined in hairlines as if a severe compound fracture had been set. A few slivers had been replaced by closely matched marble, perhaps quarried from the same mountain in Carrara, though it was a touch lighter, more translucent. It would have to age.

The closer he came, the more fissures appeared. Touching the arm, he could see that the entire statue had been remade from hundreds of distinct chunks of marble, some original, some new, put together like a puzzle.

The plaque, which he'd never thought to inspect before, read thus: "A Gift of Benjamin Henkel Jr. (1835-1870)." The Henkels must still be rich, Stagg thought, to have the wherewithal to put this back together or the clout to have the city council do it at its own expense.

How many pieces was the head in? And when the restoration was finished, would it carry a new aesthetic valence? Restored works, after all, always bore the trace of that labor, even if only an expert could say in exactly which details it resided.

The long bulbs attached to the beams around the statue streaked the blue-white marble with light and gave it an uncertain presence. Standing back from it, looking only upon its lower half, which was almost complete now except in its finest details, the fractures seemed to bring a kind of weight to the sculpture he'd not noticed before.

On late afternoons turning into night, as an undergraduate in the city he used to sit on the benches circling the fountain, reading Sidgwick or Hobbes, even Grote, under the statue's growing shadow. He felt he knew it better by that shadow, in fact, than by direct sight. The piece had never stirred anything in him, so he'd spent hardly any time face to face with it: the eyes long and drawn and faraway, the chin short and wide, the pose languid. All the interest, for Stagg at least, was shunted into one feature: the head's being turned off to one side, as if something had sounded in the distance.

Only this marble man's destruction, and his ongoing reconstitution, had given Stagg a reason to consider him properly, to scrutinize him as a whole, in his own right, and not merely as an element of the square. The chance to study his lines, his translucent skin, at this distance, standing within the now-dry fountain, all of this depended on his having been exploded.

He considered whether the original could truly be made to reappear, whether an entropic event could be run in reverse, an object unexploded. The viewer's eye measured the conglomeration of marble shards, their discrete totality, against this ideal, of a statue hewn from a single slab, which Stagg seemed to grasp more fully now, in memory, than he had on any of the occasions he confronted the original in experience; those times he had stood in front of it, then sat under it, sometimes looking across the fountain, over his shoulder, as the statue itself did, though his mind was still mulling the books, seeking in them too discrete totalities, parts and wholes.

A sound. This time not a squealing but an effervescing of

notes, rising, ringing, locking together in unfamiliar combinations, not clashing exactly, but making the ears skeptical. If the tones didn't keep coming that way, and if he didn't hear the rhythm section enter, he would have assumed a mistake. There was a kind of absolute strangeness to it, or something just short of that. The work of an undiscovered culture maybe.

Stagg drifted toward the tones, not yet ready to call them music. He'd come out, at Renna's request, to see Larent and his new band, which this must be. But he was still thinking of the statue. The legs alone, in their rough state, seemed already to carry a charge different from the one he recalled, one that, no matter how exacting a job was done, he thought, could never be brought entirely into line with the original's. But if the shifting by millimeters here and there; the discreet interpolation of foreign marble; the glues and plasters used to hold the exploded materials together as one; and the various hairlines that would invariably remain; if all of this altered the tone of the original, why must that be a shortcoming?

The new valence, he thought, must make a more complicated impression, and for that it might well have greater heft. Doubtless the original had to guide the reconstruction. That didn't mean it was any measure of the finished piece. As objects of art, they were two and not one.

■ ■ ■

Through the scarred doors of The Round, then, and into a welter twice over, bodies and pitches teeming. The music—it was music now—had filled out. The crowd, mostly clutching drinks, appeared a congealed mass, lacking the moving parts that might make for passage through to the back, where Larent was performing, and Renna was listening, raptly, he assumed.

The short leg of the L-shaped bar, facing out onto the courtyard, was mostly vacant, as the people crowded into the long leg to see into the cubed space beyond. But the sonic whirl was enough for Stagg. He stood at the end of the short leg, near the window, with his hands on the bar. When the bartender came he simply pointed at a sign describing the well scotch for the night. It was cheap, and tasted it: thin, sour, vulgarly medicinal.

The snack bowl overflowed with a house medley. Cheetos, Chex, Fritos, corn nuts, Lay's, pretzel sticks, and probably some other things. Any one of these made a passable nibble, but the mix was perverse, possibly by design, as it was suitable only to those well past drunk. He'd had nothing to eat since morning, only champagne and vodka. He finished half the bowl in five handfuls, slowing the alcoholic nausea he knew to expect.

Larent had moved on substantially from what Stagg had heard from him last, that night at the little café. Gone was the precision counterpoint. In its place, a diffuse harmony driven by piano and guitar: arpeggiated, key-revolving, and set in a strange motion. The progression seemed of indefinite length; or if it had a length, Stagg couldn't mark it, no better than a tone row of Schoenberg's. Structure was tacit, more felt than grasped. The percussion, mainly toms, bass, shimmering cymbals, surfaced in low rolling flourishes, barely fixing a rhythm, which was left to the contrabass—Larent's, presumably. He bowed a stream of half notes, then dotted half notes. It was the tether the ear sought in the driftlessness, grounding the harmony.

Gone, along with the counterpoint, was the ordinary diatonic scale itself. Or if not gone exactly, reformed. Except for the octave, the newly untempered notes had all been nudged up or down, so what remained was almost a diatonic scale, but not, a shadow.

The corresponding chords were shadows too, seeming just off target to the ear, precisely displaced, which retarded their uptake. The result was a music apprehended retrospectively, the chords' well-formedness established, their musicality unlocked, only after they'd given way to others that raised puzzles of the same order. The ear had no rest, and the struggle wasn't his alone. The faces along the corridor leading to the cube showed a blankness—furrows and squints self-consciously held in check—or else, imperfectly masking this, a prehensile quarter-smile attesting only to a knowledge unpossessed.

Many registers above, a lofted figure, aptly skewed, glided above the harmony before drifting down to mingle with its pitches. Quickly it returned to those first heights and fell again, a dissolving line that varied with each descent, adjusting to the drones of the new key.

Stagg cleared a second bowl of the mix. The powdered cheeses disagreed with the peat rot of the whiskey. He could feel a heat behind his eyes, the first trembles of his eyelids. The best of his night was already past. The sickness had caught him. He'd be both drunk and hungover the rest of the night, and the bowl would have played its part.

The music thinned and the joints of the piece emerged. The chords clarified around their central intervals, the fifths and thirds and sixths. There was a sonorousness to them, foreign, ineffable. The music had a dual aspect, he thought, like a Necker cube. Heard one way, it was alien beyond exotic, a deformation. Heard another, there was a sort of primordial solidity to it, an exactitude that made the tempered diatonic scale seem not a rival but only a coarsened derivative. The more Stagg's ears probed these pure intervals, the more this second aspect fixed itself. The sense of skew fell away; the factitious and the real switched places.

The drums petered out with the guitar, leaving the keyboard and bass to negotiate a few more chords, then a few fifths, then a few unisons, on their way to B♭, the tonic, a traditional resolution to a maundering piece.

A crescendo of claps was the last of the percussion, though it lacked the tentativeness that might have saved it from vulgarity. The unconstructed response, he thought, for anyone outside the vanguard of composition, was a ruffled silence. And the too-large eyewear, the too-small clothing all around him, did nothing to convince him the audience was any better placed than he was to grasp the night's singularity, seeing how far this was removed from the references they could plausibly have. MBV, maybe, or Earth.

He rose. He'd sweated through his socks and his feet felt bloated and wet in his sneakers. His head buzzed, not from trains or guitars now, but the day's drinking. He jostled his way through oncoming traffic to the back, the overlit blue room. A pink blanket with looping knits, along with a small armchair pillow, poked out of the sound hole of the bass drum, which someone was taking the toms off of. Two patinated crashes and a ride lay off to the side, halfway settled into brown vinyl sheaths.

Larent was at the edge of the stage, his face turned down toward his feet. And though there was nothing to talk over, or shouldn't have been, not as far as Stagg was concerned, Renna had her mouth to his ear.

"Carl."

His dark hair shining with water or sweat, and a joint hanging from his lips, Ravan approached him, looking in all other respects an overgrown English public schoolboy.

Larent approached and his face appeared over Ravan's shoulder. Renna came past them both and wrapped herself around Stagg.

"We played pool once," Ravan said, preempting the question on at least a couple of their minds: how did he know Stagg? Renna craned her neck back toward Ravan but soon dropped his gaze for Stagg's. "You won by three balls, yeah?" He extended the joint to Stagg, who took it without hesitation and pulled on it with his head bowed. "Took the table off me," Ravan said, "then lost it straight away to a Russian. This must have been, what, six weeks back? The place has shut since, did you know that, Carl? Renovations."

"Rundown place," Stagg said, exhaling.

"Who'd you go with?" Renna asked him.

"And how would you know these two?" Stagg said to Ravan, ignoring her.

"I was going to tell you," Renna said. "This is their first gig together, with their new guitarist. Ravan. I thought you might like to see it."

"Li and I—have you met him? He's the one taking the drums down—Li and I saw him playing this unfretted guitar in a gallery," Larent said. "It looks like it would be a nightmare to play, and it is, it turns out. He pulled the frets out with pliers and just sanded the wood down."

"Filled the cracks with wood putty, actually," Ravan said.

"Really unbelievable things came out of that guitar, I remember," Larent said. "There isn't anyone I know of, Li either, working that way. We played some of his stuff tonight. Sorry you weren't here for it," he said to Stagg.

"No, he heard it—from the bar," she said with a trace of contempt, or pity, Stagg thought.

"Oh. Good. We were more of a rhythm section tonight anyway, backing him up. We can go a lot further," Larent said.

"My head is still buzzing," Stagg said.

"Mine too," Larent said.

"She says you're a writer, Carl," Ravan said. "I did think I caught a whiff of that. You had to do something besides."

"Just some lectures," Stagg said.

"Besides what?" Larent said.

"Well, we're both rubbish at pool," Ravan said. "You don't disagree, do you?" Stagg hit the joint again. "Not stories, then?"

Stagg shook his head while holding in the smoke. "Histories," he said through a cloud.

"Colonial ones. Is that right?" Ravan said, looking to Renna.

"Imperial ones. South Asia, in the seventeenth century," Stagg said.

"South Asia," Ravan said with a smile Stagg thought might possibly be vicious, though the marijuana might have already started to encourage paranoia in him, as it sometimes did. "And your family, I understand, in the middle of it all. A serious man, you are. And there's a fellowship, she tells me?" He took the smoldering joint back from Stagg.

"No," Stagg said. "No idea. We'll see I guess."

"Oh, how can you not win it," Renna said.

He let go of her hands. Larent and Ravan collected their instruments and the four of them headed for the exit together.

■ ■ ■

They sat on the black canvas couch in Larent's living room, all but Li, who'd gone on to a party with the opening act. While the three of them passed another joint, Larent played bass in his bedroom with the door cracked open. He never smoked marijuana or anything else, and he drank only wine, as now. Renna had once mentioned his habit of getting drunk after gigs and playing like this, away from the rest. He'd been doing it since prep school. Bach's Cello Suite No. 5—he couldn't resist the clichés when drunk either, it seemed—wafted out of the bedroom, transposed to the bass.

"So this is what *you* do," Stagg said, gesturing at the air, the music that filled it. "Besides."

"Haven't seen a penny," Ravan said. "Think we will, Edward?" he said above the bass notes.

Larent stopped the bow mid-passage. "It was full tonight," he called out from the bedroom.

"But think of how small the place was," Ravan said. "And I suspect the opening act was actually headlining. How did you manage that?"

Larent released the bow and said something. A single word. Perhaps "charity."

"Yes, pity. Anyway, no, this won't do for money," Ravan said to Stagg, lowering his voice. "Not yet. I don't know how he gets by."

"His father," Renna said. She was curled up on the couch with her head in Stagg's lap.

"I've just got a fellowship of sorts myself, actually," Ravan said.

"A writer too, I guess," Stagg said.

"Nothing so noble. Meteorology."

"Channel four," Renna whispered before pulling on the joint. These sorts of comments, two in a row now, innocently undermining, they made him feel close to her. He raked her dirty blond hair with his fingertips and smiled as she let the smoke rise from her mouth.

"Oh I don't think they'd have me for a weatherman," Ravan said as he took the joint from her. "I'm taking up a provisional spot at NOAA, starting next week. Out of Princeton. Atmospheric research. With some fieldwork, from time to time, in Vegas, if you can believe it. Like you, Carl, I've got a doctorate. Not in philosophy, though. Something less sexy, that's the difference."

"Physics?" Stagg asked.

"Of aerosols."

"Cloud physics."

Ravan laid the joint on the oxidized copper table, green like the statue in the port.

"You know much about it?" he asked.

"No. Not really. But it doesn't sound so dull."

"It's sort of the family business. I don't much care for it anymore, but it is how I got on to what does interest me. The physics of sound, psychoacoustics, alternative tunings... Tell me, though, did you like what you heard tonight? Or not 'like'— what did you *make* of it?" Ravan picked up the joint by its waist and passed it to Stagg, who pinched it between index and middle fingers like a cigarette.

By this point he had nothing intelligent to say.

"Too drunk to have an opinion," Renna said. She pushed herself upright, using Stagg's thigh for leverage, and followed the music to its source in the bedroom.

"Too drunk?" Ravan said. "Too stoned, she means. She might be herself."

"I don't know," Stagg said.

"I think it quite complements drunkenness, actually. Our music. Induces something like it, if one isn't already. At least until you recalibrate. It's been extraordinary finding someone just as interested in these microtonal things as I am. Now, if only Edward and I could make a living this way. He might be right. Perhaps there's hope. But for now it's back to the physics labs, really just as a glorified research assistant."

He continued in a slightly quieter voice. "At least I'll be finished with this intelligence nonsense. We're both not long for that line of work, it looks like. Your fellowship is decided soon? Weeks? Months? She must be right, Carl. You've got to succeed. You just can't walk the streets like this anymore." His eyes mocked softly. "Neither of us. Though there is something to it. A ne'er-do-well appeal. That's it."

"Your family is here," Stagg asked, "or in England?"

"My accent you mean?"

"Your phrasing really. Your words. But the accent too."

"It is mangled, isn't it. No way around it now, though. Stuck with a mongrel tongue. My mother and father are back in Delhi, actually, after too many years abroad, first in Palo Alto, when I was very young, and then in London, at King's College, for many years. I grew up there, really, until university—college—when my father went back to his research at Stanford. I went with him, and then to Berkeley for the doctorate. My brother, Menar, stayed on in England, but he studied the same, at Oriel, in Oxford. He's with my father in India now, working alongside him. Researching. Testing."

"And you're here," Stagg said.

"Well, he's the better physicist, of the two of us. Better vision, bigger ideas. No one says that exactly but it's true. Is that why I got out?" He asked the question to himself and laughed dismissively.

As the roach consumed itself in the ashtray Ravan took out a tiny bud from the sandwich bag on the table. It was shaded olive and swathed in blue-white filaments. He tore it apart into stiff crinkled threads and set it on a rolling paper. He took a pouch from his pocket and sprinkled dark, sticky tobacco onto it and started to make a joint of it.

Stagg slid the lighter on his edge of the table across to Ravan and stole a look into the bedroom. The door was leaning against the inner wall and though it was misted with water, he could see out of the far window: the neon sign of a Mexican restaurant, El Calque, frosted pink.

The bowing of the bass had stopped for a while. It had been replaced by a steady mumbling between Renna and Larent. Stagg had strained to pick it up, any of it, and he might have if it weren't for Ravan prattling on the entire time. Marijuana always had the opposite effect on Stagg. For him, that was the point. Apparently not for Ravan.

Renna finally emerged, heavy-lidded and happy, though the reason for her happiness, the soft smile on her face, he had no way of grasping, except that it came out of a conversation with Larent. She climbed onto the couch and deposited her head in Stagg's lap, this time with her knees tucked up close to her chest and her arms wrapped around them. He tugged on her ear and she frowned playfully. He held her neck gently, four fingers against her pulsing throat. She turned up toward him with her eyes closed and her lips puckered. He laid his finger on them lengthwise and she took it between her teeth like a bone.

Ravan watched the exchange as twists of smoke leaked from his mouth and shot up his nostrils, returning by the same channels in thinner, more uniform streams. He picked up with the chatter as if there'd been no interval, and on his third joint of the night, perhaps for him there hadn't been.

"I don't actually think so," he said, "that he's the better physicist. Not necessarily. It might just be he looks harder, or that the world, the qualities of clouds, tugs on his eyes a bit more sharply. It really is his life, physics. But not mine. I think our father would have liked it, actually, if I'd turned out to have been the more committed one. But he knew I was leaning away quite early on.

"I studied music composition too, you see, along with the obligatory physics, which came very easily to me, because of the mathematics at its core. And I took as a child more avidly than he could have guessed to the sarod, of which my uncle was a master. He lived with us for a time, and he would find me sometimes in his room, tunelessly sounding notes, just kneeling over the thing, plucking randomly. I was very young then, and it was enthralling, this source of sound where any note at all could be found. The fretless guitar I've got now is modeled on it, really. Edward and I, we come at this matter of pure tunings, intonation, from such different angles. I think it's auspicious.

"So, yes, I think my father knew Menar Jr.—they've got the same name—would end up the proper colleague, not me. But his firstborn has always been a bit aloof, occasionally surly, and now to top it off he's gone and married a Muslim." He seemed to wink as he said this, or it may have been smoke in his eye. He passed the joint to Stagg.

"So they're not so close," Stagg said.

"Oh, they get on well enough, but my father and I, we get on more easily—or did, before it became clear my intentions were musical. I seem to be a better detector of his humor, which can be very sly, subtle. That seemed to count for a lot; he's not generally thought of as a funny man.

"I am, or was, probably more alive to his sense of purpose—even if I didn't quite share it—of wanting to turn the ground of our origins, our ancestors, from this flaking, sunburnt dirt that produced only hunger in any abundance, to something less violently resistant to growth. Whereas Menar Jr. always seemed to be in thrall to the physics of the project more than its potential to change things, to intervene in anything... human. At least that's how he was. I don't know why exactly, but his interest in applications, fieldwork, has picked up lately—and just as mine's been drowned out by the music.

"Still, physics has been important to me. I'm only a few years removed from it, really, and even then, I've been checking in throughout. Menar's worked straight through, of course, right alongside my father. The work is captivating in its way. Now I suppose, with the new job, I'll just have to summon a bit more of that interest. If I can't get the music right with Edward, I may end up rejoining them more permanently anyway. I don't know what I think of that."

"But what they're doing in India, you'll be doing in Princeton, basically?" Stagg asked. "Or is that not right?"

Renna's breath turned heavy and sleep-indicative. She had a habit of dozing in public, but without the narcoleptic's excuse. Depending on the occasion, Stagg found it vexing or charming. Tonight, though, it changed nothing. She had smoked, so it wasn't as ridiculous as it usually was.

"No, something similar. What we all do. Weather mod—cloud seeding lately. Only got the job, I think, because of my father. He's become something of a celebrity in applied atmospherics, for his work precipitating and dispersing clouds. Forty years he's been working on this. The original motivation was drought and famine relief, especially in Orissa, Bengal, and the inland plateaus, where we're from, ancestrally."

"Kalinga," Stagg said.

"Impressive! Yes, very good. In any case, my grandfather was a director of Project Gromet, back in the '60s, the first large-scale weather mod attempt in India. The White House backed it, actually, to relieve the Bihar drought. It didn't, of course.

"There've been a lot of cul-de-sacs along the way. Gromet was just the first. But they were all worth something. And the field trials I was a part of, they always brought me some satisfaction, whatever the outcome. My brother was always more pencil-and-paper, and more purely about results, success. I think my wider interest pleased my father, who could also take a certain delight in the flowering of a doomed experiment. I was with him through a lot of them, sometimes just in the role of spectator, to be fair. Every couple of years we would go back to India, the Ghats, from London or Palo Alto, to try something new, something big, like bringing in a monsoon out of season, say, luring it into the inland plateaus it normally avoided.

"My father understands the history of weather modification profoundly. He'd spend weeks in the archives alone, searching for the germs of ideas in those errant experiments, the truth in failure. Really it's not much different from what we're trying to do with music, Edward and Li and I.

"Anyway, you could say, in his own work, he's re-created the evolution of the field, experiment by experiment, all the salient ones. Most of the men who came up with those experiments have been dismissed as charlatans, and mostly they were, or just second-rate scientists. But even they, or especially they, through their recklessness, could strike on unconventional approaches, ones that might yield results if you applied them with a certain rigor they lacked, or if you just shifted them away from some misguided theoretical axis.

"It was about disentanglement. The experiments, any experiment, really, in physics, in music, brings a cluster of ideas together. Once you've separated them, you can try out other combinations, often with ideas gathered from entirely different experiments. And the whole thing is guided not by rules but by steeped intuition. The quality of my father's creative intuition is something everyone's aware of, he has that kind of nose for ideas, applications."

Ravan rubbed his jaw. He took the joint back from Stagg and pulled the last smoke from it before stubbing it out in the ashtray. He exhaled and sighed at the same time. "Well."

Stagg's sense of what Ravan said was vague in a way that pleased him. That he was under no obligation to grasp more than half of it, that he didn't need to pose smart questions—he'd smoked and couldn't reasonably be expected to, however interested, however bright he was or wasn't—made him want to hear more, to revel fecklessly in Ravan's words, which had poetry in them. To Stagg it was a performance, and maybe to Ravan as well, one he liked to give when he was stoned, for all he knew. The drug seemed to propel Ravan to a greater eloquence. He seemed to be enjoying it all, and set to Larent's playing, which had resumed, it formed something like a libretto. Stagg wanted a second act. "The experiments," he said. "What were they like?"

"Oh, you must have had enough by now," Ravan said. "I've already put her to sleep."

"She's not a doctor, of anything, though," Stagg said. He looked down at her and was pleased to find her asleep now. It had wiped the smile off her face that he hadn't put there.

"Funny. But your own work must make this all seem very dull. Tell me."

"It's pencil-and-paper stuff," Stagg said with a wave. "Tell me what you tried, out in the world."

Ravan shrugged.

"Really."

"Well, right… what did we try?" Ravan began. "I suppose at the very start there were the concussive strikes on moist air fronts. We were following in the footsteps of some long-dead scientists. Dyrenforth was one, and then a man named Ruggles, related, in fact, to a prominent American novelist. Do you know which?"

Stagg was finished talking.

"Pynchon, it turns out. Anyway, the idea," Ravan continued, "was that wet air—water vapor—might be made to precipitate without any clouds, that condensation could be forced by compression. We would just squeeze water out of the air, basically.

"I can remember the barometric checks, the waiting for needles to rise, the chain of cannons set against an invisible front. My father would give the order, as if to a firing squad, and the clearest of skies would be filled with flames. Each of the rounds had a charge. There were two reports, the firing and the explosion. Even through earplugs, the big ones like headphones, and even full well knowing the cannons were about to fire, they surprised you with their force. Not so much your ears, but your body. All that fire, twenty points of growth, twenty clouds taking shape—but of smoke not water droplets, so they lost their form and vanished. No rain, of course. The readings from our sensors showed no real change. Water was scattered through that air in about the same way as before, though if I remember, there was some slight rippling. Possibly.

"The team around my father thought much of this was just absurd. But then, my father himself knew it was absurd. Still, an American government précis reports this same experiment, conducted by Dyrenforth, as intermittently successful. Many of the early experiments, actually, were carried out under government auspices. The likelihood of out and out charlatanry, then, was not very large. There must have been *something* in them, even if the original experimenters never succeeded in isolating that something. They might have tripped atmospheric conditions by accident, simply through enough blind groping.

"The cannonading of the skies, though, I don't believe my father did any better on that one. I must have been ten at the time. But I think he thought, down the line, he might extract something from it, fuse it with other techniques, and see if the composite yielded a result. So he filed all the barometric data away.

"A couple of years later he tried an incendiary tack, lofting these flares, dozens of them, with high-velocity ground launchers. It was a sight. They phosphoresced, turning day brighter than day, beading the sky with mercury. I have tried, and it's just not possible to imagine anything brighter, Carl. It stung our eyes. For days I was plagued by afterimages. But it was difficult to look away.

"The point, of course, wasn't this visual revelation, a quicksilver sky. It was about shooting searing heat into pockets of cold, moist air, again with the hope of forcing condensation and precipitating them. But nothing. One more stage in the history of weather mod we could tick off.

"So, we moved on to cloud building. We'd send up columns of smoke, either from charcoal or trees or simply ignited oil. This smoke with a greasy sheen would go up, glossy black, through the cold fronts. I can't say these definitively failed, like the cannonading and flaring—these fires that raged by design, though resembling in every way some primordial annihilation.

"There were several cases where rain followed our burns. Dark brown clouds that kept their shape—proper clouds, not just collocated smoke—ones that stoked condensation and carried water. But sometimes no precipitation would follow. Replication was the problem. There must have been atmospheric differences we didn't, or couldn't, measure for.

"Again, my father was greedy for the data. How had they changed the constitution of the air? Had the burns encouraged the coalescence of microdroplets? Or had they only managed to shunt more carbon into the atmosphere—"

"And destabilize things further."

"Exactly, yes. Had we only done more damage to the climate

was the question. So he would sift the data for tiny changes, rebalancings, and compare them with the changes induced by other experiments. Menar and I helped with this, once we had the training to."

Stagg thought Ravan might be done at this point, but no, the torrent kept coming as the science (and his past) came surging back to him.

"Then came the dispersal techniques," he said. "How to kill a cloud. That was just as important. Everywhere in India, either you got too much or too little water. That's still true.

"We turned to various compounds: calcium chloride, silica gel, quicklime, a range of alkalis. We tried overseeding. The idea was to make microdroplets of water coalesce around so many condensation nuclei that any further condensation, into the bigger droplets that fall as rain, became impossible. It would all just hang as a mist.

"We tried electrical fields, using a network of magnets, either attached to planes flying in formation through cloudbanks or set up along the ground, looking like a field of telecom towers or a power grid. There were also the brute force techniques, World War II stuff. Applying continuous heat to clouds, vaporizing them, like the Brits did with FIDO. During the war, they'd run open burners the length of the runways so they could land in the thick, grounded stratus common to England. It kept their fleet airborne against the Germans. But the approach isn't practical with aerosols higher up in the atmosphere. And anyway, the amount of fuel you'd need to burn out a storm is preposterously large.

"That was simple dispersal. But we also wanted to precipitate these same clouds. Again we started with the cannonading, sending warheads on rockets basically. There's this idea that's been around a long time, of a trigger event, that in unstable conditions the eyes of monsoons, for instance, might set off an 'atmospheric collapse.' But if there are such triggers, we never found them. The storms were indifferent to our strikes.

"So it came down to nucleation: seeding flares shot from the ground or released from planes, around which, we hoped, droplets, the stuff of clouds, would coalesce and fall as rain. Again there were all sorts of agents to consider. Salt, charcoal, sulfuric acid, graphite, volcanic dust even—torrential rains often follow eruptions—and the simplest of all, water itself. A few droplets, properly placed, could precipitate whole cloudbanks. There were the more exotic nucleators too. Things like lead iodide, zinc oxide, even dry ice. Silver iodide, though, has a structure that can fool microdroplets into crystallizing into ice. It's shaped like a hexagon. So it was the most promising."

Though he kept speaking, at some point a while back now, Ravan had stopped communicating in the strict sense. No one could follow the niceties of what he said anymore, even if he were dead sober. Stagg, of course, wasn't even trying to.

"I remember our first trials with it," Ravan continued. "The flare launchers my father commissioned for this work were quite effective, burning the silver iodide, making a smoke of metal. In Palo Alto one winter, we watched a wave of these flares launched into puffy stratocumulus, a brilliant white, with not much vertical extension.

"We watched it go from the purest of whites through a cycle of grays: silver, ash, slate, and finally, gunmetal. With each change of shade the cloud seemed to congeal further, those supercooled droplets crystallizing around the ice-like nuclei. This was coastal California, where snow is basically unheard of. The crystals liquefied on descent. And it drizzled. Then it rained.

"The trick was the presence of the supercooled droplets, enough to get the process started. Lots of clouds have them, even when conditions aren't generally frigid on the ground. The falling crystals cool the regular microdroplets, reduce them to the freezing point and below, supercooling them, which stokes the process further, and primes them to condense around the silver iodide. That was our understanding, anyway, though again, consistency of results. Could it have all been chance? I don't think so." Ravan paused and squinted toward the music. "And now…"

"Where have they taken things?" Stagg encouraged him.

"Well, in the time I've been less than dedicated, they've moved beyond silver iodide. It's why their results are more or less provable at this point. It's still hardly perfect, but my father can get clouds to do what he wants sixty or seventy percent of the time.

"Now the agent of choice is a stable isotope of antimony, but subjected to a series of treatments: alloying, cooling, then returning it to its metallic form. Really it comes down to allotropic variation in the substance…

"In any case, the process is known comprehensively only to him and my brother and a few others in the Indian labs. I've kept up a bit, so I know some too. The essential thing is that antimony has a property of water. It expands as it freezes, or it does with the right impurities. And this seems to stimulate further condensation. It also seems to work at even higher temperatures. No need for supercooled droplets. Or perhaps it's just converting a very small amount of those in a cloud into a large amount, through a chain reaction. A trigger event after all, maybe.

"Whatever it is, warmer stratus and cumulus can be precipitated now, which expands the range of application by miles. And very little of the agent is required, which is good, because it is not so far from arsenic in structure.

"The technology is sought now pretty much everywhere in the developed world. The Indian government has some claim to it, though, since the work was done at the National Institute. But basically, the Americans want it, and the lab in Princeton is comping me a job in the hopes of getting it, I assume. Hoping my father will deliver it through me, or that he will sign on part-time.

"So I think I'll be doing as I please to some extent. Hurricane dispersal is the focus. There may be more as well. I'll get to go out to Vegas, where the experimental facilities are. I don't know exactly what they're working on over there, in the desert. No hurricanes, obviously. Or in Idaho either, the other facility. But it might be a few months till I stop the watch-work. It *is* interesting in a way, though, isn't it, Carl? Surveillance. There's an odd kind of gentility to it, given the history of intelligence. You've got a few more months too, it looks like."

"Maybe more," Stagg said.

"Well I would love to hear these lectures. Where? Which university? God knows I could stand to know more about India. And the mother country. Britain. They're open to the public?"

"They are. I'm not sure about the format yet, or the timing. They're for the Wintry."

"Ah." Ravan looked at Renna with red eyes. The rise and fall of her chest was even slower now, her sleep deeper.

Ravan leaned in slightly. "You know the museum, the annex across the bridge, you know how those gargoyles fell, yeah?"

Stagg shook his head and held Renna's shoulder. "Tell me." He settled in for the encore.

"They were just lying on the steps, whole, patina intact, when the police got there. During a philanthropic event—about urban education, alternative teaching, the need for a cash infusion—hosted by none other than the Wintry, on Friday. It was elaborate, the event. The attack too. Or maybe it wasn't quite an attack. Not on them in particular.

"A lot of money piled into the lobby that night, maestros of arcane instruments. And their families, beautifully made up. In the first room, just beyond where the drinks were served, there were Clementes everywhere: *Fire*, *Atlas*, *Map of What is Effortless*—all looking in on them, these big-faced, color-bleeding men, and the African animals like illustrations. Yes, a painter of 'ecstatic consciousness.'

"Right. A pop, a cascade of figures—angels with the gargoyles—zipping past the massive windows, top to bottom, knocking on the broad, shallow steps below. Strange to think most of them survived. Then the slow rattle down the steps to the bottom. Not much damage done in the end.

"The windows went next, rattling, then cracking, just the tops. Daggers of glass fell—harmlessly, I should say, as the crowd was tucked away from the entrance by this point. That left behind another set of daggers, stabbing upward, and sideways as well, jags of lead glass still seated comfortably in the frame.

"Inside, the floor is dressed in canapés, bits of Ibérico, overturned sterling trays, bowl-less glass stems twirling on their bases in circles. Good wine's running, pooling in places. The debutantes, they're cowering. And rightly so. A third wave of charges releases the chimeras walking the very top of the museum's frontispiece, its lineaments.

"The explosions were all external. It kept the philanthropists pinned inside the museum, prone or crouched down among the hors d'oeuvres, the wine grabbing at their silks and wools. It seemed like a desecration, more than anything. That's all we seem to get."

Ravan bit his lip and frowned. "Talking of wine," he said. He got up and poured himself some from a bottle Renna had found too readily, Stagg thought, in the shelves beneath the bookcase. Larent must hide his wine there, for whatever reason. "You want some of this plonk, Edward? Yes, yes you do." He poured more wine into Renna's glass, still a quarter full, and took it with him to the threshold of Larent's room, pinching the stem.

Bach's suite continued without pause. Larent had been playing the entire time, so steadily the music had seemed to disappear. Now they were suddenly aware of it. The gigue had been reached, its articulation smoothed by drink, making the music elastic and droning in a way Bach never was.

Ravan came back to the table shrugging. Stagg waved off the

glass in his hand. "Maybe when she wakes," he said, setting the wine down in front of her on the table.

"You haven't heard about this, then?"

"Parts of it," Stagg lied.

"You have."

"Just what anyone knows. From the Internet."

"Oh." Ravan tilted the glass, anchoring it on his lower lip. "And of course the two squares, the fountains, both exploded."

"And rebuilt."

"Well, not quite, not fully." He leaned over again. "You know Celano has resurfaced, but across the water, in Henning."

"I did know that," he lied again.

"No more girls have turned up."

"Right."

"The museum could well be his and Jenko's work. I'm quite sure the Wintry's discussions lately—about the resistance to popular orders, about linking voting, political clout, to knowledge or wisdom or whatever you want to call it exactly—this *can't* suit Jenko's constituency of workers. More than that, we both saw how expertly their own meeting space, the pool hall, I mean, was destroyed not a week ago. If anyone had both the inclination and the resources to do it, well, you'd have to think about the Wintry. Or the government, of course. But we can't really be destroying *everything*, can we? And Jenko is certainly no friend of the Wintry, as far as I understand the matter.

"But then maybe I don't. I was sent in to the museum just to take stock. I suppose we're not really the brains of this operation, just the registers, the scribes. I've filed it with my boss, and yours, Penerin. The main subject I interviewed is someone you must know, probably quite well. That's why I mention all of this."

"Oh?"

"Harry."

"Harry?"

"The director. Harry Kames. You did say your talks are at the Wintry, right?"

"Ah, Harold. Sorry, that's the way I know him."

"So you do know him."

"Of course. It makes perfect sense he was there, though the thought didn't cross my mind till now. But I don't know him well."

"I interviewed a few others, and they corroborated various details he offered. But really he seemed to have taken in the most, felt the happenings most acutely. Just the sweep of his picture. You might think he'd be more shaken for it, and he was definitely shaken, but he was in no worse shape than the others."

"Better shape, I'd guess. He's really not society. He is *of* them, but he's *not* them, not at this point, not for a long time. I can't see him being as surprised as the donors, the supporters, by the things you describe, on some level. Or as angry even."

"That must be right," Ravan said. "That's the way it seemed."

"While they—well, not all of them, I think the real robber barons are probably not that surprised either. But they must be angrier. Their sons and daughters, their wives, I can't say what they must be. Probably they don't know as much."

"Yes, well, the breeding, the markers, they were there in Kames. But he didn't seem to share the vanity. That particular sort of vanity, I mean. He seemed plenty vain. That Brahmin drawl. But not in the way that makes shock possible, the kind that comes just before indignation. He was, well, something different, when I met with him. Quite calm. As if that night was gone for him, already. Even the present. There was only the future."

Suite No. 5 closed, officially, but Larent hung a fermata on the last note and seemed reluctant to let it go. "Well done. Well done, Edward. Now come and have a drink." From the bedroom came the sound of glass rattling against glass, then the extended gurgle of a heavy pour. The bow slapped against the floorboards. Larent didn't come out, and he said nothing. "We can wake Renna up if you like," Ravan called out to him. His eyes shined with faint malice as he nodded at Stagg and drank the rest of his wine.

Stagg drew his fingers together at the base of Renna's neck, pushing the blood from the surface, leaving blanched tracks on the pale downy-laden skin that filled in a redder shade of white. He angled his fingers to bring his nails into play and caught a tiny fold of skin between them as they met at the base. She revived.

20

JEN DREW BREATH CHILLED BY LAST NIGHT'S SPIR-
its. That morning, from the reaches of her mouth, at the throat,
along the gums, and most of all in the vague tissues beneath the
tongue, neutral grain returned to her as a vapor. It seeped from
the skin inside her face. Brushing didn't help. Ten minutes later
the flavorless, alcoholic cool cut through the lesser cool of pep-
permint paste.

Reed had moved out of her place a few weeks ago, and she'd
spent the time since regressing. For almost three days now she'd
lived on Fanta and Smirnoff—a sort of ersatz screwdriver—
along with a few protein bars.

Renewal, though, was promise of the afternoon. It's why
she'd made the effort today, through a crippling hangover, to
come to this tiny airless studio across the river from Halsley, for
her first day in a new, or newish, line of work.

She hadn't lied to Stagg about the kind of thing she'd be
doing. It *would* free her from the fears of the city's hookers. That
blackjack, really. He should be happy with that, and she'd tell
him so the next time he called.

She knew violence couldn't be dodged, of course. In some
sense, it wasn't even to be dodged. Life was sculpted out of it,

the Romans had taught her that much. Homer too, all the pillage and piles of bones burning for the gods. The only question really was which flavor you'd have.

What she'd heard is that this one went down easy. Other escorts she knew were starting to make the same shift. The money wasn't usually quite as good or quick, and for the first time, it was actually going to be taxable. But everything was controlled. No more surprises. You knew exactly what was going to happen to you, even if it wasn't any prettier. The material did end up online, it was public, but how long could she keep worrying about that? What wasn't online? Even some of her hooking had probably been recorded discreetly and posted by some of her johns. It's just what people did. In any case, without her brother around, she needed a job, the kind she could fit around benders like the one she was coming off of now. There were only so many like that, and none were attractive exactly.

She rubbed her toe along the time-darkened grout of the kitchen floor. The tiles it framed iridesced from a solvent's residue. Fingerprints plastered the black refrigerator, and its noisy compressor ran almost continuously, even with the dial rolled to five, its warmest setting. The racks of the dishwasher, sea green cages, stretched out from the machine, holding acrylic plates and cups that steamed. Smaller cages held steak knives with sodden wood handles and forks with tines that failed to form a plane.

Sitting conspicuously on the counter, next to the burners and the smoke-stained fan, was the blender—pastel yellow, with imperial measures embossed on the dingy plastic of its jar.

Jen leaned a hip against the counter and pulled the tank top away from her stomach, breaking the seal of sweat. She popped watery blueberries more gray than blue from a perforated plastic box while the two men, mid-thirties and unshaven, misted the fridge with cleaner. They used wads of toilet paper to wipe it down and the streaks iridesced like the tiles till they burned off under the hot floods overlighting the kitchen.

They were going to need to quiet the fridge before they started. They squatted on either side of it and nudged it forward before angling it away to one side. The skinnier one, his forearms dressed in paisley tattoos, worked his way into this new space behind the machine. He reached down and switched off the compressor at the base of the fridge as his chin bit into the cold metal.

The other man, shorter and less useful, started putting the forks and knives in the dishwasher away, into a kitchen drawer. The tattooed one came out of the crevice and pushed the fridge back in by himself, closing the space. When he saw what the other man was doing, he slammed the drawer shut. The other man quickly shut the dishwasher. They wiped it down with the dirty wads used on the fridge. It looked neither cleaner nor dirtier for it.

Jen put the box of blueberries back in the fridge and took a pair of muscle relaxants from her pocket, the last of the Soma prescription. How useful they'd been, how necessary, after the beating. Today, though, nearly healed, she might find them more necessary still, if necessity came in degrees.

■ ■ ■

"I could really use a pick me up," Lisa said as she re-entered the kitchen in flannel pajamas strewn with elephants and monkeys. She opened the fridge wide. "Blueberries!" she said. "I love blueberries." She pulled out the plastic box she'd just been eating from and set it on the counter. "What else do we have? Oh a papaya. A nice one." The fruit, somewhere between red and yellow, rolled along the counter until the box of blueberries checked it. "Then a banana," she said, pulling one off the bunch in the rattan fruit-basket on the opposite counter. "And kiwis too. This all looks so good." She turned back to the open fridge and found a green carton of two percent: "Got to have milk."

Her brow furrowed without nuance. "You know what else we need, though." She swung the freezer door open. "Ice!" Her hands emerged clutching cubes she'd dug out from the icemaker. Before she could deposit them in the salad bowl, several fell to the ground with a crack. The handfuls were greedy.

"What a long night! Cramming is so exhausting. And I've got to be fresh for the test." She took a potato peeler to the kiwis, scuffing them with artless strokes and divesting the fruit. She skinned the overripe papaya and drew the short blade against the sopping fruit, hewing chunks from the slab, gathering them in one hand, and dropping them into the jar of the blender. By the same process she transformed the naked kiwis.

"Now for the banana." After freeing it from the peel she broke it into pieces with her hands and tossed them into the jar one by one. "And what about citrus? I thought I saw an orange in there," she said, referring to a large tangerine in the basket. After that, the blueberries went into the mix. "A little milk now." She tore away the green plastic strip from the milk cap, popped it off, and tipped a cup's worth into the mess of fruit. "And ice. Can't forget the ice." The ice went into the blender in the same way it had come out of the freezer, in fistfuls.

The machine was quieter than she'd expected. As soon as she turned it on, the ice sank from the top of the jar while the blade made its way through the mix. The mash jittered at the base, splashing against the plastic higher up in ribbons, the colors marbling, passing through the rich purples of pure blueberry pulp, the pinks of papaya cut with milk, the cream tones and texture of banana melting, before going pastel orange as the tangerine fused with it. In the midst of the purple of the blueberries, though, orange, green, and even red proved recessive. Everything settled into a smoothness and simplicity when there was nothing left to resist the blade.

The cycle stopped. Lisa pulsed it a few times as sweat came down her temples. Her body goose-bumped everywhere, though, and she wished for layers over her pajamas. She poured the blend into a tall, narrow glass with shaky hands and sipped more than she was supposed to from it. She was starving, literally. "So good." She went to take another unauthorized sip but stopped short and furrowed her brow again. "Hm... there's just one thing missing. And there's still time before school."

■ ■ ■

The chill came from without now. It rose through the rainbowing tiles into Lisa's neck, her bare shoulders. The glass was gone. Her breasts hung near her collarbones, which were still sore and swollen, and her legs and back rose up along the cabinet. She was inverted. The white key light, blocked in spots by her dangling feet that were vainly searching for a comfortable position, turned her pupils to points, barely visible against emerald irises. The light shone down on the hair in her crotch, producing, from her point of view, a fuzzy silhouette in the space between her legs.

She could feel the wood knobs bearing into her back. The inversion made her whole body hurt. It was just too soon to be in a position like this, after the beating she'd taken.

"Ready, Lisa?" The man with the tattoos pried her legs apart. She felt another chill now, a drip, a pooling slick. Just behind that she felt the pressure of plastic, then a collapse, then a pure presence. Her stomach tightened.

A click of the speculum and she felt the distance. Another click. Three more and a shiver shot up her back. The man fed the slick. Some of it fell straight down inside her, some clung to the walls, coating and cooling them. One more click and she grabbed his wrist.

"Okay?" he said.

He disappeared without waiting for an answer. A few seconds later, she saw the backlit glass of purple puree held up between her legs. Sweat rolled up her belly and breasts to her chin, which was pressed against her chest. It crossed her cheeks into her eyes, forcing them closed and drawing tears that fell into her hair.

"Here you go, honey."

"Oh, I can't wait," she said sweetly, though her eyes were stinging.

She felt another chill, much cooler, denser, than the slick. It built. It made her stomach cramp and her legs twitch. He grabbed them, held her stomach, and kept pouring.

"It's thirstier than you," he said.

Lisa thought of ice-cream headaches. From some point within her, near the pelvis, the cold climbed up her tailbone. "I think you're full," he said. There was a convulsion then, and as if something gave way, the coolness shifted in her, to a place near her center.

"There we go," he said. "Just needed a sec to swallow." He started to pour again. More contractions. He called these gulps. Finally the chill ran half the length of her torso. The space was gone.

The glass clinked on the counter. He pulled the speculum out without reducing its compass. She felt the stretch she'd forgotten about vanish. It spurred a new coolness, though, of her outsides. It flowed up her back and stomach. She squirmed and twisted, opened her eyes. Her belly was streaked in purple.

He caught her before she fell. "Whoops. Maybe that was a little too much. No, you're okay, you're okay," he said in singsong. He held her in place and wiped her down gently with a kitchen rag. His arms were strong and took away her fear.

He guided her body down off the cabinet and she lay on the cold tiles with her knees in front of her. She spread her fingers on the floor and hopped to her feet. She leaked smoothie. The man was gone and she stared into the glass eye of the camera that iridesced like everything else.

"Oh, that's cold," she said, rubbing her stomach. "Now just to finish it off." She began to jump in place, ungainly leaps and turns facing the camera, in profile, and then away from it too. Soon the jumps turned to spins and rocking hips and lithe glides and coy shakes. The sweat made her face shine.

Her muscles ached from a hangover accruing from a full week of drunkenness. Her hands trembled as they had before, from the blackjack. She was dizzy now too. The vapor of grain alcohol filled her mouth again, overriding the blueberry aftertaste. She dry heaved once but in a controlled way. No one noticed, she hoped. She was in no shape for this much movement, and there were pains in places she hadn't felt since the beating. It would have been easier, she thought, to lie there and get fucked. Maybe that's what she'd need to do the next time around. Probably these same two men would shoot it. There'd certainly be more cash in it.

"Okay," she sighed, losing a little of her brightness. She held her stomach and rubbed it in circles. She felt very strongly like shitting, just as she had after the morning's enema. "I think it's done!" she said, finding some vigor for the camera.

She put the glass on the floor. The lens dipped with her as she squatted and stared out of frame, above the camera, as if in contemplation of a weighty matter.

Before she could settle into position and bear down, the smoothie squirted from her, onto the outside of the glass and the floor, purpling the grout lines. The incontinence brought a twinge of embarrassment to her. She felt like a child with undeveloped faculties, or a geriatric with worn out ones. Quickly, though, she tamed the flow and shot it into the glass.

She turned down to look at the rising puree. There was an animal satisfaction to the expulsion. As the movement came to a close she bore down harder, forcing stringy yellow mucus into the drink. She was empty now, and this gave its own kind of satisfaction, to be voided, to have purified the vaporousness she felt herself to consist in, after sixty hours now of living on little more than spirits. She'd been asked not to eat before the shoot, for her own benefit, mainly. It would make the cleanse simpler. She'd forgotten the instructions, but other forces, her compulsions, drove her to much the same.

The glass was more than half-full. She reached between her legs and lifted it, but as she rose out of the squat she stumbled to one side and sloshed the glass. She found her balance and held the drink up near her eyes. "Look what I made," she said. She stirred it with a spoon from the drawer and began to drink.

It was less cool now—it had taken on some of the heat of her guts—but as if in compensation, the flavors had bloomed: the floral tones of the papaya, the tartness of the kiwi, the simple sweetness of the banana. There was a new sharpness to it as well, an acridity that complicated the drink, deepened it. It was more than sugars now. It was something that defied the appetites.

Texturally there was fresh interest. Amid the uniformity of the puree, the tiny points of evenly distributed fruit, she could feel the mucus slip around her tongue and mouth in long bands like egg whites. They clung to her throat as she swallowed, so that sending them down with the rest took more aggressive gulps.

She could taste the incompetence of the morning's enema. The saline never really ran clear. Twice she fell while squeezing the rubber balloon. The hangover had taken her patience with her balance.

But she was ravenous. And though bitterness remained at the heart of the drink, she found herself emptying the glass. The more she took in, the more repulsed she grew. Yet there was no stopping. Two warring instincts and hunger won.

The two men watched from behind the camera. Often a girl would balk after a sip or two, and they would have to cut the shot and threaten to pay half or nothing at all. Not that the girl didn't know what she was supposed to do when they started the shoot. Only the seasoned shameless, though, could be counted on to keep their nerve when the brew was served.

Lisa set the empty, slimed glass on the counter.

"Am I ready to ace this test!"

The men marveled. Few debutantes gave such committed performances. But then, in her famished state, it was hardly that. Aspirations, obligations, they were idle.

They cut the camera.

"You did great," the shorter one said. "Perfect, really. How was it?"

"I think it went okay," Jen said.

"No, the shake."

"Really?"

"You pounded it."

"It wasn't bad."

"Five hundred bucks and you didn't even have to look at a cock," said the tattooed one.

She burped. They all laughed. Jen could taste the salutary rot. This, finally, might keep the spirits at bay.

21

BONEYARD: I've been waiting for #4 a long while. No previews at Evil Angel yet. Ah!

ARCELOR: That's cuz Elegant not Evil produced it. Angel.

PTERODACTYL: No I've seen... amazing. She is so sweet and giggly.

BONEYARD: Dactyl send me a link in Private? Tx.

MATCHMAKER: 1st anal! Takes it like a champ. That's a big fucking cock.

BONEYARD: Dirty Debutantes was 1st anal, Match. Like a minute of it till she pulls him out. His cock isn't even that big. Didn't get more than the tip in. *Real* first time maybe?

ARCELOR: No no—camera angle / bad lighting. It's in her pussy. In missionary, right.

BONEYARD: Yeah that's it. It looks like it's in her ass though. But she does have one of those assholes that's really close to her pussy, so maybe not. But on top of that she reaches down like it hurts. Then he pulls out and it seems like after he puts it back in she's not in pain.

ARCELOR: First taste of porn cock—it hurt.

MATCHMAKER: Of course you know.

ARCELOR: Three months now Match and you still can't keep up. Boneyard, you can blow that shot up. There's no switch. She licks her hand and rubs her pussy. Just dry.

VIOLETSKYE: Hi guys just wanted to clarify this is my FIRST anal scene. I saved it for Elegant to get it right. It was scary but exciting too. So glad I finally did it. Hope you guys liked it most of all.

ARCELOR: Welcome Violet!

BONEYARD: VIOLET!!! So Debutantes had no anal—you can confirm?

VIOLETSKYE: I hear that all the time but no it really is lighting and the distance of the shot. Now you know! They should spend more. Maybe they would have got it.

ARCELOR: Bet the director likes the rumor though. Couldn't have hurt sales.

VIOLETSKYE: ;)

PTERODACTYL: The new scene looks so good. No condoms. Just waiting to see the whole thing.

BONEYARD: Congrats on your best-new-starlet nomination, Violet. And best three-way too!

MATCHMAKER: Yes congrats that is great news. Totally deserved.

VIOLETSKYE: Thank you Matchmaker. That scene was even scarier. And being nominated too!

ARCELOR: That nom, that was just your first three-way wasn't it?

PTERODACTYL: That's how good she gonna be.

VIOLETSKYE: On camera, yes! My first three-way ever was a private session. Not a fun one actually. Sketchy. Creepy. But this one went great. Jeremy H. is such a good director. Makes it easy on the girls.

APACHI5: Shooting any features now? Would love to see you in character again. And doing interracial! (We can dream…).

VIOLETSKYE: I'm not shooting any right now but there have been more offers since the nominations. They pay better but I don't think I'm really into the playacting thing. It's distracting enough with the lights and crew. The gonzo stuff, pure sex, is better for me, if only it paid. And no interracial I think. Sorry.

MATCHMAKER: You're so adaptable though. And you don't talk as much as the gonzo girls.

VIOLETSKYE: Deer in the headlights :) I can't do that on purpose though. It happens or it doesn't and it's happening less now. Too familiar. You've got to actually play the part once you can't just react and expect guys to get hard from the wide eyes.

MATCHMAKER: But you can be so natural in character. Your scene in *Ransoms* is amazing.

VIOLETSKYE: You mean I look scared and confused tied up on the bed. But I was! Not from being tied up but from being on a porn set fucking strangers in costume. So I just got lucky. Even that—I wouldn't be scared now. That's going away and then the roles just seem silly. I can't help smirking, even during. Some girls do that I know, make it sort of ironic, but the scenes aren't very hot then. Irony and sex don't mix.

PTERODACTYL: You and Sasha. Philosophers of sex...

VIOLETSKYE: The best ones don't let that show. They actually have some commitment or they never lose the wide eyes and keep turning the guys on that way, not with the character. Or the role just has fear or confusion built in like *Ransoms*.

VIOLETSKYE: Ha! Don't really know her but would like too. Another generation. She has that sexy jawline.

APACHI5: But you can do both can't you? No need to choose.

VIOLETSKYE: I can but now I just want to fuck without the gimmicks and get paid. That sort of honesty turns ME on. Otherwise I'll end up one of those bored Vivid girls. Unhot.

ARCELOR: I think it's so cool you have your own take.

MATCHMAKER: Your last few scenes have been getting wilder.

VIOLETSKYE: This new scene, it's cool. I'm happy with it. It's a feature so you think it's easier. But I tore my anus doing it. It was swollen for three days and shitting was a nightmare. I barely ate.

BONEYARD: That sucks! I'm so sorry Violet.

VIOLETSKYE: And then it turns out someone hadn't even had their PASS test cleared yet. So I'm sure I'm fine but I have to wait to be sure I don't have HIV now.

KIRKPATRICK: Occupational hazards ;)

VIOLETSKYE: That was a feature film. So what's the difference? The money. I don't think gonzo should be second-class. Everything interesting in features comes from gonzo. It's the lab.

APACHI5: I thought you got banned.

KIRKPATRICK: Ten days.

ARCELOR: Why do you waste your time here? No fucking life.

KIRKPATRICK: Same reason as you.

BONEYARD: Get back to yr bridge and suck Scottie off, Kirk.

VIOLETSKYE: Lonely like us ☺

KIRKPATRICK: Have the mods even verified that this is Violet

Skye? She shows up in this thread out of nowhere. And she doesn't talk like the deer on camera, does she.

VioletSkye: How should I talk?

Kirkpatrick: I met you a month ago, at the convention in LA, and you didn't sound anything like this. You were just a ruined child. A fool. You should be banned not me.

PteroDactyl: More bullshit from this guy.

Boneyard: Prob. should verify though, even if Kirk's just trolling.

CassandraMason: No I can tell, it's her. Some of us have been to college, guys. Sorry to lurk.

Kirkpatrick: Have you? Not community. A real one.

VioletSkye: Cassie!

CassandraMason: Congrats on the nominations. You are going to WIN, sexy. I will see you in Vegas at the awards.

VioletSkye: Thank you!!! Yes just two weeks left, see you then. Would love to work with you someday cutie. You have such a pretty pussy.

Boneyard: WE ALL WANT TO SEE THAT!

Arcelor: Kill the all-caps please.

CassandraMason: I want to eat yours V.

KIRKPATRICK: Bet Cassandra's a fake too.

VIOLETSKYE: Wish we could ask the same of you Kirk but you can't be a fake because you aren't anyone at all.

CASSANDRAMASON: HA!

KIRKPATRICK: Clever for a worthless whore.

MODERATOR 2: Cassandra you are already registered with us. Can you do the same Violet?

{User Kirkpatrick deactivated}

VIOLETSKYE: What a shame. Honest guy. This is why we do this.

VIOLETSKYE: Yes will do.

MODERATOR 2: So glad to have you! Don't worry about the trolls. We'll take care of them.

■ ■ ■

While Janice sat at the kitchen table, staring into him, Lewis, on the other side of it, could think only of the foundering of his latest chat-room impersonation. Whatever was wrong with Kirkpatrick, he'd managed to sniff Lewis out. It could take a hateful man with all the wrong intentions to see things as they were. Especially lately.

In truth, if you were observing neutrally, and not through the inflamed imagination of a fan, who was elated to be in any kind of touch, even virtual touch, with the object of his fantasies, it wasn't hard to see that the stories and theories Lewis put in Skye's mouth were incredible. There were too many barbs, however oblique, directed at the very people she was supposed to be courting. That was the point of these "adult" chatrooms, after all. Porn promotion. There were also the places where Lewis would break character to make overly intellectual points—that porn had a way of destabilizing the viewer's sense of self at least as much as the actors, say—or where he would reveal the banal brutalities of industry life in terms that were impossibly detached.

But the men in the chat rooms, in thrall to the idea of flirting with their dreams, were not in the frame of mind to notice the liberties he was taking with character. They took Lewis's indictments at face value, and were forced to see them as emanating from the most sympathetic of sources, under the circumstances: the actresses themselves. Their fantasies were terrorizing them.

Lewis didn't know Skye's civilian details, so there'd be no fooling the moderator. He clicked the page shut. Better to flee the site, he thought, than to let them prove that he wasn't her, only a simulation, an impostor. His ideas might survive then, even in the heavy shadow of Kirkpatrick's doubts, living a kind of twilight existence, subtly shaping their thinking.

He'd turned to the porn forums only after breaking off his physical interventions in the city. At this point, he felt, he could only be a beating or two away from arrest. Anyway, the last of the hookers, Lisa, her calm had exhausted something in him. He couldn't explain it to himself, but he knew he'd rather not look these girls in the face anymore, especially with the streets as clear as they were these days. The rewards no longer justified the risks. Isn't that how his father would have put it? In the end, there was nothing that wasn't an investment.

That didn't mean there wasn't more work to be done. Just not in Halsley. Scale was the question. He'd first grasped its importance, in the realm of politics, a decade ago, when he'd helped Kames and the Wintry expand into Providence. The group was fragile back then. Now they were a force.

How to answer the question of scale in his own case, given his own ethical imperatives? How different were they really, though? Lewis's sensibilities owed more to Kames than he'd like to admit. The two hadn't spoken in years, except through the odd email. Still, Lewis had listened to him lecture dozens of times. It must have left a mark.

Pornography, Lewis thought, might well be the bigger canvas he needed now, and these chat rooms might be his inroads. He'd grown up, like most men, thoroughly at home with porn, in both its public and private guises. It shadowed him, but so closely he had a hard time seeing it as something distinct from himself. But in the last few months, as he'd withdrawn from the world and tapered off his meds, the fetish had come plainly into view as something attached to him like a parasite. Once he saw it this way, he found it impossible to get off to it. Lately he seemed to feel it less necessary to get off at all—by himself, with Janice, with anyone. It felt like evolution.

One of the things he liked about the forums—and he'd liked this about his pre-assault chats with the hookers too—was that they forced him to improvise, react in the moment. He didn't come to them with scripts, fixed ideas, or stories to lecture them with. The situation would draw fresh ideas out of him, extend his thinking in unpredictable directions.

The chat rooms took things a step further, though. Now, he had to react from the very point of view of the ones he held in contempt. It was a way of putting himself in the girls' shoes—in its way a compassionate act. He felt more empathic for it, and his moral thinking seemed suppler to him. He was learning something, not just about himself, or even the girls, but about the space between them and how it might be closed.

Skye wasn't his only character. He had others going at rival forums, some of which were dedicated to more extreme pornography. In one case, the raw fact around which he built his lies was that Maya Haven, a Czech newbie to Porn Valley, was to star in the latest Piss Mops flick. Lewis-as-Maya had so far explained to the fans in the chat room how, in shooting the scene, the taste of urine was not unlike white beer; that though the first sip was always jarring, no matter how many times you'd had it before, by the third swallow, there was something quenching in it, even if the aftertaste was worse and more persistent than beer.

In shooting the scene, he, Maya, had kneeled in the bathtub. Her patellas ached from the ceramic. Each man—there were three, though in the most heroic scenes in the series, there might be twice that—each man undid his jeans, just slightly off camera, and the first man up, his cock would dangle into frame. Lewis described the initial spurt onto the tongue; how Maya was encouraged to gargle with the piss; how she let the first stream, a golden brown, leak down her chest, running over her tits and belly through her legs.

But to the surprise of all, including herself, with the second stream she began to drink. She angled her head so that the piss struck the back of her throat and disappeared directly down her gullet. By the end of it, she'd consumed more than two pints. The men clapped spontaneously as she stood and twisted the shower knob. The sound of the falling water merged with the extravagant claps as the image went dark and she rinsed the piss from her hair and body. Just this once, she nearly forgot about the money. The director even threw in an extra hundred for drinking.

So far, no one had called Maya out, questioned her reality. The forum members seemed entranced, touched, disgusted, and yes, slightly shamed by Lewis's tale. Which was his hope. It was also a funny story, he thought, and nothing hurts like humor.

But would the real Maya ever discover what she'd said in the forum? And would she be shocked by the odd detachment of her words, the self-lacerating wit? Or would she reluctantly recognize her reflection in them and hate herself more for it?

Maybe she'd even learn something about herself from Lewis, just before she reported the deception to the moderators.

And then Violet, who was becoming far more famous than Maya. What would she think of what *she'd* said, which was altogether more reflective, if equally troubling? Maybe she'd be proud, and want to take up the challenge, live up to the portrait. Maybe one day soon she'd give it all up, this twisted image of the good life. Unlikely, but not impossible.

The only woman's thoughts Lewis didn't seem to speculate about lately were Janice's. He spoke to her mostly in freighted trivialities now. Overall he simply spoke less, and even before he'd stopped getting off on porn, he'd stopped getting off on her. He was willing enough to go through the motions for her, she found. But she wasn't. So they didn't.

She of course could speculate about no one's thoughts *but* his anymore. It felt to her as if he were flattening out, shrinking. There was less of him to inhabit now, to live in or with. At the same time, she had the odd feeling he was also deepening, growing, and rapidly. But the growth was taking place far away from her, on the other side of him, a place she knew existed but always left alone out of respect, love. Now it seemed ground was being gained there, so much that it was dwarfing all she knew of him. It was changing too, seeming no longer merely unknown, though available in principle to her, if she felt it important to know. It was becoming unknowable territory, and it chilled her. She had to admit that what she had left of him now was mostly abandoned land, scorched earth. No one could survive here for long.

He shut the laptop. She shut the window and left him to himself in the kitchen.

22

IT'S BEEN TWO WEEKS NOW SINCE THE GREAT MU-
seum's facade was pocked. Tiny plastic charges, military grade
RDX, arranged with art. The paintings escaped damage, the
guests and patrons too. The event did not. A philanthropic gathering, hosted by the Wintry, dedicated only to strengthening political literacy in the city's charter schools—put simply, an education fundraiser—dispersed like that. It will be restaged. Most
of the funds, we hope, will be collected, perhaps through online
auctions, if in-the-flesh meetings remain fraught. (There is every
chance they will.)

The bare idea of introducing a discussion of weighted voting, of power indexes, of *phronesis,* fundamentally, into our
schools—readers of this magazine must wonder: how, and
whom, does it disturb?

Before this, we had the leveling of the Morlen Center, which
federal and city officials had planned on using to address, first
privately, then in a series of town halls, what they have come to
call the background instabilities, and what I prefer to call the
quiet dissonances, of the last year and a half. Three people did
die in the destruction. But that seems, from what we know and
have come to expect, beyond the intention. The means were

primitive, effective, they could even be symbolic. Ammonium nitrate—ANFO—packed tight into minivan casings. (Fertilizer, in essence, in a doorstep detonation.) Those talks have been delayed, will have to be moved, and one expects security will have to be ratcheted up again.

Then, three weeks ago, there was the careful disembowelment of a downtown pool hall that doubles as a meeting place for labor. It's Emile Jenko's. The talks held there were organized by a fine speaker, quietly convincing, so far from his roots: Javier Celano IV. Now he must seek a new place to lecture, to beseech, to plead. Another of Jenko's halls, perhaps. It's not known where he's spoken, if at all, since the attack. The meetings, if there have been any, must be of a smaller scale, less visible. Perhaps he is gathering his thoughts, privately. Perhaps he finds other ways to speak.

And the source of the implosion, of the hall, the first in what can seem—though this cannot be known, or is not, yet—a chain. Whom can *it* trouble? Celano speaks, yes, for the lay, the common. But must that put him at odds with those wondering, like us, how character, knowledge, habit, and influence—political influence—should relate? If the education, or better, the life-training, on which the apportionment of political power properly depends were to be made available to all—the charter schools need only be the beginning—why should that be so? Even the most extreme electoral reweightings needn't create *inherent* disadvantages. All those I have heard floated, anyway, call for a phasing-in, where the relevant opportunities would be made available beforehand.

I should say, I have no settled opinion if any of those proposals are worthy, though for predictable reasons, it is assumed I and others of the Wintry do, that we want things to come out a certain way. But public debate might well lead, probably would lead, only to quite moderate revisions of our understanding of political say-so. In fact, and this bears emphasis, we might well end up only reconfirming our existing arrangements, that brute, biological one: one person, one vote. Why not, if the basis is as sound as we have been assuming, collectively, it is, all these years?

This is all to say, then, that the gathering in the museum that night should not be taken, eo ipso, as a threat to Celano and his causes, which, however obscure they are—and they are quite, which I'll say something about presently—has to do with the conditions of today's workers, whether they labor in factories or storefronts, part-time or full. The assumption of a clash of class interests, tempting as it is, is superficial. And we can say that while granting that the venue of our event, the museum, is certainly itself a *symbol* of orthodox power—anything can become a symbol of anything, though—and that the patrons, it is true, were ones of great means.

The proposals discussed that night—the provision of education was the issue, nothing more—intersect with the problem that really afflicts Celano's people: even when their true interests stand revealed, the unskilled, however much in unison they may vote, are destined to be overruled in any system of decision making that is egalitarian, majoritarian, and self-interested at the level of the individual vote. It is not, then, *proposed* political arrangements, like the ones considered by the Wintry, that are his problem, not in the first instance anyway. It is the present, not the future, that is the obstacle.

Perhaps our pictures differ. I am sure they must, in some ways, though the differences may not be nearly so deep as imagined. At this point, they are irrelevant anyway. There may be doglegs we will discover down the road. But that is down the road.

Now, does Celano, the Old Rosean, see things this way? Sometimes I think he must. He's experienced too much to go in for the face value, in present circumstances, when the face value is everywhere a screen—not a blank one, but a screen nonetheless—or at least a potential one, onto which motive powers are perpetually being thrown, superimposed from a distance. And incredibly, not always with intent. That doesn't stop meanings from forming.

If he is thinking clearly, I can't see how he could see things otherwise. Perhaps he's just unsure whether the Wintry does too. He can be assured that we do. It is the sensible view.

But then, nothing around us conduces to clear thinking. Since that attack on the pool hall, there has been a level of scrutiny at the Wintry, a presence of police, plain clothes and not, that, though no formal accusation has been made, must mean we are under some suspicion (though that will be denied). Celano may take that attack, and equally that scrutiny, as evidence against us.

I am sympathetic. There is at least the ring of truth to it. But that ring attends every specious proposition too. Today the truth appears to be sounding out everywhere and all the time, and everything simply cannot be true. Facts are facts, of course. There is no question of truth. There are no false facts. But propositions are something else. And the attribution of cause and effect, for all these happenings, it could not occur at a more vexed moment, from the standpoint of what can be decisively known. Circumstances aren't exactly *un*favorable to seeing the Wintry as an actor here, somewhere behind the destruction of Jenko's hall. I must acknowledge that frankly.

But then, if *that* is the standard, how many more events might one implicate the Wintry in? How about the waste station that was recently compromised in one of our less affluent neighborhoods? And what of these beaten escorts, the community of sex workers? Would they not make as good a target, even if they are not yet politically organized? A preemptive strike of sorts? How different are they from Celano's great unwashed? Some of them work legally too, after all, in the adult film industry.

I wonder, then, when Celano does surface, whether he also will face greater suspicion, in his case for the profaning of the museum and our fundraiser. I suppose I don't wonder but know. The evidence there paints an even more damning picture, though it is still nothing so strong as conclusive, the very idea of which—conclusive evidence—has receded lately, hasn't it, into a sea of probabilities. It will be, as they say, something for the police to decide. (I hope, of course, it turns out he has little to do with this, if his thinking is as probing as I hope it is, going by some of his prognostications.)

The forced fact, whatever the truth, is that both of us are now under surveillance. The government's license implicitly expands. So one wonders, again, about the origins of both attacks. It is hard not to notice that though the materials involved differ—small guerilla charges in the museum, a single sophisticated leveling device in the pool hall, one that could incinerate the place without causing a hint of structural damage (the buildings on either side have been virtually undisturbed)—the manner of their deployment is eerily on a par. The elegance and economy. The practiced precision. There is the perfection of performance here, so perfect one doubts any private organization could manage it.

One can't help but observe these unities. Who gains from Celano and I being locked in a conflict that can only be internecine? In some sense, many do. The Christians and Muslims. The libertarians. But they have their own waves of crises. It's just not their turn. So, in the largest sense, who gains—who is strengthened—by the sight of so much strife between all of these rivals, as we head toward elections? We may say this much, I hope, without danger: these clashes can only imbue the elections themselves, along with the government responsible for holding them, with greater authority. Very likely the government will win them too, if they are seen to bring stability now. Conveniently, they can probably choose whatever means they please in bringing it. In a state of emergency, the people grow eager for a heavy hand.

In any case, Jenko's hall is being rebuilt, and the insurance has not even been necessary (though that will come). He's said that donations have streamed in. Some have been quite large, we understand. He will not name the donors, which is wise, not least because of the misunderstandings every revelation, even the innocent ones, seems to generate.

Now, this financial support cannot be assumed to be an endorsement of those labor meetings transpiring within, which represent only a fraction of the activity of the hall. It might really just be support for *him*, Jenko, given his broader business interests, which extend now, from his beginnings in this pool hall—a London import—deep into construction, much of it conducted jointly with Celano's father and a network of other developers. A threat to Jenko threatens much else.

We owe to them the reconstruction of the waterfront of southwest Halsley, destroyed last fall by those twin hurricanes that swept through in succession, John and Mark. And equally we owe the quiet rise of that little island in the river as a residential and commercial force.

What these donors make of Jenko's staging of Celano's meetings, I cannot say. Perhaps it's considered an eccentricity of his, or his philanthropic side, and through him, *their* philanthropic side. We do know their friendship, Jenko and Celano's, goes quite a ways back, not just in time, but in distance, to Europe. And by all accounts, Jenko's convictions about the needs of the workers are genuine. Many of his developments compensate them in unusually generous ways, shall we say.

Perhaps the donations coming in to Jenko are just a kindness, as one of Halsley's burgeoning landlords. (His tax revenue is appreciated by the city, I'm sure.) The halls are only one small dimension of his concerns. But this hall, it will be better than before, more modern, and more secure. Everything, it's said, will be indestructible.

Will Celano's meetings return as quickly, though. One fears

there may be a point where the destruction of property, vicious as it is, is not quite the end of it. Why should that barrier remain unbreached? On all sides, actually, the tumult, this thousand-sided Möbius strip of a conflict, has remained below this threshold. What does it say about the operative forces here that it has? Perhaps we are meant to think there are limits.

Celano's position has always been obscure. Sometimes it appears to be simply about mobilizing votes. Sometimes there is a sense that something greater is at stake, and it is this that has made things more complicated. But there is something unstateable about the position. It seems to require the provision of a language that is either dead or unborn.

Certainly it is not a classical socialism. Is it possibly anti-democratic even? Does it require a silencing of the reigning masters? Or is it rather a call for a different form, a more perfect vehicle for our original national principles? Some of his essays, attributed and not, suggest this. But welding these arguments together, the strategies they recommend, seems impossible. The elements will not jell, not yet anyway.

Are they, though, *meant* to lie discretely, as a series of piece-meal, even inconsistent interventions in our political life? Can justice really be schizophrenic in this way? Or is that a characterization from a point of view he wants to explode? Even still: can justice be a disruption? Can it exist as a kind of negation? Or is that only a clearing of a space, a prelude to something more well formed?

It is just this disunity of approach, together with his capacity to effect certain sorts of change, indeed massive change, through his diffuse allies, that makes it possible to impute such an array of motives and actions to Celano, and impossible to cross his name off any list. He can apparently explain almost any eventuality, micro or macro. The Wintry too has a varied program, but then, we aren't articulating or defending any single position, though many claim the opposite. In any case, haziness, I hope, is not a basic quality of anything we do.

But the ease with which Celano can be invoked, it has made him less predictable, not more. Is that, finally, what he is after? A blurring?

So, the museum: on its surface, yes, the building, the Wintry gathering, can seem natural objects of his animus. Targets. Given that his own meeting ground was destroyed just prior, motives line up nicely. Or they can seem to. That's the trouble. It depends on which pronouncements of his we take most seriously: the ones about the corrosive social properties of wealth, say, or the ones about its capacity to emancipate, in which case, we are not opposed.

Firm conclusions, then, aren't possible, not unless and until his doctrine jells. This is a recipe for self-implication, martyrdom even, of a certain sort. I'm sometimes of the mind that he owes it to his followers, and to the broader collective, to make his views cohere; and other times of the mind that, so long as he is listening carefully, and is cautious about making assumptions of the other actors, especially the ones that are nearest to hand, that he might more effectively maintain a certain kind of public scrutiny, that he might sharpen all of our eyes, by remaining in the shadows. Sometimes it is the veil that keeps the attention where one wants it, and where, I agree, it is needed.

I hope, personally, that he does not, and never did, assume the destruction of his hall, Jenko's hall, must somehow issue from wealth—private wealth, anyway (the state is another matter). In fact, as I say, I hope to find that he sees no necessary moral divide between his causes and the notions we proposed that night.

We must wait, I suppose, for events to unfold.

Stagg replaced the magazine within a rectangle of clear floor. All around his desk, the ground was covered in papers, set at odd angles, but never more than one or two layers thick. He'd put the first documents down with no regard, hurriedly tossing them onto any empty area while he carried on with his research. But as their number grew and space contracted, the articles and legal pads and printouts had to be wedged between what was already in place there. Sometimes this wasn't enough, and to make room, papers would have to be resettled, like people, shunted to one side or the other, or pushed up against others.

Sometimes even this wasn't enough, and he was forced to layer, offsetting the top document from the one beneath, like a pair of cards. That way, everything remained surveyable from the point from which his work radiated: his old chair.

Squat and hard-backed, extracted from his childhood home—he'd not thought of the place, out in L.A., since it had been sold off, almost fifteen years ago now—he'd done all his grade-school homework in this chair. It seemed the homework never finished.

Stagg leaned back and felt the chair cradle him. In the present apartment, with the present desk, it came up short—it was in no sense adjustable—leaving him to type upward, with his hands held out across from his chest rather than his stomach. Once he'd thought to get a lower-set desk; but then, it had come with the apartment, and it was attached to the bookcase.

Getting a taller chair would have been simpler. But the over-constructed original, made of too many planks, had decayed unrepeatably. It was something he'd never been able to replicate. The weakening of its joints, the legs and back, the wood itself: the chair seemed never to resist him, compensating for the tiniest shift of weight or pressure with a bend or a twist.

At first, the pliancy made him feel as though the chair would collapse beneath him. But it had remained that way for at least a decade now, perpetually on the brink. Somehow this was its most stable state, and what he'd first apprehended as weakness proved instead to be a kind of peculiar responsiveness.

Responsiveness to him, anyway. The proportions of anyone else's body might destroy it. Sometimes he put clothes on it to discourage Renna from using it. Sometimes she sat on top of the clothes. Other times she would sit on top of him while he was in it, and they would both feel sure they would collapse in a pile of wood. It never worried her. He'd shoo her away then with a smile, or lift her up and set her on the bed.

He leaned back still further in the chair and wondered where she was. He hadn't seen her for a couple of days now, since that night at Larent's, with Ravan, where they'd all given up their minds to various substances. He'd taken her home in a cab and she slept all the way. He woke in the morning and she was somewhere else already. She'd texted a few times since then as she scampered around town, working, schmoozing. He'd dutifully responded. But she'd said nothing concrete about meeting and he wasn't going to be the one to do it again.

The only woman he should have been calling was Jen. In some ways she might need him more than Renna. Anyway it was his job to follow up. He wondered where she was now, and what exactly she was doing, or what Roman she was reading. Lucretius maybe. It's what he was reading. He still had nothing to tell her, really, so he'd wait until he did.

He let the front legs of the chair come down and opened his eyes. Now that he had it here with him, he found it hard to work, or rather to think, without it. His most probing ruminations seemed to occur in its arms, leaning back away from the desk, with his eyes falling on an empty wall.

It was the only furniture that felt necessary. A duvet on the floor could suffice, and his computer was a laptop. It would be easier to bring everything else in the room in line with the chair than the reverse.

Ultimately, though, he changed nothing. The comfort that was good for thinking was not, it turned out, good for writing. Between the chair and the desk there was a useful mismatch. The slight but continuous strain it caused brought Stagg a greater consciousness of the act of writing, and this awareness seemed to produce sharper, more definite lines of prose. It was as if, given the extra effort involved, he didn't want to have to spend anymore time typing than he had to, so he would try to get it right the first time, or nearly so. Typewriters, he understood, had the same effect. Perhaps the pen as well. The costs they imposed concentrated the hand and the mind. His essays, or whatever they were, had benefitted. The roots seemed stronger.

He stood and just as quickly sank face first onto the bed a short yard from the desk. Penerin had emailed him a link to this same piece by Kames, but he'd had the magazine itself handy. Probably it could only be published under Kames's name, and in the Wintry's own monthly, *Lebenswelt*, it was so loose, so oddly voiced and full of circling repetitions.

Kames's intellectual pedigree was irreproachable, though. His doctorate in political theory, begun at Princeton and finished at Chicago, won him a fellowship year and then a tenure-track post at Berkeley. But rather than revise his dissertation, *Paradoxes in Voting*, into a book, he shelved it, along with the formal apparatus he'd developed that put a new complexion on decision theory.

He turned instead to composing a commentary on *The Crisis of Parliamentary Democracy*, by the notorious and brilliant Weimar (and then Nazi) legal theorist Carl Schmitt. Schmitt had written of the possibility of democratic dictatorship, and Kames was trying to see what he could do with the idea, stretch it, break it even if that's what it took to see oneself through to a viable state. He was also seeking a fresh conception of *demos*, and like

Leo Strauss, he was reaching back to the Greeks, to Athens, to find it.

The result of his labors, fully intelligible only to a few Schmitt scholars, was as keen in its critique of liberal democracy as it was troubling in its positive proposals. The essence of it was simple. Kames thought there might be ways of bolstering democracy— or salvaging it, it was not always clear—that traded on a notion already of great currency. Selves, it was almost common sense now, were something formed, acquired, not natively endowed, even if certain endowments might form preconditions on self-hood. But if that is what identity simpliciter was, it was only custom, and probably cowardice, that made an exception of political identity. One's political significance, like any other, was a matter of what one did, the forms of life one participated in, the know-how one acquired and deployed, the moral and political character one developed. It wasn't merely what one was, as a brute biological matter: a creature falling under a certain genus and species.

Political selfhood was a kind of *second* nature; unlike first nature, it was necessarily always up for grabs, accessible to, and losable by, all. It was an achievement. Which meant, among other things, that it was perfectly possible to exist biologically and not politically. At most, Kames thought, biology guaranteed only the most rudimentary form of political citizenship, nothing like an equal hand in steering the ship that was society.

He married this to the thought that commerce could abrade character, that in some cases it could make one unsuitable for politics. Stagg felt closest to Kames on this point: A contractual approach to politics had catastrophic social and cultural consequences. Some read this as a dangerously reactionary stance. But it felt natural to them both, and seemed now to them, at this point in history, like a new kind of progressivism.

In any case, it was with this proto-position in hand, and a growing frustration with the limits of the seminar room and his colleagues walking in lockstep, that he founded his research center, naming it after the fount of wealth necessary to do so, his great grandfather, Franklin Wintry, the British zinc baron whose sons would settle in the New World.

Kames couldn't stand to hear it called a think tank. The phrase smacked of something shallow, intellectually second class, and depth was at the core of the project, though it was inflected in a new way. It had brought him notoriety, as he and his colleagues injected ideas, like this essay, at once incisive and ambiguous, into settings where they might make contact with ripe circumstances.

With help from friends like Leo Eldern, Kames had transformed the Institute into a national force. At this point, he had to be heard. So publishers obliged, pushing aside their normal concerns, sometimes of clarity, always of length. But this piece was unusual, even for him. It seemed more of an artful jotting, a pretty ramble, fit more for a good blog. It might have been pride alone that prevented Kames from publishing it that way, what made it necessary that it appear in the print issue.

But then it might also be that the note was not a note at all, with its suggestion of incompleteness and approximation, but the finished version of a form Stagg failed to recognize as such. The essay's apparent imprecisions might actually be a set of carefully inscribed double- and triple-entendres and, indeed, occasionally, red herrings. And why not? These days, if you were to flourish or even survive, everyday life seemed to demand the most subtle exegesis. Why then shouldn't actual texts? Which meant, Stagg thought, that Kames's article might well be as perfect for what it was, and what it was meant to be, as *Madame Bovary* was a novel, what *its* author had hoped for it, and for her, Emma.

This struck Stagg as more likely, knowing the value Kames placed on rigor. Anyway it had been a while now since one worried about a prestige gap between print and digital. Even Kames, in his mid-60s now, was not so antiquated. In some ways, he was seeming as modern as could be. Probably more than Stagg himself, who seemed more interested in the past than the future.

Stagg slept with the lights on, in his clothes. It was cold and the heat was unpredictable, so this was not only easy but practical. He left the thinking for the morning, when there would be two of them, he and Penerin.

■ ■ ■

The same essay, printed out on paper that had been wet at some point and had dried wrinkled and stiff, was sitting on the desk when Stagg came into the office. A Venn diagram of coffee rings marked it along the margin, and it was turned around, as if he should read it. He picked it up. There were only a couple of underlines, most of which seemed not to correspond to anything of outstanding importance: "museum," "plain clothes," "a fine speaker." They must have been stray markings as Penerin followed along with his pen. But then they seemed too definite for that; they showed through on the reverse side of the pages.

"Strange, right?" Penerin said from the doorway. His voice was soft, as if he were standing farther away than he was.

Stagg nodded and set the sheets down. Without looking at him, his boss walked around to the desk and sat slowly in the mesh swivel chair.

"I can't see what this *does*, or what it's about... really about," Penerin said in almost philosophical tones. "Can you?"

The question sharpened his voice, and his eyes, which finally fixed on Stagg, held a new intensity.

"It's definitely—"

"It's accusations, it's camaraderie, directed at this same guy, Celano," Penerin interrupted. "And Jenko too. Then there's the insinuations about us, but just fuzzy enough for him to deny.

And then the academic jargon that I don't know what." His voice was sharper still.

The fluorescent loop overhead, veiled by frosted glass, crackled faintly and continuously. Stagg waited a few beats to see if Penerin was done.

"Ravan spoke with him," Stagg said.

"About the museum, right. He collected the facts—a strange bunch of them."

"Strange events."

"No, but what he put down, what Kames gave him, the emphasis is all wrong. It's more about the wine than the bombs. It's bizarre."

"Is that Ravan or is that Kames, though."

"Jesus fuck, Carl, this isn't about distortion, you have to see that." He paused, calmed himself. "What about this essay then? These are Kames's words, right? He chose them. So whatever is odd *here*, there's no excuse, no messenger, we know it's him. And it is *weirder* than anything Ravan reported. For one, why is he talking about the assaults on the hookers like this? Of all the things he could have chosen, why was *this* his example of something you could just as well accuse him of?"

Stagg avoided his eyes now.

"Any ideas? Even just about how this guy thinks?"

The contempt in his voice was unconcealed now, and a good part of it must have been directed at him. Stagg shrugged vaguely.

"No? Then any idea why we still have no clue why the beatings tailed off since Best?"

"Not yet."

"Not yet. That's great. You realize we have every right to be paranoid now, right? There are weeks till we're supposed to pick a president. Are you paranoid?"

Stagg nodded.

"See, that can't be true. I can't see how, anyway. You haven't said a single useful word about Kames today. Which means you think there's no point worrying about him, or you just don't know anything about him. But of course, you *do* know him. So you must not be worrying about him, and you should be."

Stagg didn't know what to say. For a moment the hum of the bulb took over.

"We had to look into the Wintry, obviously, after this," Penerin said, holding the printout up. "They tell me your name is on the schedule, for a lecture. So does Ravan."

"It's not—"

"There's nothing wrong with that. Prestigious place is what I've heard, whatever the controversy. You're there for your research, I guess. History? Politics?"

"Yeah."

"You must consider that your real life, the one you'd rather be living all the time instead of sitting here with me. But see, this is history too. This is politics, what we're doing. So this *is* just as much your real life as anything."

"I never said it wasn't."

"Then you can take it just as fucking seriously, can't you."

Stagg gripped the cool chrome armrests that sloped away from him. He slid his hands down the metal tubes, loosening his grip to prevent them from clinging to the metal, which seemed damp. But that may have just been his sweat. He lifted his weight with his elbows and pushed himself further into the chair until his back went straight.

"Look, you don't have to do anything *that* different—it's just noticing," Penerin said. "Same as always. So you bring up this article with him, show some interest in the details. And maybe you end up finding out a tiny bit about what he's really playing at. That's all. There's nothing for us to argue about really, Carl. I'm not angry you work at the Wintry. It could actually be a good break we caught here, really."

"I'm only applying to work there at this point. But what you're saying now, it—"

"Wait. What have I said?"

"Well, I'm thinking now maybe I shouldn't—"

"But I haven't said anything. Or, okay, no, I am saying there are things we don't understand, Carl. And as long as that's true, nothing's right, nothing's wrong. That sounds like freedom, I know, but it's also a very big fucking problem. You can see that, right? Because it won't last. Because after the fact, after people die, or an election's derailed, when none of us can do anything about it, we—not "they," but us, all of us—we'll say this was wrong, that was right. I don't know that it makes any sense that we do that, but we do that, and we'll do it here too. If we're lucky, you could help us see which is which a little quicker, and we'd have a tiny bit of choice in how we come out. In history.

"Understand, I'm not saying Kames must have done something wrong," he continued. "It's always possible there's nothing there. Mostly there is nothing, right, you've already seen that by now. But we're coming at this from several angles. Ravan will be involved too. Our numbers people have been working. You're just another arrow in the quiver, one we didn't even know we had till yesterday. We're grateful. We need you."

"And how would you know that yet?"

Penerin rubbed his eyes.

"Let's just see what I see."

They listened to the light.

23

1. From the East, from that town, there came a spark the size of a glowworm. Growing ever bigger it came to the center of Kolamba, waxed here to unmeasured size, and burned up everything at once. On that day, in consequence of its splendor, the enemy who had penetrated to Sirivaddhana took flight with the haste of those who are threatened with peril.

2. The Ruler of men guarded his son, who grew by degrees like another moon.

Darasa weighed the passages against what he knew. Senaratana, the "Ruler of Men." Rajasingha, his son, born to Queen Dona Catherina, the Portuguese princess and wife previously to Senaratana's brother and predecessor on the throne, Vimaladhammasuriya, who was now dead. And the "cruel and brutal" *Parangi*—Portuguese—merchants "puffed up with pride," who "waxed very strong" in Colombo.

General de Azavedo had seen this glowworm spark in his dreams and scattered his forces in the hours before dawn. The Portuguese scrambled to their forts locked safely in the forests, leaving the great port of Colombo clear. This was in the decades after 1600, in which the Portuguese were still strong in the south of the island, before the Dutch arrived.

The threat of the spark deferred, the king would have made his way to Sirivaddhana, a jagged and unassailable land. He divided the kingdom between three sons, two being his dead brother's, and the other his own. On three leaves, the names of the three provinces were inscribed: Uva to the east, Matale to the north, and then the Highlands in the middle surrounding Kandy. The boys reached down to the overturned leaves at the base of the mounted relic, which held a molar said to belong to Siddhartha Gautama. To his blood fell the prize, the impregnable Highlands, safest from European advances. Seven years hence, Senaratana died and his true son, soon to be known as Rajasingha, ascended to the throne.

Darasa sat at his desk in fine dawn light in the town of Nillemby, not far from Kandy. He reached for the stylus and drew the nib from the bottom of a shallow black pool of ink. In a broad book of palm leaves, he copied the passages from the Lesser Chronicle, which took account of the years between 1604 and 1635 in a thousand words, on a sheet of palm leaf fifteen inches square and started to annotate it with these thoughts.

The length and complexity of the text determined the size of the sheets. When it was sprawling, like the Chronicle, it would have to be divided across many small sheets, as now. Other times, when it was possible to see the piece as a whole, in one sweep, the giant palm leaf would be left uncut. Once, in commentary on the Jataka tales, part of the Pali Canon, he amassed 547 whole leaves, one for each life of the Buddha described. The stack remained in the attic of Kandy's main temple, several feet high and hopelessly bound with twine.

The margins, top and bottom, left and right, usually dwarfed the text itself, which he would inscribe in the center of the leaves. As he annotated, he would box paragraphs, sentences, phrases, words—not always nouns and verbs, but conjunctions, definite articles, simple negations, all the way down to the smallest atoms of sense. A light line led from each of these items to the margins, where Darasa would set the relevant comment.

The technique was unique. The other monks simply numbered passages from the text to correspond with their annotations in a separate palm book. But Darasa's strategy encouraged commentary of much greater length; the sheer size of the margins seemed to call out for detail, otherwise the sheet would appear empty and the labors of the commentator slight. More than this, his approach revealed hidden relations between annotation and text, and between annotation and annotation. A network of sense emerged, the nodes playing off each other. Only on its basis would Darasa compose his finished commentary, in a standard palm book.

For this reason, his rooms appeared less like a scholar's and more like a draftsman's. During his working sessions, leaves of various sizes would drape most of the furniture, covering the bed, the chairs, the floor. The eyes of his guests would invariably drift from his own toward these annotations overrunning his quarters.

But the results were difficult to dispute. His work threw a light much brighter than most. There were perhaps only a half dozen monks in the country with minds both as expansive and exacting as his (it was the combination that was rare). His eccentricities—not just his quixotic approach to commentary, but his avidity for maps, seamanship, and foreign theologies, as well as the special interest he took in the Europeans in the kingdom, which some of the conservative monks had once (and perhaps still) found perverse—mostly induced reverence rather than ridicule.

Commentary was only part of his work. Together with twenty other monks of scholarly repute, he was responsible for adding to the historical record of the island. This was done under the eye of Rajasingha, who was not, however, in a position to edit or guide the monks, not openly or explicitly, anyway.

Here too Darasa found a way to apply these same interpretive techniques. Most monks knew the Chronicle well. A few knew it nearly by heart. But none of his contemporaries spent more time annotating it, wondering after its mode of composition, the potentially variable intentions of the chain of authors from Mahanama onward. None searched with quite the same vigor for interstices, elisions, interpolations.

The prevailing thought in the priesthood was that their role was to write the present, not interpret the past or consider the veracity of the Chronicle, which was, after all, composed by *them*, their predecessors in the temple. This was especially so of recent portions, where the language resembled the vernacular and interpretive measures were not required as a matter of course, as it was when proto-Sinhalese was involved in the earlier periods. Those parts of the Chronicle demanded a fusing of horizons, which, depending on how the monk managed it, affected his grasp, and the grasp of any reader of the Chronicle, of even the simplest matters of fact.

For Darasa, though, even when the language of the past dovetailed smoothly with that of the present, and it was an option to take the Chronicle at face value, it was a mistake. The present—the activities of the king and his court, the role of the priesthood, the changing constitution of the island's population (Indian, Chinese, Arabic, European)—should, and in a way could, only be recorded in the light of a fuller account of the past.

But the chapters of the Chronicle were heavily condensed. What he needed was a way of regenerating the original heft of history from the distillate left in the Chronicle. (Some auxiliary records did exist, of course, which partly explained Darasa's interest in the Europeans, the records they kept.) Only then could the present be set down with the right weighting and balance.

In fact his ambitions extended further, though he never spoke of this. He hoped earlier sections of the Chronicle might not only be reinterpreted but reweighted—redistilled—which might alter the complexion of the era while respecting the facts.

But revisions were not something considered by the priests. Their predecessors had direct access to the full spread of facts. It was thought that later revisions could only introduce distortions, bending the past to the needs of the present. But in Darasa's view, the present affected the past, or anyway the present affected the history of the past. Potentialities contained in events, invisible to the contemporary eye, might reveal themselves only to the future.

But perhaps this sort of account was not to the point. Previous chroniclers might have meant to capture the past as present, the lived past, illusions and all, and not the past as past, a living past whose tail might grow ever sharper. If the goal was to record a people's consciousness, the psychological texture of an era, its truths, its madnesses, the Chronicle as it stood might well be the better guide.

However it was with revising the past, in composing provisional text for the Chronicle, where his hand was freer, Darasa applied his usual exegetical methods, annotating the older record heavily, teasing out the implications and presuppositions to draw excluded material to the surface, or even implicit material the original authors may have only accidentally deposited in the text. With this fuller history in hand he would make sense of his time.

The committee of monks would write up the same events. The texts, unattributed, were then compiled. The monks would meet and take each from the stack and read it out to the assembly. Line by line they debated its merits, compared it against the others. Twenty versions of the near past were sifted this way. Notes were taken on suggestions for a composite text, and a rough outline was settled on. One monk would then be asked to whittle, meld, and rewrite as necessary, developing a draft version to be voted on by a group of seven senior monks, who would ratify the text, typically unanimously (though five votes sufficed), or else send it back to the monk with corrections until an acceptable version emerged.

■ ■ ■

Darasa was taken from sleep by a warbling groan. Soon it appeared a chorus, just out of tune, sometimes two voices, sometimes three and four. Occasionally it thinned to a single plaintive whine, but never would it cease. Like the chants the fellowship practiced, a voice always carried through.

This went on for several minutes, Darasa in a semiconscious state. Footsteps began to sound in the midst of the droning voices, then mutterings. Panicked ones. He raised himself from the mat and kneeled at the window: a comet, bluer than the moon and larger than the stars. Another glowworm spark. But the child, Rajasingha, was now a man.

In the courtyard in Nillemby, the black was unstained save for several spheres of light. Four of these, separated from each other by a few yards, were thrown by the palace torches mounted along the entryway. At the base of each lay a sentry. Two were curled on their sides, wriggling. One was prone. The nearest to him was on his knees. A flash of metal shot from his chest into the dark, the orange light of the torch imperfectly camouflaging the red staining his chest. The wailing persisted.

There was a banging. Two more spheres, barely overlapping, hung in front of the palace doors, which had just swung shut. At the same moment a rifle may have discharged, the sound was so sharp, and one man fell to the floor in front of the doors. Others, cloaked in royal garb, lay along the wall of the palace, creating a further background groan Darasa hadn't noticed till then. Men in the same attire—turncoats, presumably—pried at the doors alongside several others carrying scabbards, men of good birth.

One ran his sword down the slit between the doors, striking the heavy bolt. From the other side came the murmurs of Rajasingha's men, the loyalists who had managed to shut themselves in, and also the most trusted guards, stationed in the interior, who were known to carry formidable European weaponry. More men, aristocrats down to peasants, judging by the varied dress, shot through the spheres at the entryway and reappeared seconds later within those at the palace doors. There they stayed for hours. The courtyard rapidly filled with rebels. They would wait the king out, assumed he would surrender.

Darasa knew the king would not give himself up. The palace grounds sat on the v-shaped edge of a plateau that descended into a valley widely thought to be covered in impassable forest, making it unapproachable from anywhere but the front. The monk knew, though, from some of the great men of the court— intimates of his own distinguished family, who had delivered him, as was the practice, to the priestly order when he was a boy—that a steep, barely visible path only partially cleared of brush led down into the valley. With the heavy arms of his men, and with the two elephants he kept at the back of the palace, for his own amusement, but also to break through the remaining brush, Rajasingha had a strong tactical advantage over anyone who might be stationed in the valley, supposing the rebels could envisage this possibility, which they almost certainly could not.

Until day broke Darasa watched the crowd with a steely calm. Some of the lead rebels came early in the night to assure the monks of their unconditional safety. The four resident monks, a couple of them in a panic, asked Darasa to speak with them, but he saw no need. He told them simply to wait in their quarters as he was doing in his.

Rajasingha never emerged. In daylight the rebels found one

of the king's cannons in the village and thought to use it to breach the palace. Soon after they found one of his elephants and changed tack. The beast was whipped repeatedly, apparently to no effect, until finally, irate, it lunged through the palace doors. The building was deserted. They went to the back of it and found the trampled brush.

A party of thirty or so was dispatched in pursuit down the valley path. The senior rebel leaders—several were nobles familiar to Darasa—stood in the palace doorway and addressed the crowd. Having flushed the king from his palace, they thrust forth one of their number, an aristocrat not of Rajasingha's bloodline, but of one dispossessed of any royal standing centuries earlier. He emerged from behind them and stood before the throng, looking on timidly.

In the village that day, the rebels celebrated, chanting in the streets. Word was sent out to the rest of the country that Rajasingha's reign was finished, that a historical wrong had been righted. In the evening, many of them were put up by residents. Others squatted in the courtyard.

The next morning, the new king did not come out from the royal quarters of the palace. Eventually the guards opened the doors. The room was empty. He was searched for but never found. Perhaps he feared a counterattack from the former king. Or he may have simply had no interest in ruling. What was certain was that he was not the driving force behind the revolt, but a pawn of the rebel leaders, who were nobles without claim, however slight, to the throne.

News of his absence spread to the courtyard. In short order pledges to Rajasingha began to resound, first a few here and there, but soon everywhere, in a torrent, as rebels smoothly mutated into loyalists. Most of them took to proving their allegiance by murdering the rebels around them, declaring them traitors. By nightfall, the courtyard was tiled in bodies, as was much of the town. A smaller group remained, several dozen, all rabid loyalists by now, many nursing wounds from the melee.

News of the rebel collapse reached Rajasingha. But he did not return to the palace in Nillemby, preferring the securer location, Digligy, he found himself in now. In his stead he sent his men. The crowd, smaller still, as the wisest had fled, greeted the men warmly, cheering the king's reign. Every one of them was dispatched, as was any local suspected of conspiracy. Nillemby was made a ghost town, except for the temple, which, as usual, was left alone.

The comet passed; order returned.

■ ■ ■

These events weren't likely to find a home in the Chronicle, not like this. Darasa anyway had the feeling that much of the Chronicle existed subterraneously. This must partly have been a practical matter. A more detailed history, one that included all the smaller events occurring during a king's reign, would have run to many thousands of pages; and the monks, especially the less scholarly of them, could not be relied on to know it thoroughly. Since common knowledge is what bound them as an order, a universal frame of reference was vital. The two Chronicles covered two thousand years. Keeping them to a manageable size meant excluding much, or rather, he thought, leaving much of their substance to be inferred.

Some of the exclusions had more interesting reasons behind them. The canonical mode of the Chronicles was tributary, an exaltation of kings and the kingdom they'd shepherded through the ages. To inscribe in it a failed rebellion in support of a noble with only the most tenuous claim to the throne would be to disrupt the sense of inevitability. It might suggest the fragility of both a king's rule and the people he led.

In the island's history there were four successful rebellions against reigning kings, where a leap of succession had to be written into the text, there being no other choice. But they were remarkable, Darasa thought, for always being understood as restorations of some earlier ruling bloodline, from which the new, heretofore unrecognized king invariably descended. The succession was merely a correction, a redress. So the arc of destiny, of narrative, remained undisturbed and the paean proceeded without interruption.

Had the recruited man been the brother of Rajasingha, even this failed rebellion might have qualified for treatment in the record, sibling rivalries for the throne being common and accepted, as they offered no real challenge to fate. In fact it was rumored that one of his brothers was in hiding in India or the North Country. He too might have walked away from the burdens of kingship. No one could say.

Might any of the four successful revolts have been driven by the people and not by the king-to-be and his claims to the throne? In two of the four cases, once in 400, and again in 1543, the Chroniclers describe not the motive force of the revolt, but only the justice of the outcome, in terms of the rules of legitimate succession. If these were in fact populist disruptions, it took no fabrication on the part of the Chroniclers, only omission, to mask that.

Reading the Chronicle, Darasa couldn't help but feel, by the way certain events were skeletally described (as here) and others were repetitiously overattended (a king too lavishly praised); or by how a train of events suddenly yet artfully veered contrary to the momentum it seemed initially to carry; or by how in certain periods the priesthood's doings are dwelled on, with little attention to the broader kingdom, that the monks had succeeded in suggesting a deeply variegated historical unfolding, an unthinkably complex narrative. Sometimes it seemed as if a passage, simply in its cadences, contained reverberations of something that rubbed against the surface gloss, though—and this was remarkable—without tarnishing it. These reverberations complicated each other as well, while others synchronized in surprising ways, deep beneath the text. Sometimes it felt to him as if five or six versions of two thousand years on the island were intertwined, with only one accented at any point. The pattern of emphasis, the cycling between dominant motifs, it could occur at intervals as short as a paragraph, sometimes even just a sentence, and as long as several chapters.

He wondered how he might freight his portrait of Rajasingha's reign with the pressures exerted on it by this stillborn rebellion. What would be his glowworm spark? Whatever thread it linked with—perhaps with more than one, or perhaps the various narratives could be taken as a single motley unit, a dissonant chord—it would have to be expressed through a pattern of muteness. But the means escaped him.

24

"I LIKE THIS," KAMES SAID, HOLDING STAGG'S ES-
say in his hand. He was standing on his balcony at the Wintry Institute in a cardigan and corduroys, a cigarette, a boutique
brand, it looked like, burning down between his fingers. The sun
silvered his gray hair as a light wind mussed it. "I like this but I
wonder if it serves."

Stagg held the wrought iron rail with both hands, the weight
of his frame on them. Three stories down, eucalyptus and oak
trees running along the eastern edge of the lawn brought shade
to the pond, turning its water black.

Kames had taken no more than three drags of the cigarette.
He might have taken just one. Mostly it sat between his fingers
as he talked.

"You'd like to deliver this piece first," he said. "It's not that
it isn't interesting. But it's almost a meditation—never mind the
pun—on historiography. That will be good to get into, but it
seems a complicated place to start. Better, I think, to give us
some history to work with, before we confront how it *becomes*
history."

The wind sheared an inch of ash off the cigarette. "The other
thing is that there is nothing much here of the struggle between

the Europeans, your ancestors in particular, and the Sinhalese. Isn't that the crux of the project?"

He let the butt fall from the ledge and re-entered the office. The door was made of thick glass but it took Stagg the merest swipe of the fingertips along its edge to close it behind him.

"Oh, let me just show you what the fellows' offices are like. I said I would do that. And thank you again for coming so early. I've got to be elsewhere by ten, my wife needs me."

They wound their way down the central staircase, marble, a soft white. The steps were deep and unusually broad, as if meant for the traffic of a major university library.

"I haven't exactly used the monk's methods," Stagg said. The stairwell was also rock, a speckled gray granite, and his words boomed. He lowered his voice. "But the problems with history, his ones, my ones, aren't totally unrelated. It's not a correspondence—that's too strong—but an affinity. Interpretation, evidence, expression, we're both figuring out how to do history. It would be one way of setting up the other lectures, since historiography itself is at issue. But there are other ways, yes."

"Right, well," Kames said as he reached the base of the stairs and led them out through a corridor of offices. They were each trimmed in dark wood on three sides and sheathed by a glass door, tinged blue, on the fourth. Only the last office on the right was in use. The man within, sleeves rolled loosely just below the elbows, clicked lazily at a mouse. *Principia Ethica* was open, facedown on the black desk, colored stickies poking out on the sides and bottom. "That's Max. A philosopher too. But we are going to leave him alone this very early morning."

The corridor merged with a wider walkway flanked by two larger offices with cherry doors ajar, both looking out onto courtyards through far walls of glass. Kames tapped the doorframe of one. "This just came open," he said. "Better, I think." Stagg peered in for his sake. Besides stacks of boxes not much could be seen, though there were the vaulted ceilings, and the walls were covered in a creamy paper that looked like cloth. "He's returning to academe, Chicago. Nothing as nice as this. I think we may have spoiled him."

They passed through to the atrium, which functioned as the central reading room. The ceiling, thirty feet up, was a single slab of glass, as were the walls to the left and right. Beyond one was the pond, still shaded. The water had more blue in it from here, and the surface, stirred by the wind, had more texture. The clouds shifted, redistributing the sunlight, and from the fringes of the pond a red cloud of rose finches ascended to the branches of the trees.

Beyond the other glass wall was a manicured lawn. Violets circled the bases of oaks. White rocks circled Japanese beeches. Fifty yards into the grass stood a high stone wall with a semi-circular entrance cut into it, and farther back, at what Stagg assumed was the edge of the property, he could see, just above the wall, the tops of trees arranged like the pickets of a fence.

The two of them sat at a large circular table in the middle of the atrium, empty of all but rows and rows of books on all sides.

"Did you need coffee?" Kames asked.

"No."

"Good. Well, the lecture. The approach to historiography."

"I think there is an affinity," Stagg said, "but that isn't the only reason to start with it. It does get into the domestic politics. Whatever tensions were present there, they weren't simply imported. There's an internal tension that gets complicated by external forces. My thought had been to begin with that. The distribution of power between the priesthood—a lot of their authority came from being the minders of history—and the king and his court. Then there's the warrior class, which overlaps with the court but isn't always allied with it, sometimes siding with the priesthood. Some of the rebellions seem to be spear-headed by it.

"I get into the present-tense of that internal struggle, which happens in the midst of external pressures. But I leave those offstage until later. The complications. The Europeans. The interplay."

Kames gave no response. He was waiting.

"There's also the other lecture I showed you, just before, which starts with Rutland's encounter with the monk. I just think... it's not as if our own problems, today, are mostly like this, with insides and outsides. There's no outside anymore. September 11, yes, then, maybe. And that jump-started something. Opened a door, as you put it.

"But now, no one now thinks these things in the news, the hall, the convention center, really have, or *have* to have, anything foreign about them. Maybe it's more economic than cultural now."

"Intra- rather than trans-. Right," Kames said. "Wherever there are conditions for friendship, really. And its other half, enmity. I think Schmitt was right about that much. But we can't assume economics is always the basis. We never could."

"Yeah. But money does make friends. Enemies too. Think about the museum—"

"Well that's certainly the way it's being set up in the press. It misses the mark, and pretty badly." He turned sharply to Stagg and stood. "You might be interested in something I've just written on this. I have it in the office."

"I am. And I read it yesterday."

Kames stayed on his feet. "So?"

Finches continued to ascend from the pond, not in groups now but singly.

"Shall we walk?" Kames said. "It is cold. The garden you haven't seen. It will bring back England. Cambridge. I remember Caius had something very like this, for the fellows. Here, though, we are all and only fellows. And you can walk on the grass if you want. Do you miss England?"

Stagg only smiled. He followed Kames past the shelves of

books, through the automatic doors and onto the pink pebble path cleaving the lawn. He wrapped his hands in the wool of his pockets as a high gust lashed his eyes.

"So you disagree with my little editorial," Kames said.

"Only about excluding the economics, in that case." Fog trailed from Stagg's mouth as he spoke. "But you don't really do that."

"No, that's right. But I make room for the possibility, even the probability, that it's not strictly relevant in this instance."

"That Celano is idle."

Kames paused on the path and Stagg did too. "That's more possible than it seems," Kames said. "I do think that, yes. Why shouldn't he be? He's very clever, I understand."

"But he would have a reason to retaliate."

"Well you haven't read very carefully it looks like. He and I and you have so many reasons."

"But after the pool hall—"

"It's their force that matters, when we talk about reasons, Carl. Their felt force really, how they appear to the parties involved at the moment of decision, under whatever circumstances prevail. It's got nothing to do with how rationally compelling they are *in fact*, how persuasive they *ought* to be found by them, given their interests. As if we even know, reliably know, what our own interests are. And that's putting aside how willing we are to reveal them to others. Do you see what I mean?"

They started to walk again.

"This is all very hard to calculate," Kames said. "So, in the face of this, we simplify. We abstract. We assume likenesses between parties, and in doing that steal all the nuance, the eccentricity, from them. From whatever's actually driven them to act, I mean, which is often many-faced and not infrequently touched by some element of delusion or self-deception. Even then, though, knowing how un-illuminating it is, we'll insist on the formulas: 'Certain sorts of actors are likely to find reasons of such-and-such a kind persuasive.'"

"That the sorts of people Celano backs are just the sorts you'd want disenfranchised, you mean?"

"That's one assumption we can count on people to make, yes. But it tidies us up, perfects us in a certain way. Celano too. I mean it falsifies us. Grounds, even very good grounds, for hatred don't guarantee hatred. That you've every right to draw a distinction doesn't mean you will. Political economy can make us mean if we're not careful, whether it's Smith or Marx or any of their descendants. We may be prejudiced. We certainly are, actually, and that's not always a bad thing. But we needn't be simple too. We're more interesting than that. I think Celano may be as well, and not just him. All ingeniously discriminating, in enmity, in friendship."

He stepped through the semicircle and into the open-air chamber, thirty yards square: a private garden, composed only of vines with blue flowers climbing along the trellises on the high stone walls. In the center, a ring of burnished wooden chairs faced out. Tightly clipped grass and a wide, heavily built well sat within the ring.

"Simple, right? The well produces very good water, though it isn't used much. It was here before the Institute was built, sealed over. So I thought we'd build the garden around it. The superstructure is a bit well-like, isn't it. That was Zirilella's idea, the architect. You get this changing configuration of light because of the gaps, like windows, cut into the east and west walls."

Brilliant blue patches capped thick pipes of light coming in through the gaps. They sat down in the ring of chairs, facing off in different directions, as the configuration didn't allow sight-lines to cross. The chairs were immovable and so wide that their arms didn't reach the rests. Only a race twice the size could have comfortably occupied them.

"But yes," Kames continued, "it's not necessarily untrue that

Celano's constituency ought to be discounted, given what they are *now*. But why should they remain as they are? Why should they want to? Wisdom is mostly acquirable. And if they transform themselves, well... You know, many of those rich old men at the fundraiser, giving their own money, *they* would be discounted too. Their problem is worse, in some ways. Commerce has deformed some of them, probably permanently. Character is flexible only up to a point. And some of those men are old dogs now. So, yes, they too have misconceptions about who they are. Who will disenchant them I don't know." Kames shook his head. "And all these simple lines. Between Celano and I. And Jenko. Must he also stand on the other side?"

"But they're being drawn all the same," Stagg said.

"Yes."

"And that will bring attention."

"It has."

"And you're prepared for that? A wrong impression made on the right people—"

"You know, I've always found it funny, the way you can draw all the wrong lines and still the picture you end up with is right in a way," Kames said. "And not just as a matter of chance. It's managed to catch something along the way. But it's a kind of rightness that can leave you casting about when it comes time to figure out what to do." He rubbed the blood back into his fingers. "No one is wrong to think there is passionate intensity around. Even among the best now. Yeats would be surprised."

In the light there was shadow and movement. The rose finches had clustered in the windows of the walls; their forms cut shapes out of the light. One shot down into the garden, its shadow contracting to nothing as the bird lighted on the very spot it had been thrown onto among the flowers and vines.

"Anyway, yes, I suppose the domestic situation is fraught enough," Kames said, no longer as ruminative and more conciliatory. "That makes this piece no worse a place to start, to understand how one layer of complication grafts onto another. But it's still very thick with exegesis. Perhaps we can backload some of that, even move it to a later talk, and you can build a bit on the relations between the various political bodies?"

"I'll see if I can find the right materials, from the journals, to interpolate. They might not exist. I'd rather not do it through exposition. But if the material is there, sure."

"Yes, I can see you are set on that. I think we'll give it a go, without a real frame then."

The cold had seeped through their clothes. They rose at the same time, facing away from each other. "Even historians need performance art," Kames said. "That must be your feeling."

25

BLUE TITS, A HALF-DOZEN OF THEM, JUST BELOW the window, hopping about on a branch in crisp Valley light filling the thinnest sky, translucent blue and shading off quickly at its upper edge toward a moon still sharp and clear and of a phosphorescent gray bespeaking death and life both.

Jen loved California for this light, and it was the memory of it, from her first trip out West, that clinched it for her. She was only three weeks removed now from her life back East, in the old apartment, under that ambivalent light that barely lit the place, or Halsley itself, it seemed like.

Whatever she thought of the light, though, she would have had to move—or be moved, forcibly. She'd learned from other actresses she'd met that the adult industry was really a possession of the West. On the East Coast, there wasn't enough work for them, and the scenes didn't pay as much as they should have. Since that first shoot with the smoothie, she'd done a few soft-core videos, ones where she'd only been called upon to kiss girls or self-penetrate. But the pay was modest and couldn't offset the rent and the booze (and the pills). She was also finding out it was sheer fantasy to think you could make real money in the business merely fucking yourself. A guy had to give it to you for that to happen.

At that point, she wasn't quite broke yet, but on the cusp of eviction anyway. The landlord wanted her out, her neighbors too, though she'd been so out of it, she could only partly recall the episodes that explained why. Had she managed to apologize to them, for any of it, or had she only dreamed that she had in drugged slumbers? Either way, they didn't want to hear it.

Carl had called a few times in those weeks. Early on, she picked up, choosing occasions when she was pleasantly buzzed rather than wasted to do so. She dodged his questions about her new job and steered their conversations toward a common love, books, especially the ancient ones. In the fourth and last of the calls, they talked about ancient history—Herodotus—for at least twenty minutes. It confirmed what she'd suspected, that he was marvelously well read in just the things she found most captivating.

She stopped picking up after that. She didn't care, or want to care, about what was happening with the case, with the one assaulting the whores. Talking to Carl made that harder. She didn't care to know about the other girls either, even Mariela. Nothing that really mattered bound them together. She wasn't interested in false connections. The only person she'd actually talked to with any fondness or frequency in Halsley lately was the Palestinian running the corner liquor store. She thought he had a good heart.

And then there was Carl, of course. That only gave her another reason not to answer. She didn't want to tell him about the drinking or have to lie to him about it either. But he kept circling back to it. When they'd spoken last, he'd asked about her drinking with a kind of curious concern that seemed to reach beyond his job. He didn't ask about anything else that way, not books, not even the case itself. It felt personal, and she was glad he asked but gladder not to answer. It wasn't his problem that booze had overcome her since her brother moved out, or that her parents refused to send any more money. (Was that Reed's doing? She hated to think so but felt it must be true.)

She also knew from their conversations, from what she'd said about the ancients, about pictures and profiles, the past and the future, that she'd won some bit of respect from Carl, this transparently educated man slumming it as an agent. She didn't want to give any of it back. She liked the gentle arrogance of his manner, actually, and the way she could put it under pressure from angles he didn't expect.

At that moment, though, she was in no position to do that. Things were too hard, that's why she'd moved out so suddenly. Maybe she would call him when she could stand, or else when she could barely crawl, things had gotten so bad. Not now.

Instead she focused on the light she lacked, that all of the East did, Bethesda too. Four days later, after her usual taper from vodka down to wine, she gave up the apartment—she wasn't leaving much behind, really—and for the second time in three years landed on a college friend's couch in Los Angeles. Jen had been a lot less scattered that first time, she knew this from the way her friend carefully observed her now.

Staying there kept Jen from returning to liquor, though, and in any case it took her only a little over a week to find a new home, in the San Fernando Valley, on a tip from a porn actress whose tits she'd sucked for a pittance back in Halsley. A group of girls all shared a huge house with a talent agent, Frank C., who was influential enough to guarantee a steady stream of work for them.

For the moment, Jen had the room to herself; another girl had left that week, for unexplained reasons. The other bed, also a queen, rested against the far wall and was made up primly in a bright red quilt with thick pillows in yellow cases resting on top of it. She hoped the bed would stay just that way, empty and pretty, at least for a while, until she settled in. Everything was gorgeous.

"Jen!" came the muffled yell from a man three floors down.

"Okay," she replied, in a voice she knew would not carry back to him. She was still in her underwear. In the third drawer of the dresser, nestled in a bed of socks and pajama bottoms, she found the only things she was careful to bring with her from Halsley: a row of plastic orange bottles, some of which had sat unopened for weeks during the last vodka binge. She took two pills from the leftmost; one pill from the second; skipped two bottles, irrelevant for the moment; took one from the next; skipped another—relevant, but too strong for the early after-noon—and tapped out two more tiny ones from the rightmost. She'd drunk nothing stronger than wine the past two weeks and the meds were a part of that story, though they did cloud her mind in a different way.

"Jen!"

"Okay," she replied with more urgency but no more volume. She pulled two hangers down off the garment rack next to the bed: very fine white fishnets that she sheathed her legs with, and a stretch dress that clamped around her, making a bra mostly unnecessary.

Through the hole left in the rack by the clothes she'd taken down, she looked into a mirror. It threw back only a generic California tart. She'd seen girls like this in Venice Beach at dusk, just after landing at LAX. Later, as she got acquainted with her new state, she would find other species of the genus in Malibu and Newport and Laguna.

Her face was already painted, pink dashes along the cheek-bones fading to a feathery white further down, near the jaw. She tied her hair back in a ponytail. Her eyebrows were care-fully shaped, black, narrow, and short, and the lashes around her eyes were conspicuously false. The chests of many of the girls in the house were as well, though her own, so far, was not. It was generous, given her size. She was a wispy one, uncommonly small-made. They'd had to size down the stockings.

Before the man could fire off her name again she stepped into the hall, shoeless. Downstairs they'd have all sorts of heels and boots.

"Honey, come down now," he said. "We need to see how we want this to work."

"Okay," she said. Finally her voice was loud enough, and traveling through few enough barriers, to reach him, Frank.

From another door a blonde emerged, short, small breasted, and holding a pair of blue pumps by the heels.

"Jeff's putting me in this scene too!" Amanda said. "Just more fun. Frank tell you about it?"

Jen bobbed her head vaguely. Amanda took her arm and trotted down the spiral staircase with her in tow. Her hand slipped from Jen's biceps to her forearm to her hand as the distance between them grew. She stopped and waited for Jen to catch up. "What else are you listing, besides boy-girl? Three-way? You want to work your way up, though, to the crazier stuff. Double-vag, things like that. That's what Liz and Annie tell me anyway. It keeps directors coming back. Once you've given it all away, it's harder getting hired. So you want to stretch it out, like a strip tease."

Jeff, the director, had four small DV cameras set up in the vast cube of a living room. It opened onto a patio of a nameless shape and a pool so large the Olympics immediately came to Jen's mind. No one was outside past the glass, just that crisp, directionless light hanging above the shallow hills the pool melted into. Their hardy greens and browns were flat and even and without shimmer.

There were several flat-roofed mansions in pastel pink, and one in stark maritime blue, probably looking much like the one she was looking out from, she guessed, though she'd never observed one of them like this, from a distance, from inside another. How long she would stay here she couldn't say, but it looked like a perfect beginning.

Frank met them at the base of the stairs, shoeless like her, but in Nantucket shorts. Thin white frames with rhomboid lenses sat on his pulpy nose, and his orange-toned skin looked thick and chafed. "So, these girls are new," he said, looking at them but talking to Jeff, who was squatting in the middle of the living room, fingertips spread wide for balance, examining the angles. The furniture was modular: segments of white leather, some backed, some not, that could be freely reconfigured.

"One's newish, one is really new, right?" Frank said. Amanda frowned in mock objection and squeaked past him toward the cameras with a peck on his cheek.

Jen stopped on the last step, leaving her level with Frank, who clasped the back of her head with one hand. His fingers ran above and below her ponytailed hair, the way one would hold a cigar. "You'll like Amanda," he said. "Doesn't matter if you've been with a girl before or haven't even thought about it. She's that sweet. And your check'll be that much bigger." He slid his hand down her neck to her shoulder and rubbed it. "This is the easiest sort of shoot because we just do it in the house itself. It's kind of a famous set now, this house. Shoots beautifully."

"We'll start outside by the pool and bring things in," Jeff said as he made his way over to them. "Oh, I like this," he said, gesturing at Jen. "The tiny ones. I'm Jeff."

"Lisa," Jen offered. She may have crossed a continent, but she was still the same working girl.

■　■　■

A round of Ativan set the mood. They laid Lisa out over one of the segments, with Amanda's cunt just inches from her face. This was new. Lisa hadn't truly been with a woman—kissing, fondling, didn't count—and the fragrance startled her. She knew it only on a man's breath, or from his cock. But then it was adulterated with saliva or pre-come, and often booze. She had of course caught a whiff of it on her hand, after she'd masturbated, though again, that was not the smell of cunt itself but of its secretions on a foreign body. When they were still tucked within the organ itself, she knew now something else was produced, a complex of sweat and skin, mucus and piss, all distilled and decocted in the airless space between the legs. Amanda's legs. There must be something common, though, she thought, to this musk and all others of womankind. At least a family resemblance.

Amanda slid down and Lisa's nose ran up to her clit. Their lips met in a cross. "Take it in," said the stunt-cock, as the girls had a habit of calling his kind. He grabbed her ponytail and thrust her nose down into the cunt.

"Just stick out your tongue," Amanda said. Lisa's tongue came out. Amanda took the ponytail from the stunt-cock and steered Lisa's head, and with it her tongue, into her. The taste was also a complex, and it seemed to Lisa utterly uninferable from the smell. She didn't mind either of them, really.

He buried his cock in Lisa. Few if any johns had a cock like this, none she could recall, and this was with the benefit of muscle relaxants. While he fucked Lisa from behind the stunt-cock thumbed her asshole open. After some work he got three fingers in. He pulled them out, spit on the asshole, evacuated the cunt, and filled her asshole in a single thrust that, for all the Soma, drew a sharp yelp from Lisa, though Amanda's crotch muffled it somewhat. The two of them pinned Lisa's face there until she felt less from both orifices. The sense of taste seemed to disappear from her mouth, the touch from her asshole, except when he would pull out to make it gape for the cameras, which she would later find out it did. Frank said she was a gaper.

First there would be the ache of decompression. On reentry she would be struck by a pain like a paper-cut made by thick stock, the unsealed envelope from a luxury stationary set maybe. The cock would rub the cut crossways as it entered, until the head was past the fissure. Then only the smooth base of the cock would worry it, a background irritation she soon forgot.

"You want to clean this up, sweetheart?" the stunt-cock said to Amanda. She let go of the ponytail and took the pressure away from Lisa's face, one of two pressures she'd been feeling. The second disappeared as he pulled out of her.

Amanda stuck her tongue into Lisa's gape first. This felt like nothing to Lisa, not just because of the Soma, but because of the size of the gape the stunt-cock had created. He pulled Amanda away by the hair, replacing the tongue with his cock. Then he slipped the cock down Amanda's throat until sputum came up.

"You taste so good," Amanda said to her. Lisa didn't know what to say. So she said nothing as she lay there, the leather ottoman holding her up, the stunt-cock going back and forth between her gape and Amanda's mouth.

There would be no ass to mouth for Lisa, though. Frank didn't want to spook her. She'd only been in the house a couple of weeks and this was her first taste of hardcore.

The stunt-cock pulled out and brought Lisa around with her ponytail to where Amanda was. She wobbled and tripped to the ground; the Soma was turning her to jelly.

Flanked by the girls, their faces on either side of his cock, he stroked himself off. Lisa could smell her own bowels on his cock. They were familiar to her from the smoothie shoot back East. He kept jerking while the girls waited. Amanda squeezed her tits together and gargled his balls sympathetically for a while to encourage him. But he was tiring. He switched hands and his strokes got jerkier. Amanda was starting to look as if she felt sorry for him. Lisa was having trouble simply staying on her knees; the pills wanted her to lie down.

Eventually his face began to bob with belief. All three of

them brightened. In an impromptu maneuver, he got to Lisa's side and burst across both their faces. The two girls separated their cheeks and long strings of come fell on their thighs. Come hung from Lisa's chin. Amanda clipped it off with her lips. A beat went by that felt like a call for reciprocation. Lisa slurped the come off of Amanda's gummed eyelids. The blonde giggled and pecked Lisa on the lips with guts on her breath.

26

LIKE A TAMBOURINE CONTINUOUSLY SHAKEN, GO-
ing on twenty minutes now. This, the sound of crashing keys.
They bristled from the ring in copy-proof cuts, circular, tubu-
lar, square. The brassy rattle of the keys against the dashboard
had been almost pleasant at first, softening the rumble of the
ancient jeep's engine. It distracted Ravan from another rattling,
of his body, as they drove over the mud saucers of the flats of
Death Valley, the common origin. Now he'd reached a second
phase. Rather than diverting him, the jangle melded with the jarring of his viscera, encouraging the sickness.

"Why so many?" Ravan said with his palms flat on the scarred
dash, eyeing the keys.

"Lots of doors in the national labs," Menar said.

"No, but why did you bring them all over with you from
India?"

"I didn't think not to, really."

"Well, you could separate the key for the ignition."

"But then this lovely music would go," Menar said, gesturing
at the keys. "Wouldn't you mind?" The suggestion of a smile
breached his face. Only a relative could see this.

"No."

"Okay, I will do when we get there. Ten minutes. The way back will be a whisper if you like—except for this yappy engine, of course. I just hope we'll get to play baccarat before I leave. I've never been to Vegas, you know."

The station appeared ahead, a C-shaped aluminum tube with entries on both ends of it and a broad pair of doors in the recessed middle, raised up like a garage. Everywhere the ground was paved in hexagonal mud scales, a chemical signature of the valley soil that produced this kinetic signature in passing vehicles.

Ravan looked in the rearview mirror and saw nothing but dust.

"Your NOAA people tell me these stones—see that one?—they leave trails. Only no one has ever seen or recorded them move. That can't be right."

"I really don't know."

"Sailing stones."

"Yes."

"They also mentioned an unplayable golf course somewhere in the valley."

"Did you bring your clubs then. For the challenge."

"What people you work for, Ravan."

"With."

They exchanged a family smirk, Ravan's wryer than Menar's. A resemblance held them together, the smirks. Otherwise the brothers did not look much alike, except for a shared softness in the eyes. Menar was the taller, by half a head, perhaps 6'3". He had a long, clean-shaven face with a sharply tapering chin. His skin was a pale tan, a shade or two lighter than Ravan's, and he wore his hair short and neat, the inverse of his brother's.

"It's a craggy salt bed," Ravan said. "The Devil's Golf Course."

"Well, as I say…" Menar trailed off, or referred back to something Ravan couldn't pinpoint, something indefinite, a general idea, maybe, or several at once, even an infinite conjunction. Menar said a lot when he was in the mood for it.

They pulled into the station under marbled, pregnant skies.

"Well timed," Menar said.

"Dr. Peshwa, we are so pleased to have you here." A bearded man, not so old, in a light blue button-down and dark blue jeans approached them as they hopped out of the jeep. Two more men stood within the station.

"We have a live feed set up so the rest of the team can see back East," the bearded man said.

"Ah, hello Michael," Menar said. He squinted and twisted his face. "And please—it's Menar. You don't call this one doctor, do you?" His hand trailed back toward Ravan, who approached from the back of the jeep with two white duffle bags.

"So the matériel has arrived, I take it," Menar said.

"Just over there," Michael said. "Dispersers on the left, seeders on the right."

"Slakers and makers," Ravan said softly as he passed by his brother with the bags.

The garage held a central server, four workstations, a bank of laptops, and a large monitor some hundred inches wide. Beyond the workstations was the storage and lab facility. Ravan set the duffels on the ground next to the weather missiles crowding the racks.

Menar stooped and lifted a seeder up to his chest. It was the height, if not quite the weight, of a dwarf. He cradled it in his arms. The head of the missile, the end of the rocket stage, was ringed by six smaller missiles, copper darts, each about a foot long. The two technicians moved to help him but he nodded them off. He set the rocket roughly on the central steel table in the lab. It clanked and rolled several degrees, planting on a fin. Michael trotted to the back wall and switched on the lights above the table, which were startlingly bright. They turned the silver rocket a watery white.

"It doesn't take much of a payload to activate clouds, or to dissolve them either," Menar said, tapping one of the darts. "It used to be thought you needed to dump huge quantities to get anything going. That was actually a mistake. Too much agent retards the reaction. You just need to get the formula right. That, and the mechanism of distribution. My father sent you the specs."

"Some, yes," Michael said. "A one-pound charge in each?"

"That's right. The tiniest warhead. You can launch them from the shoulder too, if need be, when a platform isn't practical. Easier with two men, but a strong one can do it alone. On-board altimeters activate the charges, and rather than explode, they make the powder, treated antimony, smolder and stream smoke." He looked at his brother. "So, you've got these set to discharge at what, seven thousand feet? Eight thousand?"

"I was going to send them up to six, to eight, and to ten," Ravan said, "one at each elevation, and then draw them right across."

"That sounds right," Menar said. He pointed to the rack of missiles and looked at Michael: "These are based on the latest Starstreak, you know. The Mark III. Can you see the resemblance? I don't know exactly how much bleed-through there is from military technology to your atmospheric R & D. I'm assuming rather a lot," he said with a gesture of outspread fingers and tightly closed eyes. "Just like us." He shook his head with vigor and a smile. "You and the Brits appear to share the Starstreak now. Thales builds them, in Belfast, but Lockheed's helped tweak it for your army. Actually," Menar said after a pause, "I have seen quite a lot of them deployed in Kashmir, and in Pakistan, launched by the allies, principally the two of you. More versatile than the old Stinger. Good for striking lightly armored vehicles, low-lying helicopters. Defeats jamming. No infrared needed. And with the darts, the odds of making contact expand." He caressed one of the darts. "They were certainly effective there, we can all agree, I think."

Michael looked to one side of Menar and nodded slowly without saying anything. He sucked in his lower lip, drawing the blond whiskers of his mustache down past it.

"And now they've proved more versatile still," Menar said.

Michael smiled and fixed Menar's eyes. "They have, yes," he said.

"One more use for them, and again, it's all in the darts. Did you know any of this?" Menar asked.

"Not exactly, not really," Michael said. "But what your father has managed to do here is very interesting." The two techs stirred and nodded along.

"He's a gift. And it's much more than interesting." Menar paused again, a habit of his. "The formulation is mostly his work. Delivery, how to aerate the substance, that was up to me. That's why I talk of the rockets."

"Well that's not really true," Ravan said. "You've done plenty with the formula. And it's nothing without distribution. It's really all one thing, not many."

"Is it?" Menar said. Again there was the suggestion of a smile on his face, invisible to all but his blood, Ravan. "You know, I think it would be possible to do both today."

"Both?" Michael cocked his head slightly.

"Seeding and dispersal. The same storm, the same patch of it even. We've done it in parallel before, at a distance of some miles. We precipitated a cloudbank in one place and vanished it in another. But why not try the very same cloud. Let's seed this one now. After we have it going, we'll switch it off, scatter it. We can try, anyway. It's not foolproof. None of it is, actually. There are definitely still unknown variables in play. But we've reduced their number more than anyone. More than the Chinese. More than you too, otherwise I wouldn't be here. We are far beyond chance now." He looked at the techs. "Shall we get these outside, then, before the water falls?"

Michael looked slightly confused.

"Before it comes down on its own," Ravan said, pointing through the opaque roof to the heavily clouded skies beyond.

"Ah," Michael said.

The technicians each picked up a seeder and headed outside, ducking under the back doors before they had fully risen. Michael and Ravan helped move them while Menar took out a laptop from one of the duffels and logged onto the network. "Oh, good work," he said as Ravan left with a missile in his arms. It drew a smile from his brother.

The two launch platforms were side by side, just behind the station. They looked like squat traffic lights, but without the lights. There were only holes where they should have been. The wide poles, painted in a textured, heat-resistant green, were moored deep in the dirt, far below the mud tiles, with support struts fanning out from the base along the flats. Thick rectangular panels with three holes, each a foot deep and stacked vertically, hung off one side of the poles. The panels could be remotely flattened out to any degree, and the poles themselves could be rotated.

Low-lying stratus clouds, vertically developed, hung overhead. A tiered deployment of makers, as Ravan had suggested, would be ideal. "So, rotate them out ten degrees each," Menar said. "That should get us enough of a gap between them."

Michael and the technicians stood between the launchers while Ravan dialed in the platform angles from his terminal. They whirred in opposite directions, turning the warheads away from both each other and the three men standing between them.

"Better to get some distance for launch, I think," Michael said, withdrawing into the station, the techs in tow. He positioned himself over Menar's shoulder, near the edge of the lab table, which Menar was using as a seat. The deployment code he'd been tweaking on the flight over from New Delhi, the algorithms that charted the missiles' course, the darts' sub-course, and the moment of payload ignition, flashed across the screen of his laptop. Ravan thought of their father, Menar Sr., as he watched his brother make final adjustments in front of the matrix of data. The other three lab men, just as in Ravan's childhood, stood quietly awed by the maestro.

Menar scanned the last of the figures. One final look out at the platforms and then a glance at Ravan: "So, here we go." Everyone but Menar moved to the edge of the station's open doors.

The tail of the first seeder went a deep, dark red. Suddenly it was orange and shimmering the air as the rocket took flight with a rowdy hiss that quieted as it ascended. They watched the narrow contrail form, lither than any airplane's, tethering the rocket to the launcher like a harpoon.

On entry its rumble was muffled by the cloud. At just that moment, with another keystroke, Menar deployed the second rocket. It went up just like the first except for the debris that fell from it: a ring of metal, red with heat. "Was that from the platform?" Menar asked.

The second contrail took shape just below the first, which had, owing to the mix of fuel and heavy atmospheric conditions, congealed in place. The final seeder, which was meant to prepare the lower third of the cloud, fired off cleanly and revived the fading hiss of the second rocket just before it too died in the clouds. Menar had adjusted the platform panel so its path fell between the other two, but lower, creating a configuration of contrails that looked, when viewed from the monitor, which drew its signal from cameras stationed beneath the platform, like a V in three dimensions, thousands of feet deep along the z-axis.

The rocket stage of the final missile fell to earth as the six darts parted ways. They fanned out in smooth parabolic arcs until they ran parallel to the cloud base, just beneath its surface, and it was only their color, a sharp yellow from the smoldering antimony, that made their slender contrails visible against the grayscale backdrop of clouds.

A star like an asterisk formed as the darts diverged from the origin at speed. The contrails grew pale, their color thinned by cloud as the darts sliced through the gauzy base, burrowing further by the second. The lines gave out and the star peaked when the darts were too deep to see.

"Eighteen darts make three stars," Menar said. "The other two, at the higher elevations, we can't see, but they're there. And that's it." He scrolled through the onscreen values, the mathematical trace of the darts.

"This is the definition of a warm-water cloud," he said. "It must be a hundred degrees today, and without the sun. If there are any supercooled droplets at all in that cloud, there aren't many."

Menar went outside and the others followed.

"The darts run very hot," Menar said, "creating tiny updrafts. The antimony particulate is taken up in them, you get greater diffusion. That's the root of natural condensation. Then the binding of particulate with water microdroplets, the coalescence threshold drops, and the microdroplets suddenly turn macro. No simulation of ice crystal nuclei at all," he trailed off. "That would be pointless in a cloud like this, it's so warm. There's nothing to crystallize." Menar turned and said, "You can send the drone through again, Michael, and see the difference we've made already."

Michael had kept the tiny unmanned plane in a holding pattern nearby, continuously recording data with a battery of sensors for other experiments carried out earlier in the day, but ready for use should they need it here. He made a call to the pilot and in a few moments it cut through the cloud like a larger dart, a desert tan to the dart's reflective copper, flying upward until it emerged from the top. "Temperatures are up and rising," Michael confirmed as he joined the others outside. The cloud thickened and yellowed, the bottom edge darkened, the black bands widened.

"You know, we do use—Ravan has probably told you—a propagation approach sometimes," Menar said. "Identify a pocket of supercooled droplets, get it to overtake the rest of the cloud, freeze the whole thing. We've also tried creating that pocket ourselves, if we can't find one. Nitrogen flares—"

Just then Michael's eyes disappeared behind a splatter of water. He pulled the glasses from his face with a startled grin and grabbed Menar's shoulder.

"Well then," Menar said. "We should probably go back inside. These artificial rains can be monstrous."

The drops were sharply formed and proportioned to a monsoon. They burst on the skin like tiny balloons, and the water released felt almost sticky. There was an uncommon discreteness to the downpour. It produced the sort of precisely articulated patter on the mudflats, like a continuous drumming of the fingers, one might expect from a much harder, more resonant surface, like the aluminum roofing of the station (though the earth had more bass to it).

The saucers started to come apart. Fissures appeared and filled with water that overflowed the cracks running like grout lines between the mud tiles. The crisp attack of the rain slowly gave way to a gurgling.

Menar leaned up against the steel table with his hands wrapped around its edge.

"Well," Ravan said softly, sitting down at the terminal directly behind the table. The storm had transfixed the NOAA men, holding them where they were.

"Yes, well," Menar said. "If you hadn't seen this before, you'd be just as stunned as they are."

As the storm swelled, the raindrops lost their form and

merged into ropes. The saucers were invisible now beneath a roiled, viscous layer of water, the rain falling faster than the ground could take it in.

"This is striking, Menar, really striking. Especially with warm water," Michael said, turning away from the storm to face him. Water ran into the station in thick rivulets, amplifying the brightness of the corrugated steel floor.

"But I am starting to worry this could become a flood," he continued. "We should close these doors or—"

"Well if you've seen enough, let's switch it off," Menar said. "As I say, we've never dispersed a cloud we've provoked into storming, certainly not like this. I do wonder if the two agents will interact in some way. They shouldn't. But let's see. Close the doors, I think. The monitor will serve."

The techs brought the door back down, muting the falling water. Menar re-adjusted the position of the eastern platform, five degrees to the west. The seeders were identical to the dispersers in appearance, save for the darts, which were a darker copper and slightly larger, carrying a 1.5 pound payload.

"We call these dispersers 'slakers' for a couple of reasons," Menar said. "One is that, though the cocktail's complicated, unslaked lime—treated lime—is a vital ingredient. But much less of it than is usually necessary to make it a desiccant or a significant source of heat. In bulk of course it's deeply toxic, burns the eyes, and so on. But we've managed to get round that problem with the auxiliary compounds we've bound it with."

He tapped the track-pad and the first rocket ascended in just the manner of the seeders. But the digital monitor presented it differently, more instructively, and in peculiar ways, more viscerally, than direct sight could, odd as that sounded. Under magnification the contrails seemed more deeply textured and bubbly, and also discontinuous, having a patterned structure of thicknesses harnessed to each other: a cotton rope that looked as if it were being thrown to the sky. The launch cameras caught a sun-bright gleam of orange, then gray smoke, then a missile-tipped contrail.

"Deployment's pretty much the same," Menar said. As before, the first rocket slid through the base of the cloud, on its way to the upper reaches. Just as it disappeared, Menar sent the next rocket up.

"The separation between launches, is there a reason for that?" one of the assistants asked. "Do the upper layers need to be activated first?"

Menar seemed surprised he could speak. He smiled. "Yes. Nothing technical, though. It's just so the rockets and darts don't collide. It's happened in trials, darts going straight into missiles. No charge in them, but the impact and the heat exploded the fuel tanks. Just a mess."

"And one more," Menar said, releasing the final rocket. "Here we'll see something. Limelight."

"Limelight?" Michael said. "Oh, as in—"

"As in limelight. Candoluminescence."

"Right, yes."

"A real show," Ravan said.

"Actually, raise the doors," Menar said.

"Really?" Michael asked.

"Yes, why not? You can't be worried about this little shack, can you? Surely you've got the funding to bear a little water damage. In the name of science. Or art."

"No, of course we can." The assistants opened it and a small wave of water rolled in, giving out after a few feet.

"Oh, that's not so bad," Menar said. "Now look."

They could see virtually nothing of the third rocket, the sky was so heavy with rain and black clouds. Then its contrail bloomed a supersaturated white at its far end. It seared their eyes. Squinting, they watched the light dilate, divide in six. The rocket fell away, limp, useless, and dark as a new star grew against the storm. This time the smoke was terracotta, and the radiating darts luminous, which turned the clouds directly above their path a greater intensity of white, and, through contrast, darkened the more distant parts.

"As I say, limelight," Menar said.

The NOAA staff looked on as water pooled around their shoes. Absolute white and sizzling in their ears, the darts broke the plane of the cloud and dug into the storm. The men watched these haloed dots of white, still surprisingly bright, as they continued to race away from each other, though the rust-colored lines of the star itself disappeared, cloaked now by cloud.

Their eyes dealt more easily with the veiled limelight, and they continued to follow the expanding circle of lights. When the darts had finally exhausted themselves, they marked the vertices of a star twice the size of the terracotta one they'd just painted on the underside of the storm above.

Menar looked back at the laptop. The spent darts would be descending now, unlit and unseen.

"So let's see," he said. It was still storming hard and the mudflats outside had become a lake of red, as they did in flash floods. (Nearby Furnace Creek also reported unusually heavy rains.)

Ravan thought he could hear the beginnings of a decrescendo. The roiling waters filled the ears less fully now, and it was easier, it seemed, to attend to the rest of his senses. The first thing he noticed were his sopping shoes. The lab assistants pulled heavy towels from a storage closet and threw them to the ground, working them around with their feet, mopping up what they could.

"You can give the drone another pass," Menar said. Michael radioed again with the orders. "It must be quite hot now."

They all sensed the diminishing patter of water on the roof. Outside on the flats, the ropes withered to beads, first swollen and oblong, but then, sooner than seemed reasonable, just tiny dots, specks.

"Very much hotter," Michael said, staring into a screen.

The cloud itself was losing substance, not through collapse but expansion. As it distended it turned wispier, vaporous, ever more transparent, the gray and black ribbons seeming to lighten as they dissolved into simple air.

The lightest drizzle persisted, but the extent of the transformation left the NOAA people nodding vaguely to one another and pointing up at the faltering cloud.

"What you have here is something real," Michael said without looking at Menar, who was seated on the table, playing with his laptop, his mouth bent this time into an insouciant smirk visible to anyone who cared to see. Ravan, shoeless now, joined the other assistants looking out onto the watery flats, his heart beating harder but not faster.

27

IN A LIGHTLESS ROOM HE AWOKE TO HER WEIGHT, a leg strewn across his, a palm planted in his chest, a chin tucked above his collarbone, a mouth set against his neck. She'd rather he not wake. He knew this. Probably she thought this was the surest way of stopping him. At the very least she'd be hoping he'd wink at her delayed arrival, once again past midnight.

"How was the night?" Stagg's voice was uneven and weak from sleep. It pleased him not to have to simulate this, though he would have, had he been awake, say, for hours in the dark, waiting.

"Good," she whispered.

For a moment he let Renna believe that was it, and she began to take the long, even draughts of air that bring sleep.

"Good," he said into the silence.

He put his hand over hers, the one on his chest, and she rubbed his fingers, pressed her lips more firmly against his neck, but without a pucker so it made no sound. Thalidomide kisses, she called these. He'd been the first to offer them, nameless then, and she disliked them, shuddered when he placed them on her cheeks in jest. Tonight, though, she must have thought they made a kind of sense.

He squeezed her fingers together, running the tips over one another, and put his free hand behind the knee of the leg that ran across his own.

"I got you the cinnamon-lox thing," he said. "Sounds disgusting. But it's on the desk."

"No it's *so* good. I had some," she said. "Why are you so nice to me?" This time she kissed him properly on the neck, held his skin between her teeth. She slid her hand down his stomach. He caught it.

"And those three were how?" Though no louder, his voice was more substantial now, more committed to wakefulness.

"Just rehearsing." Her voice was firming up too, though reluctantly. "There was marked-up staff paper everywhere. The way your papers are. I think I stepped on some of them in the dark just now." She scratched the hair on his chest. "You're not mad, I hope."

The laugh he gave was inaudible, but the tightening of his chest was enough for her to know.

"Ravan can read music?" he asked.

"Yes. And well. He's as serious as Edward."

"And Li."

"He wasn't reading. Not sure he can't though."

"And you can, still?"

"Sort of. But I would never have been able to read this stuff. Partly it was so heavily corrected. There were slashes of ink everywhere, strikeouts, notes that had been written over, woven right into the passages. So it was hard to read off what was left through all of that. But even if it had been clean, the notation is just really weird. I think a lot of it they've just made up, for all the microtonal things.

"They're working on this long piece, symphony length, with some parts that are electronic, tape loops, things Edward's always been interested in," she continued. "There are all these sweeping lines linking sections, and little scratchings and symbols in the margins and between staffs, for notes that don't belong on the lines. A bunch of different sharps and flats too, and a bunch of fermatas, caesuras, which made the page that much more crowded and weird."

"I'm supposed to know what those are?"

"Caesuras? Well, I guess there's no reason you should. But you do, don't you."

This time his laughter made it to their ears.

"And the sound?"

"I'm still thinking about it. Sort of a wall, I guess. But it felt like it was taller and wider than the room. It's hard to explain. Like it was only part of a whole that wasn't all there to be heard. But really it was the whole. That was it."

"And?"

"And... it sounded strange at first. The chords. But as you got used to the structure, the motion, that sense of incompleteness, it sounded even stranger, but in the details now, the textures." She paused. "Ravan's done a lot of the writing, I think. Or at least the rewriting. It didn't look like Edward's handwriting, or only partly, so I'm guessing."

"But it was only notes."

"You can still tell someone's handwriting."

"Clearly."

"They work together in this weird way," she said, ignoring the minor provocation, which was her way. "They write over each other's music, so the score is just dripping with ink by the end of it. That's what it looked like. Sometimes one of their hands is dominant, these heavy marks fixing the other's sketchier ones. In other parts it's the other way around. They just keep rescoring this way, going back and forth, without going to clean paper, and somehow they can still read the result. It's a true composite, though. It's rare."

"Hm."

"And what did you do?" she asked. "Did you call the hooker again? What's her name, Jen?"

"No."

"She's okay now?"

"I don't really know. I don't see how she could be though."

"But is she *cute*, Carl?" Renna had never been jealous of another woman in her life, and her glibness about it grated on him.

"I thought," Stagg said.

There was a long silence.

"You thought what?"

"No, that's what I did tonight. Think."

"Just like this?" She patted his chest with the hand that was still under his, again sidestepping the tacit rebuke, the conversation it might open.

"Basically. With the lights on, part of the time."

"Did you revise at all though?"

"I don't think I need to. It's more about order, placement. I'll just read that piece on exegesis later in the series. Really I'm changing course a little, and I'm not sure if Kames will like it. A new introduction. But I'm not going to try to sell him on it yet."

"Do you ever think, though, Carl, that at least for now, that maybe you should withdraw?"

"What? Because why?"

"Because what your boss said about Kames, what you told him Kames said to you. It's possible, isn't it?"

"It's hard to say exactly what Kames meant, though. Penerin's paranoid. And there are three days left now till the first talk, Renna. Nothing's going to change in that space. And easy for you to say."

"I'm only worried! I don't know why you have to make everything into something besides love." She made a fist under his hand and thumped his chest with it before flipping away from him.

"There'll only be one lecture, if you're right," he said in a cooler voice. "More reason to do things the way I want, I guess. And if there's only going to be one, it should be about my family, and the escape. That's what Kames was saying he wanted anyway."

"Maybe," she said. By the shifting of the bed he could tell she had pulled her knees up to her chest, as she did when she was fed up, or worried, or tired, depending.

"Maybe what?"

She said nothing. He drew breath.

"How was Larent?" he asked.

"Fine." She was curt.

"He asked you over?"

"He and Ravan."

"You don't know Ravan."

"Edward told me he wanted me to come too."

"Li asked you as well, I guess."

"No."

"You don't know him?"

"I do. You know that. Edward just didn't mention him."

"And I guess you have to accept every invitation."

"You can't do this, Carl. I offered to cancel."

"You don't want to be rude."

"You can be such an asshole." Her eyes were rolling, he knew this. That he couldn't see this didn't matter.

He rolled on his side, toward her, and pulled her to him with one hand between her breasts. "An asshole?" he said. She squirmed and thrust her legs out straight and grabbed his hand. "I thought you can't be rude," he said. He slid his hand up her chest to her long and graceful neck and held it without a hint of compression. "Just to me, I guess."

Her own hand, still on his, went limp in a familiar way. Her lips ran across his cheek as she turned her face toward him, as if it were possible to look him in the eye in the dark. Their lashes touched as she blinked. Her eyes, millimeters from his, they'd be deathless now, earth-inheriting and faintly defiant about it. There would be that suggestion of a snicker in them. And why shouldn't she look at him? The dark was as good as the light for what she was searching for.

"What do you get from this?" he said, keeping his hand where it was. She turned past his face until he could feel her breath on his ear. He thought she might bite him, so hard he'd need stitches to close the gash.

"I thought you weren't going to drink on your own anymore," she said. "This doesn't happen otherwise."

"From him."

"Nothing. I'm not getting anything from him. There's just history, that's all."

"And what does that have to do with now?" His grip may have tightened.

"Don't talk to me."

"Oh, but you love to chat."

She lunged for the light but he held her just out of reach. Her fingers grazed the metal string dangling beneath the bulb and it struck the lamp rhythmically, four times.

"I am with you every night," she said.

"And our time together. We're either unconscious or fucking. Day or night."

"I am *always* thinking of you. I talked about you till they told me to stop."

"That's thoughtful."

"This isn't going to work like this. He's my oldest friend."

"There's nothing wrong with him. He's fine. I just don't get what he does for you."

"Do you really not get friendship? Is that actually possible?"

"If it were for the magazine it would be different."

"Do you really not understand it?"

He took her face, which was pressed down into the pillow,

in his free hand. He torqued it toward him and stared into the spots where he thought her eyes must be. They could have been closed.

"Do you get that he's nothing next to me? I really don't give a fuck if he's played with the Concertgebouw, or that he composes shit that's too ridiculous to fit on a staff."

"I do get that," she whispered. "And you are *such* an asshole for making me say it again." It was his hand that went limp now. She sat up and pushed herself back against the headboard. He waited for the light but it never came.

"He has qualities," she said in a tone that had turned deathless like her eyes. "He has gifts. Different from yours. Not as great maybe. But he has them. You've said that. You'd be disappointed in me if he didn't."

"The pale-faced fag with the bow in his hand."

"He can be charming, in this soft, quiet way. Elegant. I think you even like that about him, though you won't admit that now. And he would never talk about you like this, he doesn't have the crassness, the churlishness in him."

"Churls. Okay."

"You wouldn't think it's possible. You can outshine him when you want to, in every way that matters most to me. But you don't seem to want to anymore. You'd rather be *this*. It makes no sense, but you've chosen it, you keep choosing it."

"I haven't earned the right to this feeling, you mean? Of course I haven't. But you wouldn't think of me like you do if I didn't already believe that something, capital-s Something, is going to come from me, and that it isn't all that far off now. And that it's all a fait accompli, before I can prove that it is, or that there's any such thing as one."

"I know."

"That's the balls of it, and the trouble with it. Justifying—"

"What?" she taunted. "Justifying what?"

"I don't know. Contempt. You know, there's this story that

back before everything, before he had the books, Wittgenstein told Russell how distressed he was, justifying his contempt for the philosophers around him. For all the ones who couldn't or wouldn't clear it all away, untie themselves from everything they knew or thought they did, and try to recover the world from that mess. Justifying, because he hadn't recovered it himself yet. But the way he was going at it, untangling knots, it was only a matter of time. But he couldn't hold himself to a standard that demanding, ask that of himself, without the contempt. It was the fuel. They were one thing. However fucked up that is, they were."

A long silence followed.

"Wittgenstein," she said.

"Whatever. Naipaul then. The feeling came long before the right to it, that's the point. And if you see me as in any way the same as Larent—"

"But you just said how, basically. What he's trying to do in music, isn't that untangling knots?"

"No, still, if you see me as operating on the same *plane* as that meek shit—or any of these literary men you go on about, their pathetic shticks. Charming, right." He felt himself beginning to flail.

"Look, I don't," she said. "I don't. And I know who you are, what you are. That's why we're here. But I can't keep telling you who. My angel."

"I am always, always waiting," he said. His voice was brittle and dark now. "Always there's something between you and me. Does it make sense to you that I, not me, really, just anyone like me, should be waiting? And fine if you run into a greater mind on the way home, but not this effete—. He can't be why I'm waiting. Or any of the others. But if you find a Wittgenstein out there, yeah, by all means, take him home. Or bring him over. I'll suck him off too."

"He was a fag, right? Wittgenstein?"

"One way to clear all the dumb cunts out of your life."

"You can't really think you can talk to me like this. Maybe the hooker, I don't know. But not me."

The bed rocked sharply. What came next was the sound of glass breaking glass, two ways, a doubling. The ambient hum of night entered and it made the room seem somehow blacker.

He pulled the sheets over his head after that, just as the switch snapped and the light annihilated something. Now there was the sound of cloth sliding, the swoosh of a long zipper, the rustle of laces, the clack of boot heels on wood and the hushed click of a gently closing door.

28

JENKO'S INTELLIGENCE WOULD ALWAYS BE GREAT-
er. He had more eyes than Penerin, and they were trained without training. His men had grown up in these untoward neighborhoods. It lent them the kind of easy attunement that the
state's agents could never quite match.

Jenko's stake in the matter was also greater, which gave him
the advantage of urgency, one the police couldn't have felt,
not for this demographic. Half the maimed hookers were his,
though even the victims wouldn't have known they belonged
to him. Jenko operated at a remove. His girls answered directly
to a committee of pimps he'd handpicked, or rather, that his
assistant had. Two removes then.

Tending to the beaten girls cost Jenko much; but then, there
had to be some benefit to working for him, splitting their earn-
ings with him instead of going out on their own (though that
had its own risks). He would pay for the girls' hospital care, and
then for some time afterward their rent, nursing them back to
health. Erin, Mariela's friend, was the last of his that had been
hurt, many weeks ago. She was better now, back to maximum
capacity, seeing one or two johns most days of the week.

It took longer than expected to identify the source of this

cost, the one troubling Jenko's girls. But in time the profile his men developed, the portrait they painted, turned singular. Its subject, Lewis, came into view, though he remained as obscure as ever to Penerin and his agents.

How to deal with him, though? A warning of some sort? A tit-for-tat beating? The only rule Jenko insisted on observing in this business: no deaths.

"So that's him," Aaron said. "Lewis Eldern." It was midday, and he and Jenko were in their not-yet-reopened pool hall. Its windows were still boarded. Aaron was Jenko's assistant, the one he used for the operations Jenko suspected his business partners, especially Celano, might not smile on. Prostitution, say.

In a Platonic sense, the old friends shared a politics. But Celano's blood was bluer, his money purer, so the ordinary world, the one of flux, did less violence to his ideals.

This is how Jenko explained the complications. Certainly he himself believed the country had failed the weak. He was in fact only a few generations removed from having that very same grievance, though against another country (Slovenia), on another continent. Equally, he was doing what he could to arrange the world in a way that fortified labor, though he left the details to men like Celano. He'd spent far too much time and money on Celano's political projects for that to be gainsaid.

But he also believed he was part of a family enterprise. He drew no line between his own fortune, his father's, and his father's father's, and felt more than a little duty to keep it in good health. And a fortune, a business, an empire that wasn't growing could never be in good health. So he'd done his part and expanded it, overseas, in America, in partnership with other developers like Celano.

It was true that the Jenko empire wasn't pretty from all angles. It hadn't been in the beginning either, when it was just in London. There were girls then too. But it had to be said, Jenko thought, that until the state might be remolded to provide decently for these sex laborers, he was giving them a livelihood, as well as protection. There was something stark about the arrangement, of course, nothing like ideal, but this was what Celano didn't understand: the world that is has a claim on us that the world that might be must settle before it can come into being.

Anyway, on the broader issue, Celano must have felt the same duty toward his own father's business concerns, to keep things growing. He was just lucky they were cleaner, purely in construction and real estate, or at least seemed to be. There were things Celano, his dear friend, must be keeping from him, after all. What exactly was he doing in Spain now, for instance, so soon after the museum defacement? The unannounced trip had left Jenko to answer most of the police inquiries into the attack alone.

But really he didn't mind that he didn't know. No man can reconcile all the facts about himself, for another or for himself. No man should be asked to. What Jenko needed to rely on Celano for, in construction and in politics, he could, and vice versa. That was enough.

Aaron pointed at the lean man in rolled French cuffs on the wall-mounted screen, viewable from anywhere in the now partitionless hall. The place gleamed. The virgin felt was as rich as green could be, and the wood of the tables was an oily reddish brown: matched rosewood, bought from black-market stock and inlaid with ebony. The bar itself had doubled in size since everything had been burned.

The image of Lewis on the screen was not very new. It had been collected from the cameras of several strip clubs and bars Jenko had a stake in. The tapes couldn't have been turned over to the police, even though Jenko would have liked nothing better than having the police solve this problem for him, protect his investment, his girls. They carried too much self-incriminating evidence for that.

They wouldn't have been enough anyway. Lewis hadn't been

singled out by footage alone. It took the pooled capacities of a community of traders in contraband, sex most of all, steered by some of Jenko's higher ups, to detect him. None of this data could be passed on to the police, for the same reasons the tapes couldn't. The clubs would have been seized the next day and Jenko would have found himself a new home, in prison.

So he'd ordered his own investigation. Jenko's men were all given simple instructions: whoever they talked to in the streets and clubs, whoever seemed like a candidate for the crimes, nudge things toward the dark, toward hookers and violence especially, and see what appeared. This came naturally to most of the men; the innuendo involved wasn't so different from, say, selling drugs or girls. What made it even easier was that they shared in Lewis's violent fantasies. Grittier versions, if anything.

The men could almost be themselves, then, so much so that sometimes they would forget that they were acting on orders at all. The difference was mainly one of restraint, namely, letting their own war stories be bested by the targets'. They had to let them emerge as the victors in recklessness, in contempt. This was more difficult than it sounded. They were used to winning that game. They were also told to convey a willingness to collude in whatever schemes the targets floated. This came much easier to them. Looking for an angle, that was just life.

They talked to dozens of false leads, men who seemed to have done plenty wrong, but not the particular wrong their boss was interested in: the beatings. Finally a promising incident occurred. One of Jenko's men, Terry, got a strange reply to a standard question in a local dive. He tried to sell a bleary-eyed regular he recognized from the tapes on a hooker for the night. But the man didn't just accept or decline. Instead he said he'd had his share of girls, and he couldn't be less interested now. In whores? Terry asked him. Whores, yes, but more than that, the whole thing disgusted him now, sex itself. Which you really don't hear.

"And what did Terry tell him?" Jenko asked.

"He let him rant for a while," Aaron said, "about sex, money, porno. They got drunker. Eventually Terry got his name. So we checked him out."

"Well?" Jenko ask.

"He rented a cargo van from our little fleet, out of Boston though, just a few months back. We had the girls look at that particular van, and Erin said, yeah, it had the same little dent in the door she remembered. Then we showed her the footage and said he looked right, though he'd had sunglasses and a baseball cap on then. She couldn't be sure. But the other girls confirmed it was him."

"So what will we do?" Jenko asked himself aloud.

"This is the thing. Terry kept encouraging him that night, about what he wished would happen to all those 'disgusting' people. Lewis started saying some strange stuff... He talked about wanting to give."

Jenko laughed. "Give?"

"Give, yeah."

Jenko peered at the image on screen, Lewis caught mid-stride, a leg hanging in the air. "He does have the look of money. Money hard done. His name, his father."

"Leo, the trader."

"I kept money with him at one time," Jenko said. "He did well for me. Twenty-five percent, year on year. But I don't think he or his son has anything much to give now. Everyone pulled out of that fund. Trust is everything—and Leo couldn't be trusted anymore."

"A half million is what he said."

"That sounds like drunk talk to me. Bragging."

"That's not what we think."

"Well, I suppose things could have improved for Leo. Sure. It's possible. So then, how will the son 'give'?"

"He didn't know exactly," Aaron said. "He kept talking about these porno awards—"

"In Vegas."

"Yeah—"

"What about them?"

"He wished he could give those people something."

"Not the money, I guess."

"He wants them—I mean, the way he put it, he wants them to get some air."

"Is that a joke? If it is, I don't think I get it."

"This is nuts, but Terry thinks he meant, like, halothane or BZ. Gas. At the ceremony. For the half mil."

"Ah." Jenko smiled and tapped the table twice with his middle and ring fingers. "You believe this."

"Not to hurt anyone is what he said. Only to make them 'see things.'"

"And exactly how gone was, he when he said this? Or how gone was Terry, that's what we should be asking."

"I mean, it's true, he did look like he hadn't slept in a while."

"The fantasies we have."

"But he also sounded like he could mean what he said. Terry wouldn't have bothered me with this otherwise."

"And Terry's very bright?"

"Look, we already know he kicked the shit out of all these whores. Isn't that fucking crazy too? Why couldn't he mean it?"

The two of them held a long look.

"So what did Terry say to him, after hearing all this?" Jenko asked finally.

"Nothing, of course. He just listened. Lewis had no idea he was basically talking to you. But we can get back to him. It'll be easy to find him now, see if he's really game to go through with this. And if it's all bullshit, we'll know. Nothing's lost."

"Five hundred thousand is actually not enough to fill an auditorium with an airborne agent, even just an incapacitator. There are the usual risks for us. Every incident, every event, brings another risk with it. And this one would be very large. The logistics, getting to all the vents without detection. But then, it *is* a life sentence for Lewis."

"Probably."

"And if you add the beatings, that's more than life."

"But we don't want to touch those, right. A bunch of those whores are ours. It could lead them here."

"Can you *please* stop calling them whores?"

"Girls, I mean."

"Better. So then there's the gas. Let's talk to Leo's little boy and check his nerve. Terry can handle it, if you feed him the information?"

"And if he's looking for some time off."

"Otherwise someone else. Somebody's always looking."

"So, halothane, BZ, what?"

"Do we actually need it? To make this work for us? If we have everything else set up and call in the anonymous tip just before, we could probably just pretend about the agent itself."

"Oh. Well, I guess—"

"But check the labs. Talk to him first, of course, make sure this is real. And then, sure, we can think about doing exactly what we say this time. It would be easier to bury Lewis in a trial with everything being authentic. Trust, you know."

29

FOUR TALL STEPS AND STAGG WAS UP ON THE DAIS, a maroon folio tied with raw leather string in his hand. Kames clasped Stagg's shoulder and gave him a single deep nod as they passed each other near the lectern.

It surprised Stagg to see the auditorium as full as it was—at least three quarters—not just because of the arcane topic, or his lack of visibility in the field, but because of the tension surrounding the Institute lately, one he assumed would keep a crowd away. Maybe the turnout meant the full measure of that tension, great as it was, could only be felt by those with special knowledge. How many that was, he couldn't tell.

A good portion of the audience looked about his age, and of the same background. Some of them must have undertaken watch-work themselves, for reasons like his own. They would know bits and pieces of the tale, even how some of those bits and pieces fit together, just as he did. Some might well know more.

It was a condition of getting the work, of course, that one concealed the fact, though some confidences would inevitably be made to intimates. And in fact these were calculated for by the agency. But most of the people here were, overtly at least, only intellectual colleagues, or would-be colleagues, and information of that kind, which would have shown them to be colleagues twice over, would not be exchanged, not least for the implication that one was reinforcing the very political order being worried, from all angles, by the Institute.

Kames's introduction had been kind and Stagg was about to falsify it. His essays were *not* critiques, not in any clear sense, even to him. Or if they were, they transcended his intentions, not only his past ones, but the ones he had now, which seemed to extend no further than reading out the pages he'd brought with him.

Worse, these pages were ones Kames hadn't reviewed. Stagg was taking a detour. Renna was right, the future of the Institute was uncertain now in ways deeper than its director could know. Deeper even than Stagg knew, probably. What he'd reported back to Penerin, of his last conversation with Kames, in the garden, had made his Second Watch supervisor cagey about his own plans in a way that was new to Stagg. Penerin probably had other information by then as well, perhaps from Ravan. Not that he was going to share all of it with Stagg. In truth, their dealings were only partly above board. Penerin told him only as much as he wanted to. Just like Kames. When matters got complicated, both his bosses turned elliptical.

The thing that was certain now was that a shift had occurred. By the time the elections came and went, there might well be no possibility of a Wintry fellowship left. Penerin's evasions suggested as much. Their ambiguities had turned his words, like Kames's, into a cryptic—or better, encrypted—poetry.

Now it was Stagg's turn. Instead of the main essays, he'd brought only scattered appendices with him, bits that captured the tiniest flashes of light and no more. If the earlier pieces were shards, these were specks. But wasn't it possible, he thought, that they reflected more, like a dust of diamonds? They felt realer to Stagg in their discreteness than the longer tableaus he'd assembled with such pain. Perhaps they managed to say more, in their compression, about him and his several selves, his family, and about history, than the rest of what he'd written, even if he was less sure he could fully survey their meaning. That was the problem, the virtue, of poetry. It outran you.

They might also achieve what any one of the essays could not. In the space of one lecture, the only one there might be now, he could still suggest a whole narrative, a destiny, this way. Because even dust could be shaped into a trail. What mattered was arrangement, order.

In fact he would be telling two stories at once, one about the past and another about the future. If he was betraying Kames in not delivering the more lucid lecture they'd agreed on, the one centered on the monk, he was also showing him a kindness. The trail would be an arrow. It would tell what Stagg knew about the circumstances, the tension, but without telling. The same way Kames liked to tell. From there, it would be up to him.

Though he wasn't close to Kames, and didn't especially trust him, he owed him something for giving him the chance to speak. More than that, there was kinship. Kames wasn't wrong in thinking the country had reached a liminal moment in its history. Penerin and his kind wanted to deny this. They said everything could be recovered. But there were such things as faits accomplis. A world built around seducing the man in the street had managed to turn all the world out into that street. Now, almost everyone found the free world unlivable, chaotic, coarse. The invisible hand, Kames liked to say, turned out to have a very strong grip. It finally had *all* of them by the neck now, it seemed. Maybe he was right. It was time to lop it off.

Stagg unknotted the leather and pulled the small sheaf from the case. Tapping the pages on the edge of the lectern, he caught Kames's eye, far in back and with his face already made up in a furrowed expression of concentration. He might have other things pressing on him just now. Stagg thought to say something that would suggest the change of plan. He thought to thank Kames. But no, both ideas might only corrupt the simple intention he had left, to read.

■ ■ ■

I.

Around that great table they sit in silence. Rajasingha's attendants, noblemen in their own right, look on from a smaller table nearer the lake as the king takes his daily meal. So as not to contaminate the great man's food, each wears a mask, sewn from the sun-bleached fibers of the coconut.

In all there are twenty dishes set out this afternoon: sambhur of the Highlands stewed in a thin, turmeric-laced gravy that is almost a broth; breadfruit garnished with cinnamon and lychees; river fish in a chili and cardamom curry; steamed pittu flecked with cashews, served with a tamarind sambal; fritters of rice-flour and jaggery; and fifteen besides. He will eat of only four or five of these.

The king makes a faint gesture toward the pot of boiled jack-fruit and lime. The nobleman closest ladles it onto a corner of the banana leaf from which the king is eating slowly, methodically, alone. Today's meal is unusual only in that it is taken by Lake Kilara, at the royal retreat, the pleasure house. He's here three or four times a year, usually for a few days only. The makeshift palace in newly royal Digligy, and in fact his very grip on the country, is under muted and perpetual threat. A populist rebellion forced him from the palace in Nillemby, westward into the mountains. And the Dutch have been making incursions eastward into the heart of the island, from Colombo, ever since making landfall on the southwestern coast four decades ago, around 1640. The twin forces have made Digligy his home and Lake Kilara his refuge.

The king finishes his meal and dismisses the others, who

make their way beneath the overhanging lattice from the gazebo to the main complex. The noble servants, unmasked now, as the king has finished, take away the dishes. This will be their meal. He steps from the gazebo to the banks, thinking of the evening's return to the palace. The sun has made a mirror of the lake. Dressed in a white tunic embroidered in red, his scabbard once again at his side, he begins to circle the lake, turning over the options.

Van Holten had said the Dutch forces stationed near Colombo were mounting a fresh campaign to capture the Highlands and the kingdom, that their flatteries, of defending His shores from the Portuguese, had always been hollow, from the time they'd arrived. The possibility now occurs to the king of making the Dutch, after all these years, finally mean what they say, by bringing them into a more profound conflict than they intend with their European brethren, the Portuguese, the kind that might weaken each enough to flush them both from the island.

The information had not been offered up of Van Holten's will exactly. The king had first seen the soldier chained and starved outside the royal court, alongside other European captives. He'd been left behind by a retreating Dutch squad led by one Commander Haas. Only after weeks of being kept like this, exposed alternately to withering heat and violent rain, was Van Holten brought before Rajasingha. He was offered a peasant's meal and some shade and that was the end of it. He told what he knew.

The king completes his circle of the lake. He's decided to host the latest set of Dutch envoys offering a false peace. Back in the pleasure house proper, he sends his messenger down to the coast to invite their leadership to the royal court as guests of honor.

II.

Rutland walked in late to find Knox sitting on a stool, drinking palm whiskey in the living room. Before Knox could comment on the hour, Rutland set the Bible down over the brass rivets of the trunk, which had been pulled from the *Ann*, their captured frigate, twenty years ago by the Sinhalese. The spoils had spoiled, though. The rations were rancid and the clothing, stored in a separate compartment, had rotted not much differently from the meat. The Sinhalese had lost interest in the shrunken, sea-sodden box, and it was left to the two of them, Rutland and Knox, to discover its only remaining value, as furniture.

Knox leafed through the pages and his shipmate wondered if he would go through the same stages he himself had, now almost fifteen years ago, when the monk had given him the book: whether the surge of awe and gratitude would be overtaken by a stubborn sense of smallness.

But Knox's eyes never lost their wideness. Immediately Knox's father came to Rutland's mind, the fevered one, delirious in his last days, talking mostly in Biblical snatches to his son and his earthly keepers, the two Sinhalese. They seemed to be the last fully formed sentences he possessed, at least the last of any complexity. It was as if their syntactic force, or else the depth of their entrenchment, had equipped them to crowd all else out of his mind. To Rutland this seemed an elevation of the Book at a cost to the man's psyche, or else just the reverse.

He could see that Knox was also thinking of him, the old man endlessly apologizing for bringing his son along on this unholy "mission of exchange." They were exchangers, Knox Sr. had said.

Sitting on the floor across from Knox, Rutland undid his boots, the leather rough and cracked. Knox started reading out passages of the Bible, lines his father had fixed on, near death and long before, back in England; lines he wanted to deliver now to his dead father, to Rutland, to all three of them. Each page was a trigger. On seeing the first few words, or even just the arrangement of the page, taking it in with a sweep of his eyes, the rest of the passage would follow like a stream. He would intone the words he saw in his mind, his eyes floating up to the other end of the house, the wall, the door, or the window, but never to Rutland.

Then he would turn a few of the supple vellum sheets—what merchant was missing this now?—take in another page, the flow and frame, and light on another line. Rutland hadn't been much moved on seeing many of these lines himself, but he was moved by the effect they had on his friend.

Knox set the book down on the trunk and sat in silence. The flask of arrack shone in the light of the candle. Rutland took it to his lips but only a trickle of spirit remained, just enough to numb his tongue. Knox excused himself with a half-hearted wave, taking the Book with him into his room, which left Rutland to watch the tallow burn.

III.

Scabbarded men stood along the edges of the main hall, facing its walls like dunces in a room with too few corners. They'd each slipped a stopper out, eye-level and wide as a face. Through these gaps in the wall they looked out into the torch-lit court. Along the thick outer-court walls, in the hollow spaces scattered throughout, another set of men positioned themselves the same way, facing out into the broader village, where conversations were had, trade was conducted, life was lived.

Then there were the roamers, and sometimes he, Rajasingha, was one of them. Only the very closest to him knew. On these nights, his face was darkened a shade, and his locks, usually pristine, were made stringy and left to hang haphazardly around his ears, like an old warrior's. The king would be clothed like the middling ranks of the court (he had several swords marked with the shields of modest nobility).

Only after he'd officially retired to his quarters, not long after dark, would he begin his walk. Two guards stood by his chamber doors as he wandered the court, the night's gossip begun. He talked to no one, only listened, and if called out to, or interrupted, he pretended not to hear, and sometimes not to see.

His purpose was, primarily, ostensibly, security. From his watches and guards much intelligence came to him, but the mediation introduced impurities. Depending on the messenger, the information would be colored in one way or another, and this was not always, or even often, intentional.

He was sure there was much that was being misapprehended, when it wasn't simply missed altogether. It wasn't arrogance or vanity that made him think few of his officers could hope to see as he did. Keeping his kingdom alive this long, through the many years of tumult, coming from all directions, within and without, demanded an otherworldly sense for tone, for gesture: a capacity to see the future in things.

He didn't acquire this sense through ruling. It came first, and it was what marked him as a ruler, the almost disinterested pleasure he took, even as a child, in understanding the effects of his actions: what would become, when he no longer needed a guardian and ascended to power, the ripples of his rule. A king had to take this relish, directed to no end, to stay king.

Nearly every night-walk shuffled the order of faith he had in the great nobles of the court. There were, in truth, many in the middle who neither rose nor fell much, being neither confidants nor traitors. But some near the lower margin, the threshold, would rise high up into safer territory, sometimes to a place that made them for a time unimpeachable. Others would fall from these heights to somewhere near the margin. The problem only occurred when a great man already near the margin fell, thereby crossing the threshold.

Reasons would then be found. When treason could be imputed, the execution was public. When the case was harder, a vanishing followed. Sometimes this was an exile; usually it was a private execution.

There were a very few cases, no more than half a dozen, where, owing to discoveries made about the man, usually during a later watch, either by the watchmen or the king himself on one of his night-walks, a noble who had fallen below the threshold would right the wrong that had caused the fall before it was feasible to have him disappeared or killed. Curiously, none of these men ever fell out of the king's graces again.

Against the wishes of his aides, Rajasingha would pass the inner wall of the court and roam the village, a less manicured space, freer in form, centerless and so more hazardous. Here he would stroll through the lanes and splitting byways on which the village houses and markets were arranged. His stride would shorten, or he would pause altogether, and by his expression pretend to decide whether to enter a shop, say, or take a rest on a rock.

When they'd started these watches, soon after the rebellion, Rajasingha frequently heard unflattering things said about his rule. But open criticism soon disappeared after the watches began, as the Court always seemed to know what the people said or did, even in private.

Dissatisfaction fell away into code. A second language, compounded out of the first, in which hybrids of existing phrases, placed back to back, came to mean something else, took hold in the kingdom. Everyone was soon bilingual at least.

When this tongue drew notice—the watches grew bilingual too—these sentiments were shunted into gestures, looks. But from the many eyes of the king these were no safer. Use of these codes and gestures, when discovered, led to various sorts of seizures, always disguised, tailored to the circumstance, and laced with the moral significance, the cruel wit, of parables. A man's yard might be taken for use by the state in the cultivation of a public garden, if he'd been found to have complained, in the wrong tones, about the condition of the village. Cattle might be led away on an alleged suspicion of disease—for the king's use if they were grand, to slaughter and destruction otherwise—if the grievance concerned inadequate supplies of water or cattle feed, which were regulated by the councilors. Or a son might be conscripted for a servant's role in the temple if a family's objection was to the coziness between royals and monks.

Repercussions could be more serious, if the king was in the mood: the destruction of crops on which taxes had failed to be paid in full, apparently through natural disaster, but in reality through localized flooding in the night. Or something as simple and devastating as the outing of a couple having an affair, as the king, though estranged from his own wife, was faithful still, and held fidelity in high regard.

To some villagers and townsmen, this was all the simple meting out of justice, and a miraculous one at that. It seemed to them that the king really was a god now, so much did he know about their lives. Their complaints stopped in all its forms. It was churlish and vain, they thought, to question the divine order, one that the king's newfound omniscience gave them a greater faith in than ever before.

Others, though, turned to a different kind of silence. Strictly faultless, always possibly meaningless, a mere lull in the conversation, silence was recruited to indicate unsayable points of dispute with the kingdom. What exactly the interlocutors took from these silences, what idea was ultimately exchanged, couldn't be known. It was never used systematically enough for that, which made it safe from interception, from translation, by the king's watches. In truth it was less an exchange than an improvisation, one man intuiting, with only silence as his guide, what was felt by another.

IV.

Dressed in the clothes of a European man he never met, whose fate he didn't know, Rutland entered the royal martial quarters, a few miles from Digligy, and sat on the broad wooden bench near the door.

There was Haas, captured in a night raid on a Dutch fort, smiling and chatting in his mother tongue with Van Holten, his comrade, who sat next to him with a swatch of cloth in his hand, polishing an already gleaming snake, the delicately wrought hilt of a longsword. There was Marco da Silva, heavily stubbled, black hair falling in rings down his bright collar, whistling a tune—trying, it appeared, to drown out the Dutchmen, if only in his own ears. Then there was Michel Veneres, pacing the room in high brown boots and a flowing vest that seemed to have tails, idly drawing his finger across the shields hanging from the walls.

The room doubled as an armory. Some of the arms were European, some were local but forged in their style. Like Rutland, Veneres was a volunteer, an unlucky trader of a nation with no stake in the island, not a martial capture like the Portuguese or the two Dutchmen, though he'd committed some time ago to the group.

It had been two weeks since, against Knox's advice, Rutland agreed to join the European squads the king was assembling to train and lead his Sinhalese brigades. The Englishman and Frenchman, though traders only, were added to this, one of the lead squads, for the prestige, it was thought, of having all-European units.

All of them had been in captivity on the island at least several years. None longer than Rutland, though, who'd been held almost two decades now. All knew some Sinhalese. But the Dutchmen knew more English than Sinhalese. The Frenchman knew more still. The Portuguese and the Englishman knew only their own languages. The group spoke an immature pidgin, still rough and prone to breakdown, drawn from these languages.

They were given the finest arms in the king's possession. Frequently this meant being reunited with their own or their brethren's, the spoils of Sinhalese raids on their forts. Haas's arquebus hung from the wall.

Haas stood and greeted Rutland, though by this time he was already seated. The four of them, their glances happened to lock in a circle, two standing, two sitting, each one's eyes on the next. The circle broke. Their eyes wandered again. The moment had served, though.

Veneres paced and spoke to Rutland for the group, in fine English, about their treasonous task. With a hard-edged vagueness that astonished, he talked of difference, of sameness, of the future. These three together, he said, formed a dial, like the cindric mal, the flower clock used by the priesthood to time their chants, to bring them to a close, and to begin them again. The room fixed on Rutland, all but Veneres himself, who carried on fingering the arms.

V.

The king watched Rutland walk away, finely outfitted, his gilt scabbard catching the light, with a royal message for Knox. Rajasingha found himself on the cusp of a clearing, a new era, built on the backs of Europeans: four squads of fair-skinned men, sent down the mountain in a false alliance with the imperialists. They'd be disguised as plunderers, marauders, and escapees of his kingdom, talking of inroads, of exploitable weaknesses in Digligy and Kandy. The king's own men, dark-skinned, many dozens of them, steeped in ambush, would be trailing just behind, guns and swords leering from the shrubs, ready to pounce on the invaders.

It would be the choice of Rutland and the others in these European squads. If they turned on the natives, and sided with their blood, they would be killed with the rest of the whites—first, in fact, as they were nearest the Sinhalese forces following behind. At the same time, retreat, if necessary, would still be possible for the king's men. If, however, they remained loyal to the king, and Rutland and the others managed through their tales to disarm their own countrymen and convince them they were allies, victory would be simpler still. The reinforcing Sinhalese brigades, combined with the king's European forces, would be too much.

Tomorrow the king would meet with Rutland's squad. He thought of the 547 lives of the Buddha. He wondered how many he himself had, and which one this was.

VI.

The light came only from stars, and the stars were weak, so it fell just short of the world, leaving it visible but not quite seen, everything bathed in graphite blue. They'd arrived at the outer wall at the back of the palace. It was formed of rough-hewn stone drawn from the thickly forested valley they'd just crossed in the night.

Da Silva tested his grip on the wall. A rustling was heard. He lifted himself up off the grass. Haas signaled for him to wait till Van Holten and Veneres emerged from the brush—at the last minute, Rutland had abandoned the plan—but whether he understood or not, he began to climb. He had no sword, just a wide, short blade in his boot whose hilt rose up to Haas's face as he ascended. The temptation to pull da Silva off the wall passed, partly because Haas wasn't sure he'd get the better of him. The Portuguese was agile, a master of weaponless combat, and good with a blade too. They'd found that out in training. Da Silva had the knife to Van Holten's throat when Haas intervened.

Da Silva stopped at the top without cresting the wall. The other men had collected at the bottom. Side by side, all but one started to climb. On the order of Veneres, the one playing watch at the base, they slipped over the top and into the darkness within.

The limed walls of the palace proper shone blue-white, the stars sufficing only to bring light to things that gave all of it back.

Veneres came over the wall and settled in the grass. Another rustling came. A snake perhaps.

They saw no sentries at the back, at the two short palace doors. Above the doors, every few yards, there were black squares lining the wall. The king's windows. Trees rose over the sides of the palace, twisting over the wall in both directions, creating broad patches of a slightly richer black in the yard.

The men crept along the semicircular wall in the darkness that reigned at its edge, headed for those windows, the king. As they approached they made out a massive form a third shade of black within the trees ahead. They decided it was a boulder. Then it was rumbling toward them at speed, cutting through the tall grass, squealing like an elephant. One by one, the men found themselves overtaken as their own squeals joined its, as life, this life, was stamped out of them, expelled from their bones.

VII.

Mud and water waist-high, Knox and Rutland inched through the mangroves with their bags held over their heads, looking for a way back to London, and finally, in Rutland's case, to Kent. His bag was heavier than it should have been, but the journals and papers counted for a lot. The last one that went in was Darasa's note. It had been sealed with an inscrutable stamp when it arrived by messenger, and it suggested just enough about the king's treacherous plans for the European squads, Rutland felt, to impel him to flee with Knox into the northern swamps, looking for their people's vessels along the upper coastline, if they could make it that far this time.

Rutland had delivered the king's message to Knox, a spoken one, before Darasa's arrived. Its complexion altered in the light, or perhaps the dark, of the monk's note, as did the monk's in its. In fact, Rutland had dispatched the very first of the three messages, to Darasa, about the circle of eyes he'd seen in the martial quarters. Now all their words could only be seen through the veils of the others'.

Rutland had taken his letter to the temple himself, in the early morning. He gave Darasa the Bible back at the same time, the pages speckled with water stains, or tears, it appeared, and marked by Rutland and Knox at passages that might be of special use now to the monk.

What Darasa had made of the note, and of the markings, Rutland didn't know. An exegete of his caliber had every chance of cracking it. Both their notes, in fact, provided for the possibility of discovery and, by those means, the forestalling of a connivance. But courage couldn't really be ascribed to the authors of these letters, since to the extent their messages were recovered, a duty, one attending the knowledge so imparted, was shunted from writer to reader.

It should be said, the king's own message to Knox, in plain, bright language, yet so plain, so bright, it couldn't be seen at all—Rutland and Knox never settled on an understanding of it—shared in this same negativity.

■ ■ ■

Stagg searched the remaining paper-clipped bundles for one that might serve as an epilogue, or one that might be collided with the rest, to react it. But before he could choose, or choose to finish where he was, a strong, quick clapping, the work of a single pair of hands, came from the back. It was Kames.

Soon there were other hands. The noise swelled. Judging by the space between Kames's hands, the great width of his clap, it was his applause that was most vigorous. It was the kind reserved for finales, though, not intermissions. He might have been trying to save everyone from embarrassment, Stagg's talk was so peculiar. And the crowd, bemused by the lecture, followed the director's lead. Stagg couldn't continue now, though perhaps he wouldn't have wanted to. Kames might have understood all he needed to, about Stagg and his dividedness, and about himself. There was no need for endings.

The director's face was out of sync with his hands, though. It failed to express, or even simulate, quite the same pleasure. That didn't mean he took none. He might have evinced another pleasure, or several even, but if so they were of subtler sorts, not the ones of airy eyes and upturned mouths, slightly ajar, with teeth shining within, also ajar. What else, besides pleasure, was in that face? Recognition, Stagg hoped. Kames more than anyone should know that in a scattered world, everything hinged on your capacity to put the pieces together.

The clapping peaked. Normally at these talks Kames would be walking up the aisle to the microphone near the stage to moderate questions. But he remained where he was until the clapping died. Stagg sucked in his lower lip and gave two quick nods to no one. He left the pages on the lectern. Kames could study them later if he liked, for the niceties he had encoded in them. He snatched the folio, pinching it from the foldover, and strode off stage with the unknotted leather string dangling.

30

"I WAS SURE WE WOULDN'T HAVE THESE FOR A long while," the lab director said. "Nice to get them so soon, put them to work. Federal approval's been simpler than usual too."

"Because the storm's so big," Ravan said.

"And so fast. I think we just have days now. A clear category five. But it's also because of what they saw you and your brother demo in Death Valley. I can tell you from watching it from here, it was shock and awe." He spread the emphasis evenly across the last three of these words in a way that didn't neutralize it.

Men wearing the orange and black of Princeton Tigers wheeled the metal cabinets across a bare concrete floor polished to such a smoothness it seemed wet to walk on. The director's leather soles made a crack with each contact and then slid along the surface, failing to find purchase as he put his weight on them. Ravan's topsiders and the sneakers of the workers did better, silently.

Each cabinet was loaded with weather rockets, twelve of them, settled in the u-shaped grooves of the steel matrices within. The storage space amounted to a vault recessed into the far wall, held at sixty-three degrees Fahrenheit.

Ravan spent his days just on the other side of that wall,

plowing through masses of figures, checking the ideality of simulations against the raw jags of the world. The data came from tests carried out in the airless heat of Nevada; the frost of Idaho (he'd seen twin blizzards induced in October); and, just recently, the simmering wet of Florida's Everglades, on light storms rolling in off the coast.

Trajectories, temperatures, displacements, and payloads, a cocktail of reagents forever recalibrated: thirty-four primary variables in all, collated by proprietary software engineered in the atmospheric labs of his father and brother in India.

After several years away from the daily details of weather research, Ravan's handle on the intricacies of the software's algorithms paled next to theirs, and even next to some of his colleagues in the Princeton labs. Yet his easy way with mathematics, especially his natural bent for ratios, semblances, pairings and functions, and most of all divergences (latent or nascent), was enough to make him essential to the lab. He was fast, and with the storm approaching, speed is what they needed most.

The director looked over the phalanxes of rockets as the two walked alongside the men rolling the last of the cabinets into place.

"Amazing that we have these now, Ravan. Something so concrete."

"And semi-predictable."

"All our research, it's already being taken more seriously now, after Death Valley. That there can be productive yields in our lifetime, that it's not just speculation anymore," he said. "Now, I just hope your father's rockets work as well over the ocean as they do in the desert."

"Well, you've seen the footage from India," Ravan said.

"I have. Though nothing's as convincing as a live performance. But I guess you were there for those trials too."

"For one of them, the first. We burst a monsoon just off the northeastern coast. By landfall it had totally bled out. By the time it reached the Ghats, this trivial thing was left, not even a drizzle so much as a mist just heavy enough to fall rather than hang. It felt like Disneyland in the summer, all that mist. They've done that twice since. So why not a hurricane like this."

"Why not."

"There've been failures, of course. More of them than successes. I've told you all this. But we have yet to make a storm worse."

"Of course. And all the usual precautions are being taken anyway. Halsley's surge barriers too, which might be adequate by themselves, we don't know. But if we can stop this storm from even making landfall, well, why test the barriers? Not making the storm worse is really all NOAA is asking of us. The rest is hope. Intelligent hope, though. That's the big change."

"It's more than hope. The conditions here are colder, but I don't think that will alter the action of the cocktail, introduced the right way. Menar doesn't either. I think we can count on changing things."

■ ■ ■

Ravan fingered the triad, his thumb climbing over the back of the sanded fingerboard barren of frets, to stop the low E string. He ran his nails across the strings with his other hand and something like a minor chord came from the tiny practice amp in clean, reverbed tones. There were several beatings between notes, long and slow. He resolved them without lifting his fingers. Instead he simply leaned them up or down the board, a shifting of weight more than a change of position. The tones bonded and the chord, till then something small and discrete, appeared to emanate from the room itself rather than anything in it.

The chirp of Skype accented the third of the chord. Ravan tapped the mouse and one of the *Disintegration Loops*, an etiolated six-note specter of a piece, an echo stripped of its origins, resumed on the loop he'd set up. He'd let it run all through the night, many times through. He dreamed through it.

The black of the sleeping computer screen was replaced by his brother's face, and beneath it, a smaller face, less formed: Menar's son's.

"Ravan," Menar said, just before the child lodged his fingers and much of his hand in his father's mouth. He coaxed the hand back out. "You have the shipment now, yeah. How did it all look? And what *is* that?"

"What are you seeing?" Ravan asked, looking down at the guitar still in his lap.

"No, the sound. Can you turn that down?"

Ravan nudged the slider partway down with the mouse.

"Actually can you turn it off?"

"Don't you like it?"

"So this is what's become of music, is it?"

"You can hear me fine it looks like."

"You've got a lot left to fill in, don't you. It sounds like nothing."

"It's not me, actually. But as far as I know it's finished. Polished nothing."

"You'll do better."

"Oh, I don't know. It memorializes 9/11. It's very deep. I slept to it last night."

"So when is this concert of yours?" Menar asked. "I told Dad about it. He just stared at me."

"Saturday." He unplugged the guitar and strummed the strings he was choking with his other hand.

"After the show, Ravan, can't you use a break? From all this industriousness. Dad would like to see you. So would this little one." Menar resettled the boy on his lap. For a moment the baby's eyes, the bridge of his nose, took up the entire screen.

He'd lunged over the keyboard. Menar pulled him back and the giant became a child again.

"The storm is coming in," Ravan said. "I'm pretty sure the lab will want me here."

"They will. But I can put in a call to your boss. You owe it to yourself to come back this way. The family hasn't seen you in a while, not all at once. You can sift data for them so long as you're on the network. The seeding missiles are what count. They're all marked. The ones with gold decals should go to the naval platforms, the Coast Guard."

"I know."

"The gold ones are calibrated for your storm, the colder air. The other seeders are standard, but can be added if necessary, or used later in trials."

"Good, good, yes." Ravan wasn't looking at the screen anymore but the fingers he was forming chords with now.

"So..."

"So..." Ravan didn't look up.

"You know," Menar said, "I was thinking just today how tricky it all is, really."

"What."

"Preparing these rockets."

"Hm."

"Do you appreciate that? Probably that's what you don't quite grasp. You've been too busy with this music to notice."

Ravan let go of the guitar and let it swing from the strap around his neck. "Actually I know quite—"

"You know a lot, yes. But not as much as you should. The hundreds of steps we take each of the seeders through, the treatment of the antimony at the core of the formula. You see, beyond the allotropic phases, the cooling and heating, there are all the isotopes. Some are more useful than others. Most are benign. But if the starting materials are off just a little, or if we overtreat them a fraction, a couple of kinds of radioisotopes appear."

"Right."

"One of which, post-treatment, is worryingly radioactive. A very short half-life, but within that window, a big problem."

Ravan unstrapped the guitar and leaned it against the amp. "I've been paying that much attention, yes."

"The margins are just so fine. That's why this has been as expensive as it has been, the precision that's demanded."

"I know the dangers."

"In theory, you do. But the thing of it is, it's actually already happened once in trial. Just last year we launched a few seeders into clouds deep in the Indian Ocean. They failed to make rain. Fine. Nothing so unusual about that. But they succeeded in doing something else. They charged the cloud with the radioisotope, loaded it like a gun. When the storm finally did break—by this point it was an odd pink, or red—it broke in the middle of the ocean. That was our one bit of luck. The waters were sampled and tested, as always. And they were more than a little toxic. We dodged a bullet. Did you know all that too?"

Ravan shook his head slowly and switched off the amplifier.

"Now you're paying attention. Good. You see, I'm a bit closer to Dad on these matters than you. The music's taken you away from some of this. Your government has been leaning on us for these rockets for a while now. Bringing the Starstreak missile home, for properly humanitarian purposes this time, they say, by converting them into cloud seeders. But do you suppose they can cleanse these rockets of their former purpose entirely? Or will we find, down the road, that it was merely dormant, and at just the right moment these missiles will come chasing us again, but as weather this time?"

"I don't know how we can say." Ravan said this only after a complicated pause, one that consumed all the distance he usually felt toward his brother's line of work.

"And isn't that just the problem, Ravan?" Menar said gently. "In any case, you'll know they've asked for this batch last minute, and we've obliged and rigged these seeders up quickly—more quickly than they really ought to have been. All just to deal with your storm.

"Now, in fairness, it does look to be a true monster. That's why clearance was so easy on your end. The storm we had that problem with in India, it was quite small, and it was not a bet to make landfall. But yours, well, if we don't burst it, it will certainly come ashore, brutally. And all that coastline, the nerve center of the country. I don't know if there is any surge barrier that can cope with it. It's more than a category five, really. We just don't have the right scale for it.

"Given its size, we are sending up a lot of seeding agent. I have complete belief in our chemists, of course. The odds are small, objectively speaking. But these things, well..."

Menar kissed the back of the child's head and finished the thought in a lower, slower voice. "Nothing is perfect. And no process, none at all, is really, truly stable."

Ravan needed no convincing.

The child squirmed and cried, stretched out his hands to one edge of the screen. Menar's wife broke into the frame. Ravan had met her only once, at the wedding. She was a gentle, fine-boned woman with a translucent complexion, the signature of the Muslim clan his brother had married into a few years ago.

The union had driven a slight wedge between the two Menars, Sr. and Jr., though they still worked closely together. After the marriage, work seemed to become the central plank of their closeness, and this was not lost on the son. It changed him, his father's chilly response to his wife and her family, which included higher-ups in the Pakistani military his father thought needlessly radical, and moreover who seemed to be suspicious of his own research collaborations with the U.S. government—though, infuriatingly, they would always stop short of saying so.

She took the Indo-Aryan boy to a place off-screen without saying anything to Ravan.

"Look, however it is, I'm glad you've got everything," Menar said. "The gold ones, I know I've said this, are the ones that will do what's needed. God willing."

The smirk made the briefest of appearances. Then a hot stare shot down somewhere near his feet. Finally there was a firm smile back at his brother.

"Got it," Ravan said.

"You really must come and see this boy," Menar said, looking off-camera with a softer smile toward his wife and child. "Before he gets any bigger. You'd be a fool not to."

31

THE NAP OF THE CLOTH WAS AS DENSE AS JENKO'S
pool tables, but the green was deeper, carrying thick casino light
that broke up the dark between games of cards. Lewis thumbed
it in a slow spiral, felt the trapped warmth. He ran his finger over
the cold white paint of the stenciled box, and then the card sitting face-up within it, a ten of diamonds. The second card came.
He was looking for an ace, a blackjack. A king arrived instead.

Lewis's hand froze beside the pair. There was no hitting a
hard twenty, so he waited for her, this young Vegas dealer with
a face like an arrow and a platinum blond ponytail bobbing
behind her head. She had a six showing. He nodded to show
he would stand. She flipped her hole card. Another ace, giving
her a soft seventeen. She pulled another card from the dealing
shoe, still four decks thick and resistant to counting, though he
wouldn't have known how to anyway. He wasn't a real gambler,
just passing time till the show. Now a second face appeared, not
a king's but a queen's. Twenty-seven. Dealer bust. She pushed a
small stack of chips toward him.

He and the blonde had been going heads up for an hour now
since the others had dropped off, first the old woman with the
bottomless cosmopolitan, then the young man whose unfussed

boredom suggested he was a local. Lewis was left alone with the dealer, who played, as she had to, like a machine, standing and hitting by rule alone. He was ahead, on intuition.

Janice was gone. She wouldn't answer his texts even. There was no fight, he'd been too stunned. She'd called her sister and quietly moved out of their apartment. *His* apartment, he had to get used to that now. The two sisters packed Janice's things up while he lay hungover in bed, pretending he was asleep while everything was taken away. She said he'd already left her in every way that mattered. Whatever its truth, he resented her resort to a breakup cliché. They didn't fuck. They didn't talk, for a while now really. He'd stopped asking about her life, the kind of restaurant she dreamed of opening someday, and he didn't answer her about his.

He'd left himself behind too, she said. That was less of a cliché, but it was also less true, he thought. Yes, he didn't paint, didn't work, didn't do much but go out at night, without her. And whom was he meeting, she wanted to know. No, she didn't really want to know. But there was no one else, if that's what she meant.

He hadn't left himself behind, he felt, only a promise of what he might have been that turned out wrenchingly false: that he might be one to transmute life into paint and back into life, reformed. Should he apologize for the gift he didn't have? Maybe she would rather see him die trying, vainly trying, for what was beyond him.

Really, he'd only resuscitated an earlier version of himself, the one he'd left behind for art, after college and those Wintry seminars. He was back to politics again, and in the most straightforward way. He'd never been so practical. He was going to transmute life only into life, without the indirection of either art or theory, the Wintry and its talks, this time.

Even just before the end, though Lewis and Janice would go to bed on separate sides of the mattress, they'd wake in the morning tangled together. She would separate herself from him then, resent the false intimacy. There was nothing less false for him. It was what was left of them: the quietest, most sustaining part.

There were no more of those tangles now. She was gone. And he was gone in one way at least, the flesh and blood of him. Without her he was an abstraction, a thought-in-the-world, not a being.

It diminished him in every way but one. When the world fell away, its costs and risks did too. Bringing to life the idea he was now—even on the largest scale—suddenly seemed possible. He owed it to Janice. He'd put all but fifty grand he had into this scheme, including the money he'd earmarked for her restaurant.

He was here in Vegas alone to see his handiwork tonight. He thought he was alone, anyway. Past the humming slots discharging coins, in a cave of a bar shielded from the light, he saw the creamy shoulder blades and the dark hair nipping at them, and then just the edge of her jaw. She was facing away, toward the bar and an assemblage of bottles backlit in the color of bourbon. But her profile, the unusually sharp angles, was enough to kindle something in him, a vague displeasure, a mild sense of shame or fear, twinned to a gauzy curiosity.

She was sitting in a raised, short-backed chair, talking to a very old man in a very good suit who stood rather than sat. Going by the man's posture and expression, the two didn't know each other intimately but would shortly. She put her hand over his and with the other she lifted a broad martini glass to her lips. An olive looking twice its size through the vodka or gin rolled around the base of the cup.

The blonde waited for Lewis to ante up. Instead he gripped the two stacks of chips he'd won and poured them into his pockets. He left nothing for her, not even a smile. A few seconds later, though, he found himself walking back to the table, reflexively pulling chips from his pockets. He placed a few of them on the lip of the green without checking their value. Tens. She didn't notice the chips, or perhaps pretended not to, offended by their meanness at a table with fifty for an ante. But that was luck.

The falling coins kept chiming in the slot machines as he sought a better view of that woman at the bar. But her face stayed angled away from him, so the improving image only clarified what remained beyond it.

The last row of slots receded and the noise of the casino turned mute and distant as he crossed into the cavernous bar. He moved to one side as he approached, carving around her, but just as more of her face came into view, and his memories began to stir again, she twisted away from him. He waited for her face to return, but the man was whispering in her ear now, and she was listening, and it seemed they would stay posed that way forever.

He reached the bar and ordered a drink by touching one of the beer taps. A few customers separated him from her. The old man looked at Lewis as he talked into the woman's ear.

"Do you really?" she said, finally, just as the bartender served Lewis's pint.

Familiarity came all at once. The last of them—she'd called herself Lisa, in the street by his open car door, and under the overpass just before he'd done what he'd had to do. Three words and that was enough for him to know. Somehow she'd made it here. A shadow. Was she on the flight over? Three rows up, in a seat on the other side of the aisle, there was the dark hair, the pale skin of the legs. But again, the face out of view.

The bartender had just said something, clearly and loudly and definitely to Lewis. Except for the soft scratching whispers of the old man in Lisa's ear, no sound competed. But still Lewis didn't understand the words.

Before he could form a thought, Lewis searched his pockets to pay for the drink and rid himself of the bartender. His wallet was wedged beneath the chips. He scooped out as many as he could and set them on the bar, returning to his pocket to fish out the wallet.

The intervening customers, silent men he hadn't realized were a group, paid for their drinks and left together. Now only empty space separated him from Lisa, the one girl he couldn't read. He'd failed with her, it looked like. She was unchanged, still hooking, thousands of miles away. How many others had he failed with?

The bartender gestured and said something more, and Lewis, in fear or confusion or frustration, pushed the beer and the scattered chips toward Lisa and walked out of the bar into an indistinct chaos of noise, which was matched only by the confusion of light streaming down into the atrium at all angles, in several colors and as many intensities, freighting the air.

■ ■ ■

His father had told Lewis once about the time he saw Mike Tyson fight in this arena, with business colleagues, just a year before the boxer fell from greatness. It was not much of a fight. His British opponent's reflexes were betraying him with age. But then, every boxer's reflexes seemed to fail him against Tyson. The fight was over in five rounds, on a TKO. It would have been shorter still, Leo told him, had the Brit not taken to clinching from the opening bell.

But he had no thought of winning. It was a foregone conclusion that Tyson would triumph. Somehow this didn't manage to dim the moment. The trick can't be repeated too many times, but Tyson had only recently come to seem indomitable. For a while it was a thrill simply to see that status confirmed.

The bout turned from sport to theater, classic repertory work. There was almost sympathy for the Brit, as the only question was how, not whether, he would succumb.

Tyson seemed playful during the match, Leo said, shooting

around the ring in little leaps, smiling through his mouthpiece, tossing the other man around with his forearms. All the while he was finding his timing. The opening came on a separation, the conclusion written in five punches: a double jab, a right cross, a tight left hook that sent the Brit's mouthpiece into the front row, and an overhand right on the way down that sent his chin into his chest, making a mess of his tongue as he sprawled onto the canvas. He spat mouthfuls of blood as the victor, preordained, stood on the ropes over a turnbuckle, hopping down seconds later to congratulate the Brit on the part he'd played.

That day, decades ago now, Leo Eldern had been ringside. Today his son was in the closed circuit theater next to the arena, watching in, as if through the one-way window of an interrogation room.

Pornography awards not being prizefights, the theater was only half full, though the industry's sex workers, hundreds of them, completely filled the auditorium itself. Lewis, who had calmed himself some since stumbling upon Lisa earlier in the day, scanned the seats right around him, but there wasn't enough light to make anyone out. He wondered what sort of person would pay for a screening like this, assuming the ceremony was to unfold roughly as planned, that the vents in the auditorium gave nothing but chilled air. Some must be raincoaters on other nights, he thought, in other theaters, and they'd leave only after they'd made the floors sticky.

For the next three hours, he studied the screen, its glossed women and the ponytailed men, no less glossed and steroidal in appearance than the women, yet not merely of secondary interest but of hardly any at all. Their words, few though they were, and even less significant than they were few, barely caught his ears.

Most of all he monitored the master of ceremonies: a former queen of porn, now a producer and figurehead for her own adult studio. She was the ideal barometer, as she was onscreen most, and through the whole length of the ceremony. If the atmosphere was changing, it should show in her first.

But between the three-way and costume design awards, and between those and the girl-girl prize, had her skin flushed any? She'd been red to begin with, presumably from the Vegas sun outside, so it was hard to tell.

He listened carefully to her too, for botched words, names, stutters or any other struggles of the tongue. There were some, but then there were always some, even in the speech of the best. A decline is what he needed, and he couldn't find one.

There was eye contact to assess. The auditorium was filled with the distractible. You wouldn't arrive, and certainly not survive, in the industry if you weren't. But was the hostess any more distractible toward the end, as the best-new-starlet award approached, than she was at the start? Did her eyes flit faster now? Did she forget the films, nominees, punch lines, and stories of the year that was in Porn Valley, only hours away in California? When she looked into the camera, did her gaze miss the lens, or the point beyond it, where the consciousness of the viewer lay?

There was her stride to attend to. She started the night with a textbook whore-strut, lightly pasteurized by the ease of Valley life. It was a carefully coordinated gait, its moving parts were many, and it could break down in any number of ways. But it didn't seem to alter. No collapse into a lopsided swagger or a beach stroll, no retreat into a common strip-mall hustle. If there was any change at all, it was only in the direction of greater command. Whatever contempt there was in it at the beginning remained to the end, when she called up the best new starlet, Violet Skye, who trotted onto the stage with the sexualized power that five-inch heels a waxy red guaranteed.

All the while, Lewis was listening to the room itself, to the gaps between speeches and the hostess's drivel. A presumed silence. There was always a hum, though. Was there any change in that? Was a hiss growing, and could this be picked up through the theater screen? Or did one need to be in the auditorium itself for that?

Could the hiss correspond to a draft from the vents? Could you see collars rustling, single strands, or tufts even, of bleached hair twirling, the lightest earrings swaying in it? Or was it too delicate a change for that? Could you only feel it, this cooling vapor on your neck, from inside the room, through a sense the screen couldn't provide for?

Lewis heard nothing and saw nothing. Not even Lisa.

The curtain was falling as the hostess, still unfazed, invited everyone back for next year's ceremony. As the cameras whirled about, the guests rose. The audience of which Lewis was a part, in the theater, mostly stayed put. They would wait to watch the sex workers file out before they did the same.

Lewis's mind whirled like the cameras, and there were only more questions everywhere he turned. Could they be immune to the gas? Could their plastic poise not be taken from them? Were their senses beyond further derangement? Was their compass so true that nothing could disorient them? Could they not be made to sleep either? Was it unnecessary, for the deathless?

He could feel himself flushing. His mouth had already gone dry. He got to the aisle but nearly fell in the dark, his thigh crashing into armrests several times along the way toward the exit.

As he opened the doors the lobby lights overwhelmed his eyes, forcing them into the tightest squint. He opened them slowly and the world reformed, first as two men in police blue, stock-still. Four more men in the same blue materialized in front of the exits off to the side of the popcorn machines and the candy under the long glass counter. The employees of the theater, dressed in green uniforms and gathered together, were the last to take shape, on the opposite end of the lobby.

A feeling distilled many times over, from an ether, in days long past, down to this barely viscous thing, like glass—it filled

Lewis completely. He had no name for it. Nothing was more familiar.

No one moved.

32

THE FLOOR WAS SMALL, THE WALLS ENORMOUS. Four hundred people made arm's length unachievable, yet the warehouse, a silo for carbon black before it burned down in an unprovable arson, remained nearly empty. It felt it, too, even with them crowding the floor. All that space hovering above, a sealed sky.

Some of the damage from the fire remained. Most of the windows lining the top were missing or shattered, and thick soot covered a ceiling that had yet to be scrubbed or blasted. Streaks of bleach stained the walls, as did grand blazes of rust formed by the rainwater that would have rushed in through the broken windows in the weeks since. The smell of coal-fire was everywhere. There was a hint of soil in it too, and a polymer that lent a saccharine note.

In the gray space between laws the owners, chemical suppliers mostly to experimental labs in the region, had rented the silo to the bands for the night. The last group had just taken down their gear, and Larent, Moto, and Ravan, the closers, were setting up their own. The monitors blared Reich's *18 Musicians*. They weren't quite eighteen in number themselves, but they'd brought enough other musicians along with them to fill out the sound and play everything that needed playing.

Dozens of small speakers sat convexly behind the audience, along the curve of the silo wall. Directly across, they set up Larent's collection of oscillators, two MPCs rigged to laptops, a frequency modulation synthesizer, several rack-mounted amplifiers, and a Marshall stack for Ravan's fretless guitar.

Moto's drums were out in front rather than behind all of this, and had been whittled down to a bass, a snare, a floor tom, and a series of splashes with no true crash. Between the drums and the electronics were the strings and brass: the cellos, a violin, Larent's double bass, and a quartet of trumpets.

Three hundred rungs up, perched on an iron grating at the top of the tower, Renna and Stagg watched and listened. They hadn't talked about that night yet, the one that ended in broken glass. The music meant they didn't have to right now, which pleased them both. Language was hurting more than helping lately. It was better simply to sit together, alone.

But the ladder rattled and faces started to appear. A half-dozen of the crowd below had found their way up. They'd come with Percocet and marijuana at least. Recompense for the intrusion, that was the way Stagg thought of it. He waved off the marijuana but accepted a clutch of the familiar off-white pills, the ones Jen had softened her tragedy with. Instead of popping one, though, or handing one to Renna, he pocketed them all and went for the ladder in search of an emptier grating. Renna gave them a sheepish smile and followed him down. She was getting sick of that smile, the one she seemed to need more and more around him.

The two had hardly made it down ten rungs when a rising wave met them from below, 440 hertz shooting up at them from the lens of speakers on the factory floor, like the ocular beams once thought to leave the eye. At the same time that this filtered sawtooth traveled the length of the tower, bouncing off the ceiling, its pitch spiraled upward through the series of over-tones, a second per.

The sheer height of the silo gave it reverberative powers greater than most cathedrals. But the acoustics were flawed. There was especially the coldness of the sound, which must have been augmented by the concrete and further distorted by the tunnel-like shape of the building.

Stagg lost the rhythms of his descent in the wake of the saw-tooth, the coordination between hands and feet. He paused and Renna's foot came down on his hand. He pulled it away from the ladder and twisted around before finding his grip. As the wave disappeared above the 46th partial, into the inaudible range, the two of them continued their descent in a countermotion to a music they could no longer trace.

The strident buzz of a naked square wave replaced the saw-tooth. This time it was Renna who paused. Stagg looked down, his hand still hurting, and saw Larent working the oscillators, peeling away partials, paring down the brute wholeness of the wave with the same slip-stick motion he would use to hold a note on the double bass, his rosined bow alternately catching and sliding across the strings.

Around this synthesized core the musicians they'd hired arranged an organic, pure body: doublings, pure fifths and thirds, and a pure major sixth above it, all played in measureless notes, the instrumentalists ducking in and out of the chords at will. Having dialed in the oscillators, Larent triggered the MPC samples and joined them on the bass, bowing the lowest A.

Harmonically the piece was simple, the motion generated through synthesis, additive and subtractive. Ravan ran a kind of interference with his guitar, injecting tempered notes just micro-tones off from the rest, shading the music away from purity. Quickly these beating tones, these wolves with intent, went from peculiar accents to percussion more vicious than anything pro-vided by Moto, who pounded out a beat on bass and snare made up of the fewest strokes necessary to imply the time signatures revolving every sixteen bars: 3/4, 4/4, 5/4, 3/2.

Renna and Stagg dropped onto a vacant grating about half way up the silo and took half the Percocet. Over the next minutes, or however long it was, by infinitesimal increments that evaded the ear the music grew extraordinarily loud. Stagg hadn't noticed any discrete bump in volume, but now that he'd sensed the scale of the sound, it was unignorable and still expanding.

As the music grew, the audience shrunk in proportion. Since the silo doors couldn't be seen from where they were, the contraction too occurred by imperceptible intervals. Every few minutes, though, they could see, with a detachment the opiate permitted, that the crowd was that much smaller and the music that much larger.

Sick from sound, they took the rest of the pills. Everything dimmed, the sound transforming from an exogenous crush to a simple flush of space. They leaned against each other and stared down at the band. At Larent. Neon green peeked out of his ears. Plugs. Prepared.

They passed out on the grating, or fell between sleep and wakefulness, whether from shock or the drug or both. An abrupt silence woke them. They looked down to the floor and it was empty. Only the band members remained. Larent stared up at them inscrutably. Ravan was smoking something.

33

THE RINGS WERE HARDLY LOUDER THAN THE ringing in his ears. Several came and went before Stagg noticed the doubling. He reached down from bed, groping for the source, and found it in the pocket of his pants, which were strewn on the floor, inside out, and still buttoned at the waist. The belt was buckled too. He must have pulled himself out of them somehow. He couldn't remember. Even now he was dazed.

Before he could separate the phone from the pocket the ringing stopped. He dialed back.

"Well, you're an asshole," he said just as Ravan picked up.

"Oh, you weren't supposed to stay to the end, Carl! Only the fools did," Ravan said. "Or the ones with earplugs, like us. How could I have known you'd overdosed—and fifty feet up at that? You made no sense after you climbed down."

"Because of whatever you call what you were doing."

"Because of the pills you took, I'd think. You came quite close to falling from the ladder. Renna too. Plenty of suspense in it. And what I call it is music. It was quite classical in some ways. The score was agonized over, you know, by Edward and me."

"It was more like theater."

"Well, the volume bit was really Edward's idea, if that's what you mean. Did you think it ruined things? Funny, he said you're the first person he'd bounced the idea off of. You'd liked it then."

"My ears are fucked."

"So you've changed your mind," he said. "I'll let him know. Anyway, it'll all come back, don't worry. My ears have nearly bled after some of the things I've heard. And you weren't even that close to the speakers, like the people on the floor. If anyone should be worried... but tell me this, it must have been a sight from up there, looking down on this factory floor just disgorging people, fleeing, essentially, hands over their ears."

"I don't know what I remember."

"I suppose it doesn't matter. To have seen everything perfectly, to have been changed, you don't have to remember a thing," he said. "But this isn't really why I called. This storm, you see, there's a chance, a meaningful chance, it's going to be much worse than expected."

"My part of town doesn't flood, however bad it is."

"That's not it. Anyway the barriers should save most of the city from the floodwaters."

"Then?"

"It might be worse in a new way, where the problem's not its size or speed."

"I haven't heard anything about this."

"You aren't going to. And I'm not going to go through meteorological stuff that won't mean anything to you anyway. Ionic charges, isotopes, and such. I'm just telling you what we know now, or anyway a few of us do, here in Princeton. It could create a kind of... imbalance... in the atmosphere, one we haven't quite seen before. It could last for days, even weeks after the storm's officially dead."

"Which means?"

"Which means it's the perfect moment for a trip."

"No, I—"

"You could go out to Vegas. That's what it means. See exactly who this man—Lewis Eldern—we've been looking for all this time is. Extraordinary that it took some anonymous tip to bag him. We weren't even close, were we? What a waste of money we've been."

"But why would I care that much, to go out there?"

"Don't say that," Ravan said with a laugh. "After all, he did hurt that girl you've been looking for. The last one, Jen."

"I'm not looking for her."

"Really? I'd heard you'd been calling. He might know where she is."

"It's not important."

"You're sure?" he asked. "Well then, aside from that, Lewis *is* the one who's mucked up your plans. That must be important to you at least."

"We'll have to see what happens."

"Oh, come now. That Kames hasn't seen Lewis or his father in years, it makes no difference. There's too much history between them, too many common motives, *not* to investigate the Institute, given all the other evidence. Penerin's been wanting to anyway, for lots of reasons. You know that most of all. And it'll be closed until they're done. It could take months. They'll drag it out. And who knows what it'll turn up. I think we both know they're going to find something. At some point, there has got to be something."

"Still. Seeing Lewis, interviewing him, isn't going to change any of that."

"For the gambling then, Carl. The whores. Nothing's keeping you here. No lectures. No fellowship. Penerin will probably send you out there anyway eventually, unless you quit first," Ravan said. "But now you can't afford to quit, can you?"

"And where'll you go? Jersey's not escaping, they say."

"India. I don't recommend it."

"Your family."

"Take Renna somewhere."

"Right."

"You have to. You'd be a fool not to, Carl. More than that."

Stagg switched off the phone. Renna stretched her leg across his and he wrapped up her head in his hands.

"Hm?"

"Hm?"

"I still feel sick," she said.

He tapped out two Advil from the bottle on the windowsill and swallowed them. He tapped out two more and slipped them into her mouth. "Water?"

She swallowed without any.

"I can't hear anything."

He smiled. "So, Dakar."

"Dakar what."

"This weekend."

"Oh, stop."

"Really. We could go."

She sat up. "Why?"

"What do you mean?" he asked. "It'll be fun."

"But all of a sudden."

"That's the thing. It has to be."

"What?"

"We could stay a few weeks even, depending. We could make it up to England too. We could both get what we want."

"You mean the hurricane?" she asked, incredulous.

He sat up.

"But that's why they built the barriers," she said. "It's not *that* big a deal anymore."

"They might not help, in this case."

"And how would you know?"

"Ravan just called."

"Of course he did. There's nothing about him that's not fucking weird."

"Well, he would know, wouldn't he? Of anyone we know?"

"And what about everyone else in the city? What are they going to do about it? I haven't heard of anyone else evacuating."

"They should probably go too. You can invite them."

"I can't, not just like that."

"What happened to the whimsy, little girl?"

"I'm interviewing someone Monday. And anyway I can't get vacation right now, even if I asked." She touched his whiskered face.

"Let's just go."

"Carl! Just because there isn't any fellowship now, I'm supposed to drop everything? I'm sorry about what happened but—"

"No, you know—it's fine." She could keep Larent company. Really, the guy would like that. Maybe she would too.

"No it's not. It's terrible. And I'm really sorry."

"Later then. We'll go, sometime."

"Really, really soon. In a few weeks even." She kissed him on the lobe of his ear. "We *have* to stop fighting, though. Clean the slate. I don't even think this was about a storm."

"No?"

"More like a test."

"Of what?"

"I don't know."

34

STAGG WAS ON HIS WAY UP NOW, TIGHT AGAINST
the window, listening to his ears pop over the ringing that persisted. The clouds ahead were heavy and swirling, but nothing
like what they were farther out, he assumed, with the storm
coming in over the Atlantic. He could see the Coast Guard on
the horizon, six ships bound for a fury they'd try to calm, just
days now before the elections.

This was the last flight out. The seat beside him was empty
but there was a young woman in the aisle. Tall, pale, and elegant, she didn't seem to want to talk and he hoped she wouldn't
change her mind. She was someone the English would call the
right sort, he knew that almost immediately. She'd said nothing more than, "No, that's fine," when he'd stooped over and
slid his briefcase beneath the seat between them with a defer-
ential glance. But she'd done it in the pure cadences of received
pronunciation, the ones he knew mostly from his grandmother,
who'd agreed, to his surprise, to let him stay at the country
house in Kent indefinitely, whether he was researching or not,
or coming with company.

Something indefinite appealed to him now. If he wanted, he
could scrap everything he'd written and just live in that library,

reading. And if the elections were thrown into chaos by the storm, or if they weren't, and the results were adverse or simply meaningless once more, what would it be to him, at home, abroad, and free, finally, of Penerin's heavy thumb?

For all he knew, this woman could be headed to Canterbury too, going by her accent. Or if not her, by sheer force of intuition—he'd not told her he was going anyway, without her, he'd just packed and left—Renna might be. (It wouldn't have shocked him.) Or else, by the vaster powers of chance, which were really just the sublimities of miracle, maybe even Jen.

A tone sounded twice as they found themselves within a turbulence they'd been briefed on. The shades were wide open but they might as well have been closed now for all he could see through the windows whited out with cloud. The plane started to shake, first in a fine, even tremor, then less regularly but more viciously, sinking and rising and sinking again in a wind that seemed made of strands, tiny streams with their own natures, traveling at their own speeds, braided together like rope.

The plane steadied. The windows became windows again.

"Sorry about that," said the captain. "At least you won't be in Halsley for it."

The woman took out a sterling pen and opened up a notebook, four by six, already much used. She began to write slowly, thoughtfully, in a cursive hand too small for Stagg to read; though if he looked closer, somehow he felt he might find only a wavy line. He wasn't tempted to test the feeling, not now. Looking did have limits.

A different tone sounded and a flight attendant spoke over the speakers: "Feel free to use your wireless devices now." A rose glow began suffusing the plane, a peculiar rose he'd never known, though he must have seen night fall, the sun set, dozens of times from above like this, shuttling back and forth between continents. Perhaps, though, there was never an hour, an atmosphere, quite like this.

He ran his fingers over the cold screen of his phone and thought of the two women he'd left in the dark, to find their own way. He watched the dark ink of this woman's pen run onto paper, watched her illegible, undulating line deepen as the pulped wood pulled it in. She paused, held the broad nib against the book, wondering, he supposed, how to continue, just as the finest point bloomed before them both.

THE GLACIER A NOVEL BY JEFF WOOD

"Gorgeously and urgently written."
—*Library Journal*, starred review

"It seduces you slowly, the reader hypnotized from the first page."
—*Heavy Feather Review*

THE ONLY ONES A NOVEL BY CAROLA DIBBELL
* **One of the Best Books of 2015** —*Oprah Magazine*, *Washington Post*, *Flavorwire*, *National Post*

"Breathtaking. It's that good, and that important, and that heartbreakingly beautiful." —*NPR*

"A heart-piercing tale of love, desire and acceptance." —*Washington Post*

HAINTS STAY A NOVEL BY COLIN WINNETTE
* **One of the Best Books of 2015** —*Slate*, *Flavorwire*

"[An] astonishing portrait of American violence. The rewards of *Haints Stay* belong to the reader." —*Los Angeles Times*

"A success... *Haints Stay* turns the Western on its ear." —*Washington Post*

SOME THINGS THAT MEANT THE WORLD TO ME
A NOVEL BY JOSHUA MOHR
* *San Francisco Chronicle* **Bestseller**
* **One of the Best Books of 2009** —*Oprah Magazine*, The Nervous Breakdown

"Mohr's prose roams with chimerical liquidity." —Boston's *Weekly Dig*

THE CORRESPONDENCE ARTIST
A NOVEL BY BARBARA BROWNING
* **Lambda Literary Award Winner**

"A deft look at modern life that's both witty and devastating." —*Nylon*

"*The Correspondence Artist* applies stylistic juxtapositions in welcome and unexpected ways." —*Vol. 1 Brooklyn*

NOT DARK YET A NOVEL BY BERIT ELLINGSEN

"Fascinating, surreal, gorgeously written, and like nothing you've ever read before." —*BuzzFeed*

"...suspenseful and haunting... This is a remarkable novel from a very talented author." —*Publishers Weekly*, starred review

BINARY STAR A NOVEL BY SARAH GERARD
* **One of the Best Books of 2015** —*BuzzFeed, Flavorwire*

"The particular genius of *Binary Star* is that out of such grim material in constructs beauty." —*New York Times Book Review*

"Rhythmic, hallucinatory, yet vivid as crystal." —NPR

A QUESTIONABLE SHAPE A NOVEL BY BENNETT SIMS
* **Winner of the Bard Fiction Prize**
* *The Believer* **Book Award Finalist**
* **One of the Best Books of 2013** —*Slate, Salon,* NPR's 'On Point'

"[*A Questionable Shape*] is more than just a novel. It is literature. It is life." —*The Millions*

THE ABSOLUTION OF ROBERTO ACESTES LAING
A NOVEL BY NICHOLAS ROMBES
* **One of the Best Books of 2014** —*Flavorwire*

"Kafka directed by David Lynch doesn't even come close. It is the most hauntingly original book I've read in a very long time. [This book] is a strong contender for novel of the year." —*3:AM Magazine*

RADIO IRIS A NOVEL BY ANNE-MARIE KINNEY

"Kinney is a Southern California Camus." —*Los Angeles Magazine*

"[*Radio Iris*] has a dramatic otherworldly payoff that is unexpected and triumphant." —*New York Times Book Review*, Editors' Choice

CRYSTAL EATERS
A NOVEL BY SHANE JONES

"A powerful narrative that touches on the value of every human life, with a lyrical voice and layers of imagery and epiphany." —*BuzzFeed*

"[Jones is] something of a millennial Richard Brautigan." —*Nylon*

HOW TO GET INTO THE TWIN PALMS
A NOVEL BY KAROLINA WACLAWIAK

"One of my favorite books this year." —Roxane Gay, *The Rumpus*

"Waclawiak's novel reinvents the immigration story."
—*New York Times Book Review*, Editors' Choice

CRAPALACHIA
A NOVEL BY SCOTT McCLANAHAN

* **One of the Best Books of 2013** —*The Millions, Flavorwire, Dazed & Confused, The L Magazine, Time Out Chicago*

"McClanahan's prose is miasmic, dizzying, repetitive. A rushing river of words that reflects the chaos and humanity of the place from which he hails." —*New York Times Book Review*

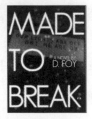

MADE TO BREAK
A NOVEL BY D. FOY

"With influences that range from Jack Kerouac to Tom Waits and a prose that possesses a fast, strange, perennially changing rhythm that's somewhat akin to some of John Coltrane's wildest compositions."
—*HTML Giant*

MIRA CORPORA A NOVEL BY JEFF JACKSON

* *Los Angeles Times* Book Prize Finalist
* **One of the Best Books of 2013** —*Slate, Salon, Flavorwire*

"Style is pre-eminent in Jeff Jackson's eerie and enigmatic debut. The prose works like the expressionless masks worn by killers in horror films." —*Wall Street Journal*

I SMILE BACK
A NOVEL BY AMY KOPPELMAN

* Now a major film starring Sarah Silverman and Josh Charles!

"Powerful. Koppelman's instincts help her navigate these choppy waters with inventiveness and integrity." —*Los Angeles Times*

ANCIENT OCEANS OF CENTRAL KENTUCKY
A NOVEL BY DAVID CONNERLEY NAHM
* One of the Best Books of 2014 —NPR, *Flavorwire*

"Wonderful… Remarkable… it's impossible to stop reading until you've gone through each beautiful line, a beauty that infuses the whole novel, even in its darkest moments." —NPR

THE PEOPLE WHO WATCHED HER PASS BY
A NOVEL BY SCOTT BRADFIELD

"Challenging [and] original… A billowy adventure of a book. In a book that supplies few answers, Bradfield's lavish eloquence is the presiding constant." —*New York Times Book Review*

"Brave and unforgettable."
—*Los Angeles Times*

1940 A NOVEL BY JAY NEUGEBOREN

"Jay Neugeboren traverses the Hitlerian tightrope with all the skill and formal daring that have made him one of our most honored writers of literary fiction and masterful nonfiction. [*1940*] is, at once, a beautifully realized work of imagined history, a rich and varied character study and a subtly layered novel of ideas, all wrapped in a propulsively readable story." —*Los Angeles Times*

BABY GEISHA
STORIES BY TRINIE DALTON

"[The stories] feel like brilliant sexual fairy tales on drugs. Dalton writes of self-discovery and sex with a knowing humility and humor."
—*Interview Magazine*